M a.

The exciting passion-filled stories of the O'Connell family – sexy, wealthy successful – they're about to gamble on love!

THE O'CONNELLS *Dynasty*

Business & Pleasure

Three powerful, intense and satisfying novels by one bestselling and award-winning writer:

SANDRA MARTON

Praise for
The O'Connells
by Sandra Marton

"The first book of the O'Connell series, *Keir O'Connell's Mistress*, vibrates with charismatic characters and a tight, page-turning plot. No one delivers consistent must-reads like Sandra Marton!"

"Romance does not get better than a Sandra Marton story. *The Sicilian Surrender* has power and passion evident in the strength and compassion of an exquisite hero and the heroine's courage to create a new life. Together they are a formidable couple."

"*Claiming His Love-Child* by Sandra Marton is a truly remarkable love story. Though she begins with a common premise, Marton crafts a compelling tale filled with emotional highs and lows for her protagonists."

"With *The Sheikh's Convenient Bride*, Sandra Marton delivers an elegant, yet simple love story."

"Sandra Marton gift-wraps a juicy tale filled with tension, high stakes, a to-die-for hero, passion and romance. This is a very engrossing story."
[The One-Night Wife]

"The emotion and passion are vivid."
[The Sicilian Marriage]

—*Romantic Times*

THE O'CONNELLS *Dynasty*

Business & Pleasure

SANDRA MARTON

Harlequin Mills & Boon Limited, Eton House,
18-24 Paradise Road, Richmond, Surrey TW9 1SR

ISBN: 978 0 263 87704 5

012-0210

Harlequin Mills & Boon policy is to use papers that are natural, renewable and recyclable products and made from wood grown in sustainable forests. The logging and manufacturing processes conform to the legal environmental regulations of the country of origin.

Printed and bound in Spain
by Litografia Rosés S.A., Barcelona

KEIR O'CONNELL'S MISTRESS

SANDRA MARTON

Sandra Marton's popular O'Connell family saga
collected together into two special volumes.
Satisfaction & passion guaranteed!

February 2010

THE
O'CONNELLS
Dynasty

Business & Pleasure

March 2010

THE
O'CONNELLS
Dynasty

Conveniently Wed

Sandra Marton wrote her first novel while she was still in primary school. Her doting parents told her she'd be a writer someday and Sandra believed them. In school and college, she wrote dark poetry nobody but her boyfriend understood, though looking back, she suspects he was just being kind. As a wife and mother, she wrote murky short stories in what little spare time she could manage, but not even her boyfriend-turned-husband could pretend to understand those. Sandra tried her hand at other things, among them teaching and serving on the Board of Education in her home town, but the dream of becoming a writer was always in her heart.

At last, Sandra realised she wanted to write books about what all women hope to find: love with that one special man, love that's rich with fire and passion, love that lasts forever. She wrote a novel – her very first, and sold it to Mills & Boon. Since then, she's written more than seventy books, all of them featuring the sexy, gorgeous, larger-than-life heroes that have helped make Sandra a bestselling author. A four-time RITA® Award finalist, she's also received eight *Romantic Times* magazine awards and has been honoured with *Romantic Times* Career Achievement Award for Series Romance. Sandra lives with her very own sexy, gorgeous, larger-than-life hero in a sun-filled house on a quiet country lane in the northeastern United States.

Look out for Sandra Marton's latest exciting novel, *Blackwolf's Redemption* (May 2010), available from Mills & Boon® Modern™.

CHAPTER ONE

Late summer, on the road to Las Vegas:

THE sun was a hint of gold lighting the rim of the desert as Keir O'Connell crossed the state line into Nevada.

The road was empty and he was driving fast, the black Ferrari eating up the miles like the powerful thoroughbred it was. A sign flashed by, so quickly Keir couldn't read it, but he didn't have to. He knew what it said.

75 miles to Las Vegas. Welcome to the Desert Song Hotel and Casino.

Seventy-five miles. At the speed he was driving, little more than half an hour away.

Keir eased back on the gas pedal.

He'd been on the road for two days, driving almost non-stop, knowing he'd pushed things too far and if he didn't hurry, he'd miss his mother's wedding.

The thought was almost enough to make him smile.

Missing the duchess's wedding wasn't an option. She'd wait until all six of her children were gathered before taking her vows with Dan Coyle. Afterward, she'd peel the hide off whichever of them had caused the delay.

No, missing the wedding wasn't a possibility. Besides—Keir checked the dashboard clock—besides, he'd make it in plenty of time. The ceremony wasn't until tomorrow. He'd told himself he was driving hard because he wanted the chance to visit with his family and that was part of it, yes, but the greater truth was that driving fast relaxed him.

He knew, from long experience, that taking a car almost to its limit, seeing how far he could push the speed until he was hovering on that razor-sharp edge between control and the loss of it, was usually enough to drain him of tension. That, or being with a woman, but that was the last thing he wanted now.

He hadn't touched a woman in the thirty days he'd been gone…in the month since he'd made an ass of himself in a moonlit Texas garden with Cassie Berk.

One month. Was that all the time he'd been away? Had he really made so many life-altering decisions in four short weeks? It didn't seem possible, especially for him. He'd spent a lifetime with his brothers teasing him about being such a vigilant planner.

"Be careful," his mother had said the year he'd gotten his pilot's license, and one of his brothers—Sean, maybe—had laughed and hugged her and said there was no reason to worry, that Keir would never have an accident unless he planned it first.

Keir frowned.

Then, how come he was about to sign off as Chief Operating Officer of the Desert Song and move twenty-five hundred miles across the country to a vineyard in Connecticut—a vineyard into which he'd sunk a small fortune?

Keir shifted in his seat and tried to find a better angle for his legs. The Ferrari had more room under the dashboard than some cars he'd driven but it was built for speed, not comfort, especially if you topped six foot two.

What he was going to do would make anyone edgy. And, yeah, why lie to himself? The prospect of seeing Cassie again bothered him, too. It bothered him a lot. Nobody went through life without doing something stupid; despite what Cassie had called him, he wasn't arrogant enough to think he was the exception to the rule. But what he'd done that night…

He owed her an apology. She'd be calmer by now, willing to let him eat crow and say he was sorry he'd come on to her. It had been the mood and the moment, that was all. Too much champagne, too much slow dancing, too much of the enforced togetherness that came of him being Gray

Baron's best man and Cassie being Dawn Lincoln's maid of honor.

It was his fault, all of it, and he was prepared to admit it. He was her boss, dammit; he knew the rules about sexual harassment. Knew them? He'd *written* them at the Song, not just rules about harassment but others that clearly laid out what he expected of people.

Logic. Reason. Common sense. He believed in those principles. He'd built his life on them…and forgotten every last one, that night with Cassie.

"You're an arrogant, self-centered, stupid son of a bitch," she'd said, breathing fire when he'd done the right thing, stepped back and tried to say he was sorry.

Had she let him? No way. She'd rounded on him with fury and the worst of it was that the things she'd called him might have dented his ego, but they were true.

He'd made a move on her he never should have made and put her in the position where she'd been damned if she responded and damned if she didn't.

She'd responded, all right.

He'd taken her in his arms in a dark corner of the garden at that Texas ranch. A second later, she'd been clinging to him, opening her mouth to his, moaning as he'd bunched up her skirt and slid his hands under her dress, that long, gauzy dress that made her look like an old-fashioned dream instead of a Las Vegas cocktail waitress…

This kind of crap wasn't going to get him anywhere. He was maybe fifty miles from Vegas and exactly thirty days and nights from what had happened—what had almost happened—in that garden, and why was he thinking about it again?

He was hungry, that was why. His stomach wasn't just growling, it was snarling. He'd pretty much been living on black coffee and catnaps, just pulling off the road long enough to fill the car with gas and his system with caffeine. It had been a long forty-eight hours from Connecticut to Nevada.

If you wanted to get philosophical, he thought, goosing the car back to speed, it had been the longest journey of his life.

Other cars were feeding onto the road now, all of them heading toward that glittering Mecca in the desert. Keir slowed the Ferrari to what seemed a crawl.

He'd gone to New York on vacation, though that hadn't been his original plan. He'd intended to drive to Tucson, then to Phoenix, just get away for a couple of weeks, enjoy the feel of the car—he'd bought it only weeks before—on the long, straight desert roads.

And then, right after the ceremony, his mother and Dan Coyle, the Desert Song's Head of Security, had taken him aside.

''Keir,'' the duchess had said, clinging to Dan Coyle's arm, ''I know this will come as a surprise…darling, Dan and I are getting married.''

Keir smiled.

A surprise? Yeah, but once he'd thought about it, he realized it shouldn't have been. He'd caught Dan casting longing looks at the duchess for quite a while and caught her blushing like a schoolgirl in response.

So he'd kissed his mother, clapped Dan on the back, and after they'd laughed and maybe cried a little, the duchess had taken his hands in hers and told him that he was to take a month's holiday, at least.

''Orders from on high must be obeyed,'' Dan had said with a wink, when Keir had begun to protest.

''You deserve a real vacation,'' Mary had insisted. ''Just be sure you're back for the wedding.''

Dan had grinned, told him that they'd chosen a date, even a time, and then Keir had kissed his mother, shaken Dan's hand, said if he expected him to start calling him Daddy he was in for a rude surprise.

And when all the good wishes and jokes were over, Keir had taken a deep breath and said he thought it might be time for Mary to take over the management of the Desert Song again, and for him to move on.

Dan had urged him to reconsider.

"Is it because I'm marrying your mother? Keir, that isn't necessary. There's no need for you to leave."

"No," Mary had said softly, "of course there isn't." Her smile had trembled a little. "But he wants to leave. Don't you, Keir? Running the Song was never what you wanted to do in the first place." She'd touched his arm. "I think I've always known that."

It was the truth and Keir hadn't denied it. They'd talked a bit, the three of them, of how things would be with him gone and Mary in charge.

"With Dan sharing responsibility," she'd said firmly and Keir had nodded his agreement. He liked Coyle; he'd be good for the duchess and if anyone could keep her in line, Keir figured Dan could.

After that, he'd gone back to the wedding festivities...

And Cassie.

Keir frowned, took his sunglasses from the visor and slipped them on.

He'd intended to start for Tucson early the next morning but after the fiasco in the garden, he'd tossed his things in his car and headed east instead of west, not just in search of a holiday but in search of his own life.

It was one thing to be free of the responsibilities he'd assumed six years ago, but free to do what? The only thing he was sure of was that he didn't want to go back to arbitrage. He'd made a fortune in the complex world of stocks and bonds before taking over the Song, but that was the past.

He had yet to glimpse the future.

To that end, and, yeah, maybe because he'd figured that keeping busy would block memories of how stupidly he'd behaved with Cassie, he'd made some discreet inquiries of colleagues once he reached New York. Within a couple of days, an attorney representing a French hotel conglomerate approached him about a five star facility planned for the East side of Manhattan. They wanted his expertise and were willing to pay handsomely for it. A lunch, then a couple of dinners, and Keir had begun thinking about becoming a consultant in New York. The idea pleased him. He loved the pace and power of the city and started looking to put down roots.

That was why he'd been standing on the terrace of a penthouse a few mornings ago, the realtor beside him gushing over the view, the rooms, the lap pool and spa, when suddenly her voice seemed to fade and Keir had found himself seeing not the view but himself, forever trapped inside a paneled office, forever doomed to wear a suit and a tie and sit behind a desk.

What had happened to the boy who'd wanted to be an astronaut? To the kid who'd wanted to slay dragons? A penthouse suite, a private pool and an expensive view had never been part of those dreams.

How could he have forgotten that?

He'd turned to the realtor, told her he was sorry but he'd just remembered an appointment. Then he'd gotten into the Ferrari, pointed it north and let the car eat up the miles until he'd found himself in Connecticut farmland.

He'd been driving without an agenda, figuring on turning back once he knew what in hell he was doing, but the weather was beautiful the car was purring. When he pulled out a map while he filled up at a gas station, he realized that if he went just another few miles he could check out the Song's competition. A couple of northeastern Native American tribes had opened casinos and hotels in Connecticut. They were very successful. Why not combine business with pleasure and take a look? He might not be running the Song anymore, but he might find something interesting to pass on to Dan and his mother.

So Keir had piled back into his car and headed a little further north and east.

The Native American casinos had proved enlightening.

He'd spent the rest of the morning strolling around, discreetly observing the operations. Then for reasons he'd never be able to fathom, he'd gotten back in the Ferrari and driven another hour, hour and a half, until he'd ended up on a road that knifed through tall stands of oak and maple, where his car was the only traffic and the only sound was the cry of a hawk, circling overhead.

He'd almost missed the sign.

DEER RUN VINEYARD, it read, *Luncheon and Dinner Thursday thru Sunday, By Reservation Only.*

It was Thursday, Keir had thought, glancing at his watch. It was almost two. A little late for lunch and besides, you needed a reservation but, what the hell?

So he'd turned down a narrow dirt road and found, at its end, a scene that might have been a painting: a handsome old barn converted into a small restaurant, a garden surrounding a patio filled with umbrella tables and a profusion of flowers, and beyond that, row after row of grapevines climbing a hill toward a handsome old stone house set against a cloudless blue sky.

Keir felt a tightening in his belly.

Yes, the hostess said, someone had just phoned to cancel a reservation for the second seating. If he'd just wait a few minutes…?

He'd accepted a glass of wine and gone for a stroll up the hill, walking through the rows of vines, drawing the rich smell of the earth and the grapes deep into his lungs…

And suddenly known that he belonged here.

He'd asked the owner to join him for coffee. Keir came straight to the point. He wanted to buy Deer Run. The proprietor beamed. His wife was ill; she needed a change of climate. They'd decided to put the place up for sale just days before. What a nice surprise, that Keir should have turned up wanting to buy it.

Keir hadn't been surprised. Until that afternoon he'd never believed in anything a man couldn't see or touch but something—he didn't want to call it fate—*something* had been at work that day.

He'd looked at the books, had data faxed to his accountant and attorney. Before the sun dipped behind the gently rolling hills, he'd become the new owner of Deer Run.

Stupid? His accountant and attorney were too polite to say so. What they *did* say was "impulsive."

Keir speeded up a little and changed lanes. Maybe they were right, but he had no regrets. He needed to change his life, and now he'd done it.

Las Vegas, ten miles.

The sign flashed by before he knew it—before he was ready. He slowed the car to a crawl.

He was not a man who ever acted on impulse and yet he'd done so three times in the past few weeks, walking out on the French deal, buying a winery…kissing a woman he shouldn't have kissed.

Why regret any of it?

The kiss was just a kiss, the five star hotel and the penthouse in New York had been wrong for him, but the winery…the winery felt right.

No, he thought, he had no regrets at all. Not even about Cassie.

Keir turned on the radio and heard the pulse of hard, pounding rock. One thing he'd learned during this trip was you could tell where you were by listening to local DJ's. Back east there'd been lots of Dylan and Debussy. The closer he'd come to the middle of the country, the more he'd heard Garth Brooks. Now, with the desert behind him and the Vegas strip just ahead, the sounds of rock and roll were kicking in.

Actually, what he liked best were the old standards, the stuff nobody played anymore. He'd grown up listening to those songs, *Embraceable You* and *Starlight* and the rest; his parents had always seen to it that music like that was featured in at least one lounge at the Desert Song.

The band had played lots of those numbers at Gray and

Dawn's wedding, especially as evening came on. He'd been dancing with Cassie, the two of them laughing as they moved to something by the Stones, when suddenly the music had become slow and smoky.

That was when he'd gathered her into his arms, as if the whole day had been leading up to that moment.

He knew the reasons.

People did things they'd never think of doing when they went to weddings and parties where the wine flowed and inhibitions got tossed aside.

How many toasts had he drunk? How many dances had he danced with Cassie, watching the flash of her long legs, the way her dress clung to her body when the summer breeze blew? How often had he inhaled her scent when he leaned close to ask if she wanted something from the buffet?

Why wouldn't she have suddenly seemed a beautiful, mysterious creature of every man's hottest dreams instead of a woman who might have been around the block more times than he wanted to count?

As he'd danced her into the garden, away from the lights, away from the other guests, he'd even imagined asking her to go with him the next day. He'd thought of what it might be like to be alone with her in some quiet, romantic hideaway.

''Cassie,'' he'd murmured, tilting her face to his in the darkness. And he'd kissed her. Just kissed her…

Until she made a little sound, moved against him and dammit suddenly, his hands had been all over her, molding her to him, lifting her into him, sliding under her skirt against soft, silken skin.

Keir tightened his grip on the steering wheel.

Great. He was right back where he'd been when he'd pointed his car east the night of the wedding, feeling like a damned fool for having hit on a woman who worked for him, who'd probably been afraid to say ''no'' or maybe figured making it with the boss would improve her chances of being something better than a cocktail waitress…

He could still feel the way she'd stiffened in his arms, hear the sound of her voice.

"Keir," she'd said, "Keir, no."

That was what had brought him back to sanity, the way she'd said his name, her voice shaking, her body losing its soft, warm pliancy—and maybe that had been part of the act, a game designed to make him want her all the more—except, if he'd wanted her any more, he'd have exploded.

Keir cursed, stepped on the brakes and brought the car to a skidding stop on the side of the road.

Okay. He'd made a fool of himself but he'd done that before and survived. Not with a woman. Never with a woman, but he'd done his fair share of dumb things. Like making cold phone calls as a trainee at a San Francisco brokerage house and being set up by one of the other trainees so that somehow he'd ended up phoning the wife of the firm's CEO.

He'd sold her three hundred shares of stock.

Now there was Cassie. Well, yeah. He was sorry he'd kissed her, but seeing her again, apologizing, wasn't going to be any problem at all. Wasn't there some old Irish saying about a little humility lightening the load and being good for the soul?

If there wasn't, there ought to be.

As for buying the vineyard… Keir took a deep breath and pulled the car back into traffic. Enough introspection. He was minutes from home, his mother was getting married tomorrow, and he had the feeling he was in for one hell of an old-fashioned, rowdy O'Connell family reunion.

Up ahead, a creature that looked like a small, slow-moving tank stepped out of the scrub. It looked from side to side, took a cautious step forward, then an equally cautious step back.

Keir braked, swung wide, and left the armadillo in the dust.

* * *

Half an hour later, he pulled into the employee lot at the Desert Song and parked his car in its usual space. The security guard at the back entrance gave him a big smile.

"Hey, Mr. O'Connell. You're back."

"How're you doing, Howard?" Keir stuck out his hand. "How's your wife? That baby's due any time now, isn't it?"

"Yes, sir. Couple of weeks. How was the vacation?"

"Terrific."

"And now it's back to work, huh?"

"Something like that." Keir clapped the guard on the shoulder. "Take care, Howard. Be sure and let me add my good wishes when the baby gets here."

Keir stopped smiling as he stepped inside the hotel and walked down the hall that led past a series of offices. He could almost feel the place swallow him up. Even dragging a breath into his lungs seemed difficult.

A month away, and now he really knew how much he wanted out.

He stabbed the freight elevator call button, tucked his hands into the pockets of his well-worn Levi's and tipped back a little on his heels.

The duchess had made it clear that she'd understand, if he left the Song.

Would she, really?

He'd come to Vegas to help run the place after his father's death. He was the eldest son, the O'Connell offspring who'd proven himself Responsible with a capital R. Cullen wasn't. He'd just left college, a dozen credits short of his degree, to do God only knew what. Sean had been—well, nobody had been quite sure of what Sean had been doing or where he'd been doing it. And the girls—Megan, Fallon and Briana—had all still been away at school.

"You'll just stay for a bit," his mother had said, "only until I can handle things on my own."

After a year, he'd suggested they hire a Chief Operating Officer.

"I don't know that I'd feel comfortable with someone outside the family," Mary had told him. "Can you stay on a little longer, Keir?"

He had, and just when it looked as if his mother was ready to take the reins, she'd had a massive heart attack.

Keir pressed the call button again and made a mental note to have Maintenance check the elevators. There were only two cars in this bank and they got heavy use from employees. One, at least, should have been moving.

Now, by a twist of fate, he was free of the responsibility of the Song. Thanks to another twist, maybe he'd found what he'd been looking for, even if all he knew about wine was how to drink it.

Better not to think like that. Whatever he knew or didn't know about grapes and wine, he was glad he'd bought Deer Run, glad he was finally getting on with his life. He felt as if it had been on hold for years, not just the six he'd spent working for his mother but the years he'd spent taking university courses that bored him.

He'd never let himself think about that while he was in school or even afterward, but during the trip east, the car eating up the miles, he'd felt something pushing for acknowledgment inside him, as if what had gone on in that garden had only been the first step toward acceptance of the truth.

He was restless.

He'd *always* been restless, though he'd fought against it. He'd kept it hidden like a dirty secret, even from his family.

"My strong, dependable boy," his mother had told him once. "You're just like my Ruarch."

Dependable? His father? Ruarch O'Connell had been a gambler, shifting them all from place to place on the turn of a card and never giving a damn for a plan that stretched further than tomorrow.

The last thing he wanted was to be like his father. Keir believed in laying things out so you knew what was coming next. And he'd never so much as fed a coin into a slot machine in his entire life.

So, why was he gambling now?

He tightened his jaw and pressed the call button again.

Investing in a property wasn't gambling. It was logical. Reasonable. As reasonable as knowing, *knowing,* dammit, a woman wanted you and then letting her pretend she didn't…

He cursed under his breath, pounded a fist on the call button and glared at the light panel above the door.

What he needed was a shower, a quick nap and a meal. Then he'd have his head together. That was why he was going to his suite the back way, so he didn't run into the duchess or any of his brothers or sisters, who were probably at the Song by now.

He certainly wasn't going the back way to avoid seeing Cassie.

Funny, how he'd never much noticed her until that night in the garden. She was an employee. He probably wouldn't have known her name if she hadn't been Dawn's friend—and the duchess had taken an interest in Dawn.

Hello, Cassie.

Goodbye, Cassie.

That had been the extent of his involvement with her. He didn't even know how long she'd been working at the Song, just that she was there, serving free drinks in the casino, dressed in what he thought of as the casino uniform. A short black skirt topped by a low-cut blouse. Black fishnet stockings. High heels. Vegas was a town where scantily dressed women were the status quo. Why *would* he have noticed?

But she hadn't looked like that in Texas. Maybe that was the reason he'd become aware of her. Okay, maybe he had noticed her once or twice before. Even in a town like this, where beautiful women were a dime a dozen, Cassie's looks were special.

She'd gone into the night with him, let him touch her and kiss her, and then she'd said "no." Why? She'd been as turned-on as he, as eager for what should have come next…

Keir's mouth tightened.

Maybe she'd expected him to ignore that breathless little "no." Maybe she'd expected him to offer her something to sweeten the deal. Whatever the reason, it was a damned good thing she'd decided to stop him. He'd been lucky to get out in time.

What was it his brother Sean had once said about men and hot-looking women? Maybe it was Cullen who'd said it. Not that it mattered. The message was what counted.

Men suffered from ZTS. Zipper Think Syndrome, meaning when it came to sex, guys thought with their zippers instead of their heads.

Keir grinned. Yeah, that was it. The old ZTS theory.

The light above the elevator was moving at last. Twelve. Ten. Eight. Six. Two. Keir gave a relieved sigh as the car announced its arrival with a soft ping.

Okay. One problem solved. For all he cared, the doors could slide open, the Berk babe could be standing there with nothing on but her skin and it wouldn't mean a damn.

Except, that wasn't quite the scene. Cassie was inside the elevator, all right, wearing that little skirt, the clingy top, the high-heeled shoes…

Correction. She had only one shoe on. She was bent over the other one, which seemed to be stuck to the floor, her cute little bottom pointed straight at him. Either she was too busy to know she had an audience or she just didn't care.

And he was having trouble remembering that he was too old to be led astray by ZTS.

Man, he'd been on the road too long.

Keir cleared his throat and donned what he figured was his best Chief of Ops polite smile.

"Hello, Cassie."

She jolted upright and swiveled toward him, the look on

her face going quickly from surprise to recognition to displeasure.

"You!"

She filled the word with loathing. Well, he could hardly blame her. Her memories of the last time they'd met probably were no better than his. Be pleasant, he told himself. After all, he owed the lady an apology.

"Yeah, that's right. Me." Keir nodded at the shoe. "Having a problem?"

"No," she snapped, "I always stand around like this, with one shoe on and one shoe—"

The car began to move. She hadn't expected it and she jerked back.

"Careful!"

Keir grabbed for her but Cassie flung out a hand and caught the railing.

"Don't touch me!"

So much for being polite. "No problem. You want to break your neck, be my guest."

"I'm doing just fine on my own."

"Oh, yeah. I can see that." He watched, arms folded, as she tried to pull the shoe free again. "Stop being foolish, Berk. Let me help—or would you rather I put in a call to Maintenance and have them send up a work crew?"

"What? Those idiots? They're the ones who left this damned piece of wood here in the first place." She leaned down again. "I'll fix it myself."

Maybe. But he couldn't promise what he'd do if she kept bending over like that.

"Not on my time," he said sharply, "and not in my elevator. Dammit, why argue over something so simple?"

"Go ahead, then. Who am I to argue with the man in charge?"

"'Thank you' might be a more gracious response." Keir squatted down, yanked the shoe free and rose to his feet. "Here. Next time you decide to wear stilts—"

The car shuddered to a halt. Cassie yelped, stumbled, and Keir caught her in his arms.

She caught her breath. So did he. She was pressed tightly against him, her back against his chest, her bottom against his groin. Don't move, he thought, God, don't move…

The doors swooshed open. Keir heard a sound. A snicker? No. A snort of laughter. He swung around, taking Cassie with him, and saw two very interested, all-too-familiar faces.

Cassie gave a little moan of despair. "Your brothers?" she whispered.

Keir nodded.

Sean and Cullen O'Connell simply grinned.

CHAPTER TWO

CASSIE'S day had gone really, really well.

She'd worked a double shift to cover for one of the other girls who'd either come down with the flu or had a new boyfriend—nobody was quite sure which—but that was okay.

No problem. She could use the extra money.

The only thing was that she'd started the first shift tired after a tough, three hour exam, the final one before she got her degree in restaurant management. Cassie had taken the course on the Internet after signing up, mostly out of curiosity, two years ago. The work had been interesting and, to her surprise, she'd done well at it.

Soon, she'd start looking for a job as far from Vegas as she could get. She'd already decided on an employment agency, a place called TopNotch, because the gossip mill said TopNotch provided almost all management employees to the Desert Song.

If it was good enough for the Song, it was good enough for her.

By the time her second shift was drawing to a close, Cassie was totally exhausted. Her mouth felt stiff from constant smiling, her eyes felt tired from the re-circulated air washing over her contacts, and her feet…

No. She wasn't going to think about her feet. Rule One in Cassandra Bercovic's Survival Guide: dancers and waitresses should never think about their feet until they no longer had to stand on them. Once you admitted they hurt, you were in deep trouble.

She was already in trouble.

Cassie winced as she eased one foot just a little way out of its silken, stiletto-heeled prison. Her toes felt as if they'd been jammed into a ball, her arches ached and the soles burned as if a sadist had gone at them with a blowtorch.

She sighed, plucked an empty glass from beside a silent slot machine and put it on her tray.

Toe shoes had been the bane of her existence until she'd given up ballet the day after her seventeenth birthday. Back then, she'd thought bloody feet were only the province of ballerinas.

Talk about being wrong…

Okay. Enough of feeling sorry for herself. Her feet hurt. Big deal. The good news was that she was almost out of here. It had to be close to seven. There was no way to tell because there were never clocks in casinos. The only time that mattered was how long a guest spent at the slots or at the tables.

She knew the time, though. She'd asked Chip on her last stop to put in an order at the bar.

"Pushing 6:15 in the old A.M.," he'd told her.

Thank God.

Cassie swallowed a yawn. One last circuit of the room and that would be it. The casino was almost empty at this hour. Only the diehards played between dawn and breakfast, and there hadn't been too many of them this morning.

"Miss?"

She knew who it was before she looked. The sweaty-faced guy at the dollar slots. Rule Number Two of the Bercovic Survival Guide: you could count on a minimum of one pig turning up, each and every shift.

"Yes, sir?" she said politely.

"Gimme another orange juice. And this time, do like I said, okay? I want a double shot of vodka, not a single."

"It was a double shot the last time, sir," Cassie replied, even more politely.

The man glared as he slapped his empty glass on her tray. She shot a quick look at the tall paper cup that held his coins. Last time she'd come by, it was full. Now, it was almost empty.

"Listen, toots, I can tell the difference between one shot or two, and that wasn't no two. I want a double. You got that?"

Cassie could almost feel her blood pressure soar but she'd been a waitress long enough to manage a smile.

"Yes, sir. I'll be right back with your drink."

Her smile turned into a scowl when she reached the bar.

"Pig," she muttered as she slapped down her tray.

Chip grinned. "Nothing's as much fun as the early morning players, Cass. You should know that by now."

"Yeah, yeah, yeah." Cassie sighed. "Another OJ, double vodka."

"Comin' up." Chip reached for a clean glass. "Guy's an asshole, huh?"

"You got it."

"Well, the shift's almost over."

"How soon?"

Chip pushed back his cuff and checked his watch. "Five minutes to go."

"Hallelujah! I'm so tired I'm liable to fall asleep standing up."

"Yeah. Me, too." He cleared his throat. "Coffee would help, right?"

"I don't know if anything will help. I'm totally wiped."

"Trust me. You need coffee. Espresso, black, lot of sugar to double the jolt."

"You're probably right."

"And some food," Chip said, adding OJ to the vodka. "Which is why I figured we could go someplace for breakfast, say a little place just opened a couple of blocks off the Strip."

Cassie sighed. "Thanks, but all I'm up for is going home, taking a shower and falling into bed."

"Alone," the bartender said, with an easy smile that made it okay, "right?"

Cassie smiled, too. Chip was a nice guy and if she'd been interested in getting involved, he'd have been a good choice—but then, when it came to men and to life, she'd never managed to make good choices. One thing she'd learned, though. When it came to life, you had to take whatever it threw at you.

Men, at least, you could swear off, and she definitely had.

If only she'd remembered that before Keir O'Connell had come on to her at Dawn's wedding.

"Keir keeps looking at you," Dawn had whispered when they had a moment alone after the ceremony.

"Don't be silly," she'd whispered back. "He's probably just trying to remember where he's seen me before."

Dawn had laughed, just as she was supposed to, but it was true, Keir *had* been looking at her, the way a man looks at a woman, giving her those sexy little grins, leaning in closer than necessary to ask if she wanted anything from the buffet, and he'd been so gorgeous in his tux, so dangerous with those dark as midnight eyes…

"If you change your mind about breakfast…" Chip said, and Cassie looked up and smiled.

"Sure."

"Ouch. Was ever a word said with less enthusiasm?"

"Chip, I'm sorry. It's not you, it's me."

"Double ouch. That's the great-granddaddy of all brush-off lines."

Cassie blushed. "Honestly, I'm just—"

"Hey, I'm teasing. It's okay. Can't blame a guy for trying, right?"

"I'm just not dating anybody for a while. You understand?"

"Sure." He put the double OJ and vodka on her tray. "Bet the guy who ordered this hasn't tipped you yet, right?"

"Clever man."

"He gives you any trouble, you need any help, just sing out."

"Will do. Thanks."

"Hey, no need. I live to serve."

Cassie laughed, plucked a couple of cocktail napkins from the stack on the bar and brought the drink to the guy at the dollar slots. She dipped her knees the way you were supposed to, put a napkin beside him and the glass on top of it.

"Your drink, sir."

"I hope you got it right this time."

"Double vodka and orange juice, just as you ordered."

The man picked up the glass, slurped half of it down while he fed tokens into the machine. Cassie started to walk away.

"Hey! You take this back to that bartender and tell him—"

Coins began to cascade from the slot machine. Music played, lights blinked, and the river of silver kept coming.

"Lookit this! I hit the jackpot."

It certainly looked as if he had. Coins were still pouring out.

"You must of brung me luck, little lady." Grinning, the man stuck a beefy paw into the shimmering explosion of silver. "Here. This is for you."

Cassie lifted her eyebrows. "Why, thank—"

The words caught in her throat. He'd handed her two dollars. She narrowed her eyes, opened her mouth—and felt a hand close around her elbow. Inez, her replacement, marched her away from the machine.

"Do not," Inez said through a toothy smile, "tell *el puerco* what you think of him."

"Two bucks," Cassie hissed. "That's what he gave me, after four drinks and a couple of hours worth of nastiness." She craned her head, looked back over her shoulder. "He must have hit for a thousand."

"Six thousand," Inez said, still smiling and still hustling Cassie toward the employees' exit, "and he is the slime of the universe, but you want to keep your job, right?"

"Inez…"

''Remember the rules, Cass. Employees are always polite to guests.''

The rules. The Desert Song's rules. Keir O'Connell's rules, not Cassie Bercovic's. If she told the guy what she thought of him, O'Connell would sack her.

Too bad the boss didn't have rules that governed his own behavior.

''Here.'' Inez took Cassie's tray and handed her the small purse she'd left behind the bar. ''Now, go home.''

''Once, just once, I'd like to tell a guy like that what I think.''

''Wait until you're ready to quit. Then come into the casino and security will give you special dispensation to clobber the sleazebag of the night.'' Inez grinned. ''Okay?''

Cassie sighed. ''Okay.''

''Until then…you're rude, you're crude, you lose your job.''

''I know.''

''Good, 'cause the big man's serious when he tells that to employees. If you have a legitimate beef with some SOB, you take it to O'Connell and let him handle it.''

Inez was right. That was Keir's policy, and wasn't that amazing because if you wanted to talk about rude, crude sons of bitches, he was your man.

And why did she keep thinking about him this morning? She wasn't going to do it again, except maybe to consider that as bad as the guy up to his wrists in silver was, Keir was worse.

''Okay,'' Cassie said, with the stretch-the-lips smile she'd learned putting in six nights a week strutting across a stage with the Eiffel Tower on her head. ''I'm going home.''

''You do that. Just leave Mr. Big Tipper to me.'' Inez fluttered her lashes. ''I'll be so sweet when I talk to him that he'll pass out from a sugar overdose.''

Cassie laughed and gave the other woman a quick hug. ''Good night.''

''You mean, good morning.''

''Whatever. Have a good one.''

"Yeah. You, too."

Cassie thought about taking the stairs to the basement locker room but she was just too tired and her feet really were killing her. Maybe it was these shoes. They were new, and the straps cut into her flesh.

She pressed the call button for one of the employee elevators. Sighing, she slipped one foot from her shoe and rubbed her cramped toes against the carpet.

Wearing three inch heels wasn't fun, especially if you'd spent most of your life torturing your tootsies.

Rule Number Three of Cassandra Bercovic's Survival Guide, Cassie thought, grimacing as she pressed the call button again. If you started doing *pliés* at seven and high kicks at seventeen, forget about high heels because your feet would be a hundred years older than the rest of you by the time you hit twenty-nine.

The problem was, Rule Number Three was pitched into the dust by Rule Number Four.

The Higher The Heels, The Better The Tips.

It was the truest rule of all, and she needed every penny she could come by if she wanted to hold out for the right management job. She didn't know where she'd find it or when. Her only criteria was that the place had to be small and pretty, and light-years from Las Vegas.

Then she could trade in these torturous stilettos for a nice comfy pair of orthopedics.

The thought made her smile.

Sighing, she slid her shoe back on, stepped out of the other one and flexed her toes.

Except for the one jerk, she'd had a pretty good shift. Two shifts. Most people had been pleasant, the tips had been decent, and the only guy who'd tried to hit on her was so decrepit that she'd almost felt sorry for him.

Cassie glanced up at the unblinking lights on the panel over the cars. What was taking so long? That hot shower and soft bed were calling to her...well, maybe she'd wait on the bed part. She'd sign on to her computer, see if, by some miracle, her grade was waiting in her e-mail in-box. And there was something she wanted to check on, a question she was pretty sure she'd gotten right on the exam but she wanted to look it up and be sure.

Tired or not, she preferred going online early in the day, while things were still relatively quiet in her apartment complex. It had been tough, getting into the habit of hitting the books after you'd been out of school for almost a dozen years, especially when you'd been such a miserable failure while you'd been there the first time.

Maybe that was why she hadn't told anyone she was taking the course. This way, if she flunked out, nobody would know except her. She might have told Dawn, who was her best friend, but she'd sensed that Dawn had enough trouble of her own without having to worry about offering encouragement to a terrified student.

And then Dawn had fallen head over heels in love and she'd plunged into planning a beautiful wedding at Gray's uncle's ranch in Tex—

Cassie stiffened.

Uh uh. She wasn't going there again. Forget Texas. She'd wasted enough time the past month, going over what had happened, what she'd said, what Keir had said, trying to figure out how she'd ended up in that garden, letting him make a fool of her.

Actually, it wasn't was all that difficult to understand. The romantic setting would have softened even the most dedicated cynic. Add buckets of champagne, dreamy music, the no-way-out-of-it amount of time the maid of honor was expected to spend with the best man…

The best man. What a joke. The *worst* man was more like it, and where was that damned elevator?

Cassie banged on the call button.

She missed Dawn. All those late-night chats at the kitchen table, the two of them pigging out on pizza or take-out Chinese. If Dawn were still here, she'd not only have told her about the restaurant management course, she'd have told her about Keir O'Connell, too, how he'd gone slumming, how amazed he'd been when she'd stopped him from making love to her…

…how relieved.

Cassie's mouth thinned.

Oh, his face when she'd told him to stop. All she'd meant was that things were moving too fast but Keir had blanched under that all-year tan. He'd let go of her so quickly that she'd almost fallen.

"Cassie," he'd said, his voice hoarse. "Cassie, I'm so sorry…"

What he'd meant was, *What the hell was I doing?*

She knew, because she'd seen that look on men's faces before, when she was a showgirl. You met someone, you hit it off, things were fine until the guy asked what you did for a living.

"I dance," she'd say.

"Where?" he'd say.

From there on, it was all downhill.

By the time she'd been desperate enough to strip, she'd known better than to talk about it.

She wasn't either a showgirl or a stripper anymore but it didn't matter. She was still Cassie Berk and some things never changed…and where was that miserable elevator?

To hell with it. History was history. With a little luck she'd be out of Vegas soon enough. No more hearing the ping of the slots, even in her sleep. No more guys thinking she was smiling just for them. No more turning her feet into aching, leaden weights.

Best of all, no more seeing Keir.

He was away. On vacation, everybody said, as if it were a miracle the great man would do such a thing.

She'd already known he was going away.

"I'm taking some time off," he'd told her as they sat alone at one of the little umbrella tables, smiling at each other because smiling had seemed a good thing to do right then.

He'd said her he was going to New York and then he'd

hesitated as if he were going to tell her something else, and just for a minute, for the tiniest bit of eternity, she'd thought maybe, oh maybe he was going to say, "Cassie, come with me..."

The light panel blinked to life; the elevator doors slid open. Cassie was trying to jam her foot back into her shoe when the doors began to slide shut.

"Hey!"

She lunged forward, hobbled into the car and stepped on some plywood sheets one of the maintenance guys must have left on the floor. One heel sank into the wood.

"Idiot," she mumbled, as the elevator doors closed.

She grimaced, tried to jerk her foot free, but the heel was wedged into a knothole.

"Major idiot," she said, and jerked her foot out of the shoe. Tongue between her teeth, she bent over and began working the shoe free. It wobbled under the pressure of her hand and she knew she'd have to be careful or she'd snap the stupid heel off. It wasn't just high, it was also thin, sharp and unstable.

Too bad she hadn't been wearing this pair of torture devices at Dawn's wedding. If she'd planted a heel like this in Keir's instep, he'd still be limping.

"Dammit," she hissed, "would-you-let-loose?"

The shoe didn't budge. Maybe it had better sense than she did. If *she* hadn't budged, hadn't gone into that garden with him...

How could she have made such an ass of herself? She'd spent her life living by Rule Number Five, or maybe it was Six. Who cared what number it was? The rule was what mattered.

Never Make It With The Boss.

It was the most important rule of all, it let you avoid a whole mess of trouble, and she'd almost broken it. And what about the rules he'd broken? All those sexual harassment things that said employers were not to hit on their employees.

What about that?

She'd been foolish but no question, Keir was to blame for what had happened. Coming on to her, when he was her boss. Maybe he did it all the time. She'd never heard even a hint of gossip but when men who looked like he did—tall, broad-shouldered and altogether gorgeous—they set their own rules.

What was with this damn shoe?

If she never saw Keir again, it would be—

The car jerked to a stop. The doors slid open. She heard someone clear his throat and she almost laughed, thinking what a weird sight she probably made…

"Hello, Cassie."

She froze. That voice. Male. Deep. A little husky. As removed as if they'd never had that midnight encounter in the garden.

But—but it couldn't be. Keir was away. He was—

He was here, looking at her with a smile so polite she wanted to slap it away.

"You," she said, and she knew her loathing for him was in the one word because that polite smile slipped from his face.

"Yeah, that's right. Me." He looked at her foot, then at her face. "Having a problem?" he said, his voice tinged with amusement.

"No," she snapped, "I always stand around like this, with one shoe on and one shoe—"

The car began to move. She hadn't expected it and she jerked back.

"Careful!"

Keir grabbed for her but Cassie flung out a hand and caught the railing.

"Don't touch me!"

"No problem." His voice was cool. "You want to break your neck, be my guest."

"I'm doing just fine on my own."

"Oh, yeah. I can see that." He watched, arms folded, as she tried to pull the shoe free again. "Stop being foolish,

Berk. Let me help—or would you rather I put in a call to Maintenance and have them send up a work crew?''

''What? Those idiots? They're the ones who left this damned piece of wood here in the first place.''

She glared at him, then at her shoe. The truth was, he could probably free it in less time than it would take him to make the call. Besides, if the maintenance guys showed up, they'd have a good laugh and spread the story all over the hotel.

Cassie lifted her chin. ''All right.''

'''Thank you' might be a more gracious response.'' Keir squatted down, grabbed the shoe, yanked it free and rose to his feet. ''Here. Next time you decide to wear stilts—''

The car jolted to a stop. Cassie stumbled, yelped, and Keir grabbed her before she could fall.

Grabbed her, so that she was pressed back against him, so that she could feel the warmth of his body, feel the swift hardening of it…

Somebody was laughing.

Keir swung around, still holding her. Cassie's eyes widened. Two men were standing at the open doors of the elevator, taking in the scene with big grins on their faces.

They looked nothing like Keir or each other…and looked everything like Keir and each other.

Her heart dropped to her toes.

For days, the staff had been talking about the O'Connell clan, all Mary Elizabeth's daughters and sons, and how they were going to descend on the hotel for the duchess's wedding to Dan Coyle.

''Your brothers?'' Cassie said, even though she already knew the answer.

Keir nodded, his brothers chuckled, and Cassie wondered what the odds were on the bottom falling out of the car so she could simply disappear.

CHAPTER THREE

BEYOND the perimeter of the Desert Song, the Strip was as brightly-lit, as busy and noisy as if it were midday instead of midnight, but everything was hushed deep within the hotel gardens. The lights in the oversized pool had been dimmed and emitted a soft, fairy glow.

Nice, Cullen O'Connell thought, as he drifted on a float in the warm, silky water. You could even see the stars. Not the way they blazed in the blackness over the vast grasslands of the Rift Valley or on a rare, clear night high on the snow-laden slopes of Mount McKinley, but nice, nevertheless.

Even in Vegas, it was nice to know that the stars were still there.

"You counting stars again, like when we were kids?" Sean O'Connell spoke softly, from a float just a few feet away.

"Better to count stars than count cards like you were doing at the blackjack table a little while ago," Cullen said lazily.

Sean chuckled. "Now, Cullen, would I do that? Counting cards is illegal—if you do it when you play a hand, and I was only watching, not playing."

"Counting stars is safer," Cullen said with a smile in his voice.

"Considering that we're back in Sin City, maybe the only thing we should be counting is babes."

"Like that summer, you mean?" Cullen smiled up at the sky. "When I saved my allowance the whole year so I could buy a telescope? And Pop found you using it to girl-watch instead?"

"You mean, Pop found *us* using it."

"Yeah, well, I was easily corrupted."

Sean gave a soft laugh. "I'd almost forgotten that. Remember the blonde in the corner room on the fourteenth floor of the east wing?"

"How could I forget? She was the reason the old man threw out my telescope and paddled my behind so hard I couldn't sit for a week."

"Two days, and admit it, she was worth it."

The men drifted in silence for a while, and then Sean spoke.

"How many times you think we sneaked out here at night, buddy? I figure it must have been at least a couple of hundred."

"Heck, we probably got *caught* a couple of hundred."

"Yeah. And got our bottoms warmed. Never stopped us, though, from sneaking out again."

"That's 'cause it was worth it, coming out here late at night, getting to use the pool without sharing it with a couple of trillion strangers."

The brothers sighed, at ease as they drifted on the water and three decades of shared memories.

"So," Cullen said, "where were you when you found out about Ma's engagement to this guy?"

Sean turned over on the float and cushioned his face on his folded arms.

"Monte Carlo. At a private casino. I was up fifty grand when I got the cable." His voice roughened. "I must have lost ten years of my life, just opening the envelope. I thought—"

"—that Ma had had another heart attack. I know. It was the same for me. I was downloading my e-mail and there was this message marked 'urgent,' with the Desert Song's address on it and I figured..." Cullen sighed. "I was so relieved that it took me a while to start worrying about the actual message, you know? That she's marrying this Dan Coyle, a man nobody knows."

"Keir knows him, and seems to like him."

"True."

"And Ma's crazy about him."

"Well, those are both good signs, right?"

"Right." Sean sighed. "It's good to be back."

"Temporarily."

"Oh, yeah. That goes without saying. I wouldn't want to live in this fishbowl again." Sean dropped his hand and let his fingers glide through the water. "We owe Keir."

"For taking over here, after Pop died? Yeah. Big time."

"He looks… I don't know. Edgy."

"You think?"

"Maybe that's the wrong word. I just get the feeling he's got something on his mind."

"The fox in the elevator, maybe." Cullen grinned. "Man, what a scene to walk in on. Keir, holding an armful of female, looking at us as if he wished he could have dropped right through the floor of that car…"

Sean rolled off his float and into the water. "You think there was something really going on there?"

"In an elevator, in the Desert Song? That's not big brother's style. He's too buttoned up to try something like that."

"Too bad we didn't get much chance to torment him about it."

"Yeah. Bree's and Meg's timing sort of screwed things up." Sean's voice warmed as he spoke his sisters' names. "It's good to see the two of them. Last time we were all together was, what, Christmas?"

"I know. Well, it's tough, with you traipsing around the world, me in New York, Bree in San Francisco, Meg in Boston, Fallon God knows where—"

"Paris, last I heard, for what she calls a fashion shoot."

"Meanwhile, Keir's trapped here in Vegas."

"You think that's the way he feels?"

"It's the way I'd feel, in his place."

Cullen hoisted himself out of the pool and dragged the float up beside him.

"You know what? I'm going to get him alone and ask him. I mean, maybe he wants to go on managing the Song, but if he doesn't… Ma's okay now. She looks wonderful, in fact. Seems to me it's time we made other arrangements, like convincing her to hire someone to take over."

"Someone *is* going to take over," Keir said, stepping out of the shadows. "Under the duchess's supervision, of course."

"Of course," Sean said, smiling. "How'd you get her to agree to that?"

"Actually, she suggested it." Keir loosened his tie and tucked his hands into his pockets. "Her doctors gave her a clean bill of health and she's been chomping at the bit, wanting to get back to work."

"She's up to handling things alone? Well, with the help of a Chief of Ops?"

"She won't have to. She's going to be a married lady this time tomorrow, remember?"

"Actually, we wanted to talk to you about that. This guy Coyle. He's okay?"

"Yes. Definitely okay."

"He'd better be."

"I think he was pretty okay to you guys when you tried that CIA interrogation at dinner." Keir grinned. "Considering he's a retired captain of detectives with the New York City P.D., he let you get off easy."

"Hey," Sean said, straight-faced, "you can never be too careful about a man you're going to call 'Daddy.'"

"Tell him that, why don't you?" Keir said, his tongue firmly tucked in his cheek.

"I did. That's when I decided he was probably all right."

"Because?"

"Because he said he'd slug me one, if I ever tried it."

The three brothers laughed. Then Sean climbed out of

the pool, dumped his float over a *chaise longue* and thumbed his wet hair out of his eyes.

"So, let me get this straight. Ma's going to hire somebody to manage the place, and he'll report to her and Dan?"

"That's the plan. Just to set your minds at ease, I trust Dan completely, not only because I ran an in-depth check on him before I brought him into the Song a few years back but also because I've gotten to know him well. He's definitely one of the good guys. And he knows the Song, inside and out." Keir shoved aside the damp towel Sean had tossed over a lounge chair and sat down. "That sound okay to you two?"

"It sounds fine," Sean said.

"Fine," Cullen echoed. "But where does that leave you?"

Keir cleared his throat. "I'm, uh, I'm moving on."

The simple words stopped conversation. Until now, Keir hadn't realized how ominous they sounded.

"Moving on?" Sean said. "Where?"

Keir hesitated. His mother had looked at him as if he'd lost his sanity when he'd told her his plans. Would his brothers?

"I'm going east. I bought a business in Connecticut."

"You serious?"

"Dead serious. It looks like it's going to be a lot of work. I mean, it's small, but I think, given time, I can build it into something."

"What kind of business?"

Keir shrugged. "A small one, like I said."

"He's being deliberately vague," Sean said to Cullen, as if Keri weren't there.

"Yup. In fact, I get the feeling BB doesn't want to tell us what this business is," Cullen replied, his grin hidden by the darkness.

"Don't call me that!"

"Can you imagine? He doesn't want to call him BB and he doesn't want to tell us what this business is." Sean gave a deep sigh. "What's the good of having a brother if he won't let you in on his secrets?"

"A Big Brother," Cullen said solemnly.

"Uh huh." There was a pause. "With a pair of capital B's, for short."

"Will you stop calling me that? And I didn't say it was a secret!"

"Should we tell him he didn't have to?" said Cullen. "Should we remind him that we're his very own flesh and blood and we can read him like a book?"

Keir looked from Cullen to Sean. Despite all their teasing, they were worried about him. He knew, because he'd overheard more of their conversation than he'd let on. Well, why not tell them now? Get it over with, instead of dragging it out until after the wedding tomorrow. That was what he'd planned but being pronounced insane by all five of his siblings at once might be just a little intimidating.

"Okay." He took a deep breath. "You want to know what kind of business I bought?" Another deep breath. "A vineyard."

For what seemed an eternity, neither Sean nor Cullen said anything. Sean was the first to break the silence.

"Did you say, vineyard? As in, where they grow grapes and make wine?"

"That's right. With a small restaurant as part of the set-up."

"A vineyard," Sean repeated.

"Yes."

"In Connecticut," Cullen added. "With a small restaurant as—"

"Dammit, will you stop that? Yes. A vineyard. And a restaurant. And I don't care if you guys think I'm nuts or what, I'm glad I bought— Hey! Hey, what're you doing?"

What they were doing was clapping him on the back hard enough to have sent a smaller man to his knees.

"Man, that's terrific," Cullen said happily. "I mean, it's

crazy as hell but it's time you did something crazy. Right, Sean?''

''Absolutely. It's so off the wall, it sounds like something I could have done.''

''And that's a compliment?'' Keir said, laughing.

''Damn right. Listen, you need to get in touch with anybody who's into wine, let me know. I took a marker I never got around to collecting from a guy playing *chemin de fer* last summer. His family owns a vineyard in Burgundy.''

''And if you need legal advice, I'm your man,'' Cullen said. ''I know you have your own attorney but since you'll be doing the deal closer to my turf, back east—''

''Wait a minute.'' Keir stepped back and looked from one of his brothers to the other. ''So, you don't think I'm ready for a rubber room?''

''Well, of course we do but then, we've always thought that. Right, Cullen?''

''Absolutely right.'' Cullen gave Keir a light punch in the shoulder. ''Seriously, congratulations.''

''Yeah. I mean, thanks.''

''Just for the record, I'm impressed.''

A smile curved Keir's mouth. ''Yeah?''

''Yeah. Sounds like an interesting proposition.''

''Well, that's good to hear because the vote, so far, is three to one that I've lost all my marbles.''

''Who's voting?''

''The duchess. My accountant. And my lawyer pretty much made it unanimous.''

''Ma'll come around. As for the accountant and the lawyer—all the more reason to dump them.''

''You think?''

''Absolutely. Megan'll be your CPA. I'll be your attorney. We'll only be a couple of hours away and besides, why deal with people who'll look for the hole in your head each time you sit down at the table?''

Keir laughed. ''You have a way with words, pal, you

know that?'' His smile tilted. ''You want to know the truth, there've been moments I've doubted my own sanity.''

''Just because you're starting to live dangerously? Hey, that's what life's all about.'' Sean elbowed Cullen. ''You got all this straight? The man's bought himself a vineyard. He bought himself a restaurant. And if it hadn't been for us, he'd have made it in the elevator with Cinderella.''

Keir's mouth tightened. He'd been expecting this ever since his brothers walked in on the scene with Cassie.

Then why did the teasing words make his belly knot?

''We were not about to make it in the elevator, as you so delicately put it.''

''Whatever you say, big brother.''

''I hardly know the lady.''

''Well, that's good news for me. Just tell me her name, give me her number—''

''Keep away from her.''

Keir's voice was suddenly tense with warning. Cullen and Sean stared at him. He glared back, and then he groaned.

Cullen was only kidding but even if he wasn't, so what? If he wanted to hit on Cassie, let him.

''I mean,'' he said carefully, ''we embarrassed her enough. Besides, she's an employee. She works in the hotel. She's a cocktail waitress.''

''Well, that certainly explains why the two of you were wrapped around each other. Doesn't it, Sean?''

Keir folded his arms. ''You're never going to leave me alone about this, are you?''

''No,'' Sean agreed pleasantly, ''we're not.''

''Look, the elevator stopped and Cassie was in it. And—''

''And?'' Cullen said, with a lift of his eyebrows.

''And,'' Keir said briskly, ''her heel was stuck.'' Two pairs of eyebrows lifted. He decided to ignore the warning signs. ''Somebody from Maintenance had left some plywood on the floor, and her heel got wedged in a knothole.''

Sean gave a deep sigh. ''Dangerous combination, plywood and elevators.''

Despite himself, Keir's mouth twitched. ''Listen, I'm warning you both—''

''No, it's cool,'' said Cullen. ''We understand. As some men get older, they need more of, uh, more of a stimulus before they can get it on.''

''Older? I'm one year older. One year!''

''He's right,'' Sean said. ''It wasn't senile male hormones, it was a galloping case of ZTS.''

''Okay. It's not going to work. I've explained what happened. You want to get some more mileage out of it, go on. Be my guest.''

''Trust us,'' Sean replied solemnly, ''we will.''

Keir looked from one of his brothers to the other and saw the laughter dancing in their eyes. A familiar warmth spread through his veins. This was the way it had always been, two of them needling the other, and it had never mattered which two it was because it changed from day to day. Hell, it changed from minute to minute.

But what bonded them together would never change. Shared memories and shared blood would always unite and sustain them, just as it had when they were growing up. Being the sons of Ruarch O'Connell had not been easy, despite the duchess's misty-eyed memories.

He felt a catch in his throat. He'd missed his brothers. Missed this. The teasing, the laughter, the knowledge that nobody in the world knew him the way they did.

''All right.'' He nodded, sighed, offered all the signs of peaceful surrender. ''You guys want details, you'll get them. Just come in a little closer…''

He moved fast, as if they were all still kids and these were the old times, when they'd played their own version of touch football whenever they'd been in one place long enough to find a flat field. He took Sean out first, his shoulder connecting with Sean's flat belly and then he spun and got Cullen before he could sidestep. Both of them yelped and fell backward into the pool hard enough to raise a geyser of water that rivaled Old Faithful.

A spill of feminine laughter erupted behind Keir. He swung around and saw his three sisters standing next to one of the softly-lighted palm trees that ringed the pool.

"Hey." He grinned. Briana, Fallon and Megan grinned back.

"And to think," Fallon said archly, "that Mom sent us to find you gentlemen because she was afraid you were sitting around, having a long, solemn talk about what would happen now that BB's leaving."

Keir raised one dark eyebrow. "You see those guys in the pool? One of the things that put 'em there was calling me Big Brother."

Megan rose on her toes and peered past Keir. "Poor babies," she crooned.

Something in Briana's smile made the hair rise on the back of Keir's neck.

"What?"

Bree fluttered her lashes. "Enjoy your swim," she purred.

He yelped as his brother's hands clamped around his ankles. Keir hit the water hard, went under and came up, sputtering and laughing, between Sean and Cullen.

"Is this the respect you show your big brother?"

Cullen sighed. "All of a sudden, he wants the title back."

"Damn right." Keir smiled. "You know what? It's great to have you home."

"We agree," Sean said, and he and Cullen proved it by shoving Keir right back under the water.

Keir awoke at five minutes before six the next morning. He reached out and shut off his alarm clock before its shrill cry could pierce his foggy brain, then sat up and swung his feet to the floor.

Four hours sleep was all he'd had. He and his brothers and sisters had ended up here in his suite, where they'd sat talking and laughing for hours. There'd been a lot of catching up to do. Only the prospect of having to look bright-eyed for their mother's wedding had finally sent them scattering at almost two in the morning.

Keir yawned, got to his feet and walked into the bathroom. The wedding wasn't until noon but he needed time to check on things, make sure the flowers, the music, the food and champagne were as close to perfect as he could get them.

It wasn't every day a man had the chance to oversee his mother's wedding, he thought as he stepped into the shower.

He had some last minute things to do for himself, too. Falling asleep last night, he'd decided there was no sense in delaying his departure. The sooner he left Vegas and began his new life in Connecticut, the better.

This morning he'd phone his attorney, tell him to fax some documents to Cullen's New York office, then instruct his accountant to fax his files to Megan's office in Boston. He'd already arranged for Deer Run's vintner to stay on, but the woman who managed the restaurant had accepted a job in Florida.

"Too many cold New England winters for me," she'd said.

That meant he'd need a new manager.

The restaurant was handsome and the food was great. Service had been a little erratic—his main course came out at the same time as his soup—but all that could be dealt with. Instinct told him there were probably other details that needed improving.

He didn't know what, specifically. Restaurants weren't his specialty. For the last six years his talent had been managing people and if he'd learned one thing, it was that the key to success was finding the right people, then trusting them enough to do the job.

Finding the right people was relatively simple. Whenever he'd needed a manager, someone with the necessary combination of talent and brass, he'd turned to the TopNotch Employment Agency.

They'd never let him down yet.

Well, why not continue dealing with TopNotch? They had contacts everywhere; they'd sent him people from virtually every state in the union.

Keir stepped from the shower and wrapped a towel around his hips.

Okay. He'd phone TopNotch, lay out what he wanted in a manager for the restaurant and leave finding the right person in their more than capable hands. Then he could devote himself to this new challenge. Deer Run. Wine-making. Life in the quiet hills of Connecticut, instead of the fast neon lanes of Vegas.

Maybe he'd even find himself a woman. Someone special. There hadn't been anyone special, not for a very long time.

Swift as a heartbeat, an image flickered in his mind. He saw a woman in a long, old-fashioned gown that clung to her lush curves with each whisper of the wind…

"Hell," he said, and blanked his thoughts to everything but his mother's wedding.

Promptly at noon, he stood with his brothers and sisters at one side of the altar. Mary had insisted that all her daughters and sons give her away. Dan's grown children stood near their father. Everyone was smiling.

Smiling—and quietly weeping.

Keir could hear his sisters sniffling into their lace hankies. He glanced at his brothers. Their eyes glittered in a way that told him their throats were as tight with emotion as his.

"…pronounce you man and wife," the justice of the peace said.

Dan took Mary in his arms. Keir hugged his brothers, kissed his sisters…and suddenly found himself scanning the room filled with family and friends for a glimpse of a woman with sea-green eyes and coal-black hair.

She wasn't there. Why would she be? And why should he be looking for her? There wasn't a reason in the world to see her ever again.

"Keir," his mother said.

He turned and took the duchess in his arms.

"I'm happy for you, Ma." Dan held out his hand and Keir shook it. "I'm happy for you both."

Mary laid her hand against his cheek. "You're leaving soon, aren't you?"

Keir drew a breath. "Yes. Tomorrow." He smiled at Dan. "Now that I know you're safe in good hands, and happy."

"I want you to be happy, too, Keir," Mary said softly.

"I already am."

His mother's eyes filled. "You need something more."

Hours later as he packed, Keir thought about what his mother had said, and wondered if she was right.

CHAPTER FOUR

Bradley Airport, Connecticut, six weeks later:

CASSIE'S plane touched down on the runway just as the first bolt of lightning tore the sky apart.

"Glad that didn't happen when we were still up there," the woman sitting next to her said.

Cassie agreed. She was nervous enough, considering that she'd flown east to take a job, sight unseen.

She took down her carry-on bag and joined the line exiting the plane.

An incredible job, from the sound of it. It was, just as the headhunter at TopNotch had said, an excellent opportunity. A management position at a small but elegant restaurant. An apartment, free of cost, fully furnished and right on the premises. And, best of all, a salary she'd figured had to be a typo until she'd cleared her throat and asked.

How could she have said no?

"Your references have checked out, Ms. Berk," the headhunter had assured her. "The manager of Tender Grapes seems quite pleased with your qualifications and since the owner's left hiring a replacement in her hands, the job is yours if you want it."

"Just like that? She doesn't want to meet me or anything?"

The headhunter had smiled an unctuous smile that Cassie suspected was meant to be reassuring, but which had exactly the opposite effect.

"Just like that, Miss Berk. The lady trusts my judgment."

Cassie was nobody's fool. Something about the whole

setup was off. Sure, she had her degree in restaurant management and several years experience working as a waitress under her belt, plus all the time she'd put in working in bars and lounges, even if some of it hadn't exactly involved waiting tables or working the cash register, but surely there had to be more qualified people.

What was the catch? Had the place been condemned by the Board of Health? Had the chef tried to poison the diners? Was the owner demented? Better still, why was the current manager so desperate to hire a replacement?

''She's not,'' the headhunter had assured her a little too quickly. ''She's eager, that's all. She'd like to hire someone, spend a couple of days training her, then move on.''

Cassie figured the truth was more complicated than that but beggars couldn't be choosers. The job was too good to pass up. So was the chance to get out of Vegas.

Ever since what she thought of as the elevator incident, she'd had waited for somebody to point a finger at her, shriek ''Elevator!'' and burst out laughing.

She knew that was silly. Keir certainly wouldn't have told anybody he'd been party to such a farce. Neither would his brothers and anyway, all three of the O'Connells had left the day after the wedding.

Good riddance. If there was any decency in life, she'd never see Keir again.

Cassie hurried to the baggage area and waited for her luggage.

The deciding factor in her decision had been a practical one. The restaurant was paying her airfare and moving expenses. A couple of thousand dollars saved was a couple of thousand dollars toward the future. Why waste it?

The luggage belt lurched to life. Cassie stepped forward as suitcases began their circuit of the baggage pickup area. Her suitcase would be easy to spot, thanks to the bright red bow on the handle that she'd taken from one of the pizza boxes at the party last night.

The girls she worked with had given her a fine send-off. Pizza, wine, even a cake.

Good Luck, Cassie, the icing on it had said. Everyone had hugged her and kissed her and laughed, and she'd joined in because that was better than bursting into tears and admitting that this all might all be a mistake.

Her suitcase finally appeared, big red bow and all. Cassie leaned in and hoisted it off the belt.

"You're so brave," Inez had said, "to move to a place you don't know and take on such a big job."

Bravery, she thought as she lugged her suitcase toward the car rental counter, had nothing to do with it. In fact, she was scared spitless. Not that she'd ever admit it to anyone. If life had taught her one great lesson, it was that the best way—the only way—to deal with fear was to look it in the eye and laugh.

The line at the counter was mercifully short. Cassie put down her suitcase.

Besides, being scared—okay, terrified—didn't change the truth. She wanted this fresh start more than she'd ever wanted anything in years. Hadn't she been working toward this moment? Managing a small, established restaurant for a salary that still made her blink was what all the studying was about. And if the new job sounded as if might come with problems attached…

Why think that way? Maybe she was wrong. Maybe her résumé sounded brilliant instead of pathetic. Besides, it was time for a change. A big one. You couldn't go on working in a place when you disliked the job, the customers, the people who owned it…

Not true. She didn't dislike Mary O'Connell. It was Keir she disliked. Disliked? Cassie snorted, loud enough so the guy ahead of her looked around, his expression noncommittal, though it changed fast enough when he saw her.

"Hello," he said, and smiled with all his teeth.

"Goodbye," she said, and didn't bother with the smile.

The guy turned the color of a rutabaga and she knew she'd been curt to the point of rudeness, but so what?

If you're rude or crude, you're out of here.

That had been Keir's dictum. He'd put it differently, couched it in some smooth talk about the importance of treating guests with respect at all times, but the employees had boiled it down to one simple phrase.

She could be as rude and crude as she liked. O'Connell had nothing to do with her life anymore. Besides, the guy who'd just come on to her was big and good-looking. Men like that deserved to be put in their places.

The line shuffled forward.

Too bad she hadn't put Keir in his instead of fleeing right after those elevator doors opened. She knew how it must have looked to his brothers. Imagine if they'd seen what had happened in the garden, when she'd been in Keir's arms not by accident but because she'd wanted to be, wanted his mouth on hers, wanted to feel all that heat and hunger…

The woman behind her cleared her throat. Cassie blinked. The line had moved forward while she'd been wasting time thinking about a man who hadn't wanted her for anything but a roll in the hay—and had ended up having second thoughts about that.

He was ancient history, not worth a minute of her time. She hadn't even joined in the gossip about where he'd gone, or why, after the duchess's wedding.

Some of the girls she'd worked with said there'd been no room for him at the Song anymore, but she didn't buy that. Maybe maternal love was blind, but all you had to do was see Mary Elizabeth and Keir together to know how much the duchess loved him.

As for where he'd gone… New York, someone said. Or Paris, something about a big French hotel corporation hiring him. Either place could have him. She'd had a schoolgirl crush that got out of hand. That was the only reason she'd ended up making an ass of herself that night, Cassie thought coolly, and stepped up to the counter.

* * *

Moments later, she was behind the wheel of a rental car and on the highway, feeling better and better as the tires ate up the miles. The road was wide, the traffic light, and the storm had moved off. Trees flashed by on either side, dressed in the brilliant orange, red and gold of a New England fall. When she let down the window, sweet, rain-fresh air filled the car.

Cassie took a deep breath. Nice. Very nice, especially for someone who'd never been further east than Austin.

This was going to be great. A good decision, a good move… A good career step.

Eyes glued to the road, she dug her hand into her purse and pulled out the written directions the headhunter had given her. The only part that looked sticky came after she left the highway and took a state road that intersected the town road that led to the turnoff for Tender Grapes.

"Louise Davenport—the manager you'll be replacing—says to keep your eyes peeled," the headhunter had said. "The turnoff from Fenton Road to the restaurant comes up quickly and it isn't well-marked."

"But there *is* a sign, right?"

"Oh, yes. Ms. Davenport says it's just not as visible as it might be. She says it makes people turn up late for their dinner reservations all the time."

Why not change the sign? Cassie had thought, but she hadn't been foolish enough to say it.

"No problem," she'd told the headhunter, in her most businesslike manner.

Once you'd made a blind leap into a new life, why worry about a sign?

Almost two hours later, Cassie knew she'd been wrong. She should have worried about the sign. "Hard to see" was one thing, but this sign was invisible even after two U-turns and three increasingly slow crawls up and down Fenton Road in search of it.

And, just to jazz things up, the storm that had greeted her at the airport seemed to be returning with a vengeance.

The sky was darkening; thunder, accompanied by occasional jagged spears of lightning, rumbled overhead.

Where was that damned sign?

Cassie pulled onto the shoulder of the road. She was already fifteen minutes late. Well, it was the Davenport woman's fault, for giving her such lousy directions. Exasperated, she plucked them from the passenger seat and read them again.

Highway 84 to Route 44. Yes. Proceed east for twelve miles. Yes. Make a right onto Fenton Road, which was at the intersection with the gas station on the left, the hardware store on the right. Yes.

Yes?

This *was* Fenton Road, wasn't it? That place where she'd made the turn, where she'd spotted the store with the lawn mowers and a bunch of other strange-looking machines out front *was* a hardware store…wasn't it?

Cassie sighed, dropped the directions in her lap and drove back the way she'd come. Rain pattered against the windshield, lightly at first, then more heavily. The intersection was just ahead. Gas station, check. Hardware store, che…

''Oh, hell,'' she said wearily.

It wasn't a hardware store, it was a place that sold lawn and yard equipment. Well, how would you know that, unless you were a local?

Fifteen more minutes wasted, finding the correct intersection, then making the turn onto Fenton Road. The rain had turned into a downpour so hard that she kept waiting for Noah to sail past in his ark, except old Noah couldn't have navigated an ark or even a rowboat on a road like this. It was too narrow, too twisty, too overhung with tall trees that muscled right up to the blacktop.

This had to be the right road, but where was the sign? Not that it mattered. She was so late now that she could kiss the new job goodbye. Cassie had no difficulty imagining Louise Davenport giving her a cold eye and saying sorry, she'd changed her mind, she wasn't about to hire someone who turned up an hour late, even if Tender Grapes was desperate because, face it, a place had to be desperate to—

Was that a sign?

Cassie stood on the brakes. Not too bright on a wet, leaf-strewn road. The car shuddered and stopped. She backed up cautiously. Yes. It was a sign, a small one, half-buried in a tangle of wet leaves and shrubs, with what looked to be a wagon track leading into the woods just beyond it.

She craned her neck, narrowed her eyes, did everything humanly possible to read what the sign said. She couldn't, not from the dry warmth of the car.

Cassie sighed, listened to the rain drumming on the roof, then watched the water overwhelming the windshield wipers. She looked down at her plum-colored silk suit, her black suede pumps…

A long, weary breath and she stepped out into the deluge.

It took less than a second.

Goodbye, frighteningly expensive, viciously conservative hairdo. Goodbye, equally expensive, equally conservative suit. Goodbye, pumps with the stylish-yet-comfortable-lady executive heels, which sank into the muck with each step as she plodded to the sign and scraped away wet debris and leaves.

Goodbye, perfect-yet-conservative hundred-dollar manicure, she thought, and almost wept.

Yes, this was the sign. *Deer Run Vineyard,* it said. *Tender Grapes Restaurant, Luncheon and Dinner Tuesday thru Thursday, by Reservation Only.*

Deer Run Vineyard?

Cassie shoved her dripping wet hair out of her eyes, thought about wringing out the hem of her skirt, thought about pointing the car back toward the airport and flying home so she could wring the neck of the headhunter who'd sent her on this debacle of a trip…

Except, Las Vegas wasn't home. Not anymore. She *had* no home. No apartment. No job. Nothing to go back to.

No one to go back to.

She was completely alone.

The realization, which she'd so carefully managed to hold in abeyance until now, drove the breath from her lungs. She got into the car oblivious to the wet, to the cold seeping into her bones, folded her hands in her lap and stared blindly at the rain.

Alone.

But she'd been alone before.

Cassie closed her eyes. The truth was, she'd always been alone, even when she was a little girl. A mother who drank, the faintest ghost-memory of a father…

Her eyes flew open. What was this foolishness? When had she ever wallowed in self-pity?

''Never,'' she said firmly, and turned the key in the ignition.

She'd been a hell of a lot more alone when she was seventeen than she was now. She'd dropped out of high school with only six months to go before graduation, packed her things and left.

Cassie lifted her chin, put the car in Drive and turned onto the wagon track that led into the forest.

Just left, when she was almost seventeen, without an idea of what she was going to do, where she wanted to go, how she'd support herself. She'd taken her baby-sitting money, all one hundred and fifty bucks of it, shoved the least threadbare of her clothes into a backpack, walked the five miles to the bus station and bought a ticket for the first bus out of Denver.

That, she thought firmly, as low branches reached for the car like hungry fingers, *that* was being alone.

And she'd survived.

Maybe there were things she didn't want to remember, things that had made surviving possible, but she was older now, and wiser.

She had skills, too. She was a dancer, could still be one despite her bad knee, if this job didn't work out. All those years learning tap and ballet, at first because it had been better going to the neighborhood after-school program than going home and then because she'd come to love the hard work and discipline of dance. And, after that, the better part of a decade doing high kicks and struts…

She couldn't do the high kicks anymore but she could still dance for her supper if she had to, the same as she could serve a roomful of hungry customers, courteously and efficiently.

The one thing she'd never do again was strip, not if it meant taking a job cleaning toilets instead.

And she'd never wait tables in a place where the customers were jerks, like that guy in the casino the day she'd seen Keir for the last time, when he'd put his arms around her in that elevator and even though she'd known he was just trying to keep her from falling, she'd felt…she'd felt…

Cassie grimaced. "Oh, for God's sake," she said with disgust.

She was older and wiser, and done with men. Besides, why was she thinking in terms of defeat?

Through the thinning trees ahead, she could see a clearing and a handsome red barn with gently rolling hills behind it. The rain made it difficult to see much more, but she could make out a tall structure—a turret, maybe—and the rooflines of a house on the ridge of one of the hills.

This had to be her destination.

Her heart thumped.

Yes. It was. This sign was bigger and easy to read.

Welcome to Deer Run. And, in smaller letters, *Tender Grapes Restaurant.*

Except for a black SUV and a couple of nondescript cars, the parking lot was almost empty. Cassie pulled into a space, shut off the engine and tried to gather herself together. Okay. The good news was that she'd finally found the place. The bad news was that she was close to an hour late.

She pulled down the sun visor, looked into the mirror

behind it, and groaned. Who'd want to employ the creature staring back at her? She looked as if she'd been dragged through the mud.

Cassie popped open her purse, took out a comb and tugged it through her wet hair. Great. Now she looked as if somebody had plastered a black wig to her head. And what was that? Mascara, dammit! Quickly, she wet the tip of a finger and rubbed at her eye. As if a smudge of mascara was going to make the difference between looking like something that just crept out of the primordial ooze and a competent, businesslike manager.

She snapped her purse shut.

Never mind what she looked like, or that Louise Davenport would either faint or shriek with laughter at the sight of her. Never mind that she'd probably blown this job offer. She'd come a very long distance and she wasn't about to bolt and run now.

She had never run, not from anything, unless you counted that night in Texas and that had been a different situation, entirely.

Mouth set in a grim line, she stepped from the car, marched across the gravel to the red barn and the door marked *WELCOME.* The rain picked that moment to stop, just as if somebody had turned off a faucet, and a watery sun peeked out from behind a cloud.

Too bad she wasn't into omens. On the other hand, maybe Louise Davenport was. It was a thought worth keeping.

Did she knock? Or did that "welcome" sign really mean "enter"? Cassie took a breath, put her hand on the doorknob…

The door swung open. A tall woman with iron-gray hair stared at her, then reached for her hand.

"There you are. I'd about given up." The woman cocked her head. "You are Cassie Berk, aren't you?"

"Yes. Yes, I am. And I'm awfully sorry I'm so late, and that I'm such a mess, but—"

''Nonsense.'' The woman drew Cassie forward into what was obviously a small, handsomely furnished reception area. ''You're here, and just in time. Oh, have I introduced myself? I'm Louise. Louise Davenport.''

''Yes. I mean, how do you do, Miss—''

''Miss Berk, I'd love to chat but as it is, I'm going to just about make my flight.''

Cassie blinked. ''Your flight?''

''Umm. I'd hoped to show you around a bit but I'm afraid I can't take the time.''

''Oh, but—but Miss Davenport...''

''Louise,'' the other woman said, as she collected a raincoat, purse and umbrella from a chair.

''Louise. I don't understand. Don't you at least want to ask me some questions?''

Louise looked puzzled. ''I already hired you. Why would I ask you anything?''

''Well—well, we've never met. There must be some things you want to talk about.''

''Very well. I suppose there are.''

Cassie let out a breath. ''Good. Because I have some things I want to ask—''

''Are you good at getting along with people?''

''I'm fine at getting along with people.''

''Even chefs?'' Louise laughed gaily. ''Chefs with big egos, touchy temperaments and shiny knives?''

Cassie stared at the woman. ''That's a joke, right?''

''Certainly. Oh, of course it's a joke, my dear. What else would it be?''

The truth? Cassie took a quick step back. All at once, returning to Las Vegas, job or no job, apartment or no apartment, seemed like an eminently viable option.

''Miss Davenport. Um. Louise. I'm starting to think there's been a mistake.''

''Oh, no mistake, I assure you.'' Louise slid on her raincoat and buttoned it. ''I must tell you, though, I think you're a brave woman, taking on this place.'' Her eyes darkened. ''And that man.''

''What man?''

''The headhunter told me she explained everything to you, the reason for the generous salary and the rental-free apartment. My hands are clean. I didn't hide a thing, not a thing, I mean, what's the sense? So many applicants, so many people who've come and gone in two or three day's time... Well.'' Smiling she held out her hand. ''Good luck, Cassie.''

''No.'' Cassie backed away from the outstretched hand. ''I mean, you can't just leave. You have to show me the ropes and—and besides, I'm not sure I want to—''

''Louise!''

Both women jumped. The roar came from the top of a narrow staircase on the other side of the room. The voice was male and human, but it made Cassie think of an enraged lion.

''Louise, is the woman here yet?''

Louise made a face. ''His bite is every bit as bad as his bark,'' she hissed, and took a breath. ''Yes,'' she said loudly, ''she got here a couple of minutes ago.''

''Well, let's hope she's not as addle-brained as the last one you interviewed.''

That voice! Oh God, that voice. Cassie became very still.

Louise squared her shoulders as she turned toward the stairs.

''Whatever she is,'' she said coolly, ''she'll have to do, because I am leaving.''

''Louise.'' The voice oozed charm as footsteps started down the steps. ''What can I do to make you stay? I've already offered to double your salary. Can't you—''

''No,'' Louise said firmly, ''I can't.''

She slipped past Cassie, walked into the rain and slammed the door behind her.

I should be right on her heels, Cassie thought wildly, as

the booted feet and worn jeans of the man came into view. It couldn't be. It couldn't…

"I don't believe it," Keir said on a shocked whisper. He widened his eyes, shook his head a little as he stared across the room, and Cassie knew exactly how he felt, as if he were having a hideous nightmare and couldn't wake up.

"I don't, either," she said, and she turned away from that face she'd never intended to see again and reached for the door.

CHAPTER FIVE

CASSIE? Cassie, here at Deer Run?

No. Absolutely not. Keir had never been prone to hallucinations but he figured he must be having one now.

Dreaming about Cassie—hot, middle-of-the-night dreams that he thought he'd left behind way back in adolescence—was one thing. Conjuring up an illusion was another, except an illusion wouldn't drip water onto the floor, or look at him as if he was something out of her worst nightmare.

The door banging shut behind her, hard enough to rattle a display of corkscrews, brought him back to reality.

Illusions didn't slam doors.

Keir gave himself a mental shake and went after her. He heard an engine roar to life as he ran down the last steps and out the door, but the car hurtling down the driveway belonged to Louise.

Cassie was just slipping behind the wheel of hers.

"Cassie!"

She didn't even turn her head. Keir snarled an oath, reached through the open window and grabbed her hand just as she was jamming the key into the ignition. He yanked the door open.

"Get out of that car!"

"Keep away from me, O'Connell!"

"I'll say it one more time, lady. Get out of the car."

"Who in hell do you think you are?"

"Are you getting out," he said, curling his hand around her wrist, "or am I going to drag you out?"

"Let me point something out to you, mister. This is not the Desert Song Hotel. I don't work for you anymore. I don't have to click my heels and obey your orders or—"

"Okay. Okay, Berk, that's it."

Cassie yelped as he flung the door open, reached inside and lifted her out from behind the wheel. She fought back, gripping the steering wheel, then the door handle, kicking and cursing and pounding his shoulders, but he was bigger, stronger and determined.

No way was she leaving yet. He had questions. What in hell was she doing here? And why was he torn between the desire to send her packing and the hope that maybe she'd come all this distance because she'd been having the same dreams that had been plaguing him?

"Okay," he said roughly, "what's it going to be? Do I get some answers now, or do I have to carry you inside and tie you to a chair until I get them?"

As if she had a choice, Cassie thought furiously. His threat was all too real. Hadn't he just dragged her out of the car?

"Put me down," she said through her teeth.

"Answer the question first. Are you going to stay put?"

"Am I supposed to be afraid of you? Because I'm not."

"Is that a yes?"

"Put—me—down!"

He did, lowering her slowly to her feet, his eyes flat and dark. She wrenched her arm free, took a step back and met his cold look with one of her own.

"Just for the record, if you try and manhandle me again, you'll regret it."

"Why'd you run?"

"A lesson I learned, living in the desert. You see a snake, you get out of its way as fast as you can."

Keir folded his arms over his chest. "Very amusing. Now, explain yourself."

"I beg your pardon?"

"I want to know what you're doing here."

"Exactly my question, O'Connell. What are *you* doing here?"

Unconsciously, Cassie copied his action, which forced her wet silk sweater and jacket to press icily against her skin. Great. Just great. She was a billion miles from home, cold, wet and angry as hell because despite what she'd just told him, she'd already figured out what Keir was doing here. She just couldn't bring herself to believe it.

"At Deer Run?"

"No," she snapped, "at a watering hole in the middle of the Kalahari. Yes, of course, at Deer Run."

His eyes narrowed. "I own it."

Oh, hell. "You own it."

"That's what I said."

"The restaurant, too?"

He nodded. "That's right."

The confirmation was just what she'd expected. Still, it hit her with the force of a blow. She'd wanted to believe this was just some awful coincidence and there'd be a simple explanation for his presence.

Well, there *was* a simple explanation. He owned the place.

Goodbye new job, new career, new start.

"Your turn, Berk. What are *you* doing here?"

Cassie lifted her chin. "The agency sent me."

"What agency?"

"The employment agency."

"The employment agency?"

"If you repeat everything I say, this is going to be an awfully stupid conversation. You asked TopNotch to hire a manager for your restaurant."

"So?" The anger in his eyes gave way to confusion. "What's that have to do with..."

She knew the instant he figured it out. His dark eyebrows rose until they almost met his hair; his mouth dropped open. It was not the best expression for a face as good-looking as his, she thought coldly, but then, what could you expect of a man who'd just learned that some Barbie dolls could actually walk and talk?

"You're kidding."

"I have no sense of humor when it comes to this kind of situation, O'Connell. Being dragged clear across the country on a wild-goose chase is not my idea of fun."

It had begun raining again, a slow, fine drizzle that left droplets of water glittering in Keir's dark hair. He ran his hands through it, which made it stand up in damp little tufts. He looked completely baffled. Cassie almost felt sorry for him…but then his expression went from baffled to disbelieving, and she remembered that the person who was getting shafted here was her.

"Let me get this straight," he said slowly. "You're here to interview for the manager's spot?"

She thought of telling him that she wasn't here to interview at all, that the job was already hers, but why bother? She was not staying. If she had to go to Boston or Hartford or all the way back to Vegas and wait tables sixteen hours a day, she was not staying here.

"Oh, I know. I know, O'Connell. How could that be? How could I have the audacity to think I could do anything more complicated than hustle drinks to the customers?"

"I didn't say—"

"You didn't have to." At least he had the decency to blush, she thought grimly, and she drew a deep breath. "I signed with TopNotch Personnel for a job managing a restaurant. They passed my résumé on to your Miss Davenport. She interviewed me over the telephone and hired me."

"Louise?" he said, with a laugh so infuriating she wanted to slug him, "*Louise* hired *you*?"

"You're repeating yourself again. I know how impossible it seems, considering my absolute lack of credentials. I mean, years of restaurant experience—"

"Restaurant experience," he said, with a smirk.

"Restaurant experience," she said, with an icy bite to

the words. "Something you'd know nothing about—unless you think strolling through the Desert Song's facilities and nodding at the help with that—that condescending look on your face constitutes experience?"

"I did not stroll through the Desert Song."

"No. That's true. Sometimes, you hung around long enough to bestow a benevolent smile on the peons."

"Nor was I condescending," he said stiffly.

"I guess not. You never asked any of us to bow."

Keir narrowed his eyes. "We seem to have gotten off track, Berk. You were explaining how you were able to con Louise into hiring you as her replacement."

"You mean, what lies did I tell?" Cassie smiled tightly. "Sorry to disappoint you, but I only told her the truth, that I'd put in years in the trenches." She paused for effect. "And that I have a degree in restaurant management."

Could a man narrow his eyes to slits and still see? Keir O'Connell could. At least, that seemed to be one of his talents.

"A degree in—"

"Restaurant management. Yes. I have a diploma I'd be happy to show you, *if* I were going to take this job, which I am not."

"Had it printed yourself, did you?"

"Oh, certainly." Cassie batted her lashes. "Right down at the corner Quik Copy. You'd love it. Great big gold seal, lots of curlicues..." Her sarcastic smile faded. "Listen, *Mister* O'Connell, not that our little chat hasn't been fun—"

"It isn't over yet."

"Trust me. It is." Cassie shuddered. Until now, fury at the thoughtless woman who'd brought her here, at the twist of fate that had shoved her into a face to face confrontation with this arrogant idiot she'd hoped never to see again, had warded off the cold. Now, she felt it seeping through her body, invading the marrow of her bones. If she didn't get warm soon, she'd turn into an icicle. "Maybe you haven't noticed, but we've nothing further to say to each other. Well, why would we? Emperors can't be bothered about the little people."

Keir unfolded his arms and put his hands on his hips.

"That's the second time you said something like that about me, Berk."

"My oh my. Hurt your feelings, have I?"

His face turned a color that reminded her of a plum sweater she'd once owned. He was angry. Really angry. It made her feel wonderful. Had he really gone through life thinking people didn't see right through that "I feel your pain, but we have to pull together for the sake of the team?" routine?

Okay. People didn't, but she did. She surely did. There'd been a time he'd had her fooled, too, but then she'd gone to that wedding…

"Sorry," she said sweetly. "You're right, of course. I didn't mean to repeat myself."

Keir dug his hands into his pockets and curled them into tight fists. She'd meant it, all right. Not that the taunt hurt. He never dealt with people the way she made it sound.

Hell, she was impossible. Gazing up at him from under her lashes…such long, thick lashes. How could a woman this beautiful be such a pain in the butt? Better still, how could she be so beautiful when she was as wet as a cat who'd just climbed out of a bathtub?

Wet? She was soaked. Anger had kept him from noticing it until now.

"You're soaked," he said.

"Really?" Cassie widened her eyes. "How clever of you to notice."

"How'd you get so wet?"

"It was raining, just like it's starting to do now. I guess it doesn't rain in your private world."

She unfolded her arms and put out a cupped hand, to

demonstrate. His eyes flashed to her breasts, clearly outlined under her wet clothes, and he felt a faint, unwanted tightening of his body.

''You look as if you stood under a waterfall,'' he said sharply.

''Close.'' She smiled thinly. ''Now, if you d-don't m-mind—''

''Your teeth are chattering.''

Dammit. They were. Nothing like chattering teeth to spoil the illusion of contempt she was trying so hard to maintain.

''Another astute obs-s-s-servation.'' She eyed him with defiance. ''Goodbye, Mr. O'Connell. I won't say it hasn't been an in-in-interest—''

''Oh, for God's sake!'' Keir reached out, scooped her into his arms. ''By the time you finish the wisecrack, you'll be frozen solid.''

''Put me down!''

''Believe me,'' he said, as he marched toward the office, ''I intend to.''

''Are you d-deaf?'' Cassie pummeled his shoulders. ''What did I tell you would happen if you t—touched me again?''

''You try to slug me, lady, you're in trouble.''

''*I'm* in trouble? Did you ever hear of laws against k-k-kid—''

''Kidnapping,'' Keir said grimly, shouldering his way past the door. ''Did *you* ever hear of hypothermia?''

''Give me a break, O'Connell. I—I—I'm not hy-hy-hy—''

''Yeah. Right.'' Keir carried her through the reception area, up the stairs and into his office where he elbowed the door shut and dumped her, unceremoniously, on her feet.

''Get undressed.''

''What?''

''You heard me. Take off your clothes.''

''In your dreams!''

He had to give her credit. Her teeth were chattering, her clothes were soaked and she bore more resemblance to a water rat than a woman—okay, a beautiful water rat, if there was such a thing—but she was still fist-in-your-face defiant.

He thought about telling her she'd gotten it right, that she *did* get undressed in his dreams, but what would that do except provide her with more ammunition?

"Give me some credit, Berk. If I wanted to get you into the sack, I'd try a more subtle approach. You need to get out of those wet things and into a hot shower. There's a bathroom behind that door. Wrap up in a towel when you're finished. I'll bring you something to wear."

"You're crazy."

"And you're dripping on the carpet."

She looked down. Water dripped off the tip of her nose and onto her soggy shoes.

"Have it cleaned," she said blithely, raising her eyes to his, "and send the bill to me. Now, s-step aside. I'm l-leaving."

Keir reached back, locked the door and leaned against it.

"I'm going to count to five, Cassie. Either your clothes are doing a disappearing act by then, or I'll just have to take them off you myself." He paused, his gaze fixed on hers. "One."

His voice was low, almost rough. He meant it; Cassie knew that he did. She thought about what it would be like if she held her ground, if she said yeah, fine, you just try it and see what happens, buster…

"Two."

And then she thought about how it would feel to have him open the buttons of her jacket, slide it from her shoulders. Thought about how he'd react when he saw what the rain had done to her sweater, how it clung to her breasts… Or had he already noticed?

"Three."

She could feel her nipples tighten. From the cold. Only from the cold.

"This is st-stupid," she said angrily, unsure if the anger was for herself or him.

"Four," he said, and started slowly toward her.

On the other hand, he wouldn't dare undress her. He was egotistical; he wasn't an idiot. Neither was she. To give an inch would be to lose not just the battle but the war.

Cassie folded her arms and raised her chin.

"Five," she said helpfully. "Six. Seven..."

He was inches away. A breath away. Neither of them was counting out loud but she could hear the numbers booming inside her head. Eight. Nine. Ten...

Keir reached out slowly, curled his fingers around the first button on her jacket, slipped it free.

"What the hell do you think you're d-doing, O'Connell?"

"Undressing you," he said coolly.

The next button opened, and the next. "Stop it!"

"I will." His voice was still pleasant but it had become low and rasping. His pupils were dark pinpoints as he slid his hands under her jacket, under her silk sweater.

She felt her head spin, felt desire course through her blood...

Cassie sprang back. Keir dropped his hands to his sides. They stared at each other for a long moment, his face taut muscle and bone, her heart pounding, and then he stepped back, too, and put even more distance between them.

"If you don't want me to do the rest, get into that bathroom and finish up for yourself."

He spoke calmly, looked at her calmly, as if nothing had happened. And nothing had—nothing, except that she was having trouble catching her breath and her skin tingled wherever his hands had been.

She swung away from him, because that was the only safe choice, and walked to the bathroom.

"Good girl," he called after her, and she turned, eyes flashing.

"I am not a g-girl, good or otherwise. Now, get out!"

"I'm going."

"My suitcase is in the t-trunk of my car."

"Fine."

"As soon as I get out of that shower and into a change of cl-clothes, I'm out of here."

"First you're going to explain why you flew 2500 miles for the chance to work with me."

The door clicked shut. Cassie glared at it. Then she kicked off her shoes and watched with satisfaction as they hit the wall and left thin smears of mud on the pristine white paint before falling to the floor.

A small victory, she thought as she turned the lock, but a victory just the same.

The shower felt wonderful.

She turned her face up to the hot water, then bent her head and let it beat down on her neck. After a while, she reached for the bottle of shampoo that stood next to the soap, opened it and took a sniff.

It smelled like lemon. Like Keir. His skin had a faint, lemony scent. Her brain must have registered that fact without her realizing it.

Cassie frowned, washed her hair, rinsed it, and picked up the soap.

It smelled like lemon, too.

Keir's shampoo. Keir's soap.

She'd been lathering her body. Now, her hand stilled. She looked down at herself, at her breasts, her thighs, at the translucent soap bubbles clinging to her skin.

Keir had used this same soap. He'd felt its soft kiss, its sensual glide and stroke…

"Dammit," she hissed, and dumped the soap back into its dish. Again, she lifted her face to the spray. This time, she adjusted the water until it was cool, let it beat down and clear her head. Once she felt like herself again, she shut off the water, wrapped herself in an oversize bath towel and cracked the door.

"O'Connell?"

No answer. She opened the door a little further and scanned the room for her suitcase. How long did he think it would take her to shower? Or did he harbor some funny idea about what would happen once she'd finished?

The man had a lot to learn. Didn't he think she'd learned anything from that day in Texas, to say nothing of that humiliating incident in the elevator?

The elevator. Thinking about it still made her cringe. At least he could have called and apologized, but no. He'd probably been too busy making jokes with his cretinous brothers at her expense—

The door swung open. Keir stared at her. She stared back. A feeling that was hot and electric shimmered in the air before she looked away.

"My clothes," she said briskly.

"*My* clothes," he said just as briskly, tossing jeans and a sweatshirt on the leather love seat. "They won't make a fashion statement, but they'll keep you warm."

"I want my own things, thank you."

"Yeah, and I want every table in my restaurant filled on the weekends. Why should I drag your suitcase up here when I'm only going to have to haul it back to your car when you leave?" He jerked his chin toward the stuff he'd brought her. "Go on. Get dressed."

Cassie's smile was all teeth. "What's the problem, O'Connell? Can't you make up your mind? First you want me out of my clothes. Then you want me in them." Holding the towel clutched between her breasts with one hand, she snatched up the jeans and shirt with the other. "As for the restaurant…try putting up a sign people can see and you might just pick up a customer or two."

"What?"

"Nothing," she snarled, and slammed the bathroom door in his face.

Keir took a deep breath. What was the matter with him? He'd seen half-naked women before. For that matter, he'd seen *this* woman half-naked before. That outfit, the costume she'd been wearing in the elevator…

He sank down on the love seat.

A man's head could explode, trying to get a handle on the real Cassie Berk. So far, he'd seen her dressed like a princess in a fairy tale, like a sex kitten, like a poor little orphan of the storm.

Now he'd seen her in a towel. No makeup. No fishnet stockings or take-me-I'm yours spiked heels. How could a towel be more provocative than those stockings and heels, than the skirt that had flirted with her backside?

It was, though. All he'd been able to think about was that under that towel, Cassie was all silky skin and warm, feminine scents.

His mouth thinned.

How many other men had thought the same thing? How many had tasted that skin, been surrounded by that warmth? He was making a fool of himself over a woman who'd pranced around damn near naked for half the men on the planet…

Except him.

And *she* was going to tell him how come his restaurant bookings were off? He laughed. Tried to laugh, anyway, though the sound came out more a snort of self-derision than anything else.

Okay. She'd caught him by surprise, that was the problem, turning up here, and on a bad day, too. Louise had caught him by surprise this morning, telling him she was leaving in a couple of hours. She'd promised to stay on a week, to break in the new manager…

Cassie Berk. The new manager. He groaned and leaned

his head back. Talk about improbable situations, that had to top the list. There'd even been a moment, standing in the rain, when he'd felt a tug of sympathy for her, coming all this way for a job that she'd never have, but so what? He had his own troubles. The vineyard was in great shape but the restaurant had a bucket of problems. Imagine handing it over to a woman whose closest connection to running a restaurant came from serving drinks to customers.

Okay. So she had some kind of management degree. It probably came from a diploma mill. Even if it didn't, he wasn't going to be her job-experience guinea pig. And he sure as hell wasn't going to get himself into a situation where the woman who'd been sashaying through his X-rated dreams shared his life, 24/7.

Keir rose to his feet, tucked his hands into his pockets and paced the room.

This was all Louise Davenport's fault. She'd seemed so capable, so easy to deal with, when he'd first bought Deer Run, but the more time had passed, the more temperamental she'd become.

None of the candidates she'd hired had worked out, either. He'd given her *carte blanche* in keeping with his policy of delegating authority, but not one of the people she'd taken on had made it through a week.

The last one had only lasted two days.

"I can't work with a slave-driver, Mr. O'Connell," the guy had said, just before he'd stomped off.

Slave driver? Him? Keir ran his hand through his hair as he sat down heavily in the chair behind his desk. He was the easiest boss in the world. Demanding, yes, but only of the best in people. He was never unreasonable, never unpleasant. Never.

"We've run out of suitable candidates, Mr. O'Connell," Louise had told him coolly, a week or two ago. "I'm afraid we're down to the last applicant."

Which brought him, full circle, to the woman in his bathroom.

No way. No way in hell would he—

The bathroom door opened. Cassie stepped into the room. This was better. His sweatshirt, his jeans, everything huge and hanging so that he wasn't distracted by the lush thrust of her breasts or the rounded curve of her hips.

"Satisfied?" she said coolly.

Keir waved a hand at the chair opposite his. She could be polite? So could he.

"Sit down please, Cassie."

Cassie sat. She must have used his dryer. Now that he thought about it, he'd heard its buzz through the closed door. Her hair was loose and hung straight down her back in a black fall of silk. The shower had washed away her makeup. She looked young, innocent, gorgeous...

Innocent? The last thing he'd done, before signing off at the Desert Song, was to pull her file and read it. She'd been a showgirl in glitzy Vegas extravaganzas. She'd danced behind a bar in a G-string, taken off her clothes for strangers...

Keir folded his hands and forced a smile to his lips.

"Well." He cleared his throat. "I must say, seeing you is quite a surprise."

"Why?" Her smile would have made an alligator happy. "Did you think they wouldn't let me cross the Connecticut border?"

She sat back and crossed her legs. They were the longest legs he'd ever seen.

"What you mean is, how did I end up getting hired by your sainted Miss Davenport."

A muscle knotted in his cheek. "Look, I'm trying to be polite about this, but—"

"But, you can't bring yourself to believe me." Cassie fluttered those long, impossibly thick lashes. "I'll bet you were hoping I'd say I'd come to find you,'' she said in a seductive whisper.

He felt the blood rush to his head and, dammit, to his groin. He didn't have to react when she baited him. She was good at that, even in his dreams. Sometimes he awoke, amazed that he hadn't ground his molars to powder during the night.

''Listen,'' he said, ''here's the deal. I'll ask the questions, you answer them. Okay?''

Cassie shrugged one shoulder. ''Fine with me.''

Keir plucked a pencil from the desk. ''Well,'' he said cautiously, ''unless I misunderstood, you claim Miss Davenport hired you through the TopNotch agency.''

''Wrong.''

''Wrong?'' Was there a glimpse of salvation on the horizon? ''Then, TopNotch didn't...''

''They did.'' Cassie uncrossed her legs and sat up straight. The time for playing games was over. ''And Davenport hired me.''

''You mean, she asked you to come for a final interview.'' He clucked his tongue, shook his head, did whatever he figured it took to show some empathy. ''Well, what can I say, Cassie? I'm terribly sorry you were inconvenienced, but—''

''Do you have a hearing problem, O'Connell? She *hired* me. As in, she signed on the dotted line.''

The pencil snapped and he tossed the two halves aside. ''That's impossible.''

''There's a contract in my purse that says it's not.'' Cassie smiled thinly. What the hell, why not give him a few minutes of suffering before she assured him she was leaving?

Keir's eyes narrowed. ''Contracts are made to be broken.''

''Really.''

''Yes, really.'' He smiled, or tried to, and his voice took

on a conciliatory tone. "Look, I know you must be disappointed. And, I suppose, in a way, this is my fault."

"Is it?"

"Well, in the sense that I let Miss Davenport make some poor decisions." Wrong tack. He could see that in the way she raised her chin. She had a habit of doing that, he'd noticed, whenever he pissed her off. He sat back, steepled his fingers under his chin and tried another approach. "Tell you what. I'd like to be fair about this unfortunate situation. I'll pay your airfare back to Las Vegas."

God, the arrogance of the man. Did he think he could buy her off with an airplane ticket? Cassie smiled politely.

"Thank you."

His smile grew more congenial. "And, since you're being so understanding about this unfortunate error, I'll compensate you with a week's pay."

"How generous."

Keir felt the skin prickle on the back of his neck. Was there a warning in her voice?

"Yes," he said quickly, and pushed back his chair, "well, I'm glad we could resolve the matter so amicably."

"I do appreciate your admission of responsibility and your offer of compensation, Mr. O'Connell."

There was that prickle again. How come she'd suddenly started calling him Mr. O'Connell?

"No need to thank me," he said, even more quickly. "I'll just write you a check and—"

"But I'm not interested."

She spoke before she had time to think. Until this moment, she'd had every intention of walking. Defeat was preferable to working for a man like Keir O'Connell but who did he think he was, to try and buy her off? To sit there and look at her as if she were an insect that could be brushed away when it became annoying?

The man thought she couldn't run his restaurant. Well, he needed to be taught a lesson.

His smile fled in the blink of an eye. ''What do you mean, you're not interested? It's a fair offer. More than fair. If you think you can hold me up—''

Better and better, Cassie thought coldly. She shoved back her chair and stood up.

''I'm staying, O'Connell. You wanted a manager. Well, you've got one.''

''Don't be ridiculous. You can't—''

''Where's my apartment?''

''Your what?''

''My apartment. You know, the one that adjoins this building.'' Her smile was dazzling. ''The one that comes with the job, fully furnished, rent free. Where is it?''

Keir shot to his feet. ''Okay, I'm tired of playing Mr. Nice Guy. I have no intention of employing you. You don't know a damn thing about running a restaurant. There's not a way in the world I'd turn responsibility for Tender Grapes over to— Dammit, don't you walk out on me! Cassie! Where do you think you're going?''

''To get my luggage. Or a lawyer. Your choice.''

''Dammit, Cassie—''

''I'd really like to get settled in before evening.'' She flashed a thousand watt smile that had as much warmth as a tray of ice cubes. ''Despite what you think, I am fully qualified for this position. I'm sure the attorney I hire will tell you that. In the meantime, if you want me gone, you'll have to get the sheriff to evict me.''

''Listen here, lady—''

''I really think you should consider your options,'' she said almost pleasantly. ''I mean, the sheriff and a lawsuit would be bad enough, but the newspapers would just love a story about how the great Keir O'Connell tried to fire a woman who wouldn't succumb to his advances.''

''What?''

''Especially in view of what happened in Texas.''

He wanted to grab her. Wrap his hands around her throat. Turn her over his knee. Oh yeah, turn her over his knee…

"Think it over. Talk to my lawyer and try and hide from the press…or let me turn this place into a success." She cocked her head, waited. He didn't answer and she smiled. "Fine. That's what I thought. You've made the right decision, Mr. O'Connell. I'm sure you'll be delighted with the things I'll do for the Tender Grapes restaurant."

She walked past him, expecting him to grab her, expecting him to roar with fury but he just stood there, looking stunned. Stunned? Shocked right down to his toes, was more like it.

The Keir O'Connells of this world had a hell of a lot to learn about the Cassandra Bercovics, she thought grimly…and didn't let herself start to shake like a leaf in a windstorm until she was safely downstairs, trying to haul her suitcase out of the trunk of her car.

CHAPTER SIX

KEIR had the Irish gift of gab.

Mary Elizabeth O'Connell said that about all her sons and time had pretty much proven her right.

Sean had once talked his way out of a Marseillaise prison; Cullen had charmed his way into law school and Keir…well, a man didn't successfully head up a multimillion dollar resort without being able to navigate his way around a difficult situation.

Then how come he was standing in the middle of his office, as speechless as a ventriloquist's dummy, while Cassie Berk shot him a venomous look and then marched away?

The woman was trying to blackmail him. *Blackmail* him, by God!

"Hey!"

A brilliant comment, but saying something was better than standing here with his mouth open and his brain empty. Keir ran down the stairs. Cassie was already out of sight but how far could she go barefoot, wearing his jeans and shirt—and it was best not to think about how she'd looked in his clothes, because how she looked didn't have a damned thing to do with the fact that he'd sooner hire a pit viper than her.

The front door was open. He flew through it and reached her just as she leaned into the trunk of a small red Chevy.

"What do you think you're doing?" Getting her suitcase; that what she was doing. Trying to get it, was more like the truth. The damned thing was big enough to house a family of five. "Let go of that," he snarled, and grabbed her hands.

"Don't touch me, O'Connell!"

"You won't need your luggage. You can wear what you've got on. Nobody's going to give a damn about what you wear on that flight back to Vegas."

"I am not going back to Vegas," she said, grunting as she struggled to hang on to the handle of the suitcase and wrestle it from the trunk. "Damn you, get your hands off me!"

"You are not staying here, Berk. You're going to Vegas. Or to Siberia, for all I care."

"I am not going anywhere." Cassie tugged her hands free of his, straightened up and blew her hair out of her face. "I gave up my job and my apartment. I even sold my miserable car. I shipped the few things I couldn't part with here. What, precisely, am I supposed to go back to, huh? You know so much, maybe you know that!"

"That isn't my problem."

"Oh, but it is. Didn't I explain it clearly enough? You hired me. You want to get rid of me, you're going to have to fight me to do it."

She slapped her hands on her hips. A bad idea, Keir decided, because that tightened the loose sweatshirt he'd given her. Now he knew that she hadn't bothered with a bra.

Had she been wearing a bra before? Had she left it in the bathroom because it was wet, or didn't she ever bother wearing one? Why would a woman whose breasts were so high, so rounded, so perfectly suited to fit a man's hands wear a bra?

"Try listening instead of looking, O'Connell," she said coldly.

He looked up. Her voice was steady. There was a hint of color in her cheeks but he had to give her credit. She didn't flinch or fold her arms. Look all you like, she seemed to be saying; that's all you'll ever do.

Hell, *he* was the one who was blushing; he could feel the heat starting to rise in his cheeks, but why the hell should *he* be embarrassed, caught looking at what she'd let other men see a thousand times?

"I did listen," he said. "Now it's your turn. Get it straight, okay? There's no job for you here."

"I told you, I'll sue."

"Go ahead."

"Ah. I forgot. You've probably got Slimy, Sleazy and Scuzzball on the payroll."

He wanted to laugh, not at her but at the image that popped into his head of a bunch of oily legal eagles rubbing their hands with glee at the prospect of taking her on. She had a quick mind, he had to give her that.

"Actually," he said calmly, "I have something better." He paused for effect. "My brother's an attorney in New York. He'd like nothing better than to represent me."

"Oh, I'm sure." Cassie smiled politely. "Every lawyer just aches for the chance to get his name, and his client's, smeared across the front pages of the supermarket tabloids."

"Well," Keir said modestly, "I don't know about *every* lawyer, only about Cullen. Matter of fact, high-profile cases are his specialty."

"Do tell."

"Actually, he's just finishing a case right now that involves…well," he said, lying through his teeth, "I suppose it would be a breach of confidence to go into details, but you'd know the outfit, if I named it." He folded his arms and leaned back against the car. "Cullen sued a babe and her newspaper for defamation of character.

"And?" Cassie said, trying to sound bored. "What happened?"

"Cullen won and got a judgment against her and her newspaper for seven figures."

"Still," Cassie said, trying not to sound a little shaken, "all the negative publicity…"

"There's no such thing as negative publicity. You remember a while back, in Vegas, an actress caught her lover in bed with…well, let's just say it wasn't your average infidelity.'' Keir smiled again, with enough self-confidence to make her teeth ache. ''His next movie was a box-office smash. Broke all records.''

Was it true? Was *any* of it true? The suit, the bad publicity being good publicity? She didn't know, wouldn't ask, and wasn't going to be intimidated, either.

To hell with his smug smile. To hell with what he could see outlined under her shirt. Let him look and eat his cold heart out, because there wasn't a way in the world he'd ever get to touch her again.

''Thank you for explaining it to me,'' she said sweetly, ''but I'll just have to take my chances.''

''Berk, have you actually heard anything I said?''

''I heard it all. I just don't how it applies to me. I mean, what I have to lose? You want to sue me? Sue me. Your brilliant brother could win a judgment of a trillion bucks and it wouldn't matter a damn, once you saw my bank balance. It's like I said. I have nothing to lose.''

''You'd accuse me of trying to blackmail you into my bed?'' His face darkened. ''You'd tell such a lie?''

''You don't know a damned thing about survival.'' Bitterness tinged her words. ''If you did, you'd never ask me that question.''

A muscle knotted in his jaw. She was good at this. At coming on tough as nails and then, with a word or a look, reminding him that she was a defenseless woman.

Well, hell, she was. He knew damned well she really must have given up everything to come here, and even if he was the coldhearted bastard she clearly took him to be, that kind of thing only strengthened her case.

Not the one about sexual harassment. A good lawyer—and Cullen was a terrific lawyer—could put a stake through the heart of that *bête noir* without raising a sweat.

What he'd have difficulty beating was the simple fact that Cassie had given up everything she had for a job he'd offered her. Sure, Louise Davenport had hired her, but Louise was his employee. He'd ceded her the right to hire whomever she'd wanted, and she'd hired Cassie.

Check and mate. She'd won the game.

He just didn't have to let her know it.

Keir glowered at Cassie, tucked his hands in his pockets and paced toward the office. He could feel her eyes on him, burning against his back. Halfway there, he turned and paced back.

"Name your price. What'll it take to make you go away?"

A dozen possibilities flew through her mind. A month's pay. Two months. Three months. Why not? Despite the brother who was a lawyer, she had him over a barrel. He knew it as well as she did.

"I want what I was promised," she said. "The job as manager. The salary and benefits that go with it. The apartment, rent free."

Keir blinked. Back to square one, and with no way out. She hadn't backed down, not an inch. The lady had guts.

"I'll give you two months," he growled. "You screw up once in those eight weeks, you're history."

He saw the quick leap of fire in her eyes. She banked it just as fast, assumed a look that said she'd expected as much, but it was too late. She was happy. He'd made her happy.

It put a funny feeling in his gut. Discomforted, he glowered even harder.

"Are we agreed? Two months to prove yourself."

"Six."

"Three. One screwup and you're gone."

"Four, and some latitude until I'm familiar with your operation. That's my final offer, O'Connell."

He looked at her. Her chin was set at an angle that said she was prepared to battle to the end. Keir sighed and decided it wasn't worth it. Besides, who knew how long it would take him to find a manager—a real manager—to replace her?

"Four," he said. "One big-time mistake and you're toast."

"Fine, but we should agree on a definition of what 'big time' means." Cassie touched the tip of her tongue to her bottom lip. What was she doing? She'd bluffed her way into getting him to let her stay; why show nerves now? "For instance, dropping the salt shaker isn't a big-time screwup."

"No," he said coolly, "especially since we use salt mills. You do know what a salt mill is, Berk, don't you?"

There it was again, that nasty show of arrogance. Good. She could feel her confidence roaring back with a vengeance.

"I'm not going to dignify that with an answer, O'Connell. I just want to make sure we understand each other."

"Let me spell it out for you. You do anything to displease a customer, you're gone. Got it?"

Cassie nodded. "Got it." It was rude and crude time again. She could deal with that.

"Okay. That's it, then."

"No. Not quite. Two months' severance pay, should you fire me. Should you actually have *grounds* to fire me."

Keir nodded. "Agreed."

"And, despite this addendum to our initial agreement, you're going to keep to the rest of it. Pay my flight expenses, moving costs, provide health benefits—"

"You missed your calling. You should have been a lawyer. Slimy, Sleazy and Scuzzball would love you."

He was smiling. It was a joke, not an insult, so she permitted herself to offer a little smile in return.

"Hey, who knows? Now that I discovered school's not so bad..." She frowned and drew herself up. What she thought about school, or anything else, had nothing to do with him or their business arrangement. "It's been a long day, O'Connell. Mister O'Connell, I mean. If you'd show me to that apartment..."

"Keir."

"What?"

"Well, as you just realized, we can't call each other by last names if we're working together. And 'mister' and 'miss' won't sound right. Tender Grapes is a casual place."

"Casually elegant." His brows lifted and she flushed. "That's what Miss Davenport said. She said it was on the menu and on the letterhead."

"Well, she was right."

Keir moved slowly toward her. He had the grace and intensity of a big cat. Cassie wanted to take a step back but the car was right behind her. Besides, didn't all those wildlife programs say you should never show so much as a hint of fear to a big cat?

"Tender Grapes, Deer Run, our entire operation is casual but elegant." He shook his head. "Actually, I hate that word."

"Casual?" she said, a little breathlessly. He'd come to a stop inches from her, so close she could see that his eyes weren't really black but a deep, mysterious midnight blue. "Why? What's wrong with it?"

"Nothing. I mean, it's fine. 'Elegant' is the word I'd like to change. I'd prefer something a little more, I don't know, masculine." He reached out, touched his hand to her hair. "Your hair's getting wet again," he said softly.

Why was he touching her that way? Better yet, why was she reacting to it? His fingers brushed against her cheek and she felt the shock of his touch surge into her blood.

"How about—how about classy? Or—or chic? 'Casual but chic.' That would work."

"You're trembling, Cassie."

"The rain. It's the—"

"This drizzle?" He smiled, caught a strand of her hair between his fingertips. "I don't think so."

"O'Connell. Keir. I think we need to—to get something straight…"

"Yes. I agree."

He cupped the back of her neck with his hand. God, she was beautiful. He'd known lots of beautiful women, been involved with enough of them to know that women who looked like this and had spirit were rare. They were too egocentric to risk going toe-to-toe with a man. Women with looks that could send your pulse into the stratosphere purred to get what they wanted, or resorted to tears.

Cassie hadn't done either.

"Agree to what?"

To what. Yes, he remembered.

"You said we had to set something straight. And you're right. We need to clear the air, if this is going to work out."

Cassie drew a deep breath. If he wanted an apology for the way she'd forced his hand, he wasn't going to get one.

"I don't think we do. We reached a logical business agree—"

"I was talking about us."

"What 'us'? There is no 'us.' If you're referring to that—that thing in Texas, it was a mistake."

"Absolutely. It never should have happened…but it did. And I'm not going to lie to you, Cassie. There hasn't been a night goes by that I don't remember it."

He saw the pulse flutter in the hollow of her throat and he knew, *knew,* it was the same for her. The emotion that swept through him was all-consuming, hot, and dangerous. Better to deal with it now than later.

"Admit it," he said softly. "Tell me I'm right."

"You aren't! I can hardly remember Texas."

His eyes darkened. "You never give an inch."

"That's right. Never. And if that's what you hope will happen, that I'll bend—"

His mouth crushed down on hers. Startled, her hands flew up, pressed against his shoulders, but his arms went around her, drawing her hard against him, and all her good intentions scattered like fall leaves on a windy morning.

She moaned, a sweet, sensual message that went straight to his loins. Keir slid his hands into her hair, tilted her head back, kissed her relentlessly with a hunger born of endless nights and fitful dreams.

He didn't want her to bow. He didn't want her to bend. He wanted her as an equal, to play out the rest of their battle on soft sheets instead of sparring with words in a parking lot under the touch of a soft rain.

Her mouth parted under the pressure of his and he slipped his tongue between her lips, tasted her while she tasted him. He groaned and she wound her arms around his neck, lifted herself to him, wrapped one of those long, exciting legs around his.

God. To hell with sheets and beds. He was going to take her right here, against the car, pull down her jeans, drive into her again and again until they were both sated…

But a thread of sanity remained. He fought to catch it, to hang on to it. His hands dropped to Cassie's shoulders. He pulled back, and so did she.

He opened his eyes, looked into her face. Her color was high; her eyes were wide and unseeing. Her mouth was swollen from his kiss. And he—he was breathing like a man who'd just run a twenty mile marathon.

"We'll be working together," he said, his voice so thick that it sounded alien to his ears.

Slowly, Cassie nodded. "Yes," she whispered. "And that can never happen again."

"Agreed. That's why I kissed you. To get it out of the way." He cleared his throat, wondered if that sounded as ridiculous to her as it did to him. The trouble was, he meant it. Surely, kissing her would put an end to the wondering and the dreams. "From now on, it's strictly business." He let go of her and stepped back.

"Strictly business," she said, echoing his words.

He thought about holding out his hand. Then he thought about what might happen if she took it. Quickly, he reached past her for the suitcase.

"Well," he said briskly, "it's raining again."

''Umm. Yes.'' Cassie looked up as if the rain really mattered. ''Does it always rain like this in Connecticut?''

Keir laughed and grabbed for the verbal lifeline. ''Nah. When it gets really cold, it snows.''

Cassie laughed, too, as if they'd shared a marvelous joke. ''Maybe you'd better show me to my apartment, before we drown.''

''Right.'' He hoisted the suitcase from the trunk and slammed the lid shut. ''You want to walk? It's only a couple of hundred yards but if you don't want to get any wetter…''

''A couple of hundred yards?'' She shot a puzzled look past him, to the red barn that housed the office and reception area. ''It's not even a hundred feet!''

Keir began walking briskly up the driveway. Cassie hesitated, then hurried after him.

''Keir? Where are we going? Louise said—''

''Louise said a lot things. As we're both finding out, most of them were wrong.''

''She said the manager's apartment adjoined the office.''

''The tasting room adjoins the office, and if you think I'm letting you set up housekeeping in a vat of chardonnay, think again.''

''But—but the apartment… Where is it?''

''It's right there, in—''

The wind snatched up whatever else he'd said and flung the words away. Cassie tucked her hair behind her ears and ran to keep up. They were heading uphill, toward the handsome stone house with a turret she'd glimpsed on her arrival.

Keir opened the door and motioned her inside, but Cassie stayed on the top step as the wind tugged at her hair.

''Is this where you live?'' When he nodded, she went down one step. ''Forget it!''

Keir put down the suitcase. ''It's not what you think.''

''Ha.''

''Listen, Berk, I'm cold and wet and tired of standing in

the rain, arguing with you. You want to come inside, fine. You want to spend the night curled up in your car, that's okay with me. I'll give you ten seconds to think it over and then I'm going inside and closing the door."

"You're good at that 'I'll give you ten seconds' thing," she said furiously.

He grinned. "Actually, it was five seconds the last time."

"Dammit, this is not funny. I thought we just agreed—"

"One," Keir said calmly, "two, three, four—"

Cassie called him a name that cast serious aspersions on his ancestry as she swept past him. He slammed the door behind her and tried not to wonder how she could look so bedraggled and so damned beautiful at the same time.

"Okay," she said, folding her arms and tapping her foot in a fast, angry rhythm, "who gets to sleep on the sofa?"

"There is no sofa," Keir said calmly.

Cassie looked around. They were in a room that would have done a medieval king proud. An empty room, unless you counted the fireplace big enough to roast an ox, the suit of armor in the corner, and the wide stairs that swept up into gloomy darkness.

"I'm in the process of refurnishing."

"Décor by Dracula, I'm sure."

He laughed. "That's the 're' part. I'm hoping to come up with something livelier."

"Just make sure my sleeping bag's not on the same floor as yours."

"No problem." He walked across the marble floor, his footsteps loud and echoing, took a key from his pocket and unlocked a door that was almost hidden behind the stairs. "Your rooms, m'lady."

Cassie hesitated. Then she strode past him and tried to keep her jaw from dropping. She was in a living room the size of her entire apartment in Las Vegas. There were other rooms leading from it. A bedroom. A kitchen. A bathroom…

"It's a little outdated."

The understatement of the century, but that didn't mean it wasn't handsome. Cassie stroked her hand over the back of a wine-colored velvet sofa, looked at the marble floor…

"What is this?"

"It's your apartment."

She spun around and stared at Keir. "Are you serious?"

"Just let me know what you need and I'll see to it."

He tossed an enormous brass key toward her, the kind that hung on the rings of diabolical housekeepers in scary movies. She snatched it out of the air.

"The lock's old," he said, "but it works."

"Even against vampires?"

Aha! The hint of a smile, the faintest suggestion of an olive branch. Keir smiled back.

"I'll just put your suitcase into the bedroom—"

"You stay the hell out of my bedroom, O'Connell!"

So much for olive branches. Keir started to say something, thought better of it, dropped the suitcase on the floor and stalked out.

CHAPTER SEVEN

KEIR stood at his office window, drinking coffee as he gazed out over the land.

His land.

After three backbreaking, exhausting months, he was starting to feel as if Deer Run actually belonged to him. Having your name on a deed was fine but putting your sweat into the soil was what mattered.

"Sweat equity," his old man had called it, the summer they'd had to spend rebuilding a falling-down cabin on a godforsaken lake in Arkansas. Ruarch had won it in a poker game and until his luck changed and he started winning again, the cabin and its leaky roof, stopped-up toilet and sagging floors were all they had.

"You'll love the place all the more, once you've put your backs into fixing it," Ruarch had told them, but it wasn't true.

They'd all hated it, the girls for the mice that built their nests inside the old furniture, the boys for the never-ending work of trying to keep the structure from falling down around their heads. Only their mother had seemed happy, referring to the cabin as their place in the country instead of what it was, a miserable hovel on the shores of a lake that was home to an army of snapping turtles and water snakes.

Keir drank some more of his coffee.

He still despised the cabin, even in memory, but now he understood what his father had meant about sweat equity and the special feeling that could come with it when a man worked his hands raw on something that mattered to him.

Deer Run mattered.

Keir smiled ruefully. If he hadn't worked his hands raw, he'd certainly worked them hard. At Deer Run, workers harvested the grapes by cutting the heavy clusters from the vines at the exact moment they were ripe. Hand labor was costly and there were machines that did the job faster, but machines could damage the delicate fruit.

His vintner, a taciturn Californian from the Napa Valley, had expressed surprise when Keir showed up in jeans, sweatshirt and work boots the first day of the harvest.

"We have plenty of pickers, Mr. O'Connell," he'd said politely.

"It's Keir," Keir had replied, "and now we have one more."

After that, he'd worked side by side with the crew, picking grapes, unloading the heavy baskets into the pick-up cart, running the wine press and cleaning up at the end of each day. After a week, he knew more about grapes than he'd learned in the prior six weeks worth of reading and knew, too, that he'd passed some sort of subtle test when the vintner said if he wanted to learn about pruning and grafting, he'd be glad to teach him.

"Sure," Keir had said, as if the offer and his response were equally casual, but he knew damn well they weren't.

Now he felt as if he really owned these acres…or maybe they owned him.

Either way, it felt damn good.

He was happy, happier than he'd been at any job he'd ever held, and working harder than he'd ever imagined. Nights he spent at his desk in his office, writing up detailed plans for expanding the Deer Run market and reading everything he could about oenology and viticulture.

"Wine-making and grape-growing, for you ignorant beer drinkers," he'd told Cullen over dinner in Manhattan.

"Yeah," Cullen had said, "well, when you can appreciate the difference between a dark Bavarian ale and a good English stout, let me know." They'd grinned at each other.

"On the other hand," Cullen had added, "that bottle of red you sent me—"

"Merlot."

"That bottle of red," Cullen had said blandly, "wasn't bad."

They'd grinned again, talked some more, and then Cullen had mentioned, very casually, that he had a friend who was doing a feature piece for *The Times.*

"It's about people who've changed careers." Cullen had lifted his glass of Belgian White ale to his lips. "You think you'd be interested in talking with him?"

"Well… I don't think so. I'm too new to the business. I mean, I don't know a hell of a lot yet."

"Keir, are you nuts?" Cullen had pushed aside his plate and leaned over the table. "*The Times* must have a readership damn near big as the population of China."

"Yeah, but—"

"But what? You don't want all that free publicity? You don't want people in New York and most of the other civilized cities in the world opening the Sunday magazine section, turning to an article and reading about Deer Run vineyard and—what's the name of that restaurant?"

"Tender Grapes."

"Tender Grapes. Right. Which reminds me—did you ever find somebody to manage it?"

"Yes."

"And?"

"And, what?"

"And, how's the guy working out?"

Keir had thought of saying it wasn't a man, it was a woman, that it was, in fact, a woman Cullen had already met, however briefly, in an elevator in Vegas…

"Fine," he'd said, "just fine. So, tell me more about this friend of yours."

The upshot was that Cullen's pal had come to Deer Run. He and Keir had talked, a photographer had taken a couple of dozen shots and last weekend, the article had appeared in *The Sunday Times.*

There were a couple of paragraphs about the vineyard and only a brief mention of the restaurant. Keir had tried to point the guy toward it, asked him if he'd like to meet with his manager, but the freelancer hadn't been interested. It was the wine-making that had his attention. A 180 degree switch from Keir's prior career, he'd called it.

The piece had run with a photo of Keir standing on the highest ridge above the vineyard, looking out over his land.

Keir O'Connell's Kingdom, it said.

He'd taken a lot of teasing phone calls from his brothers and sisters, even one from Sean, on a yacht off the Côte d'Azur.

''Keir O'Connell's kingdom, huh?'' he'd said, laughing, and Keir had pleaded ignorance.

''I never saw that title until the paper came out.''

True…but that didn't mean he hadn't gotten a kick out of it. The phrase was presumptuous but it had a ring that he liked.

This place was his and nobody else's. The vineyards, the house, the restaurant. Whatever happened here, good or bad, would be the result of his hard work. Well, everything except what went on in the restaurant, which had turned into Cassie's kingdom.

Keir sat down, leaned back and folded his arms behind his head.

The day after she'd arrived, he'd walked her into Tender Grapes, introduced her to the surly chef and the now-you-see-them, now-you-don't staff. Cassie had said hello, how are you, pleased to meet you. The chef had grunted, the kitchen staff had shrugged, and the servers and busboys had given her looks that said why bother, when she wouldn't be around all that long.

''Listen up, people,'' Keir had said sharply. ''I expect you to cooperate fully with Miss Berk. If you think you can't do that—''

"Thank you, Mr. O'Connell," Cassie had said with a big smile, "but I'm sure the staff and I will get along just fine."

Then she'd clasped his arm, hustled him to the door and, basically, tossed him out.

Later, when they were alone, she'd told him that if she ever needed any help, she'd let him know.

"I'll whistle," she'd said, without any pretence of a smile. "Until then, I prefer to establish a relationship with my people my way, and on my own."

"In other words," he'd said, "'thanks but no thanks,' and get the hell out of the way."

"You're a quick study, O'Connell," she'd said, and that was pretty much the last real conversation they'd had.

Keir sighed, pushed back his chair and put his feet on his desk.

He had to admit, she was doing her job. It was weeks since anybody had quit or the chef had brandished his meat cleaver. Food came out of the kitchen on time, empty dishes were promptly whisked away, the parking lot was almost full at every sitting…

…And his attempts at holding reasonable conversation were a flop. He talked. Cassie listened and said nothing, unless you counted "yes" and "no" as meaningful dialogue.

Amazing, how much meaning a woman could impart with words of one syllable.

Not that he cared.

What could they have to say to each other? Would she give a damn if he said, How was your day? How do you like New England? Were those really old phonograph records I saw in that carton when the moving guys were bringing in your stuff?

None of that was his business, not even what made her laugh, or if her throat tightened when she watched the sun dip behind the hills and the sky turned to flame.

Keir frowned and swung his feet to the floor.

Who gave a damn about any of it? Not him. Cassie Berk

was his employee. So far, admittedly to his surprise, she seemed to be doing a decent job. End of story. He'd made it a point to know a little about the people who'd worked for him in Vegas but if one of them had said, *You know, I get a real kick out of watching the sun set,* he'd have figured that person was nuts.

But then, nobody who'd reported to him in Vegas had the lovely face of an angel or the mercurial temperament of a cat. A sleek, green-eyed cat who could claw and hiss one minute and purr in your arms the next…

''O'Connell?''

Cassie was standing half inside the doorway and he knew the second he saw her that everything he'd just told himself was a lie. There were a hundred things he wanted to ask her, and not one of them had to do with business.

Flustered, he pushed back his chair and stood up. Damn, she was beautiful, even at this hour of the morning. What would she look like at this same time, in bed, after a long night of loving?

''Cassie.'' He cleared his throat. ''Come in.''

She took a couple of steps into the room, then hesitated. ''If this is a bad time…''

''No, it's fine.''

''Are you sure?'' she said, and gestured toward the door. ''Because if it's not—''

My God. She was being polite. A new leaf? A new Cassie? What was going on?

''Really, your timing's perfect. I was just, uh, I was thinking about you. About the restaurant, I mean. Please, come in and sit down.''

She hesitated, then took a chair as he returned to his. He smiled politely and tried to figure out what in hell was happening. The only thing he could come up with was that she was quitting.

A couple of months ago, he'd have wanted to hear that. Not now. Whatever she'd done with Tender Grapes was working out. And even though their relationship was stilted—okay, even though they had no relationship—he liked seeing her, catching her floral scent in the entryway to the house, hearing the water run in his bathroom and knowing she was showering in hers, standing sleek and naked under the spray…

Stop it.

He cleared his throat, flashed what he hoped was a reassuring smile and folded his hands on the desk before him.

"Well," he said briskly, "how are you settling in?"

"Fine, thank you."

Silence. He searched for another topic. "I noticed you're driving a different car."

"Yes. I returned the rental and leased a car instead."

"A good idea."

"I thought so."

More silence, and she was fidgeting. Well, why would he expect her to be at ease? They hadn't exchanged a pleasant word since he'd hired her.

"Cassie." What the hell. One peace gesture deserved another. "I want you to know that I'm pleased with the job you've been doing."

"Thank you."

Was he going to have to keep pulling conversational gambits out of the air?

"Well. What can I do for you this morning?"

He saw her throat move as she swallowed. "I—I need something."

"Really." That sounded polite, didn't it? "What?"

Cassie slicked the tip of her tongue across her bottom lip. She'd gone through this scene in her head at least half a dozen times, trying to envision it every step of the way, and she'd come to one, and only one, conclusion.

You could catch more flies with honey than with vinegar.

She'd used that approach to win over the restaurant staff. The brilliant but self-centered chef had stopped threatening to decapitate the almost-as-brilliant but painfully neurotic sous-chef, who'd stopped threatening to beat up the kitchen workers, who'd stopped slowing things to a crawl. That resulted in better service, which led to better tips, which led to the servers and busboys not throwing off their signature white aprons and stomping out the door.

All in all, what had happened was proof that textbooks that emphasized the importance of getting along with those who worked for you were correct. And that led, inexorably, to the conclusion that the texts were equally correct in saying a successful manager found ways to get along with his or her boss, even if that boss was an egotistical—

"Cassie? You were saying that you needed something…?"

Egotistical, and gorgeous.

All those days he'd spent, helping with the harvest. Couldn't he have worn a shirt? It was unseemly, an employer going around like that, half-naked, his shoulders rolling with muscle, his chest lightly furred, the dark hair arrowing down into his low-slung jeans.

"Yes." She smiled. He smiled in return, looking as innocent as a baby. "Yes," she said, "yes, I do."

He nodded, still smiling, but his eyes were wary. Well, she could hardly blame him. She'd avoided him the past two months, met each of his attempts at conversation with all the warmth of a polar bear greeting a seal popping its head through the ice, and now she was doing everything but fluttering her lashes.

Stop it, she told herself sternly. You didn't need to be Miss Congeniality to impress your employer. You could do that with hard work. Besides, if she unbent too much, O'Connell would let it go straight to his zipper.

"Well," he said, still smiling, "would you like to tell me what it is you need?"

Cassie took a deep breath. "An advertising budget."

"Ah. An advertising budget."

He sounded wise and calm but she'd caught the tiniest frown, as if he'd expected something else. Well, he wasn't going to get it. One meaningless bit of chitchat, a little remark about the old records she'd seen him eyeing when her stuff had been delivered or a comment about the incredible sunsets, and Mr. I-Am-God's-Gift-To-Women would figure she was cracking open the door to something far more personal, and why on earth would she ever do that?

Keir wasn't her type. She'd never liked men that were too good-looking, too big, too masculine, too everything. They did funny things to a woman's brain and, worse still, to her heart. Hadn't that happened with the miserable bastard who was her ex-husband? Her only husband, because he'd taught her a lesson about men and trust and love that she never wanted to learn again.

"For what kind of advertising? Have you thought that far ahead?"

Had she thought that far ahead? What he meant was, wow, amazing, that she was able to think at all. That was what most men thought, when they looked at her. How come she'd imagined Keir could be different? That he'd see there was more to her than a chance for fun and games?

Not that she wanted him to.

He was her boss, nothing more. So what if he lived right upstairs? There was no reason for her to think about him, or lie awake nights, wondering how come it was so late and he wasn't home, or try and figure out where he spent his time from Monday afternoons until Wednesday evenings?

She didn't care. Besides, it didn't take a genius to figure out why he wasn't at Deer Run Vineyard.

He was with other women.

Worse, he was probably with *one* other woman, somebody with that cool Connecticut look, long blond hair and an Ivy League accent…

Dammit, that wasn't what kept her awake nights. It was thinking of ways to improve business that made…

"Cassie?"

She jumped. "Sorry. I was, um, I was thinking about your question." She crossed her legs, uncrossed them when she saw his gaze drop to her knees, and brought them close together, feet flat on the floor, ankles touching. "I've given considerable thought to the kind of advertising I'd like to do."

"And?"

"And, I think we should start with an increase in our local print ads."

He leaned forward, elbows on his desk, fingers steepled under his chin, frowning as if he was considering running TV spots on the Zambian cable network.

"Well," he said slowly, "why don't you look into the cost, and—"

"I already have." Cassie placed a folder in front of him. "I've run the figures two different ways. They're on page three."

He frowned again, looked at her again, then opened the folder and bent his head over it.

"I see. Well, that's not too bad. Sure. Go for it."

"Which proposal? The first, or the second?"

"Oh," he said, with a magnanimous smile, "the second. What the heck, if you think it will draw business..."

"I'm sure it will. So will the proposal on page four."

"Page...?" He turned the page and read through it. When he looked up this time, his eyebrows were raised.

"That's very ambitious."

"I know. But we're booked solid almost every weekend, and we fill most of the tables Thursday and Friday, too."

"And?"

"And, I've identified our target market. Affluent. Well-educated. Mostly between the ages of—"

"I agree."

"Then, I'm sure you'll agree we have to make an effort to reach it."

"But we are reaching it. Didn't you just say we're almost 100% booked?"

"We could be 100% booked." Cassie leaned forward. "If we ran quarter page ads in some regional publications—'' She named two glossy, upscale magazines. ''I've figured the cost.''

''Expensive?''

''Yes. It's on the next page.''

He turned the page, read it, then read it again. ''More than expensive. Outrageous.''

''Not when you consider the photo shoot and initial layout are one time costs.''

''It's still a lot of money to spend.''

''Not when you figure the return.''

''The *possible* return.''

''Look,'' she said, and stopped when she heard the first impatient note creep into her voice. With some difficulty, she forced a smile to her lips. ''There's risk in everything, O'Con… Mr. O'Conn… Keir. I mean, you took a risk when you bought this place.''

''A calculated risk. I knew what the land, the buildings, the label were worth. At the worst, I could have sold it for close to what I'd paid.'' Keir nodded at the folder on his desk. ''This isn't the same kind of risk. I could spend all this money and get nothing for it.''

''You ran ads for the Desert Song.''

''That's different.''

''How is it different?'' Impatience tinged her voice again. ''If you have something to sell, you have to let people know it's there.''

''I will. I'm working on a plan, and—''

''I've already put a plan in front of you!''

''Cassie. I know you've given this a lot of thought but when you've had more experience…''

''Oh, for God's sake!'' Cassie shot to her feet. ''Would you do us both a favor and get that tone out of your voice?''

''What tone? Dammit, woman, I'm just trying to tell you something.''

''That oily, self-righteous tone that says you're trying to educate me.''

''Yeah. Yeah, I guess I am. What's wrong with that?''

"What's wrong is that you don't know the first thing about this."

"Give me a break, okay?" Keir shoved back his chair and stood up. "For six years, I ran—"

"For six years, you ran a hotel."

"A hotel with six restaurants under one roof!"

"Listen, O'Connell..."

"What happened to the 'mister'?" Keir shot back, his voice as icy as hers. "You know what your problem is, Berk? You can't keep a civil tongue in your head."

"You wandered through the kitchens at the Song like—like a general reviewing his troops."

"I beg your pardon?"

"You heard me. 'Hello there, Lester. How's the wife? How're the kids?' "

Her voice was pure female, but the intonation was a nearly perfect imitation of his. Keir felt heat rising in his face.

"And there's something wrong with that?" he said, as he came around the desk. "Come on, Madame expert. Tell me how you'd have done it."

"The same way, dammit. But this isn't the Song."

A sardonic smile curved his lips. "Congratulations on a brilliant observation."

"It's a small restaurant. You take a stroll through Tender Grapes, you could be in the front door and out the back in five minutes. Instead, you used to stand around for a hour, making everybody nervous because they couldn't decide what in hell it is you wanted."

"I was being friendly. It's a hands-on management technique. Something wrong with that?"

"In a little place like this, with a prima donna at the stove, yes, there's something wrong with it. It's not hands-on, it's in-your-face. That's how the chef saw it, anyway."

"What's the chef got to do with anything? The whole damn staff was out of control."

"A small restaurant operates like a game of dominoes. Upset one piece, the whole bunch collapses."

"Another incredible observation."

"It's a fact. You upset the chef all the time."

Keir folded his arms over his chest. "Name one."

"How about when you criticized the sauce for his New Orleans shrimp?"

"Criticized?" Keir shook his head, bewildered. "I simply said—"

"He told me how you hung over his shoulder, questioning his choice of ingredients, telling him how you thought he should make it."

"He's as nutty as you are. I never did anything remotely like that."

"You told him to use less butter."

"That's not true. I probably said something like, hey, no wonder that's so delicious, Henri, there's enough butter in there to clog an elephant's arter..." Keir frowned at Cassie's smug expression. "My God, it was a joke!"

"He didn't take it as a joke."

"He never complained."

"No," Cassie said coolly, "he just waved his cleaver in the air and snarled at the sous-chef, who saved face—"

"Excuse me?"

"The sous-chef is Chinese. Old country Chinese, in case you never noticed, and when Henri gave him a tongue-lashing, he turned right around and let it out on the salad boy, who—"

"This is a joke, right? A warped version of 'For want of a nail, a kingdom was lost'?"

Cassie's eyes darkened. "Do me a favor, O'Connell. Let's not talk about kingdoms."

"Huh?"

"I'll bet your Miss Davenport tried to tell you to stay out of the kitchen."

"Not true."

"She did. I can see it in your face."

Keir glared at Cassie. Louise *had* suggested he limit his visits, but what did she know about hands-on management? What did Cassie know about it? Nothing. Not one blessed thing.

And what made Cassie think she could ignore him for almost seven weeks and then come strolling into his office, first batting her lashes and then snapping off his head when he wouldn't do what she wanted?

What kind of fool did she take him for?

"We've gotten away from the point," he growled. "You want me to sink enough money to buy a small country into your hare-brained scheme. Well, I'm not going to do it."

"Okay. You want to talk about countries, we'll talk. Like the *Times* said, O'Connell, this is *your* country. Your kingdom, and why I was dumb enough to imagine you'd be open to advice on how to run it, I'll never know."

"I don't believe this. Are you annoyed because that article didn't mention you and the restaurant?"

Cassie knotted her hands into fists. "You know what, O'Connell? You're an idiot." She whirled around, stomped to the door, then swung toward him again. He was going to fire her. Why not go for broke? "Just for the record…doing the Nero thing, playing at being a farmer, isn't going to grow this place."

"It was Cincinnatus," he said, his voice dangerously soft as he moved toward her. "You're going to toss around Roman emperors, Berk, make sure you get the names right. And is that what you think I've been doing? Playing?"

She knew better. He'd worked as hard, maybe harder than anyone else, but she was angry as hell because he wouldn't listen to anyone else, because he wouldn't see that her ideas made sense…because he couldn't see that she was going crazy, working for him, passing him on the path from the house to the winery, wondering why he'd never tried to kiss her again…

"Yes. That's what I think."

Keir didn't answer. He came to within a breath of where she stood, his eyes hard, and her heart began to pound.

Maybe he was angry enough to kiss her. She hoped so, because it was time he admitted that was what this was really all about. It was why he snarled and she snapped. She was angry but her anger had less to do with his thick-headedness than it had to do with how badly she wanted him.

All these weeks, pretending she didn't. Who had she been kidding? Her job was wonderful, better than she'd ever imagined, but what kept her up nights wasn't the job.

It was Keir.

Why had she ever stopped him that night in Texas? She wanted him. In her arms. In her bed, and to hell with whether or not he'd respect her in the morning. She already knew the answer. He wouldn't. It was why she was all talk and no action when it came to men, but she didn't care anymore. She wanted Keir, wanted him, wanted him—

"You know what you need, Berk?" he said softly.

Her mouth was as dry as the Nevada desert. "Do you?"

"Yes." His voice roughened, and she could feel her heart trying to leap from her breast. "You need a lesson, and I'm the man to give it to you."

"Keir." His name came out a whisper. "Keir..."

"What time does lunch finish up?"

She blinked. Sex by appointment? "Four, but why do you—"

"Good." He turned away, went to his desk and reached for the phone. "Be ready to go at five-thirty."

Cassie sagged against the door jamb. He wasn't taking her to bed, he was firing her.

"Five-thirty, Berk, you got that?" His eyes flickered over her. "Change into something a little dressier."

She stared at him. "Change into..."

"Something dressier." His expression was unreadable. "Nothing, uh, frilly, just something you'd wear to an expensive restaurant. You do have something like that, don't you?"

Her brain was stuck on one track. "You're not firing me?"

"For speaking your mind?" His smile was thin as a razor. "I know you think I don't know the first thing about managing people but I can assure you, whatever else I am, I'm not in the habit of firing people for being honest." Keir reached took the receiver from the telephone. "Five-thirty. Please be prompt."

Be prompt? Wear something dressy? She'd come in here with a plan she'd spent days developing. He'd not only rejected it, he'd scorned it. Then he'd let her think he wanted to make love to her—that damned well *had* to have been deliberate—and now he told her, *told her,* that they were going out on a date?

Arrogant didn't begin to cover it.

"You're joking."

Keir raised an eyebrow. "I never joke about business. You think I've been neglecting Deer Run. That I'm living out a rich man's fantasy, digging in the dirt." His eyes narrowed. "Well, you're wrong."

"Look, O'Connell, I don't really care whether or not—"

"Yeah. You care, because your job depends on what I do, or don't do, with this place." A muscle knotted in his jaw. "I know you don't approve of my management style but hands-on is the way I go, Berk."

"I have no idea what you're talking about."

She was angry and puzzled. He could hear it in her voice, see it in her eyes. Good. Did she really think she could waltz in here and accuse him of not knowing how to run his business? Of being a dilettante? Did she think a steamy look would get her what she wanted, or maybe set him up for more humiliation?

The woman figured she could read him like a book, and it was time to change that perception.

"Let me spell it out," he said curtly. "We're taking a little educational tour this evening. Why not save whatever else you want to say for then? It's a two hour ride into Manhattan." Again, he flashed that thin smile. "Why spend it in silence?"

"It's a three hour ride," Cassie said faintly. "Almost four."

"Two, when I do the driving." He hesitated, not wanting to ask, knowing he had to. "How do you know how long a drive it is?"

"I drove down last week."

His eyes met hers. "Do you know someone in New York?"

She'd gone to a seminar on wine-making that she'd seen advertised in a magazine, but that was none of his business. "I know a lot of people," she said, doing her best to sound offhand about it.

His mouth twisted. "How nice for you." He nodded to the door, the gesture bluntly dismissive. "Five-thirty, sharp."

"What if I say I don't want to go?"

"That's easy." This time, his smile was real. "I'd do what you expected me to do a couple of minutes ago. I'd fire you, and I'd smile while I did it."

A string of epithets that surely described such an insufferable man flashed through her head but she wasn't a fool. Keir O'Connell made promises, not threats.

"Yes, sir," she said crisply. "Five-thirty, sir, and in proper uniform. Sir."

"Now you've got the hang of it," he said, and watched with grim pleasure as she turned color, spun on her heel and flounced out of the room.

CHAPTER EIGHT

CASSIE looked around her bedroom and wondered if it qualified as a disaster area, or just as proof that she was certifiably insane.

Neatness counts.

She'd grown up whispering that mantra. It was something you learned early, when your mother was too drunk to notice that there was a week's worth of dishes in the sink.

Once she was on her own, she'd even thought she obsessed about being neat and she'd forced herself to let a glass languish on the counter before washing and drying it, let a blouse hang on the back of a chair awhile before putting it into the laundry hamper.

Cassie took another look at her bedroom and rubbed her hands over her face.

If a herd of buffalo had gone through the place, could it really look any worse?

Clothing was piled on the bed; shoes were strewn across the floor. Panty hose in three different colors hung on the lampshade and the few pieces of jewelry she owned lay on top of the old-fashioned dresser.

She shot a frantic look at her watch.

Five o'clock, on the nose. Half an hour to go and she'd already wasted forty-five minutes trying on and discarding her entire wardrobe.

Nothing frilly, just something you'd wear to an expensive restaurant. You do have something like that, don't you?

Nice. Really nice. Translation: He didn't want her to wear anything that would embarrass him. No feathers. No sequins. No tiny little skirts or fishnet stockings. Nothing that would better suit a bump-and-grind than his exalted company.

Cassie sat down on the edge of the bed.

Too bad she'd tossed out all her cocktail waitress outfits before moving east. Too bad time travel didn't exist so she could go back to Vegas in the year she'd worn that Eiffel Tower costume and bring it here.

Smiling, she sat back, crossed her legs and waggled one foot back and forth.

Oh, how she'd love to do that. Wear the rhinestone-trimmed demi-bra and the thong panties with gold fringe. Put on that ridiculous headdress. Yes, it looked as stupid as hell but the apparatus that held it up made you keep your shoulders back, way back unless you wanted to topple over, and that made your boobs stick out in front of you like two ripe cantaloupes. And don't forget the see-through plastic shoes with heels high enough to be declared lethal weapons.

Cassie chuckled. Too bad. If only such a thing was possible. Then, in just about—she checked her watch—in just about twenty minutes, she could watch Keir O'Connell take one look at her and fall flat on his handsome face…

Twenty minutes?

Her blood ran cold. ''Ohmygod,'' she said, and leaped to her feet.

The truth was, she didn't have anything that was 'dressy.' She'd spent a small fortune on a couple of classy suits, some blouses, a handful of dresses, all of them designed to make her look like what she figured a lady manager was supposed to look like, but dressy? Not in O'Connell's book. She'd seen him at the Song in his made-to-order suits, at Dawn's wedding in his made-to-order tux.

Cassie blew her hair out of her eyes as she pawed through the clothes on her bed.

Everything the man wore was made-to-order, probably including his pajamas. If he wore pajamas. Did he? Or was there nothing between that hard, leanly-muscled male body and the cool softness of the sheets?

Cassie frowned.

Who cared what he wore to bed? For that matter, who cared what she wore tonight? Why was she tearing through all this damned clothing a second and third time?

Neat and tailored would do fine.

Ridiculous, all this worry over what to put on. She was behaving exactly like Dawn when she'd dressed for her first evening with Gray.

This isn't a date, Dawn had kept saying, even as she said "no" to one outfit after another. She'd been wrong, of course. It *had* been a date…

Cassie scowled, put her hands in the small of her back and straightened up.

Yes, but this wasn't. It was a command performance. *Big* difference! Dawn had been shaking with excitement, even as she'd denied it. She'd already fallen for Gray; she just hadn't wanted to admit it.

Cassie went to her closet and looked inside, though there was little left on the hangers.

She certainly wasn't shaking with excitement. Neither had she fallen for Keir. Oh, maybe she got a little rush sometimes, looking at him, but a woman would have to be dead not to react to a man like him.

Besides, she wasn't stupid. What would be the sense in falling for a guy who wanted no part of you?

Only one suit remained in the closet, a black silk. The skirt was short and straight; the jacket had a mandarin collar and tiny jet buttons all down the front. The suit was elegant and ladylike but buying it had been a costly mistake. It was businesslike, yes, but a bit dressier than…

Of course! It was perfect.

She tore the suit from its hanger and tossed it on top of the heap on the bed. She'd keep the jacket closed but she had a crimson silk camisole somewhere… There it was. She'd wear it in the event the suit felt too warm and she wanted to open a couple of buttons. Add some off-black panty hose and a pair of black pumps with a nice, sensible heel… Excellent. Not even Keir O'Connell could—

Cassie paused. One pair of shoes remained in the closet, crimson suede pumps cut low in the front and with a slender, almost-but-not-quite-lethal heel. She'd bought them on the spur of the moment because they were on sale and gorgeous. They were also impractical, which was why she'd never worn them and probably never would, even though they'd look wonderful with the silk suit, especially if she actually left a couple of buttons undone on the jacket so the camisole showed.

If this were a date, that's what she'd wear. But it wasn't a date…and she was cutting it awfully close. Her watch said she had eleven minutes to go.

Not a problem. Years of making costume changes at the speed of light meant she could get completely dressed in the time it took other women to put on their underwear.

Underwear.

Cassie paused as she pulled on her panty hose. She hated panty hose. They were never long enough, no matter what brand she bought. An hour from now, these would undoubtedly be sitting down around her hips.

She glanced at the black silk suit.

For years, she'd worn a garter belt and stockings but she'd given that up when she made her career change. Demure suits and dresses seemed to call for panty hose, no matter how uncomfortable, no matter that nobody knew what she was wearing under her clothes.

A garter belt would be so much more comfortable.

A red silk garter belt, like the one in her underwear drawer. Now that she thought about it, she'd bought the shoes and the belt on the spur of the moment, right before she'd gone to Dawn's wedding. Who had she bought them for? A woman didn't buy stuff like this for herself, she bought it for a man…

Cassie frowned, pulled on the panty hose and everything else, added a touch of light makeup, discreet gold hoop earrings, a slender gold bracelet, and turned toward the full length mirror on the bathroom door.

She looked fine, from every angle. Attractive. Professional. Elegant.

She'd still look elegant if she swapped the sensible black pumps for the red suede.

Yes, but Keir…

Keir? Keir was her boss. He wasn't in charge of her life. If he didn't like the shoes, who cared?

"You manage the vineyard, O'Connell," Cassie said, "not me."

Saying the words was wonderful. Acting on them was even better. She kicked off the practical black shoes, reached for the red ones, paused…

Her watch read five-seventeen. Her heart was racing. No. It was silly. It was pointless.

It was what she wanted to do.

Cassie hiked up her skirt. Off with the panty hose, on with the garter belt and sheer black hose. What I-Am-God O'Connell didn't know couldn't hurt him, and there wasn't a way he'd ever know about the belt.

A tremor sizzled along her nerve endings like a flash of lightning.

Not a way in the world would he know about the belt.

"In for a penny," Cassie whispered. She grabbed a red lipstick, ran it over her lips, and flew out the door.

How long did it take a woman to get ready to spend an evening with a man?

No, Keir reminded himself as he paced the entry foyer, that was poor phrasing. This wasn't a date. Not by any stretch of the imagination. This was a business meeting and when it was over, the lady with the fast mouth and the nasty accusations would know just how wrong she was.

Playing, huh?

Keir paced faster.

Was that what she thought he'd been doing? Days out

among the vines, nights buried in textbooks, weekends spent shaking hands and talking until his throat was sore, convincing *sommeliers* and restaurant owners to buy his wine? That was play?

He'd been working his tail off while Cassie did a stint as amateur shrink to a chef with an attitude problem. Oh, yeah. *That* was definitely hard work.

No wonder she'd driven into the city to unwind, doing who knew what with who knew whom.

He'd have to talk to her about that. Certainly, she was free to do as she wished on her own time but Manhattan was almost 200 miles from here. She would have to understand that she couldn't make the trip when she had to work the next day.

Keir's scowl deepened.

Actually, he'd tell her she wasn't to make the trip at all. She was his manager. She had to be on hand in case she was needed. That wasn't asking much, not if she was serious about her responsibilities…

''I'm ready whenever you are.''

''About time,'' he grumbled as he turned toward her. ''I said five-thirty and it's almost five thirty-thr…''

Holy hell.

Dressy, he'd told her. And she'd complied.

Keir stared at the incredible vision in black and red. Words ran through his head. Stunning. Elegant. Demure.

And sexy. Sexy enough to start the blood draining from his head, straight into the part of his anatomy that least needed it. Everything about her screamed ''woman'' in capital letters.

That gorgeous hair, streaming over her shoulders. The spectacular face. The tiny hit of red peeking out of the half-buttoned jacket. Those long, endless legs…

And those shoes. Man, those shoes.

How was he ever going to get through this night?

Getting his jaw off the floor might be a good start. So

would breathing. Lack of oxygen only made an already bad case of ZTS worse.

Keir cleared his throat, worked up a scowl because only a scowl felt safe, walked past Cassie to the door and opened it.

"You're late," he said gruffly, "and we have appointments scheduled."

Was that a quick flash of disappointment he saw? Probably. She must have figured she'd knock him off balance, looking the way she did, but that wasn't going to happen. He was her employer. She was going with him tonight so he could teach her to think before she spoke…

Except, there were a thousand other things he wanted to teach her, and not a one of them had to do with how to run a restaurant.

It was going to be one very long night.

Keir had said they'd talk in the car, but they didn't. Cassie didn't care. She had nothing to say to him and besides, why would a woman talk to a man who so obviously resented her presence?

She shot him a quick look.

Actually, there were some things she might have said, asked him, anyway, had he given her the opportunity. Where, exactly, were they going? Manhattan, he'd said, but what did that mean? What kind of "appointments" had he scheduled?

Mostly, though, the questions she'd have asked were none of her business, like, did he always drive so fast? They might as well have been in a rocket hurtling through space.

And why had he become so angry at the sight of her?

Well, really, she didn't have to ask.

Cassie glanced down, then chewed on her lip. Foolish, to have worn the red shoes and the camisole. Her temper had gotten the best of her. Okay, so she'd made a mistake. She couldn't do a thing about the shoes but she could do something about the camisole.

She looked at Keir again, to make sure his attention was still fixed on the road. He had on a dark gray suit, white shirt and red tie; he'd tossed a black raincoat into the back of the car, which reminded her that she'd gone out the door without so much as a jacket.

If she froze into a block of ice he'd probably be annoyed because he'd have to handle her with tongs.

She glanced at him again. Such a stony profile. Such a hard-set jaw. Such rugged masculinity.

How could he look so angry and still look as sexy as sin?

"What?"

Blood swept up under her skin as he turned toward her, his eyes cold, his tone rapier sharp.

"What, what?" she said, and almost groaned at how stupid she sounded.

"You keep staring at me."

She felt her blush deepen. "Don't be silly. Why would I stare at you?"

"That's what I'm asking. Is there something you want to say?"

"Not a thing."

He made an unintelligible grunt and turned his attention to the road. Cassie waited until she was sure he'd forgotten all about her again. Good. She didn't want him to see her closing the little jet buttons. He was egotistical enough to think she was doing it out of deference to his Puritanical tastes.

Slowly, working from the bottom up, she began easing the buttons through their loops. One. Two. Three…

"Leave them."

Cassie jumped. Keir's voice was harsh and he was looking right at her.

"I'm just—I thought I'd close—"

"You look fine the way you are."

Fine. Not beautiful. Not seductive. Just "fine," spoken

with less emotion than he might have shown complimenting the sous-chef on a dish of vegetables.

She made a little sound, covered it with a cough and folded her hands in her lap. What in the world was wrong with her tonight? Fine was good. It was perfect.

It was all she wanted.

The car filled with heavy silence and stayed that way until they pulled up in front of a discreetly lit doorway on the East side of Manhattan. A large man in a maroon jacket stepped off the curb and went around to Keir's side of the car.

"Good evening, sir. Tonight's password, please?"

Cassie raised her eyebrows. "Amazonia," Keir said, handing over his keys.

The man grinned. "Yes, sir. Welcome to Lola's."

Lola's? Secret Passwords? More games, Cassie thought, as she stepped onto the curb and studiously ignored Keir's proffered hand.

Walking through the door was like walking into another world. The club, small and dark, pulsated to a DJ's heavy, electronic mix. Trees rose all around the room, vines curled around their trunks, leafy branches lifting to form a dense rainforest canopy. The air was warm and humid; water from what looked like a high waterfall tumbled endlessly beyond the raised, mirrored dance floor.

"It's a private club," Keir said, bending his head to Cassie's. "Very exclusive. And expensive."

Was she supposed to be impressed? Cassie smiled politely. "That's nice."

"Dammit, Berk, it's not 'nice,' it's—"

"Keir!"

A woman with copper skin, brilliantly blue eyes and the exotic look of a jungle cat, flung herself into Keir's arms. He grinned and kissed her lightly on the mouth.

Cassie watched with a polite smile on her face. Wouldn't it be fun to peel the woman off him, like the skin on a peach? An overripe peach. Under all that makeup, she had to be forty.

''Lola. You're beautiful as ever.''

Forget forty. More like fifty, and weren't those little suture scars under the lady's eyes?

Lola turned her pale gaze on Cassie, almost as if she'd heard her thoughts.

''And this is...?''

''Cassie. Cassie Berk.''

''Ah.'' Lola smiled politely. ''Very nice,'' she said, as if Cassie weren't there.

''Cassie works for me.''

Cassie works for me. Well, of course. He'd have to be sure Lola understood the arrangement.

Lola held out a languid hand. Cassie smiled through her teeth and shook it. Who was this woman? Was she the reason Keir left Connecticut Monday afternoons and never returned until Wednesday nights?

''Nice to meet you,'' she said politely.

Lola grinned. ''Is it really?''

Keir cleared his throat. ''Do you have a table for us? We can't stay long, so if you need to tuck us into the back of the room, that's okay.''

''You? In the back of the room?'' Lola linked her arm through his. ''Nothing but the best for you, *querida.* Come with me.''

She led them past tables packed with people Cassie recognized from the glossiest magazines, to a tiny table near the raised dance floor. A placard that said ''reserved'' stood centered on the tabletop. Lola whisked it away, insisted they sit down, gave Keir another of those butterfly kisses and paused beside Cassie's chair. She bent down and put her lips close to Cassie's ear.

''Save those murderous looks, little girl. I'm not sleeping with him.'' She gave a throaty laugh. ''Not that I haven't tried.''

"Really?" Cassie raised her voice to be heard over the music. "I couldn't care..." The music paused. "...less."

The word emerged a shout. Keir looked her with curiosity and she felt color stripe her cheeks. "I work for Mr. O'Connell," she muttered, as the sound picked up again. "That's all."

Lola chuckled and straightened up. "I hope your Miss Berk is a better manager than she is a liar, *querida.* I'll send Carlos over right away."

Keir waited until the crowd swallowed Lola. Then he leaned forward.

"What was that all about?"

"What was what all about?"

"The little cat session."

"What cat session? I don't know what you're talking about."

"Give me a break, will you? You and Lola were glaring at each other."

Cassie gave what she hoped was a negligent shrug. "You're seeing things that aren't there, O'Connell. Why not get down to business, instead of trying to read tea leaves? Why'd you bring me here?"

Why, indeed? This morning, taking her with him while he dropped in on a couple of the places where it had been the most difficult to add Deer Run Vineyard to the wine list had seemed a clever plan. Now, he couldn't imagine why he'd thought so.

What was that perfume she was wearing? Its fragrance teased his nostrils. And what about that bit of scarlet peeping out from under her jacket? Was that lace? Was that the shadowed hint of cleavage?

Was he losing his sanity?

"Listen," he said gruffly, "I've been thinking it over and—and I think we should call it a night."

Cassie blinked. "Already?"

"Yes. Yes, I really think—I think—" He drew a deep breath. "What do you call that thing you're wearing?"

"What thing?" She watched his eyes drop to her camisole, then rise to meet hers. "Oh." Cassie folded her hands tightly in her lap. "Uh, it's a camisole."

"A camisole." A muscle tightened in his cheek. "It's—it's very attractive."

Very attractive? A silk camisole, hand-trimmed in lace, was attractive? Dawn had given her the camisole as a birthday gift last year. She hadn't wanted to accept it; she knew it must have cost a small fortune, but Dawn had insisted.

"I want you to have it, Cassie," she'd said. "It's perfect for you."

But not perfect enough for her boss, Cassie thought, and smiled politely.

"Thank you."

"Yeah. I mean, you're welcome. I mean..."

Hell. What *did* he mean? Definitely, it was time to turn the car around and take her home. Or take her to bed. One or the other, before he exploded.

"Cassie. Cassie, listen..."

"Ah, there you are. Lola told me you'd just come in. Good to see you, my friend."

Saved by the bell, Keir thought, and rose to his feet.

"Carlos." He held out his hand to a tall, handsome man. "How are you?"

Carlos grinned at Cassie. "What he means is, have we sold much Deer Run wine."

"Oh. Sorry. Cassie, Carlos Rivera. He's Lola's wine buyer. Carlos, this is Cassie Berk. She manages my restaurant."

"Of course. Tender Grapes." Carlos took her hand and brought it to his lips. "I'm happy to meet you, Cassie. Keir's told me what a great job you've done."

Was her mouth hanging open? Cassie shot a look at Keir. His expression was noncommittal.

"Has he? Well—well, thank you."

"How lucky for you that you don't have to plead for more bottles of *vino* from the boss." Carlos pulled out a chair and sat down. ''We sold out, Keir. Not a bottle of any kind left.''

Keir sat back and smiled. ''Yeah?''

''Yeah. That order I placed with you? Double it.''

Keir was grinning like a kid who'd just found out he was getting a puppy for his birthday.

''When I think of all the fast-talking I went through to get you to give us a try...''

''I'm glad you did. Your wines are excellent.'' Carlos turned to Cassie. ''So, Cassie. Your accent tells me you're not from this part of the country.''

''Yours tells me the same thing.''

Carlos grinned. ''Bright, as well as beautiful. Keir, you have excellent taste in women.''

''In employees,'' Keir said in a stiff tone. ''She works for me, remember?''

''Of course. And I am happy that she does.'' Carlos glanced toward the dance floor. ''Then you won't object if I ask her to dance?''

''Oh,'' Cassie said quickly, ''I don't think—''

''Ask her, by all means.'' Keir's voice had gone from stiff to rigid. ''The lady's free to do as she wishes.''

Cassie looked from Carlos to Keir. Keir's eyes were flat and expressionless. It was the way he'd looked at her for far too long. Far too long, she thought, and she beamed a smile at Carlos and pushed back her chair.

''In that case,'' she said brightly, ''the lady would love to dance.''

Carlos rose and held out his hand. Cassie started to take it, then paused.

''Wait just a minute...'' Quickly, she undid the rest of the buttons on her jacket, slid it off and took Carlos's hand. ''Let's go,'' she said, and smiled.

For the second time that night, Keir almost forgot to breathe.

Yes, the camisole had a delicate ruffle of lace. Thin straps, too. And yes, Cassie's breasts, just their lush curve, swelled delicately above the lace. One of the straps slipped off her shoulder as she followed Carlos up the steps to the dance floor. Each time it did, she reached up to touch it and, dammit, that simple little gesture was turning him hard as stone.

He was going crazy here.

The music was hot and fast. Cassie faced Carlos and began to move.

Keir's throat tightened. Lord, could she move.

She was graceful. Sensual. Sexual. She was the essence of everything female, and he wanted to go up the steps to the dance floor, pull her into his arms and carry her into the darkness of the night.

He wouldn't, of course. He'd vowed not to repeat that one-time mistake. Okay, that two-time mistake. Besides, this was a public place. If-*if* he ever tried to kiss Cassie again, he'd wait for a quiet, private moment.

Cassie raised her arms in a graceful arc that lifted her breasts. She shook her bottom, tossed back her hair and laughed as Carlos leaned in and said something.

Keir pushed his chair back an inch.

Kiss her? Hell, he wouldn't stop at kissing her. He'd devour her, bury himself in her, take her to his bed and keep her there until they were both sated, except he couldn't imagine sating himself on Cassie. With Cassie. Couldn't imagine himself wanting to stop making love to her.

Carlos moved closer, smiling. Smiling and dancing, his hips moving, his body an inch from Cassie's, and Keir said a short, ugly word and exploded from his seat.

He snatched up Cassie's jacket and tiny purse, shouldered his way through the dancers and grabbed her hand. He swung her toward him and saw her eyes widen, saw Carlos look at him as if he'd lost his mind, but he didn't give a damn.

"Keir?"

"We're leaving."

"Leaving? But why?"

''Because I said so. That's why.''

''Keir,'' Carlos said, *''meu amigo...''* He raised his hands, palms out. ''I asked, didn't I? And you said—''

''It's not your fault,'' Keir said sharply. ''It's not anybody's damned fault but my own.''

''Keir.'' Cassie tried to tug her hand free of his. ''Keir, what are you doing? I'm not leaving until you tell me—''

''Yes,'' he said, ''you are.''

She cried out as he pulled her against him and took her mouth with his. She fought him at first, beating her fists against his shoulders, and then she shuddered, whispered his name, and kissed him back.

The crowd erupted in a wild roar but Keir didn't hear it. All he could hear was the beating of his heart, all he could see was Cassie's upturned face, her parted lips, her heat-filled eyes as he held her tightly in the curve of his arm and led her into the night.

CHAPTER NINE

MANHATTAN'S concrete and glass canyons blazed with light but within moments of leaving the city, night embraced the speeding Ferrari.

Keir had discovered a route that consisted of a series of back roads that wound between the city and Deer Run Vineyard. He hadn't taken it driving down tonight because it wound sinuously through overgrown forests and hairpin turns.

It was the way he'd chosen to return home.

Every mile, every minute, counted.

Beside him, Cassie sat silent, her hands folded in her lap. Was she having second thoughts? Did she regret letting him all but carry her out of Lola's? Had he made a mistake putting close to two hours, two endless hours, between what they'd admitted in that kiss and the hushed darkness of his bedroom?

He kept a suite in the same Fifth Avenue hotel he'd stayed at when he'd first come east months before.

"You need this place for business, huh?" Cullen had said, when they'd met one evening for dinner.

Keir had put on his most innocent look. "Hey, why else would I want a view of Central Park from the bedroom?"

"From the bed, you mean."

"Yeah, well, that too."

"Oh, absolutely," Cullen had said, straight-faced, and then they'd grinned at each other and gone on to talk about other things.

Keir shot another quick look at Cassie.

Even Briana had teased him about what she'd dubbed his love nest, when she'd been in town a couple of weeks ago.

He'd evened the score by asking her how come a kid sister knew such things and Bree had sighed dramatically.

"Go right on living in a different century, BB," she'd said, "whatever makes you happy."

Keir frowned.

What was he doing? Thinking about his kid sister's sex life was the last thing he wanted to do. He didn't want to think about anybody's sex life, except his own. So why was he wasting time driving home, when he could have had Cassie in bed by now?

Keir stepped a little harder on the gas.

He wanted Cassie more than he'd ever wanted a woman, and the hotel was perfect for a romantic rendezvous. Not that he'd ever had one there. Too busy, he'd told himself, too tired at the end of each long week…but not tired enough to stop having X-rated dreams starring Cassie.

But he didn't want a perfect setting if it meant making love to her this first time in a room filled with the ghosts of transient strangers. He wanted to carry her into the dark silence of a room that belonged only to him, to a bed that belonged only to him…

A bed where he had slept alone, all these months.

Was that logical? Keir almost laughed. The hell with logic. He'd abandoned logic the day he hired Cassie. Tonight was just the inevitable result of that loss of reason. Right now, he felt like pulling into the clearing he knew was just ahead and taking her in his arms.

Tires squealing in protest, he swung the wheel hard, stopped under the sheltering canopy of the trees and shut off the engine. Cassie turned toward him, her eyes wide, her mouth trembling, and he silently cursed himself for being an ass.

The look on her face said she regretted what had happened. While he'd been wondering if he could wait until they reached home, she'd been reliving those moments at Lola's, when he'd shown all the subtlety of a caveman.

The passion ripping through him gave way to the need

to take her in his arms and comfort her. He undid his seat belt but she shook her head when he reached for her.

''Don't.'' Her voice shook. ''What happened was—it was a mistake. Let's just—just put it aside and pretend it never—''

He kissed her, his mouth gentle against hers, his hands cupping her face. After what seemed an eternity, she sighed and he felt her lips soften. He kissed her one last time, then took her in his arms and held her close.

''I'm sorry,'' he said softly. ''I shouldn't have come on to you like that, but—''

''You don't have to explain. Like I just said, it was a mis—''

He kissed her again, over and over until she was clinging to him, her heart racing wildly against his.

''The mistake was lying to each other—to ourselves—for so long,'' he said gruffly. ''I want to make love with you, Cassie. You want the same thing.'' He felt a shudder go through her and he drew back and tilted her face to his. ''If I'm wrong, tell me so now.''

Cassie looked at him. That was what she'd intended to do, just before he'd pulled off the road. Tell him he was wrong, that this was wrong…

How could it be?

She'd never felt so alive in her life. The feel of Keir's hands on her. The taste of him. Even the sound of his voice…

''Cassie.'' He leaned his forehead against hers. ''If you don't want me, say so. Because in a couple of seconds…'' He made a sound that was half laugh, half groan. ''In a couple of seconds, sweetheart, I don't think I'll be able to stop.''

Cassie drew a shuddering breath. How could he do that? Turn her on with an admission of how much he wanted her, then touch her heart with a simple endearment that made her want to weep?

Foolish, she thought, oh so foolish. Men used words like

sweetheart all the time. They told women they had to have them, all the time. And what they said, in the dark heat of the night, was never what they meant, in the cool light of morning.

She knew all that, knew it, knew it…

And wanted him despite what she knew would happen later, the pain, the rejection, the cold light of morning's reality.

A cry burst from her throat. She clasped Keir's face, brought his mouth to hers and kissed him with all the pent-up hunger in her soul.

It was like touching a match to kindling. He said something quick and urgent, unsnapped her seat belt, pulled her across his lap, and when she gave another of those little cries he slid his hand under her skirt, feeling the heat of her skin, the coolness of lace and silk and then, yes, oh yes, the heat of her against his cupped palm.

She was wet and hot, writhing against his hand, moaning into his mouth, and it was all for him.

Now, he thought fiercely. Now, right here. Just tear off this bit of silk, free himself, bring her down and down and down onto his rigid, aching flesh…

Keir shuddered and drew back his hand.

Doing it took all the willpower he possessed. Cassie whimpered in protest, which was almost enough to make him act out the wild fantasy that had just flashed through his head, but he dragged in a deep, deep breath and clasped her shoulders.

"No," he said in a low voice. "Not here. I want to make love to you where I can see you. Where I can watch your eyes fill with me, see you tremble just before I take you over the edge."

Slowly, he took her arms from around his neck and eased her back in her seat. One last, quick kiss. Then he fastened their seat belts and took hold of the steering wheel with hands that were none too steady.

''Twenty minutes,'' he said hoarsely. ''Then we'll be home.''

Cassie nodded. She didn't trust herself to answer. Her heart was trying to leap from her chest; he wanted to see her tremble, he'd said, but she was doing that already.

Heat swept into her face. Keir was the one who'd stopped, not she. She'd been ready to let him take her here, in the car, just a couple of yards from a public road.

She'd never done anything like this in her life.

Women talked about spontaneous sex, especially backstage, killing time between numbers. Cassie hadn't. She'd listened, she'd laughed...but she'd never talked.

The other girls had joked about it.

''Cassie the virgin,'' they'd called her.

Well, she certainly wasn't a virgin. She'd fallen in love the year she landed her first job as a showgirl. Thought she'd fallen in love, anyway, which only proved how young and stupid she'd been. She'd tried to make the marriage work, but her husband hadn't understood either fidelity or love.

And there'd been men, after her divorce. Not many, but some. She was normal, she was healthy, she'd felt desire...

But never like this.

The hot, desperate need. The loss of control. The realization that nothing, *nothing,* was more important than the next kiss.

Better not to think about that. Better not to think about how this would surely end, because it *would* end, she knew that, and when it did...

''Leave it.''

Keir's voice was rough. Her eyes shot to his face.

''Your skirt,'' he said. ''Leave it the way it is.''

She looked down. Her skirt was rucked at the tops of her thighs; she'd just started to tug it into place.

''Leave it? But—but...''

He reached across the console and touched her. The heart

of her. Just once, that was all, a caress as light as a whisper, but the stroke of his hand almost shattered her.

Cassie, who had never climaxed in her life, closed her eyes and knew she was lost.

The house was dark, looming against the moonlit sky like a medieval castle.

Keir got out of the car. By the time he came around to Cassie's side, she'd started to step out.

"Let me," he said softly, and gathered her into his arms.

She began to protest but he kissed her into silence and she sighed and buried her face against his throat.

She'd never been carried to a man's bed before…

And she had to stop doing this, thinking about what had been and measuring it against what was happening now. This night might be magic but, in the end, magic was smoke and mirrors.

Life had taught her that, more times than she wanted to remember.

Just commit this night to memory, she thought as Keir mounted the steps to his bedroom. All of it. The way Keir had kissed her when she was dancing with Carlos, branding her as his in front of everyone. The way he was holding her now, as if she was tiny and fragile when the truth was, she'd never been either.

"You're too big to be a dancer, Cassie," her mother used to say, but she didn't feel that way now, not in the strong arms of Keir O'Connell.

He shouldered open the door to his bedroom, whispered her name, kissed her mouth and then let her slip down his body to her feet. Her breath caught at his hardness, the taut muscles, all that beautiful masculinity so tightly leashed.

"Cass?" he whispered, and she understood. He was waiting for her to let him know that she hadn't changed her mind.

She lay her hands flat against his chest, raised herself to him and kissed him, openmouthed, telling him what she wanted, what she needed, and he responded instantly, angling his mouth over hers as he gathered her into his arms.

She felt the brush of his fingers opening the small buttons on her jacket, felt it slip from her shoulders to the floor. Heard the sibilant hiss of her skirt zipper. He fumbled with it just a little, and that pleased her, but he didn't try to ease the skirt down her hips.

"Wait," he said softly.

He lifted her hand to his mouth and kissed the palm. Then he went to the windows and opened the drapes, letting in the light from a sky radiant with stars.

He came back to her slowly, shrugging off his jacket and tie and dropping them on a chair. Her breath caught as he started to open his shirt. The way he looked at her, eyes dark and hungry as his gaze dropped to her breasts, outlined under the camisole, sent lightning arcing through her blood.

She thought of what she wore underneath. Better yet, what she wasn't wearing. No bra. No panty hose. A crimson garter belt, instead. A black silk thong. Sheer hose.

Why had she dressed like this? Was it for Keir? Had she known what would happen tonight?

Keir's eyes met hers. He said her name in a rasping whisper, but he didn't move.

My turn, she thought, and swallowed hard. She'd strolled the stage half-naked, danced while strangers gawked, stripped off her clothes as coolly as if she'd been alone. None of it meant a thing, not after the first few times. It was just a job. Bump, pay the rent. Grind, buy the groceries.

But tonight…tonight was different. She was going to undress for Keir. And—wasn't it silly?—she was nervous. Trembling, as if letting a man see her, naked, was something she'd never done before.

She licked her lips, forced a smile. Now, she told herself, and clasped the hem of the camisole…

Keir caught her by the wrists.

"No." His voice was still soft but it seared her like the desert wind. "Let me. I want to do it."

He wondered if the words had come out right. Cassie was looking at him as if he'd spoken gibberish. "Let me undress you, sweetheart," he said, and her lips curved in a smile that almost killed him with its sweetness.

One last taste of her mouth. Then he drew the camisole off.

She was braless.

She was braless and beautiful, adorned in red lace, black silk and ivory skin, and he was in danger of losing all his good intentions about going slow.

Cassie's hair spilled over her shoulders like black rain; her eyes were wide with wonder. Her breasts were perfect, just as he'd imagined them, round, high, the tips erect with desire. He spanned her waist with his hands and knew, when he saw those long, long legs, how they'd feel when they were wrapped around his waist.

If he didn't touch her soon, he was going to disgrace himself when he finally did.

"Beautiful," he whispered, and he lifted her into his arms and kissed her as he carried her to the bed.

Was it by some twist of fate that no woman had lain in this bed with him until tonight? Or was it possible, in some way he'd never understand, that he'd bought this bed for Cassie?

He covered her mouth with his, slipped his tongue between her teeth, tasted her sweet, warm essence. She moaned and he pressed his lips to her throat, felt the swift gallop of her pulse against his mouth.

How many men? The unwarranted thought brought with it a sudden, vicious pain, but her whisper drove everything else from his mind.

"Make love to me," she told him, just as she had in his dreams. "I want you so badly, Keir. I've always wanted you."

He caught her hands, kissed her palms, then rolled off the bed, stripped off the rest of his clothing and came back to her. He ran his hands down her leg, lifted her foot, slid it from her shoe, kissed the delicate, high arch, moved up her body and kissed her breasts, her nipples, until she was crying, pleading for his possession. He watched her eyes turn black as he slid his fingers under the thong, stroked the sweet, dew-wet flower that awaited him.

"Please," she said, "Keir, please."

With a low growl, he tore away the panties and entered her, driving hard, stunned at the heat, the tightness, the silken dampness all around him.

Too fast, he told himself, too fast, too fast, but it was too late. He tried to hold back, his muscles bunching with the effort, but Cassie arched toward him and he was undone. He groaned, moved, moved again, deeper, faster, faster until Cassie's sweet, sweet cry of release pierced the night.

Keir slid his hands under her bottom, lifted her, thrust deep one last time and then the wave engulfed him, stole his breath away, but instead of drawing him, spent, into a deep, bottomless sea it tossed him up to a place where the stars burned hotter than the sun.

"Cassie," he said, "oh God, Cassie…"

Her cry ran out again and this time he let go and fell over the edge of the world with her.

Sunlight. Hot light, pricking her closed eyelids.

Cassie gasped and shot up in bed.

The night came back in a rush, images blurred and spinning. How many times they'd made love. How wantonly she'd behaved.

How she'd climaxed, again and again, come with him inside her, with his mouth on her, his hands.

The first time. The very first time, and how right that it should have been with Keir. Only with Keir, she thought, and closed her eyes.

Dawn had been a soft promise on the horizon when they'd made love the last time. She'd started to rise from the bed but he'd drawn her back against him.

"Stay with me," he'd murmured. "I want to wake up with you in my arms."

But she wasn't in his arms. He wasn't even there. She was in his bed, alone.

Cassie sat up. One night. One incredible night, but that was all. Neither of them had pretended it would be anything more and she had no idea why she was fighting back tears. Keir hadn't lied to her. Wasn't that better than if he'd made a load of promises and—

"Hi."

She jerked the covers to her chin. Keir was standing in the bathroom doorway. His hair was wet; he had a towel draped around his hips and he was—her heart skipped a beat—he was gorgeous.

"I was just—" What? Leaving? Not naked. Not with her clothes scattered all over the room. How was she ever going to get them without putting herself on exhibit? She gave him a quick smile. "I was, um, I was just going to, uh, to—"

"Ah. Sure. Okay. There are extra towels, if you'd like to—"

"No. No, that's fine." Another smile. At this rate, she could try for a job selling toothpaste. "I don't have far to go. I'll, uh, I'll shower in my own place."

"Whatever you think best." He cleared his throat. "Well…"

Damn him! If he gave her another of those phony smiles, she'd stuff it down his gullet. He'd been awfully good at pretending last night. Couldn't he pull it off a little longer, make it seem as if he wasn't in a hurry to get rid of her?

"If you'd just…" She gestured toward the clothing strewn around the room. "If you'd just, you know, give me a few minutes…?"

He looked blank. Then his eyebrows shot toward his scalp.

"Oh. So you can get—"

"Yes."

"Sorry." He stepped into the bathroom. "Just, uh, just holler when you're—"

"I will." She waited until the door swung shut. Then she flew out of bed and began snatching up her things, blushing when she picked up the garter belt.

What in *hell* had she been thinking, wearing that?

No need to wear it. All she had to do was put on the suit. Just grab the other stuff, even her shoes, and get out of here before

"Dammit, Berk!"

Cassie whirled around as Keir stormed toward her, his expression as furious as his tone. She took a couple of quick steps back, clutching the clothes to her body. Her shoulders hit the door.

"Just what do you think you're doing?"

"I told you. I'm getting—"

"Dressed," he snarled. "And running for cover." He caught her by the shoulders and shook her. "The one thing I never figured you for was a coward."

Cassie's chin lifted. "You wait just a second, O'Connell. Who're you calling a coward? I'm not a—"

"The hell you're not."

Keir hauled her to her toes and crushed her mouth under his. She threw up her hands, shoved against his chest. It was like pushing against a stone wall. He thrust one hand into her hair, fingers hard against her scalp, forced her head back until she gasped and gave in to what she felt, what he was making her feel again.

Cassie wound her arms around Keir's neck and kissed him back.

After a long, long time, he took his mouth from hers.

"I don't want you to leave," he murmured. "Stay with me, Cass."

"I can't. It's no good. You know that. Last night was—it was wonderful, but—"

"Last night was only the beginning."

Cassie shook her head. She looked up at him, tears trickling down her face.

"I saw it in your eyes a little while ago. You knew—"

"What I know," he said, framing her face with his hands, "is that I'm not going to let you go."

"We're too different."

"Yeah." He grinned, ran his hands down her back and cupped her bottom. "I noticed."

"If we make love again—"

"And again, and again, and again." Gently, he wiped the tears from her eyes, then kissed them. "Look, you want the truth? I woke up, saw you lying in my arms and panicked."

"Exactly. Like I said, we're diff—"

"You work for me. That means I broke O'Connell's Rule Number One. Never get involved with someone who works with you."

Cassie gave a sad little laugh. "It's number one on my list, too." She hesitated. "And then there's—there's all the rest of it. You know, my—my background. It bothers you, doesn't it? That I—that I was a-a—"

"A showgirl. A cocktail waitress."

"A stripper." She felt him flinch, and she took a deep breath. "See? I'm right. It does—"

Keir swept her into his arms. "I'm no candidate for sainthood, sweetheart. And all I really know is that it feels right, to hold you. To make love to you." He paused, and she could see that familiar little tic in his jaw. "To wake up with your head on my shoulder in the morning." He gave her a slow, tender kiss. "Something's happening here," he said gruffly, "and I'll be damned if I'm going to walk away without knowing what it is."

He waited, his eyes searching hers, and, at last, Cassie cupped the back of his head and brought his mouth down to hers.

He carried her to his bed, came down beside her, and as

he lowered his head to her breasts, she knew that he was right.

Something *was* happening here. Something terrifying and dangerous.

She'd fallen head over heels in love with Keir O'Connell.

CHAPTER TEN

CASSIE lay sprawled over Keir, her head on his chest, one leg draped over his. His breathing was deep and regular. He was asleep but she…she was too filled with joy to sleep.

An unexpected snowfall had overtaken the sunny morning. Fat, lacy flakes of snow fell from a sky the color of fine old pewter.

What a perfect way to greet the day, Cassie thought dreamily. She loved snow. She'd missed it, all those years she'd lived in Las Vegas. It was the only thing she *had* missed about Denver.

Keir shifted his weight and murmured something in his sleep. Maybe his arm was cramped, from holding her. Her husband had never liked her to sleep so close.

C'mon, babe, he'd say after they had sex, *gimme some room, okay?*

She started to ease away. Keir, still sleeping, frowned and drew her even closer. Cassie sighed and buried her face against his chest. Such a simple thing, what he'd just done, and wasn't it silly that it made a lump rise in her throat?

There was no comparison between Keir O'Connell and her ex. She'd known that from the first minute she'd seen Keir, years ago at the Desert Song. He was everything her husband had never been, everything she'd never been.

Keir was educated. He was sophisticated. He'd traveled and seen the world; he knew things that never mattered until you realized you didn't know how to do them, like which fork to pick up when there were three to the left of your plate instead of one.

Most of all, he'd been raised in the warm bosom of a loving family.

She'd been raised by a mother who sometimes forgot Cassie existed.

Days like this, when she was a little girl, she'd snuggled deep into the blankets, tented them around her face so that all she could see was a narrow strip of the fire escape window behind the sagging living room sofa that was her bed.

On dark nights, especially when her mother hadn't come home, Cassie would lie on the sofa shaking with fear, eyes shut tight against the bogeyman she was sure would someday pop up and grin at her through the glass.

But oh, those snowy mornings.

Cassie smiled, shut her eyes and snuggled closer in Keir's warm embrace.

Safe under the blankets, her breath pluming into the cold air of the tiny apartment, she'd imagine mountains higher than the Rockies, where castles rose into the sky. She'd imagine what it would be like to live in one of them and take walks among the clouds.

She'd lie there until the last possible minute, just before her alarm went off.

Actually, it never really went off. She was always awake before then because her mother had threatened to throw the alarm clock out the window. It was, she said, too damned noisy, and how was a body supposed to get any sleep with it blasting her ears open all the way into the next room?

Cassie had only used the clock for security. She'd never missed school, not a single day. It was warm there, and safe, and the hot, filling soup in the lunchroom that most of the kids got free, same as she did, was the only meal she could count on.

And the after-school dance program, where she could pretend to be Odette in Swan Lake, or the Sugar Plum Fairy in The Nutcracker, if only for a little while…

For heaven's sake! What was the matter with her? That minutes-old lump in the throat was threatening to turn into a rush of hot tears. What was she doing, anyway, lying around like this? Stay with me, Keir had whispered, and she had, and they'd made love again, and now it was time to go.

Even if he'd meant what he'd said, that he wanted to go on seeing her, she had her space. He had his. The best way to keep the relationship going would be to honor those spaces.

Carefully, she eased free of Keir's embrace. He muttered a protest and she held her breath, waiting, but after a couple of seconds, she could tell that he was still sleeping.

Her clothing lay in a little heap and she collected it as quickly as she could, every now and then casting looks at the bed to make sure Keir hadn't awakened. She blushed again at the sight of the garter belt, snatched it up along with the thong panties, went into the adjoining bathroom and quietly turned the lock.

Looking in the mirror was a mistake but she did it anyway. Her hair was a tangled mess, her makeup was gone and there were faint marks on her throat, her breasts…

Marks Keir had made, of his possession. Of the way he'd made love to her, taking her up and up until she'd thought she'd die of pleasure, then holding her in his arms as she trembled in the aftermath of what they'd shared.

"Cassie," he'd whispered, that last time, "Cassie, you don't know what you do to me."

She knew what *he* did to *her,* and if that was anything like what she did to him, then she understood. If he'd felt half as much of what she'd felt, she understood what he meant. She hadn't told him that because words wouldn't be adequate and besides, how much did she want to reveal? Yes, she'd come—and come and come and come—for the first time in her life, but it was more than that. Sex had never made her want to weep with happiness, never made her want to stay in a man's arms forever—

"Cassie?"

She swung toward the closed door, clothes clutched to her breasts like a shield.

Keir's early-morning husky voice sent shivers down her spine.

Carefully, quietly, she cleared her throat.

"I'll be out in a minute," she called, and hoped she sounded casual and sophisticated, the way you were supposed to sound after you left a man's bed.

"Cass." His voice lowered; she could picture him leaning close to the door. "You know what I was thinking?"

Cassie dumped her clothes on the vanity, stared at the little pile of stuff, thought about how long it would take to get it all on and grabbed for her panties.

"What?"

"A long, hot shower would be terrific."

"You're right." One foot into the panties, then the other. Careful! She'd almost tripped. Wouldn't she be a lovely sight, lying in a tangled heap on the tile? Skip the stockings. The belt. Just the camisole. Good. Now the suit.

"Cassie? Did you hear me?"

Cassie zipped her skirt, slipped on the jacket, ran her hands through her hair. She looked as if she'd been doing exactly what she had been doing all night.

She'd made it a point never to let a man see her like this. A guy who dated a showgirl expected her to look like one. Her ex had pointed that out first, the morning after they'd taken their vows at the Las Vegas Starlight Chapel.

Glorying in the special pleasure of being married, in the intimacy of it, she'd showered, then come out of the bathroom in baggy sweats, her face scrubbed clean, her hair towel dried instead of carefully styled with a brush and a dryer.

Hank had looked up from the deck of cards he was fanning and done a classic double take.

"Jeez, babe you look like something the cat dragged in. Take the time you need, get yourself lookin' like my sexy lady and meet me downstairs. We'll get some breakfast at that buffet place on the Strip, okay?"

If there was only a buffet place around now. Anything

to distract Keir from taking a good look at her when she stepped out of the bathroom.

''Cassie?'' Keir rattled the door knob. ''Are you all right? Open the door. Dammit, Cassie...''

She turned the lock, swung the door open, smiled brilliantly at the stubble-jawed, hair-in-his-eyes, half-naked, beautiful man waiting for her with a scowl on his face.

''Hi,'' she said briskly. ''Sorry I took so long, but—''

Keir cut off her words by hauling her into his arms for a kiss.

''Good morning,'' he finally said, against her mouth, ''and what in heck are you doing in that get-up?''

She put a hand against his chest and stepped back a little, wishing the room might be plunged into darkness.

''I know. I'm a mess. My hair. My makeup. And this suit is all wrinkles. Well, that's the thing about silk. Looks great until you put it on, and—''

Keir put his index finger against her lips. ''You're babbling,'' he said softly.

Cassie flushed. ''Sorry. I just—''

''Caffeine.''

''Huh?''

''You need caffeine.'' His arms went around her; he gathered her against him and smiled down into her eyes. ''Come to think of it, we both do. Plus food. Eggs. Bacon. Sausages. Or bagels. You like bagels? The kind you can only get on the East coast? I admit, they're not New York bagels, but—''

''Keir. I have to, uh, to freshen up. You know. Take a shower.''

''Uh huh.''

''Do something with my hair. My makeup. My clothes...''

''The shower idea is cool. I mean, it was my idea in the first place, remember?'' Smiling, he linked his hands at the base of her spine. ''As for the rest of it—''

''Oh, I know.'' She flushed. ''I'm a mess.''

"A mess? Cassie, you're gorgeous." His voice softened. His eyes dropped to her mouth, then lifted to her face. "Your lipstick's all gone."

"Right. Well, give me an hour and—"

"I probably kissed it off."

"Yes. I'll fix it."

"Fix it? What for?" Gently, tenderly, he brushed his lips over hers. "I like your mouth just the way it is, sweetheart."

Cassie blinked. "You do?"

"Soft and sweet, just like you." Keir smiled. "You're beautiful. Have I told you that lately?"

She felt herself relaxing, leaning back against his linked hands.

"Not for the past hour, at least."

"In that case, I have a lot of making up to do. First, though, that shower. Then, breakfast. I know a diner ten minutes from here. Not fancy but the food's great. Did you ever have smoked salmon on your bagels? They call it lox here, on the wild and woolly East coast." He smiled at the look on her face. "Don't tell me. You're into yogurt and granola, right?"

Cassie smiled. "Yogurt and fruit."

"Whatever you want, sweetheart." Keir kissed the tip of her nose. "Okay. Enough playing around while my stomach complains that it's never been this empty before. Shower time, m'lady. Right now."

She nodded and started to step back. Keir frowned.

"Where're you going?"

"Downstairs. To my apartment. To shower."

"No way. You're showering here, with me."

"But I thought—I mean, I assumed—"

"You want to take our shower in your place? That's fine, if you insist." He waggled his eyebrows. "But I'll bet my shower's bigger than yours."

Cassie laughed. "Maybe."

"And I'll bet my water's hotter than yours."

"Just like a man. You think everything you have is—"

She shrieked as he lifted her in his arms, stepped into the shower with her and turned on the water. Laughing, he kissed her. She kissed him back. And they didn't get out of the shower until the water began to run cool.

Afterward, he dried her with a big, soft towel, wrapped her in his heavy terry-cloth robe, sat her in a wing chair in his bedroom while he dressed in faded jeans, an Irish fisherman's sweater and hiking boots.

Watching him was a joy. He was so masculine, so handsome, so at ease in his own body. How would it be, Cassie wondered, to watch him get dressed every morning, watch him get undressed every night? It would never happen; she knew that.

But it was easy, painfully easy, to dream.

Then he carried her downstairs.

"It's too cold to walk around barefoot," he said, when she protested. "Besides, the sight of you in those killer red shoes might be more than I can take without some food in my belly."

She laughed and lay her head on his shoulder. Her protest had been halfhearted, at best. She loved being in his arms.

"Your turn," he said, depositing her on her feet in her bedroom.

She didn't move.

He didn't seem to notice.

Instead, he began strolling around, looking at the pictures she'd hung on the walls, touching the little mementoes she'd placed on the dresser.

After a while, she took jeans and a pair of boots from the closet, a sweater, underwear and heavy socks from the drawers. She waited.

She couldn't bring herself to shuck his robe.

"Keir?" she said, in a small voice.

He turned and looked at her questioningly. She gave him a quick smile and held up the clothes she'd gathered and he said oh, sure, he'd be in the living room.

Cassie knew it really didn't make sense. She'd been almost painfully modest when she first started dancing professionally but really, how modest could you be when you were racing off stage to make a change in just a couple of minutes? There were always other people around. Men, not just women. Male dancers. Stage managers and gaffers and the lighting crew. You'd be pulling off your costume as you came off-stage and it didn't mean a thing.

This was different. This was Keir. He wasn't a guy who'd just bought a ten dollar beer for the privilege of watching her strut her stuff; he wasn't someone who'd taken her out a few times so he could show her off.

She couldn't be casual about her nudity in front of him.

She dressed quickly, started to put on her usual makeup and paused. Had he meant it when he said he liked her just as she was?

Time to find out, Cassie thought. She opened the bedroom door, went into the living room…straight into Keir's waiting arms.

"I was coming to get you," he said gruffly.

"Did I take that long?"

"No. Yes." He kissed her, hard, his mouth crushing hers, his fingers knotted in her hair as he tilted her head back. "Let's get out of here," he whispered, "before I forget why we decided to get out of bed and put on all these damned clothes in the first place."

She liked the diner, just as he'd figured.

He could tell.

"Yogurt and fruit is all I want," she'd said, when he gave the waitress their order.

"Sure. With a little of everything else on the side."

Cassie had sighed. "We'll never eat it all."

He'd thought she was probably right. Their booth was made to seat four but when the girl piled all the stuff he'd ordered on the table, there was hardly room left for the salt and pepper shakers.

But he was starved. So, it turned out, was Cassie. She ate her yogurt, polished off her eggs, a waffle, a pancake and some sausage and when he layered half a warm bagel with cream cheese, added a strip of smoked salmon and offered it to her, she hesitated, chewed on her lip—did she know what it did to him, to watch her do that?—and said, well, okay, she'd take a bite or two…

She finished it all. No apologies for her appetite. He liked that in a woman. He was tired of taking women to dinner, watching them nibble on this, nibble on that, decline dessert even as they looked at the pastry tray with hungry eyes.

Cassie ate like a real woman. She had a body like a real woman. In all his life, he'd never dated a woman like her, so free of artifice, so honest, so lushly beautiful. He'd joked about that mystical creature called the perfect woman with Sean and Cullen but until now, he'd never thought—never thought…

He sat back, shocked by where his thoughts were taking him. Nothing in this life was perfect and besides, what did that have to do with anything? A woman didn't have to be perfect to warm your bed and share some laughs…

"…burst!"

Keir cleared his throat. "Sorry. What did you say?"

Cassie groaned. "I said, I cannot believe I ate all that. One more mouthful and I'll burst."

He smiled, tried to get back to where he'd been just a few minutes ago, sort of floating in that nice comfort zone that came after a night of incredible sex.

Incredible? Hell, it had been more than that. More than sex. Well, no. What could that mean, "more than sex"? Sex was sex, and he'd had great times before…

But not like this.

How about Cassie? Had it been the same for her, or had she cried out in the dark for other men as she had for him? Had she made those little sounds that drove him wild for other men, as she had for him?

Had she? God, had she?

''Keir?''

He looked up, fought to focus on her face. ''Yeah. Sorry. I was, uh, I was thinking about—about an order I took the other day, from, um, from The Pink Elephant. It's a new restaurant in the Village.''

''Ah,'' Cassie said, as if she cared. As if it mattered to either of them how many cases of wine The Pink Elephant had ordered.

She asked questions about the restaurant and the wines they'd ordered. Intelligent questions, knowledgeable questions, or so his frazzled brain told him, even as he wondered why in hell he was talking about business when what he wanted to talk about was what had happened last night? It really couldn't happen again, even though he'd spent an hour this morning telling her that it could, because the truth was, she was right.

This couldn't work.

They were oil and water. They didn't have a thing in common, except in bed. She was his employee. He was breaking all his own rules and anyway, it was over. The sex. He'd gotten it out of his system.

How many other men had felt the same hunger for Cassie?

''Is that your name?'' he blurted.

''What?''

''Cassie. Is it your real name?''

''Yes,'' she said slowly, ''it is. Well, my given name is Cassandra, but—''

''I thought maybe you took it when you started dancing.''

She sat back a little. Her smile tilted. He could almost feel the barricades going up. Why? All he'd asked was a simple question.

''As I said, my name is Cassandra. But nobody ever called me that. I was always 'Cassie.'''

''Oh.'' He nodded, picked up his coffee cup and stared into it as if he could read the ancient mysteries in its depths.

"Did you want to know anything else?"

Her tone was pleasant but something in it chilled him. Why was she upset? He had the right to ask her about her name, didn't he?

"No. Not really." He put down his cup, signaled to the waitress for refills. "So, what were you saying about *cabernet franc* grapes?"

She hesitated. He could almost see her trying to figure out what was going on. He was asking questions, was what was going on. What was so unusual about that?

"Well, I took a course. In New York. About viticulture, and one of the things I read about climates like this one—"

"I've always wondered. How does a woman get started, dancing in Vegas?"

She looked at him through eyes gone cold but it was only a question. He was just making conversation, was all. Why would it bother her?

"Are you asking in general, or are you asking me?"

"In general," he said, and shot her a fast smile.

"Amazing," she said softly, "that you managed the Desert Song for all those years and never got around to asking that question of any other dancer."

He'd asked. He knew all the stories. They ranged from having wanted to be the next prima ballerina to wanting to find a sheikh with a billion oil wells. Every showgirl he knew had her head so stuffed with dreams that there wasn't room left for a thimbleful of reason. Why would Cassie be different?

"You, then," he said. "How'd you come to be a Vegas showgirl?

"Me." Cassie nodded. "Well, I decided I wasn't good enough for the American Ballet Theater."

"You studied ballet."

"And tap and modern dance." Her eyes narrowed. "My first love was ballet but after ten years of standing on my bloodied toes I decided, what the heck, Vegas would be more fun.''

Was it a joke? Her expression gave nothing away. Keir decided the safest thing was just to nod and look thoughtful.

''Makes sense.''

''No, it doesn't.'' Her voice was low pitched, each word crisp and clear. ''Nobody decides Vegas would be more fun. Not me, anyway.''

''I understand.''

''The hell you do!'' Cassie leaned across the table. Her words were hard and rushed. ''Growing up, I'd loved one thing, lived for one thing. Ballet. But there wasn't much of a market for ballerinas in my world.''

Keir winced. ''Cassie—''

''Reality was, I was seventeen and my mother was a drunk, and she had a new boyfriend who gave me funny looks. So I ran away from home.''

''Cass.'' He reached for her hand but she yanked it back.

''We weren't all born with silver spoons in our mouths. Can you even imagine what it's like, trying to put a roof over your head when you haven't got a diploma or a skill? I waited tables in a zillion greasy spoons.''

''Cassie. Please. I'm sorry. I only wondered…I mean, you seem so different…I mean…''

''You mean,'' she said coldly, ''I didn't embarrass you just now by wiping my mouth on my sleeve, or by clutching my knife in my hand while I ate my eggs.''

She tossed her napkin on the table, the rage bubbling inside her like lava in a volcano about to blow and the worst of it was, she had no right to be so angry. Oil and water. They'd never be able to mix, not if they tried for a thousand years.

''What's the matter, O'Connell? You having second thoughts about making it with somebody so obviously out of your class? Or is it the stripper part that's bothering you?''

''No,'' he shot back, and then his eyes turned black as

night. "Yeah. Okay. Maybe it is. Maybe I'm finding it tough to think about all the guys who saw everything that I saw last night."

She recoiled, just as if he'd physically struck her. He saw her mouth tremble and then she got to her feet and walked out of the diner.

Keir dug out his wallet, dropped bills on the table and went after her.

"Cassie!"

She was walking fast, heading along the road that led back to the vineyard. It was snowing harder than before, the temperature probably someplace around twenty degrees, and it was at least twenty miles to the house.

"Cassie, dammit!"

She walked even faster. He cursed, got in the Ferrari, gunned the engine and took off after her. When he pulled abreast of her, he put down the window.

"Get in the car."

"Keep away from me, O'Connell."

"Dammit, you want to freeze to death? Get in the car!"

"Find yourself a new manager. Someone new to play with, too. I'm moving out of that apartment tonight."

He pulled onto the shoulder of the road ahead of her, slammed on the brakes and jumped from the car.

"Damn you, Cassandra!"

Her name, her old-fashioned name that she'd always secretly thought sounded beautiful but had never used because beautiful names had no place where she'd grown up, was like music on his lips.

Cassie stopped. To her horror tears filled her eyes. She tried to walk around Keir but he matched her, step for step, and suddenly she was weeping and he was holding her so tight she could hardly draw breath.

"I'm crazy with jealousy," he said roughly, "and I don't know what to do because I've never felt like this before."

"That's because you've never been with anyone like

me,'' she said, sobbing into his jacket. ''I told you, didn't I? We're not right for each—''

His mouth covered hers, stealing her words, her tears, her breath.

''It's because I've never cared for another woman the way I care for you. From the beginning, from that first minute I saw you that day at the wedding...'' He framed her face, lifted it to his, thought his heart would break at the tears and snowflakes caught in her lashes. ''I don't give a damn about anybody in your past, just as long as I'm the only one in your life now.''

''Those legions of men, you mean?'' Cassie gave a watery laugh. ''I have an ex-husband. Aside from that, I've probably been with fewer men than—than most of the women you know. I don't—I don't get involved with men. They want only one thing and then, poof, they're gone.''

''Not me,'' Keir said fiercely. ''I want more. And I'm not going anywhere.''

''I know you think so, but—''

''Listen to me, Cass. I'm not going anywhere. I just—I'm pleading with you to forgive me for what I said back there.''

Cassie gave a hiccuping sigh. ''It's okay.''

''The hell it's okay! I should never... I'm not a prude, Cassandra. I don't have a thing about women being virgins while men are free to tomcat around. As for stripping...that was your choice, whatever the reasons, and who am I to second-guess them?''

Cassie smiled, wiped her nose on her sleeve and clasped his face between her hands.

''Here's my story, in a nutshell. No,'' she said, when he started to speak, ''no, I want you to hear it. I left home at seventeen. I hitch-hiked from Denver, worked in diners, couldn't make enough to live on. When I landed in Vegas, the only job I could find meant doing the same thing. One day, a customer came in, looked at me and asked if I could dance. 'Could I dance?' I thought. Here it was. My big chance.''

She laughed in a way that made Keir's arms tighten around her.

''Aw, baby. Don't. Don't put yourself though this.''

''I told you, I want you to know. See, I was so young, so dumb—''

''Innocent,'' Keir said softly. ''That's what you were, sweetheart. Not dumb.''

''I took his card, agreed to show up at the Casbah hotel.'' Her smile wobbled. ''I auditioned. It wasn't ballet but I could do the routines. The costumes were beautiful. The pay was a zillion times what I was earning, so I took the job.''

The snow was coming down in almost impenetrable sheets. Keir led Cassie to the car. They got in.

''Cass, that's enough. There's nothing wrong with dancing. I never thought there was.''

''Do you know what dancing in those shows is like? Do you know that you have to audition for your job every six months?'' She hesitated. ''I had been dancing for a few years when, one night, I was running up the stairs to change my costume. I tripped, I fell…''

Keir gathered her into his arms and kissed her. ''Sweetheart, please. No more.''

''I blew out my knee,'' she said, sitting upright and looking into his eyes. ''It took a long time to get better and I thought everything was fine but just before the next six month audition, the company manager called me aside. 'Cassie,' she said, 'I thought you'd rather hear this in private.' They weren't going to hire me for the next show. I couldn't get another job in any of the revues—they all knew about my injury. So I took a job stripping in a bar.'' Her voice broke. ''That's what I am, Keir. A stripper. I always told myself I was a dancer but the truth—the truth—''

''Come here.'' Keir drew her against him, kissed her mouth, stroked her snow-dampened hair back from her face.

''You're one hell of a survivor, is what you are.'' He lifted her chin. ''And the best damned manager I've ever had.''

Cassie shook her head and buried her face against his shoulder. ''Don't say things just to be kind.''

''Me? Kind? Not when it comes to business.''

There was a smile in his voice; it made her smile, too.

''You mean it? I'm good?''

''Yes,'' he said solemnly. ''You are. You're innovative, you're tough but you're fair, you're great with people...''

''I was a lousy stripper.''

She gave a forlorn little laugh. Keir, watching the quick play of emotion on her tear-stained face, felt as if his heart was expanding in his chest.

''You were, huh?''

''Oh, I was awful. The only way I could get through my turn was to tune out where I was and what I was doing. If you don't smile, don't wink, don't look as if you're having a good time, the tips are rotten. That's what you dance for, in a bar. The tips.''

Keir tried not to let her see the rage building inside him. He wanted to beat the crap out of every jerk who'd been too stingy to tip this woman who'd had the courage to bare her body while never baring her heart. He took a couple of deep breaths, told himself to calm down, and worked up a smile.

''So you became a cocktail waitress instead, and wasn't that a fine thing to have done because otherwise, we'd never have met.'' His smile faded. ''I'd never have found you, Cassandra.''

He kissed her, his mouth moving softly over hers, and then he drew back a little and looked into her eyes.

''I'm not even going to comment on what you said about me having to find myself somebody else to play with,'' he said softly. ''As for the rest... I don't need a new manager.''

Cassie smiled. ''I guess not.''

"But you were right about the apartment. That you're going to move out, I mean."

Her smile wavered. "I don't understand."

"You *are* moving out. Tonight, sweetheart." Keir tilted her face to his. "And then you're moving in with me."

CHAPTER ELEVEN

SUNLIGHT poured into the kitchen of the manor house. The room was delightfully warm, thanks to the enormous brick fireplace that took up most of one wall; the handsome old stone floor was smooth and pleasantly cool under Cassie's bare feet.

She hummed softly to herself as she moved from the refrigerator to the oak table that stood in a cozy corner near one of the big windows, setting out glasses of orange juice, toasted scones and jam. The jam was from a farm just up the road; the scones were a special gift from the chef, who'd given them to her last night, wrapped in a pale blue linen napkin and still warm from the oven.

Living at Deer Run was lovely.

Living with Keir was the most wonderful thing that had ever happened to her.

It was hard to believe she'd never thought they had anything in common. They did. Loads of things, everything from shuddering at the sight of anchovies on pizza to midnight raids on the refrigerator to a passion for old jazz records.

She'd been right, that day she'd moved in to the apartment, he *had* been trying to sneak a look at her collection of 78's. He even had some early Ella Fitzgerald she'd searched for in every flea market within a hundred miles of Vegas, and she had a Miles Davis album he'd looked at like a kid on Christmas morning.

They both put the cap back on the toothpaste, loved English murder mysteries and hated old movies re-done in color. And if he thought today's boy rock groups were a joke while she thought, well, they were, but they were also awfully cute, she could forgive him because he was so wonderful, so incredibly wonderful, every other way.

Cassie turned off the coffee, filled a cup and added sugar and cream.

She was happy.

Happy. Such a simple word. Such a miraculous word. She was happy, for the very first time in her life.

She and Keir had been together only a little more than a month but it was already hard to imagine life without him…and that was something she tried not to dwell on because she was a pragmatist and she knew better than to think about the future.

They'd made no promises, though she would have, in a heartbeat, if only a miracle were to occur and he'd ask.

Sometimes, just every little once in a while, she let herself think that maybe he was falling in love with her. Could a man be so tender, so passionate, so attuned to a woman's every need unless he loved her?

Cassie's smile faded. Yes, of course he could.

That was the unadorned truth. The girls she'd worked with talked constantly about the men who said they loved them one moment only to toss them into the discard pile the next. Hadn't her ex done the very same thing to her, all those forever promises gone to hell in a handbasket?

How could a man kiss you off as if you were nothing? Hank had taken advantage of her so badly that by the time he walked out, she was glad to see him go.

She'd learned something, at least. She'd never let the guy be the one to do the walking, if she got involved again. *If,* because she'd vowed that she never would, not unless some miracle happened and The Perfect Man rode into her life.

Well, Keir was the Perfect Man. The trouble was, he didn't know it. He didn't know that she was his Perfect Woman, either, that she could make him happy, so very happy, if only—

"What does a guy have to do to get a cup of coffee around here?"

Cassie swung around as Keir came toward her. Seeing him made her heart fill with so much love that she felt as if it might burst.

''He has to learn to make the coffee himself,'' she said, smiling as he took her in his arms.

''I made it once,'' he said solemnly. ''Remember?''

Their cooking arrangements were simple. Cassie did breakfast, Keir did dinner, but she always did coffee, once she'd tasted the wicked black ink he brewed.

Cassie rolled her eyes and looped her arms around his neck.

''Okay, I take it back. I'll do the coffee. You get out the butter and eggs.''

''Yes, ma'am,'' he said, but instead of letting go of her, he gave her a long, tender kiss, then made a show of running the tip of his tongue over the softness of her bottom lip. ''Umm. Coffee with two sugars and a dollop of cream. Just the way I like it.''

''Sorry, pal. You'll have to pour a cup of your own.''

''I've got a better idea. You take a sip of coffee…'' His voice turned husky. ''And I'll take a sip of you. How's that sound?''

''Like an eminently fair idea,'' Cassie said softly. She rose toward him and kissed him, teasing his lips apart, sighing with pleasure when he drew her closer…

''Dammit.'' Keir sighed, clasped her shoulders and put a couple of inches of space between them. ''Baby, I'm sorry. I just remembered an appointment.''

''Oh.''

''In…'' He glanced at his watch. ''In just a couple of hours.''

''Sure.'' Cassie stepped out of his arms. ''I understand,'' she said, and she did. He had a vineyard to run. It was just that there were times, silly as it seemed, it hurt to be reminded that he was her employer, that that was their primary relationship. ''Go on, sit down and have your breakfast. How do you want your eggs? Scrambled? Fried? Poached?''

''Sorry, sweetheart. No time.''

''Oh,'' she said again. ''Well—well, fine. I'll clean up here while you get dressed.''

''No time for cleaning up, baby. Not if we're going to be in the city by noon.''

She turned from the sink and looked at him. ''We?''

''We. Definitely, we.'' Keir reached out and tugged her into his arms again. ''You think I'm going to try and pick furniture for this place all by myself?''

''What?''

''Didn't I mention it?'' he said, trying to sound casual in hopes she'd buy the story when the truth was, the idea had come to him days ago and terrified him so much he'd gotten tongue-tied, just trying to figure out a way to spit it out.

He'd never, in his entire life, wanted a woman to help him pick out anything, not even a tie.

Yes, the house needed furniture, stuff on the walls, drapes, blinds, all of that, and with winter here and things slowing down at the vineyard, he'd started to think about hiring a decorator. That was what he'd done when he lived in New York and again after he'd taken over the Song.

That had been his plan until last week when he'd awakened early one morning with Cassie's head on his shoulder and her hand on his heart and he'd thought, *Why would I want some stranger to put this place together when I'd much rather see this house through Cassie's eyes?*

A logical idea, after all, considering that they'd discovered they liked so many of the same things. There was just something about the ramifications that made it seem a—a step. A big step, though he was damned if knew toward what.

Cassie was staring at him as if he'd gone out of his mind. Maybe he had. Maybe he really had.

''You want us to choose furniture together?''

No. Hell, no. That wasn't what he'd said. Well, it was, but the way she said it made it seem so—so—

Keir cleared his throat. "Yeah. That's the general idea. I, ah, I made this appointment. With this, uh, this interior designer. I meant to tell you about it, but… I mean, I thought I had told you about it, but…" *Hell!* "Cassandra." He clasped her shoulders again, lifted her to her toes. "Come with me. Okay?"

"Okay," she said softly, and wasn't it ridiculous to have to blink back tears over such a simple request?

They drove to New York and met with the designer, who smiled at Cassie.

"Ah. Mrs. O'Connell. It's a pleasure to meet you."

Cassie turned pink. "I'm not Mrs. O'Connell."

Another "ah," and a glance at Cassie's bare ring finger. Keir narrowed his eyes and slid his arm around Cassie's waist. "This is Miss Berk. She's…"

What? What was she? How did you introduce the woman who was your lover? What did the etiquette books say on this subject, and how was it he'd never before been angry because the right word didn't seem to exist?

"Miss Berk works for me."

He felt Cassie stiffen and he couldn't blame her. Was that the best he could do?

"We're close friends."

Oh, God in heaven, had he really said that? Cassie jerked away from him and the designer uttered such a significant "ah" that Keir came close to hauling Cassie into his arms right that minute to tell her—to tell her…

"If you'll both follow me, please?" the designer said, and Keir took Cassie's elbow and dragged her with him through miles and miles of showrooms, where he finally got her to do something other than shoot him icy looks by pretending he was crazy for a tiger-print chair with carved paws instead of arms and feet.

"Don't be absurd," she said, and after that, his

Cassandra was back, saying exactly what she thought, snapping off his head when she thought it needed doing, facing down the haughty designer until the woman was reduced to saying, "Yes, Miss Berk, I couldn't agree more."

The afternoon that had started so badly ended with Keir the proud if confused owner of six figures worth of furniture and a promised delivery date of four months.

"Four months," he said to Cassie as they sat down for drinks at a table in a handsome old café in Greenwich Village. "Not too bad, I guess."

Cassie didn't answer. She was staring at her wine list and he picked it up and opened it, to see what she was looking at that was more important than he was. Nothing. That was what he could see, anyway. Nothing, because he knew he was in trouble again and, dammit, he had no idea why.

"Cass? You think that's about right? Four months?"

"It's perfect." Her smile was as phony as his. "It's a number you like, isn't it? First for my probation, now for furniture delivery."

Probation? Was she really concerned about that? Had the mention of a four month time period reminded her of it?

He smiled and took her hand. "You don't have to worry about probation, baby."

"Really."

"Of course. I thought you knew that. You've been off probation for a long time."

Cassie snatched back her hand. "I suppose it ended when I started sleeping with you."

Keir looked as if she'd slapped him. She wanted to bite off her tongue. What had made her say such a hateful thing? Oh God, she *knew* what it was, the awful realization that she had no real place in his life. She loved him and it was agony to go on pretending that she didn't.

He rose from the table. She did, too.

"Keir. Please. I'm sorry. I didn't mean—"

"Yeah," he said in a tone so cold it made her shudder. "Yeah, you sure as hell did."

"No! I swear—"

"Let's go."

He dumped some bills on the table and headed for the door. Cassie saw peoples' heads turn but she didn't care. What mattered was that she'd wounded him, and for the most selfish, stupid reasons.

What he'd told the designer was the truth.

She *wasn't* his wife; she *wasn't* his fiancée. She was just as he'd described her, his employee and his—his close friend, and whose fault was it if she couldn't come to terms with that? Keir had never, ever promised her anything more.

She ran after him, calling his name.

"Keir. Keir, please. I never thought—"

He opened the door to the Ferrari. "Get in."

Cassie hesitated, then did as he'd ordered. He slammed the door hard enough to make her jump, then stalked around to the other side and got behind the wheel.

"Keir. I know it wasn't like that. I—I'm sorry. I'm so sorry..."

"It doesn't matter."

"It does! Oh, Keir—"

He swung toward her, his eyes flat and filled with fury. "No apologies, Cassie. Hell, maybe it's time we were honest with each other."

"I wasn't being honest, I was being hateful." Tears glittered in her eyes. "I was hurt. Angry. I was—"

"What do you want from me?" he said, his words hot and sharp.

Her face drained of color. She stared at him blindly and then she began to weep as if her heart were breaking in two. Keir sat beside her, hands wrapped hard around the steering wheel, furious at himself, furious at her.

What *did* she want from him? Maybe the real question was, what did he want from her? He cursed, pulled her into his arms and kissed her until she was breathless.

"Your job hasn't a damned thing to do with what's happened between us," he said, his hands cupping her face.

"You want me to fire you so you can feel better about us being together? You want to quit working for me?" He kissed her again, his mouth hard and unforgiving on hers. "Tell me what you want, Cassandra, and I'll do it. Just don't play games with me, don't—"

Cassie grabbed his face, dragged his mouth to hers and kissed him.

"I want you," she said. "Only you."

He kissed her mouth, her hair, her eyes. She moaned his name and he knew that this time he'd never make it home. Instead, he drove to the hotel, took her to his suite, made love to her, with her, until exhaustion claimed them both.

They headed to Connecticut early in the morning, Keir clasping Cassie's hand in his over the gearshift knob. He didn't want to let go of her, not for a minute.

Something had happened last night, some bridge had been crossed. In that bedroom high above Central Park, Cassie burning in his arms like the heat of a thousand suns, he knew he'd found someone he'd been searching for all his life.

Her name was Cassandra Bercovic, a sad, neglected little girl who'd grown up to be a brave and beautiful woman.

How on earth had he ever been lucky enough to find her?

He'd held her in his arms in the soft afterglow of love-making and told her how he'd seen her as if for the very first time that night in Texas.

She'd sighed and said she'd never forget that night, the way he'd stunned her by stepping out of her dreams and into her arms.

"It was like a miracle," she'd said softly, "and when you stopped…when you made it clear you thought you'd made a mistake…I was hurt but in my heart, I understood. We come from such different worlds…"

He'd silenced the rush of words with a kiss, told her she had it all wrong, that he'd stopped making love to her that night because he'd realized he was moving too fast, but he knew she didn't fully believe him.

She *wanted* to, but she didn't.

He'd have to find a way to make her see that there were no differences between them.

Inside, where it mattered, they were the same.

He looked over at Cassie. She was asleep. He'd worn her out last night, made love to her over and over again, but it hadn't been enough.

He wanted more than that. He wanted to tell her…to tell her…

Keir swallowed dryly. Okay. This time, maybe he *was* moving too fast. He'd made so many changes in his life these last few months… It couldn't hurt to slow down. Plan things out. That was his specialty, wasn't it? Planning things calmly, logically, was always a good idea.

Deer Run lay silent and peaceful in the clear morning light. Keir parked in front of the house, stepped quietly from the car and gathered Cassie into his arms.

"Are we home?" she murmured.

Home. He smiled at the way she said it. "Yes, baby. We are."

She smelled sweet and warm as he carried her up the stairs and to his bedroom. *Their* bedroom. He told himself he was only going to undress her and put her to bed, but as he undid zippers and buttons and slipped her out of her clothes, she whispered his name. He looked into her eyes and felt his heart turn over.

"Cassandra," he murmured. "My Cassandra."

He carried her to the bed, his mouth never leaving hers, his kisses growing hungrier as hers grew more urgent.

She sighed his name, brushed her fingertips across his lips. "Keir," she whispered, "I've never felt—never felt—"

"What?" The word held all the urgency that had been building inside him. He swept her hair back from her face, cupped it, kissed her again. ''Sweetheart. Cass. Tell me what you—''

''Oh, hell!'' a voice said in gruff disbelief.

Cassie screamed. Keir swung around, fists raised, adrenaline surging through his body…

And saw his brothers, Sean and Cullen, standing in the open bedroom doorway, looking every bit as horrified as he felt.

CHAPTER TWELVE

THE three O'Connell brothers sat staring into the big stone fireplace in the living room.

Nobody spoke. Nobody moved. Nobody looked away from the flames dancing on the logs.

After a long, long time, Sean slapped his knees and got to his feet.

"Well," he said briskly, "this is an, uh, an interesting place you've got here, BB."

"Interesting," Cullen echoed. He nodded at a suit of armor in the corner. "I'll bet not many houses have a guy with a lance hanging around, just waiting for a joust."

"No," Sean said, "not many."

Sean and Cullen looked at Keir. Keir looked at them. Nobody could think of any more brilliant remarks so they went back to staring at the fire.

Time passed. Then Cullen cleared his throat.

"This room is enormous, you know? Has some nice features, though. All that molding, those great windows, the wide-planked floor…"

His voice trailed away. Sean leaped into the gap.

"Did you ever think about dumping all this old stuff? Buy a couple of pool tables, maybe a foosball table, too…" His brothers looked at him as if he'd lost his mind. "Hey, it's just a thought."

"Yeah." Keir rose and headed for the kitchen. "Anybody want another beer?"

"Great idea."

"Absolutely."

As soon as he was out of sight, Sean leaned toward Cullen. "What the hell's going on?" he whispered.

"Damned if I know," Cullen whispered back. "Only thing I *do* know is that our timing stinks."

"Man, does it ever. And, please, tell me I'm wrong, but wasn't that babe in bed with Keir the same one we saw in the elevator at the hotel?"

"I'd bet my last buck she's one and the same."

"Well, what's she doing here? Why hasn't Keir said anything about her except that she's too embarrassed to come down? I mean, I guess I can understand that, but how come he isn't talking about her? Your brothers trip over you playing games with a lady, you'd say something about the lady, wouldn't you?"

"Twice," Cullen said grimly. "We tripped over him twice."

"Exactly. So, how come he's not saying anything?"

"Like what?"

"Like what she's doing here, for starters."

Cullen nodded. "Yeah. You're right."

"I guess I'll just have to ask him."

"Let me."

"Why?"

Cullen frowned. "I'm older than you."

"What an intelligent answer."

"Look, let me handle it. I never mentioned it before because it didn't matter, but I know something… Ah!" Cullen sat up straight and shot a phony smile toward the arched doorway. "There you are, BB. Great. Another beer. Just what I wanted."

"Actually," Sean said, "I was kind of hoping to try some of your wi… No. Forget it. I guess this isn't a wine-drinking occasion."

Keir handed over the bottles and put one foot on the stone hearth.

"It sure as hell isn't."

"Look, man, if you want us to leave, you just say the word and we're out of here."

"Don't be foolish," Keir said, sounding more certain

than he felt. He shot a glance toward the stairs. Wasn't Cassie ever coming down? "It'll be fine. Just give her a little while."

Cullen nodded. "No problem. So, what were we talking about?"

"How to change this dungeon into a room," said Sean. "Remember? We were tossing around ideas, and you guys weren't clever enough to see that a couple of pool tables would do the job."

"A couple of dozen, you mean." Keir scowled at his beer bottle, raised it to his mouth and drank. "No need to do that. I already ordered furniture."

"Really," Sean said. Were they all crazy? There was a woman hiding in the bedroom upstairs, Keir was obviously upset, Cullen was hatching some kind of scheme and in the meantime, three healthy, heterosexual American males were talking about home decorating. "Let me guess. You ordered glass. Stainless steel. You know, like a doctor's office."

"Cherry."

"Huh?"

I went for cherry wood, plus some big, overstuffed arm chairs, a couple of sofas—"

"Leather?" Cullen said politely.

"Yellow and gray striped sailcloth for the chairs. Pale butterscotch suede, for the sofas."

Sean looked at Cullen. "Did the man really say 'striped sailcloth'?"

"Well, of course he did. It's a natural with the pale butterscotch suede." Cullen forced a laugh. "See what happens to a man when he moves east?"

Keir came closer to smiling than at any time in the past hour.

"*You* moved east."

"Yeah, but I didn't fall into the clutches of an interior decorator. Tell the truth. That's what happened to you, isn't it? You went someplace to buy a perfectly simple brown leather sofa and got brainwashed by a gang of decorators."

Keir sighed. ''Well, I did spend yesterday with an interior designer.''

''A designer, not a decorator,'' Sean said. He and Cullen moaned in unison. ''That's even worse.''

Keir actually managed a real smile. ''Hey, it wasn't so bad.''

''He wasn't wearing a velvet suit?''

''He wasn't a he.''

''Yeah, well, that's no surprise.''

''He wasn't a he because he was a woman,'' Keir said, and grinned. ''And we really didn't take her advice all that much. We bought what we liked.''

''We?'' Sean said lazily.

''Yes.'' Keir took a breath. ''Cassie and me.''

Silence. Sean and Cullen exchanged a quick look. Then Cullen jerked his chin toward the ceiling. ''Is Cassie the lady who…''

''Yes.''

''Let me get this straight. You went shopping for furniture with that woman?''

''Her name is Cassie.''

There was a warning tone in Keir's voice. Cullen heard it but ignored it.

''Correct me if I'm wrong here, BB, but wasn't the lady we're discussing the same one who was with you in the elevator the day Ma and Dan got married?''

Keir tilted the bottle to his mouth and drank the last of the beer.

''Yes.''

''You brought her east with you?''

''No.''

''Yes. No.'' Cullen gritted his teeth. ''Is that all you can say?''

''I can add name, rank and serial number,'' Keir said coldly, ''if it makes you feel better.''

''What's that supposed to mean?''

"That I don't like being interrogated, and I don't like the tone in your voice."

"Well, that's too bad. How do you expect me to sound, huh? You, buying furniture with a babe you were screwing around with in—"

Keir grabbed Cullen by the front of his sweatshirt and hauled him to his feet.

"Watch your mouth!"

"Let go of me," Cullen said quietly.

"She's not a 'babe,' Cullen. You got that?"

"Let go, dammit!"

The men stared at each other. Then Keir lifted his hands carefully from his brother's shirt and stepped back.

"I'm sorry," he muttered. "I know you didn't mean… Hell, I don't know what's wrong with me. I guess what just happened, you guys suddenly turning up the way you did… It was kind of rough, not just for Cass but for me, too. I mean, looking around, seeing you there… I guess neither of you ever heard of a doorbell."

Cullen smoothed down his shirt, shot Sean a look. Sean was standing with his arms folded, his face blank, but Cullen was sure of what his brother was thinking. "Let me handle it," he'd told him, but so far he hadn't done much except tick Keir off.

"Yeah, well, we rang. We even banged on the door with that two ton chunk of brass you laughingly call a knocker. When nobody answered, we tried the door and found it open, came inside and then Sean said he thought he heard somebody upstairs."

"Terrific," Sean said, with a tight smile. "Blame it on me. The thing is, Cullen's right. We're sorry we walked in on you but how were we supposed to know that you… I mean, it's mid-morning, and…" He cleared his throat. "You can't blame us for wondering what's going on, BB. First we stumbled across you and this, uh, this woman—"

"Her name's Cassie," Cullen said, shooting Sean a "you're on dangerous ground, so take it easy" look.

"Right. Cassie. We saw you with her at the Song. It was nothing, you said. She was just a cocktail waitress, you said. Now—"

"I never told you she was *just* a cocktail waitress. What I told you was, she was a cocktail waitress."

"Isn't that the same thing?" Sean asked in an exasperated tone. He looked at Cullen, who'd gone back to pretending he was the Sphinx. "Okay. Never mind what she does."

"What she does is, she manages my restaurant."

"Here?" Sean said, blowing past caution and letting his voice reflect his surprise.

"Yes, here," Keir said coolly. "Where else would it be?"

"The lady manages—"

"Cassie. The *lady* has a name. Try and remember it."

"Take it easy, man," said Cullen. "We're just trying to put the pieces together. So, you brought Cassie with you from Las Vegas?"

Keir started to tell Cullen to mind his own business, thought better of it, and took a deep breath before he spoke.

"No. I didn't. I didn't even know she'd applied for this job."

"In other words," Sean said slowly, "she followed you to Connecticut?"

"No! Dammit, she had no idea I was… Look, forget the details, okay? The bottom line is that she came here, I hired her, and now…"

"And now," Cullen said carefully, "you're sleeping with her."

Keir swung toward him, the bones in his face showing sharp beneath his skin.

"Be careful what you say," he said softly.

"Well, it's the truth, isn't it?"

"Cullen. I'm warning you…"

"Yeah. I know you are, but why? Since when are we so circumspect about our sex lives?"

''Since Cassie.'' The muscle in Keir's jaw knotted and unknotted. ''The topic's off limits. You got that?''

''How long have you known this woman?''

''What's the difference?''

''Just answer the question, okay? How long have you known her? How well?''

''It's back to interrogation time. Listen, Mr. Hot Shot Attorney, this is not a courtroom and I am not on the witness stand.''

''Hey, you two, let's cool down, okay? Cullen is just curious. Aren't you, bro?'' Cullen didn't answer and Sean rushed ahead. ''Well, if Cassie worked at the Desert Song, then Keir probably knows her pretty well. Right, Keir?''

Keir's response was curt. ''We'd never said much more than hello and goodbye until I stood up for Gray Baron at his wedding last summer.''

''Oh.'' Sean nodded. ''Well, no problem. That means you've known her for, what, five, six months?''

''Maybe you want to count the days and the hours, too.'' Keir's tone was ominous. His brothers meant well. He understood that, but there was something in the air, in Cullen's eyes, that he didn't much like. ''Or maybe you'd like to check the lady's references.''

''Keir,'' Sean said, ''we're only looking out for you.''

''Cullen?'' Keir said, ignoring Sean, keeping his eyes locked to Cullen's, ''how's that sound to you?''

''You want an honest answer?'' Cullen folded his arms and rocked back on his heels. ''I already checked them.''

''You what?''

''That scene in the elevator piqued my curiosity. It was so uncharacteristic of you that I decided to find out a little something about Miss Cassie Berk.''

''Who the hell do you think you are?'' Keir's voice was frigid. ''My life is my business.''

''You're an easy mark, Keir. You always bleed for the underdog.''

''Bleeding for the underdog, as you so graciously put it,

doesn't make me an easy mark, and what do you know about it, anyway?''

''I know what happened at the Song last year, with the girl your pal Gray ended up marrying, how she worked for you and you kept her on, even after you found out she'd falsified her references.''

''How do you know that?'' Keir demanded furiously. ''That was private business.''

''The duchess told me.'' Cullen nodded at Sean. ''She told both of us. She thought it was wonderful, how you'd done the right thing. Well, maybe it was. By ignoring the rules, you probably saved the girl's life.'' He paused. ''Well, it's your life at stake now, pal.''

Keir, hot with fury, knotted his fists, and fought to keep his temper in check. Cullen meant well. He had to keep remembering that.

''Cullen.'' He spoke softly, biting off every word. ''I appreciate your concern. I really do. Now, do us both a favor and get the hell out of my house before either you or I do something we'll both regret.''

''Your Cassie has guts, I have to give her that. Following you all the way here…''

''Shut up.''

''And she has a history.''

''I know her history.''

''She was a showgirl.''

''Get out, Cullen.''

''She was a stripper.''

''Out,'' Keir roared, pointing to the door. ''You hear me? Get the hell—''

''What you've got, BB, is nothing but a bad case of ZTS.''

Keir threw a quick right at Cullen's jaw. Cullen parried it and came back with a left. Sean yelled, jumped between them and pushed them apart with an iron-hard hand on each chest.

''Are you two insane?'' he said, looking from one red,

angry face to the other. "Since when do the O'Connells fight over women?"

"Get this straight," Keir said, breathing hard, "I'm not going to let anybody, not even you, Cullen, say anything against Cassie."

"You're not, huh?"

"No!" Keir struggled against Sean's restraining hand. "And if you don't believe me—"

"Oh, I believe you," Cullen said. A wide smile curved his mouth. "By the way, that right of yours might be quick, my man, but it isn't much."

"The hell it isn't. You want to try it again... What are you laughing at?"

"Wasn't it usually you, peeling Sean and me apart, back in the old days?"

"That was just horsing around."

"Kidstuff. And I guess we've all grown up, huh?"

"I'm not much in the mood for a trip down memory lane."

"How about for a trip into the future, where you and Cassie Berk go down the aisle? That *is* what you have in mind, isn't it?"

"Damned right, it..." Keir realized what his brother had just said, what *he'd* just said, and stopped in the middle of his sentence. "What?"

"I admit, I checked up on your lady. And I'm not going to pretend I wasn't a little worried when I found out she had a, uh, a colorful past."

"She did what it took to get by," Keir said coldly, "and that's all she did—not that she needs your vote of approval."

"No. But she has it."

"Well, that's just too damned..." Keir blinked. "What'd you say?"

"Your lady has my approval. She'll do the O'Connells proud. Besides, you love her."

Keir look from one of his brothers to the other. Cullen was grinning, but Sean looked as bewildered as he felt.

"I didn't say—"

"Give me a break, Keir. You love her. And she loves you. Obviously, she told you all about herself, even though she must have gone through hell to do it. The lady loves you, man. Not your bank account, not your name. Just you."

"You've lost me," Sean said. "Cullen? What the hell are you saying?"

Cullen gave a dramatic sigh. "It's such a burden to be the only one in this trio with a brain. Look, it's simple. I figure that any female who can talk my big brother into wandering through a furniture showroom, who can make him so deaf he doesn't hear the doorbell ring, who can make him willing to take on his own flesh and blood to defend her honor, must be very special."

Nobody moved. Nobody spoke. Then Sean began to chuckle.

"Well," he said, "well, well, well." He dropped his hands to his sides and grinned at Cullen. "When you said, 'let me handle it,' I didn't know you were going to try for an Oscar."

"I played the scene by ear," Cullen said with modesty, "but I was pretty good, wasn't I?"

"Yeah," Keir grumbled, "and a lot that little gold statue would have meant, once I'd broken your jaw."

"You'd have been in the emergency room beside me, pal, lying right on the next table."

The O'Connells looked at each other, their faces solemn. Then Sean grinned, followed by Cullen and, at last, Keir.

"You idiot," Keir said fondly.

"Same to you, pal," Cullen said.

Keir punched Cullen in the arm. Cullen passed it along to Sean, who returned it to Keir. They grinned at each other again.

''Well,'' Keir said, ''this calls for a bottle of Deer Run's best.''

''After beer?'' Sean made a face.

''You want to skip it?''

Sean smiled. ''No way, man. I'll make the sacrifice.''

Keir chose a merlot, opened it and poured three glasses.

''So,'' Cullen said, after the wine had been sniffed, tasted and admired, ''you've finally fallen in love.''

Keir felt himself blush, right down to his toes. *In love,* he thought, *me, in love.* ''Yeah.''

''So have I,'' Sean said, trying to look serious, ''at least a dozen times, but I didn't see you guys getting excited about that.''

Cullen sighed and put his hand on Sean's shoulder. ''You don't get it, kid. This is L-O-V-E. The real thing.'' He smiled at Keir. ''When do we get to meet the lady?''

It was a good question. How long did it take a woman to get over seeing two guys pop up in the doorway at the worst possible minute?

''Soon. In fact...'' Keir put down his glass. ''I'll go up and get her.''

''Maybe you want to let her come down at her own pace. Or maybe we should leave, drive around a little, you know, then come back.''

''No, don't be silly. Cassie has a terrific sense of humor,'' Keir said, mentally crossing his fingers and hoping he was right. ''I'll give her a couple more minutes, then go up and talk to her. I'm sure she'll want to meet you two. She didn't meet you, not really, that last time.''

''Does she know how you feel about her?'' Cullen asked.

''You mean, have I come right out and told her that I love her?'' Keir put another log on the fire. ''No. The words are tough to get out, you know? Tougher still to accept inside yourself, where it counts.'' He swung toward Sean and Cullen, hands out in supplication. ''But she knows. She has to know, right?''

Cullen eyed his brother over the rim of his glass. ''It's

been my experience that women like to be told these things.''

''His experience,'' Sean said, and snorted. ''Like, he knows about this stuff.''

''They want to hear the words,'' Cullen said quietly. ''Trust me on this, Keir. If you love her, you have to tell her.''

Keir nodded. ''You're right. I will. Hell, I want to.'' He smiled. ''Then I'm going to take her home to meet Ma. I have the feeling they're going to get along just fine.''

''Well, Ma knows Cassie, right? From the hotel? And from that wedding last summer?''

''Yeah, but this'll be different.'' Keir's smile tilted. ''It's not every day you introduce your mother and the woman you intend to marry.'' He paused. ''Cass will probably be nervous.''

Sean grinned. ''Who wouldn't be, meeting the duchess?''

''It's not that. Cassie has this thing about us coming from different worlds.''

''Ah.'' Cullen poured himself more wine. ''Prince Charming meets Cinderella. Not that you're a prince or in any way charming, mind you—''

''Thanks.''

''You're welcome. Yeah, I can see how Cassie would be edgy but once you give her the chance to see the O'Connell clan in action, she'll stop figuring we're royalty in, what, ten seconds flat?''

Sean reached for the bottle of wine, refilled Keir's glass and his own.

''You know,'' he said slowly, ''it just hit me… Ma's birthday is next month.''

''So?''

''So, I spoke to Megan the other day, and she says Dan's planning a big party. You'll fly home for it, won't you?''

''Of course.''

''Well, it's perfect. Bring Cassie with you.''

Keir nodded. Perfect was the word. His mother, his sisters, his whole family would have the chance to get to know Cassie…

And the chance to overwhelm her.

A houseful of O'Connells was a lot for most people to handle. You needed a strong dose of stamina and lots of self-confidence to get through a first encounter.

Cassie—his Cassie, he thought with a smile—was tough and self-confident, but she still had that stubborn conviction that he and she came from different worlds.

Would she feel intimidated?

His mother would be warm, but she'd scrutinize Cassie's every move. His sisters would be welcoming, but they'd ask her a million well-meaning questions. And his brothers would bring her into the family fold with loving, if merciless, teasing.

It would be better to fly to Vegas when nobody was around except his mother and Dan. Next week. No. Why wait? This week. He could almost imagine how wonderful it was going to be to put his arm around Cassie and say, "Ma, this is Cassie. She's going to be my wife."

"Well?" Sean gave Keir a nudge in the ribs. "What do you think? You want to take your lady home to Vegas for the duchess's birthday party?"

Keir frowned. "No," he said slowly, "no, I don't."

Cullen nodded. "Maybe you're right. I mean, that whole scene…all of us, and then Cassie… It might be a setting for disaster."

"Exactly. That's the last place in the world I'd want to take Cassie. A big family party, the O'Connells all gathered around the table? Makes me shudder to think about it. Cassie would just—"

"Keir?"

"I mean, even if things went well, Cassie might simply—"

"Keir," Sean hissed, jerking his head.

Keir turned around. He saw Cassie, in the doorway. His Cassie, so beautiful, so alive, so…

Angry?

Oh, man. Not angry. Furious. Her green eyes were blazing like the flames of hell.

"Cass," he said, going toward her, "I'm so glad you decided to come down. I was just about to come upstairs and see if you were—"

Cassie slugged him. There was no other way to describe it. She hit him, hard, in the jaw. His head flew back; his ears rang with the force of the blow. For one awful moment, he saw bright white stars against a bright red background.

"Cass," he said, bewildered, "sweetheart..."

"You—you son of a bitch!"

"Baby—"

"You no good, arrogant, egotistical, self-centered bastard!"

She raised her hand again. Keir grabbed her wrists and locked both her hands against his chest.

"Honey, what is it? I know. You're still upset because these two jerks busted in on us, right? Well, they're sorry. Tell her you're sorry, guys. Cullen? Sean? Tell Cassie that—"

"Tell me what? That the whole miserable bunch of you are afraid I might use my salad fork for the roast beef?"

"Huh? Cass, baby—"

"Do *not* call me baby! Do not *ever* call me baby." Cassie wrenched her hands free and jabbed her index finger into the center of Keir's chest. "What else, O'Connell? What other things might I do to embarrass you at that fancy table? Forget to use my napkin? Eat my peas with a spoon? Slurp my soup?"

"Cassie, you accused me of this same kind of stuff before. And I told you—"

"You're right. I did. And you told me I was wrong. Okay. Let's cut to the chase, then. My very presence would embarrass you. It's one thing to tell a woman that you don't give a damn about her past, but that story falls flat when the past suddenly counts, when the possibility arises you might take that woman home to meet the folks instead of to your bed.''

''Cassie, for God's sake, you have it all wrong.''

''No. I have it right. I *always* had it right!''

''You know what, Berk? I don't know what in hell you're talking about.''

''That's the sad truth. You really, truly don't. You want to sleep with me, make me look like—like an idiot in front of your brothers—''

''What? Cass, that's crazy. I didn't know they were going to show up. I never—''

''You never. Well, I never, either.'' Cassie took a step back. ''I categorically, absolutely, positively, never want to meet the rest of your horrible family. You got that?''

Keir looked at his brothers in bewilderment, but there was no help coming from them. Sean was studying his fingernails with meticulous interest; Cullen was showing the same concentration on the wine bottle label.

Okay, Keir told himself, Cassie was upset. It was up to him to calm her down.

''Sweetheart,'' he said, reaching out for her, ''honey—''

''Don't call me that, either, dammit.'' Cassie batted his hands away. ''And don't you *ever* kid yourself into thinking I'm angry because I give a damn for you, Keir O'Connell. I never did. You were just—just a man who offered me a good job and—and a good time for as long as it lasted.''

She spun away, ran for the door, grabbed her purse and her coat from the chair where she'd dropped them not two hours before. Two short hours before, when she'd been fool enough to imagine the man she loved was starting to fall in love with her.

So much for dreams, she thought bitterly, and slammed the door behind her.

CHAPTER THIRTEEN

KEIR stood frozen to the spot.

''What just happened?''

''Your lady's seriously angry,'' Sean said dryly, and cleared his throat, ''that's what just happened.''

Keir hadn't even realized he'd asked the question aloud until he heard Sean's response. He turned to him, arms outstretched.

''But why? Over what? What did I do, except say that I loved her?''

''Well,'' Cullen said with lawyerly caution, ''as a matter of fact, you didn't. You told us but that was about it.''

''Dammit, Cassie's the smartest woman I ever met. She must know...'' Keir drew a deep breath. ''Okay. You're right. I didn't tell her, and maybe she doesn't know, but I still don't get it. What in hell did I do to deserve all that?''

His brothers frowned, looked at each other, shrugged their shoulders and in general went through the puzzled motions of men agreeing they couldn't possibly comprehend the behavior of the exotic species known as the human female.

A car engine roared to life.

''She's leaving,'' Sean said.

''Probably going for a drive to cool off,'' said Cullen.

''She'd damn well better cool off,'' Keir said grimly. ''Hell, here I was, telling her how much I adore her—''

''About to tell her,'' Sean pointed out. ''Remember? You never actually—''

''What the hell's the difference?'' Keir growled. He stalked across the room, turned on his heel and stalked back. ''I'm in love with a woman for the first time in my life and she calls me names. I'm an SOB, she says, an egotistical, self-centered…'' He stopped pacing, folded his arms and glared at his brothers. ''Don't bother telling me to go after her.''

''Well,'' Sean said cautiously, ''you want my opinion, BB, it might be a good idea if—''

''She'll be back soon enough.'' Keir shot a look at his watch. ''An hour, max. And when she gets here, she's going to have a lot of explaining to do.''

''Uh, you want us to leave? I mean, when she gets back you guys might want some privacy.''

''Nonsense.'' Keir strode to the door and grabbed his jacket from the chair. ''Let's go have lunch.''

''Great,'' Cullen said, so heartily that Sean winced. ''We've been dying to try your restaurant.''

''It's not open on Mondays. There's a diner. We'll go there.''

''Yeah,'' Sean said, ''but if Cassie should come back while we're gone…''

''How come you're busy telling me what Cassie will or won't do?''

''Listen, I know you're upset, but…it's just that there've been times I've felt kind of the way she might be feeling. You know, on the outside, looking in?''

''What the hell are you talking about?''

Sean thought about pointing out that he was the brother who wasn't the reliable one, who didn't have a law degree hanging on the wall… Damn. Keir was right. What the hell *was* he talking about?

''Nothing,'' he said with a quick smile. ''I guess I'm just taking a page from your book. You know, bleeding for the underdog.''

''Yeah, well, let's go eat,'' Keir said gruffly. ''Cassie gets back before we do, she'll wait.''

It wasn't until they were seated at a table in the diner, everybody looking at their hamburgers and nobody actually eating them, that he let himself wonder if she really would, or if his anger at her accusations—his pain at her inability to see into his heart and know that he loved her—had made him blind to the truth.

Maybe—just maybe, he should have gone after her.

By evening, he was positive of it. He'd gone to the door a hundred times, a thousand times, opened it and looked down the driveway hoping to see her car coming up the hill.

Sean and Cullen were gone. They'd wanted to stay, but he'd told them he'd be fine, that they were right and it was best if he was alone when Cassie came home.

The truth was that he couldn't look into their eyes without seeing they were thinking the same thing he was.

Maybe she wouldn't come back.

Maybe she'd left him for good.

Keir ran to the bedroom. Her clothes were all in the closet. Of course they were. He'd have seen a suitcase, had she taken one with her.

He thought of what she'd told him about how she'd left home when she was seventeen with little more than the clothes on her back and a toothbrush.

"It's not so hard to travel light," she'd answered when he said that must have been tough. "If you're running from something you're eager to leave behind, all that matters is getting away."

Keir sank down on the edge of the bed. One silk stocking lay draped across his pillow. He picked it up, felt its softness as it slipped through his fingers.

Was he one of those things Cassie could leave behind? He couldn't believe that. She loved him. He knew she did. He'd felt it in her kisses, heard it in the way she said his name for weeks now. Why hadn't he told her how he felt? Why had it taken him so long to figure it out?

And what had he done to send her running from him?

He rose to his feet, paced back and forth like a leopard in a cage, trying to figure out what had happened. He'd been talking with Sean and Cullen. About what? About taking Cassie home to meet the duchess.

Sean had suggested bringing her to meet the family for their mother's birthday. And he'd said no, that wouldn't work, that Cassie might be in over her head.

That was when she'd come flying at him like a tornado.

Keir ran his hands through his hair until it stood up in little peaks. Had he insulted her by suggesting meeting the O'Connells all at once might be too much? Maybe. Maybe not. Maybe…

"Oh hell," he said softly.

Everything he'd said, everything she'd have heard, was coming back to him like a tape recording. Him, saying how home was the last place in the world he'd ever want to take her. How all the O'Connells would be gathered around the table and how Cassie would be lost in their midst, except he'd never gotten all the words out, never said she'd be lost.

There was more. He'd told his brothers that the thought of her being there, of taking her home with him, made him shudder.

"Cassie," he whispered in despair, knowing how it must have sounded, knowing what she'd probably thought because it fed right into her refusal to see that they weren't different, that they were meant for each other, always had been meant for each other.

And he knew in that instant that she wasn't coming back. She was gone. Gone, and it was up to him to find her and make her know that he adored her…

That if she left him, he'd be empty, forever.

Keir ran downstairs, threw on his jacket, grabbed his keys and raced out the door.

Cassie had left the house on a rush of hot anger but by the time she'd gone half a mile she began to weep.

She pulled over to the side of the road, sobbed until her

eyes were bone dry and aching. Then she told herself to stop all this nonsense and make a plan.

One thing was certain. She was not going back to Keir's house. She didn't want to see him ever again, the bastard. The rat. The…

She wept again, until she was hiccuping. Then she dried her eyes, reminded herself that crying had never solved a problem in her life and forced herself not to think about anything but what to do.

She had her purse. Her credit cards. Her driver's license and her bank card.

The solution was simple. She'd go back to where all this had started. Las Vegas. She knew people there. She could get a job. She could move in with one of the girls she'd worked with, just until she was on her feet. She could arrange to have her things packed and shipped to her.

Where there was a will there was always a way.

The one thing she couldn't do was sit here much longer because Keir would be coming after her.

He would…wouldn't he?

She glanced in the rearview mirror, afraid to see the Ferrari barreling along the road…praying to see it.

No Ferrari. No Keir.

No dream. Not anymore.

Cassie wiped her eyes on her sleeve. Where next? Could she get a last-minute seat on a flight to Vegas? Probably. Lots of planes went there. It was a popular destination. At worst, she'd fly standby.

The only question was, which airport? Hartford, where she'd flown in? Providence, which she now knew was even closer? Boston, which was further away but might have more flights?

Providence, she decided, for no better reason than that "providence" was pretty much where she was putting her trust.

She put the car in gear and headed east.

Hours later she sat in the Trans-America waiting area at

T.F. Green Airport and watched, fingers crossed, as the two clerks behind the departure desk poked at their computer terminal keyboards, then held a quick conversation.

The nine o'clock flight to Las Vegas would be boarding soon. With luck, she'd be on it.

Two other flights had already left without her. She'd almost made it onto the one that had gone out two hours ago, but at the last minute a ticketed passenger had come rushing up, panting, boarding pass in hand, and Cassie had sighed with disappointment and gone back to her seat.

This flight looked pretty good. The clerks had been paging one passenger for the last fifteen minutes. If he didn't show soon she was home free.

Keir would never see her again. Keir, who hadn't cared enough to come after her. Keir, who'd used her the same way as her husband.

Tears pricked her eyes. Cassie blinked them back, folded her hands in her lap, and waited to hear her name called so she could board the plane that would carry her away from the last man she'd ever let use her again…

A man she'd loved with all her heart.

What a fool she'd been.

Keir skidded into a parking space at the airport in Providence.

She had to be here. Dammit, she *had* to.

He'd driven all the way to Hartford's Bradley Airport and checked every airline. All that day's flights to Vegas were gone and no matter what stories he'd concocted, he couldn't get anyone to confirm whether or not Cassie Berk had been on any of them.

Maybe she'd flown out of Logan, he'd thought, in Boston.

He'd gotten behind the wheel again, raced back the way he'd come. On impulse he'd gotten off the highway and stopped at the gas station on the main road that led to the vineyard.

The guy pumping gas listened to his description of Cassie and her car, scratched his whiskery jaw, chomped on a wad of tobacco a couple of times and finally said, yeah, a woman like that, in a car like that, had stopped for gas hours back.

"Asked how to get to Providence," he'd added, and Keir had hopped back into the Ferrari and roared away. On the way to the airport he'd called home on his cell phone, called the restaurant, called the apartment Cassie had lived in before she'd moved in with him.

Nothing. No answer at home or in her apartment. No message at the restaurant.

No Cassie.

Maybe, he thought as he strode into the terminal, maybe he'd figured wrong. Maybe she wasn't heading back to Vegas.

His gut told him she was. And it told him she was going to do it from this city's airport for no better reason than the name of the place itself.

Destiny. Fate. Providence.

He had nothing else to hang on to, except that.

Keir hurried through the terminal. It was crowded, but Cassie would be easy to see. She was tall. She was beautiful.

She was his heart.

But she wasn't there. He couldn't find her. Couldn't find her…

Will passenger Arlene Nevins please come to the Mid-Express ticket counter at gate four? Passenger Arlene Nevins…

Crowded, and noisy. The buzz of people. The announcements. One after another.

Passenger Edward Epstein, please come to the Trans-American counter at gate seven.

The announcements were driving him crazy. How could he concentrate with all those damned names floating around? If only it were that simple. If only he could ask someone to page Cassie…

Keir came to a sudden stop. A woman plowed into him and he muttered an apology, looked around and went to the nearest occupied gate.

"Excuse me," he said, pushing ahead of the people lined up at the counter, "sorry, but this is an emergency." The clerk looked up, annoyed, but Keir didn't give a damn. "I need to page someone."

"I'm sorry, sir. We don't do that."

"Of course you do. I've been listening to pages ever since I came through the door." He took a deep breath. You didn't get far, coming across as a crazy at an airline terminal these days. "Look, I have to find someone." He took another breath. "The woman I love is flying out of my life from this airport. You understand?"

The clerk's eyes flickered over Keir's face. "There's an information booth. You might try there."

Keir nodded, followed directions and faced another uniformed clerk five minutes later. He thought about what to say, decided to make it as brief as possible, and worked up a smile he hoped would make him look harmless.

"I have to locate someone. Can you page her for me?"

"For what reason, sir?"

Keir hesitated. Personal reasons? No. That could ring mental alarms. For love? That could ring alarms, too. He'd been stupid to tell that to the guy at the gate desk.

"Sir? For what reason?"

"The person in question works for me." Keir pulled an engraved business card from his pocket. He knew damn well it looked impressive. Raised black letters on a heavy vellum cream stock said, *Keir O'Connell, Owner. Deer Run Vineyard, Hamlin, Connecticut.*

The stony-faced clerk took the card and read it. He looked up, and, to Keir's relief, smiled.

"Mr. O'Connell. What a coincidence. My wife and I discovered your wines just a few weeks ago. We think they're wonderful."

"Great. Thanks. Keep the card. Come by for a visit. I'll

give you a tour and a private tasting. Look, about this page…"

"We tried your restaurant, too. Excellent food, sir. And excellent service."

"Yes, well, the lady I want paged manages that restaurant." Hurry up, Keir wanted to say, stop the chitchat and get to it. He smiled politely instead. "Why not bring your wife for dinner some evening? My compliments, Mr.…" He looked at the clerk's badge. "Mr. Conway. It would be our pleasure."

"Oh, that's very nice, Mr. O'Connell. We'd love to."

"Terrific." Keir scribbled a name on the back of another card. "Would you page this lady? Please?"

"Cassie Berk." The clerk looked up. "Is that correct?" At Keir's impatient, nod, Conway drew the microphone toward him, fiddled with it…

"Will passenger Cassie Berk come to the information desk? Passenger Cassie Berk. Come to the information desk, please." Conway switched off the mike. "That should do it, sir."

Keir nodded. "Yes," he said but he didn't believe it. Cassie would know he was the one paging her and she wouldn't respond.

She was here, though. He could sense her presence.

Minutes slipped by. No Cassie, even though the clerk repeated the announcement.

Cassie, Keir thought, pacing back and forth, Cassie, where are you? Why won't you come back to me? I love you, Cassandra. I love…

He swung toward the information desk. A woman was in earnest conversation with the clerk. Keir cleared his throat.

"Madam? I wonder if you'd mind letting me cut in here."

"I'm in a rush, young man."

"Yes, but I'm desperate. The woman I love is leaving me." To hell with how it sounded. If they decided he was a nutcase on the loose they'd drag him away, but it was worth the chance. ''I have to page her and tell her I love her. I didn't, when I should have, and...'' Keir took the woman's hand in his. ''Please,'' he said.

The woman looked into his eyes. Then she smiled.

''Go on,'' she said softly, ''and good luck.''

Keir kissed her cheek, grabbed another card from his pocket and scribbled something on it. ''Try this,'' he said, shoving the card at the clerk.

The clerk read what he'd written, looked up and frowned. ''Cassandra Ber—ber—?''

''Cassandra Berk-oh-vitch,'' Keir said, pronouncing Cassie's name, *his* Cassie's name, with care. ''Page her, please.''

Cassie's name rang through the terminal. Once. Twice. Three times. And just when Keir was almost ready to admit defeat, he heard the whisper of her voice.

''Keir?''

He swung around and saw her, eyes glittering, mouth trembling.

He thought of all the things he wanted to tell here, but there was time for that. Years and years of time, if he was lucky. Right now, only the simplest words were important.

He had to say them.

She had to believe them.

Keir took a step toward her. ''Cassandra,'' he said softly, ''Cassandra, sweetheart. I love you.''

The world seemed to stand still. He waited, heart pounding, and then she made a shaky sound that was half laugh, half sob.

''Keir. Keir, my love...''

Keir opened his arms. Cassie ran to him and he gathered her, forever, to his heart.

Cassandra Bercovic became Cassandra O'Connell in a simple ceremony that April at the Tender Grapes restaurant.

Dawn and Gray Baron flew in for the wedding.

"I'm so happy for you," Dawn told Cassie as they dressed that morning. "You're positively glowing."

Cassie smiled. "So are you. You're glow..." Dawn blushed, and Cassie's eyes widened. "Dawn! Are you pregnant?"

Dawn said yes, she was, and Cassie hugged her best friend and thought, not for the first time, how amazing and wonderful life could be.

Dawn was Cassie's matron of honor. Fallon, Megan and Briana were her bridesmaids. Gray was one of Keir's best men, along with Sean and Cullen.

The bridal planner had told them, solemnly, that it couldn't be done that way. You could only have one best man and if you had bridesmaids, then you needed a matching number of ushers.

"Is that a rule?" Keir had replied politely. "Because if it is, we'll be happy to break it."

The woman had looked from Keir to Cassie. A minute passed. Then her smile softened and she said she'd always wanted to help plan a wedding where the only thing that mattered was love.

After that, all the plans fell easily into place. Even the weather cooperated. The day of the wedding was exceptionally lovely and so warm that they took their vows on the terrace. Pots of yellow and red tulips sat on the little tables; they lined the aisle that had been marked off with streamers of red and yellow silk ribbon.

Cassie, wearing a long, old-fashioned gown of ivory French lace and a matching veil, carried a nosegay bouquet of spring flowers.

She was, her groom kept saying, beautiful.

She said he was beautiful, too, in his black tux.

Mary Elizabeth O'Connell Coyle agreed with them both, but as she told anyone who'd listen, what mattered more than the bride's beauty and the groom's good looks was the simple fact that the love they felt for each other shone in their eyes.

"Aren't they a lovely couple, Dan," she whispered to her husband.

Her smile was a bit wobbly but Dan understood that. This was the first of her children to wed.

"Lovely, darling," he whispered back, and slipped his arm around her shoulders.

Cassie's matron of honor sniffled into her hanky all through the ceremony. Her sisters-in-law, who all adored her, sniffled, too. Well, all except Fallon, who watched with the kind of pleasant curiosity anthropologists afford native ceremonies.

Sean and Cullen, who were crazy about their new sister-in-law, shot Keir blinding smiles, then looked at each other, rolled their eyes and silently vowed such an awful thing as marriage would never happen to them. Gray reached for his wife's hand and brought it to his lips.

Keir and Cassie noticed none of it.

They never took their eyes from each other. When the justice of the peace pronounced them man and wife they went into each other's arms and exchanged a kiss so long, so tender, so filled with promise that the assembled guests applauded.

Some of the women wept.

Even Fallon felt a dampness on her lashes.

Surely, she thought, blinking as she looked up into the blue, cloudless sky, surely, what she'd felt was only rain.

THE SICILIAN SURRENDER

SANDRA MARTON

Special thanks to Joni Jones
For sharing her love of Sicily and its people with me

CHAPTER ONE

THE sun was a blurred golden orb in a lowering sky as the sirocco blew in from the sea, howling through the ruins of the *castello* like the voices of the rebellious gladiators who had once defended this bit of Sicily against the power and might of ancient Rome.

Stefano Lucchesi thought of those men as he mounted the last stone steps and stood on the top of the cliff. To the west, Mount Etna slumbered in the humid air. Below, the stormy waters of the Mediterranean pounded the rocky shore.

How many times had a sentry stood in this same place, watching for the enemy? Romans, Greeks, Arabs and Normans had all spilled their blood here in the name of dominion. Pirates had hunted offshore, lying in wait for unwary ships like packs of hungry wolves.

Invader after invader had conquered this land of his ancestors, until, at last, it shook free of its shackles and created enemies of its own, an aristocracy that grew fat on the sweat of those who tilled this rocky soil.

Stefano turned his back to the sea, dug his hands into the pockets of his jeans and surveyed his kingdom. Time had not treated it kindly. All that remained of the *castello* were tumbled stone walls and a handful of pillars.

Perhaps that was as it should be. There was a certain ironic justice in the way time had evened the balance sheet. What his great grandfather three times removed had built here, what his grandfather had ultimately lost in a feud so bitter it had ended in bloodshed, had long-ago crumbled to dust.

Even the land had been sold. Stefano had ordered his attorney to buy it back, piece by piece, from gnarled old men in baggy black suits who reminded him of his grandfather. Stefano had named a price that was more than fair, but the attorney's representatives had no success.

All the old men seemed eager to sell land that was basically dry and barren until they heard the buyer's name.

''Lucchesi?'' they said.

One even spat on the ground by way of punctuation.

Stefano was amazed that the name should still evoke violent emotion after more than seventy years. He'd said so to his lawyer, who grinned, shook his head and said that Stefano needed to rent the *Godfather* movies and watch them from start to finish.

''It's the Mafia thing,'' Jack said. ''How can you have Sicilian blood running through your veins and not understand? Those old guys knew your grandpa. They hated him. Why should you expect a welcome from them?''

Why, indeed?

Stefano knew little about the Mafia. He'd grown up in America, where his grandfather had immigrated decades before his birth. His father died when he was a baby and his mother, a New Orleans homecoming queen, dragged him from city to city in a frenzied search for excitement. Stefano was twelve when she died.

His paternal grandparents, who he hardly knew, took him in.

Tough, street smart, hiding his fear behind a mask of arrogance, he couldn't have been easy for them to handle. His grandmother fed him and clothed him and otherwise washed her hands of him. His grandfather tolerated him, disciplined him and finally loved him with all his heart.

Perhaps his grandfather's advanced years, coupled with Stefano having come to know him so late in the old man's life, explained why he didn't have what Jack called "the Mafia thing" in his blood. His grandfather never told him tales of bloodshed and revenge. He told him, instead, of *La Sicilia,* of *Castello Lucchesi,* of the cliffs and the volcano and the sea.

Those were the things that beat in Stefano's blood, the things he cherished without ever having seen them.

It was only on his deathbed that the old man motioned him close, whispered of honor and pride and *famiglia,* of how he'd had to abandon everything and come to America to save what he could: Stefano's father and, by extension, Stefano.

"I will get it all back," Stefano had vowed.

It took time. Years to work his way through college, though by his senior year, he was impatient. During summer internships, he'd learned to hate the falseness of the corporate life that had been his goal, to despise the "old boy" network that was already working to deny him entry, the handshake that often accompanied the knife in the back.

His college roommate felt the same way. TJ was into computers. In those days, billionaires were made overnight in Internet start-up companies. TJ was going to be one of those billionaires. He had a great idea, he had the skill, the vision…

All he needed was the money.

One winter day, his hard-earned next semester's tuition in hand, Stefano climbed into his ancient VW, headed toward Yale—and kept on going north, to a casino where he bought into a game of high-stakes poker. It was the first unplanned thing he'd ever done since the day he'd promised his grandfather to win back the Lucchesi honor, but he didn't let himself think about that.

He told himself he deserved a day off. He was a good poker player; he played for fun in school. In fact, he'd won his old VW at a poker table at a middle of the night game in his college dorm, when another guy thought he'd been bluffing with a flush showing on the table.

That day at the casino, Stefano won more than a VW. He won thousands of dollars.

The casino gave him a free room. He staggered to it, showered, slept, ate and returned to the table. Three days later, he drove back to school, dumped a small fortune on his surprised roommate's bed and watched TJ stare at the bills in disbelief.

"Whadja do, man, rob a bank?"

"There's your start-up investment," Stefano said. "I want fifty-one percent control."

A muscle jerked in Stefano's jaw. Fast-forward a dozen years.

The start-up had made him wealthy beyond his wildest dreams. Now, even though his money was invested in aerospace companies, in Texas oil, in luxury condos in Manhattan, he'd never forgotten the pledge he'd made his grandfather.

Two years ago, he'd set out to fulfill it, but it had taken the conversation with his attorney to remind him that there were places and people where ancient vendettas still made the blood hot with rage.

The hot sirocco wind beat at Stefano's back, whipping his dark hair around his lean face. He pushed the strands back and again tucked his hands into the pockets of his jeans.

"Double our initial offer," he'd instructed his attorney.

"That's far too much money. The land isn't worth—"

"No, but their pride is. Make the offer, and make it clear that I have my pride to consider, too. Tell them I'm making them an offer they can't refuse."

Jack had met the statement with a long silence. At last, he'd cleared his throat.

"You watched those movies, huh?"

Stefano had laughed. "Just make the offer and get back to me."

Now it was done. All this—the land, the cliffs, what remained of the *castello* and the view that stretched on forever—was his. So was the house he'd built, just beyond the ruins. He'd had the architect blend it into the rugged scenery and use stones from the original castle. The result was a handsome home, high-ceilinged, with walls of glass that looked over the volcano and the sea.

Stefano smiled. His grandfather, he was certain, would have been pleased.

Tonight, just after moonrise, he'd come out here again with a bottle of *moscato* and a glass. He'd pour the wine, lift the glass to the sea and toast the spirit of all those who'd come and gone before him.

And he would try to keep this place invisible to the rest of the world.

If the tabloids got word, they'd have a field day with what he'd done. It would put a sexy spin on the gossip that already swirled around him. He was building an empire, they said. He was a man of mystery. He was *uno lupo solo.* A lone wolf.

They were right about that, at least. Lucchesi Enterprises had made Stefano a public figure. Because of it, he cherished seclusion in his day-to-day life.

He'd followed his usual practice in building his new house, hiring only those who agreed to sign contracts that contained confidentiality clauses, making it clear his lawyers would be merciless in enforcing those clauses. Word would get out eventually, he knew, but this would give him some breathing room.

A little while ago, a helicopter had buzzed overhead. There was nothing unusual in that; helicopters were part of the twenty-first century. Still, he'd looked up, wondering if somehow the paparazzi had already caught up with him.

"Stef-an-oh."

Stefano caught his breath. Was it the wind? The sound of that voice, calling his name. No. It had to be the wind.

''*Stef-annn-oh.* Yoo-hoo. Don't you hear me?''

He blinked. The wind couldn't put words into sentences, couldn't paint the slender figure of a woman looking up at him from the foot of the hill, one hand scooping back her blond hair, the other cupping her mouth.

Carla? His heart thudded. It couldn't be. She was in New York. He'd left her there one morning last week, tears trailing down her perfectly made-up face, stopping when she realized he meant every word, her voice rising to a shriek as she told him what she thought of him.

The trouble had started when she burst into his apartment without warning and found him sitting at the dining room table, drinking coffee and looking at photos of the island: the windswept cliffs, the old ruins and the new house.

''Omygod,'' she'd said breathlessly, ''darling, what is this?''

There'd been no sense in saying he didn't know. The architect had put together a handsome final portfolio, and each photo was neatly labeled.

Castello Lucchesi, Sicily.

''A house,'' he'd said indifferently, as if that were all there was to it.

''Your house,'' she'd said, in that breathless way he'd once found charming and now found irritating. ''And it's perfect for the cover of the premiere issue of *Bridal Dreams.*''

''No.''

''Now, Stefano,'' she'd said, slipping into his lap, ''you know I was hired to make *Bridal Dreams* the best magazine in the world. The first issue can make me or break me.''

No, he'd said again, and she'd changed tack, twisted around so she was straddling him, put her hot mouth to his.

He should have thrown her out right then. Their relationship had grown stale; it was over and he knew it. He'd lost interest in Carla—she was self-centered and superficial, and she wanted things he had no intention of giving her—a place in his life, a future with him.

He'd been with a dozen women who'd wanted the same things and he was no more interested in permanent commitment to Carla than he'd been with the others. Carla had known that, going in; she said her life was her career, but somewhere along the way, she'd decided to change her game plan.

So he'd lifted her from his lap, told her "No" again, and as she began to weep, his phone rang. It was his pilot, saying his Learjet had been serviced and was ready whenever he was.

"Where are you going?" Carla cried as he started for the door. "You have to do this for me, Stefano. You have to!"

When he didn't answer, she'd gone from crying to cursing and screaming…

And now she was here. On his land. His island. Scrambling up the hill toward him like something out of a bad dream.

He felt his insides knot into a ball of fury at her temerity in violating this place. He told himself he was being ridiculous, that this wasn't a shrine. The only thing he had the right to be angry about was that she'd followed him on this trip without being invited, but that didn't keep him from jamming his hands even harder into his pockets and balling them into fists.

"Darling," she squealed as she reached him. "Aren't you surprised to see me?"

"How did you find me?" he said curtly.

"That's not much of a hello."

"You're right. It's a question. Please answer it."

She smiled as she rose on tiptoe and pressed a kiss to his unmoving mouth.

"It wasn't that difficult. I'm sure you think I have a bubble for a brain, but even a child could have—"

"I'm sorry you made such a long journey for nothing, Carla."

"Is that all you have to say to me after I've come so far to be with you?"

His mouth twisted. She had come for her own reasons. Being with him had nothing to do with it. He knew that, and she knew he knew it.

"—such a magnificent place, darling, and to think you didn't intend to share it with—"

"Was that helicopter yours?"

"Yes. Yes, it was. It landed in a field just a little way from here and then a taxi—"

"Go back to it and tell the pilot to take you back to the airport."

Carla blinked. "What?"

"I said—"

"I heard you. I just can't believe you'd send me away."

Tears glinted in her eyes. She was good at this, he thought grimly. Very good.

"Carla." He spoke quietly, feeling the anger inside him approaching critical mass and determined not to let her know it. He valued self-control as much as privacy. Explosive emotion was the one thing Sicilian he didn't admire. It had led his grandfather to ruin. "You're not staying here."

"You mean…" Her mouth trembled. "You mean, I'm not welcome."

He almost laughed. Did she really think a show of injured feelings would work?

"I mean," he said carefully, "I didn't invite you."

"You didn't have to. We've been together a long time."

"Four months." His voice turned cold. He knew it, but all at once, he didn't care.

"Four months," she repeated, making it sound like a

lifetime, "and now, just because I asked you a simple favor—"

"I gave you a simple answer. No one is putting my home on the cover of a magazine."

"Then, it *is* your home?" she said with a sly little smile. "You're not developing this property into a resort?"

Stefano cursed himself for being a fool. "Goodbye, Carla," he said, and started past her.

She reached out and caught his sleeve.

"I don't want it for a cover, Stefano. I want it for the entire issue."

He laughed.

"It'll be the most incredible magazine anyone's ever seen!" He tugged his arm free of her hand and began walking down the slope. Carla hurried alongside him, slipping a little in her stiletto heels. "Just listen, okay?"

He didn't answer.

"The way I've planned things will protect your precious privacy as much as it heightens the intimacy of the shoot."

They reached the bottom of the hill. Stefano looked around for her taxi. The road and the driveway were empty.

"Here's my plan, Stefano." Carla moved in front of him, face glowing under the soft lights that had just come on in the rear of the house. "One of everything. One world-class photographer, one incredible makeup artist, one unbelievably gorgeous model—"

She cried out as he cupped her elbows and hauled her to her toes.

"No! Are you deaf? There will be no shoot. No model, no photographer, no anything."

"You're hurting me."

He probably was. Carefully, he took his hands from her and stepped back.

"Where's your cab?"

"I sent it back." She smiled. "I sent the helicopter back, too."

"Wait here. I'll have someone drive you to the airport," he said, and walked away from her for what would surely be the last time.

"Stefano."

Her voice was soft; it held something that made the hair rise on the back of his neck, but he kept going.

"Which magazine would you rather see these photos in, *Bridal Dreams*…or *Whispers*?"

He came to an abrupt stop.

"You have a minute to reconsider that threat," he said as he swung toward her, "and then I'm going to pick you up and throw you off my land."

Carla's face was white. She was frightened. But she was determined, too. He could see it in the tilt of her head.

"I've already made all the arrangements. The model, the makeup man, the photographer… They'll all be here tomorrow."

He felt his jaw drop. Dimly, in a part of his mind that was observing all this with dry curiosity, he wondered what the world would think if it knew that one sentence, spoken by one woman, could have such an effect on *il lupo solo.*

"Excuse me?"

"I said—"

He moved quickly, grabbed her by the shoulders and shook her until her teeth rattled.

"What the hell are you talking about?"

"Let go!"

"Damn you, explain yourself!"

"I'll sue you for assault if you don't let go!"

It wouldn't be assault, it would be murder. He was a heartbeat away from it. Stunned by the intensity of his rage, he let her go.

"Explain yourself."

"I did, but you wouldn't listen." She wrapped her arms

around herself and looked up at him. Her voice took on timbre; excitement flashed in her eyes. ''You think you know all about making money? Maybe, but you don't know squat about magazine publishing. You debut a new magazine or relaunch an old one, what you need is to produce an issue that'll set the country talking. Just one issue, and the magazine will be so hot it'll sizzle. And so will I.''

''Sizzle some other way. No one is setting foot here without my permission.''

''We'll be here three days, no more than that. I won't insult you by offering you money for the right to do the shoot here.''

He laughed, and her cheeks reddened.

''Don't make me force your hand, darling.''

''Force it?'' he said through his teeth.

''You want to keep your life a deep, dark mystery, don't you?'' She smiled slyly. ''Offhand, I can think of half a dozen tabloids that would love an exclusive interview with the great Stefano Lucchesi's mistress—along with aerial photos of his new hideaway.''

In the ensuing silence, Stefano could hear everything. The pound of his heart. The distant boom of the surf and the sharp cry of a bird far over the rolling sea. He could feel the shadows behind him, the ghosts of the wild warriors who'd done whatever was necessary to protect this place.

''I could kill you,'' he said softly. ''No one would know. All I have to do is drag you to the top of the cliff and throw you off. By the time your remains washed up, the crabs would have eaten their fill.''

Carla's smile trembled but she moved closer to him.

''You're a heartless bastard when you want to be, Stefano Lucchesi, but killing women? Never.''

Stefano stared at his former lover for long moments. Then he spat at her feet, brushed past her and headed for the house.

So much for his dreams.

She had defiled this place.

Maybe his grandfather had been wise to have left the island behind.

CHAPTER TWO

ALL the oceans of the world looked the same from 35,000 feet…and wasn't it sad when you'd flown so often that you could think of nothing but that when you were almost seven miles above the Atlantic?

Fallon O'Connell sat back, pressed the button that fully reclined her soft leather seat and wondered when she'd turned into such a world-weary cynic.

Across the aisle, a little boy traveling with his mother sat with his nose almost pressed to the glass, enthralled by the cloudless view of the ocean miles below and by the wonder of leaving Connecticut this evening and arriving in Italy tomorrow morning…but then, the kid hadn't made this trip a million times.

She'd been as excited as he was, her first flight to Europe ten years ago.

Fallon closed her eyes.

She was on her way to an island in the Mediterranean for a one week shoot, a suite in a mansion waiting for her as well as the best makeup artist and cameraman in the business ready to work their magic…

Her mouth twitched.

A little enthusiasm might be a good idea right about now.

She sighed, sat up straight and peered out the window again.

It wasn't that she didn't want the job. What model wouldn't? The inaugural cover of *Bridal Dreams* and inside it, pages and pages of glossy photographs devoted to her.

Of course, she wanted it.

So, what was the problem? That was what her brother Cullen had asked her last night, after Keir's and Cassie's wedding.

The newlyweds had finally made their laughing escape, but the O'Connell clan wasn't finished celebrating. They'd moved the festivities from the lushness of the Tender Grapes restaurant up to the handsome stone house that overlooked Deer Hill Vineyard.

Sean lit a fire on the massive hearth.

Anybody want to roast an ox? he'd said, to much laughter.

Cullen opened another bottle of Deer Hill's prize-winning Chardonnay.

Damn good thing Keir bought himself a vineyard instead of a soft drink franchise, he'd said, to more laughter.

Cullen filled all their glasses. Sean went through Keir's collection of CDs and put on something soft and classical while their mother and stepfather settled on the sofa. Megan, Briana and Fallon kicked off their stiletto heels and groaned with pleasure.

How about taking the dollar tour? Bree said.

Yeah, Megan answered, looping her arm through Bree's. *Maybe we can finally figure out how many rooms this place really has.*

She held out a hand to Fallon, but Fallon smiled and shook her head.

"You guys go ahead. I'm going to step outside for a breath of air."

Her sisters trooped off and Cullen looked over at her. "You okay?"

"I'm fine," she said, flashing another smile. "I just want to take a look at the sky. I'm not used to seeing all these stars."

Her brother grinned. "Me, neither. Us city types tend to forget."

Fallon nodded, opened the sliding glass doors and stepped out on the terrace. The stars shone down with crystalline brilliance from a black-velvet sky; the ivory moon seemed caught in the uplifted branches of a stand of trees.

The warm air of the Connecticut summer night enveloped her.

Wineglass in hand, Fallon went down stone steps that still held some of the day's heat. She made her way slowly along the gentle slope of the hill and through terraced rows of grapevines.

There, the earth was cool and moist against her bare feet—she and her sisters had decided to forgo panty hose under their long bridesmaids' gowns. The breeze, perfumed by heavy clusters of ripening grapes, smelled delicious.

It had been a lovely day. A wonderful weekend. Her mother was blissfully happy with Dan, who'd turned out to be the kind of stepfather that gave the word luster. Spending time with her sisters and brothers was always fun, and her oldest brother was so crazy in love with his Cassie that it almost made you believe in love.

For someone else, at least, if not for yourself.

Fallon stopped walking, sipped some of the wine, ran a hand lightly over a cluster of velvety grapes.

Then, how come she was feeling so—so—

What? What *was* she feeling? Weary? Under the weather? Maybe even a little bit down? There was no reason for it, none at—

"Hey."

She gasped and spun around just as Cullen reached her.

"You scared me to half to death," she said with a little laugh.

"Sorry. I figured you heard me coming." He grinned. "I guess I have a delicate walk."

Fallon grinned back at him. ''Delicate'' was not a word anyone would use to describe her brothers. Cullen, like the rest of them, was big, six foot two in his stockinged feet.

''Uh-huh. About as delicate as a moose. What are you doing out here?''

Cullen shrugged. ''Same as you, kid. Checking the stars, stretching my legs, taking a breather. It's been a long day.''

''A long weekend, you mean. Fun, though.''

''The gathering of the O'Connell clan always is. Fewer fireworks than usual this time, at least.''

Fallon laughed. ''Probably out of deference to Cassie. I guess none of us wanted to scare her off. She scored lots of points, being able to tolerate all of us at one clip.''

''Uh-huh. She seems terrific.''

''I agree.''

Brother and sister sipped their wine.

''Amazing,'' Cullen said, after a while. ''That Keir got married, I mean.''

''It happens,'' Fallon said lightly.

''Sure, but not to us.'' They both laughed. ''It was a great ceremony.''

''Mmm.''

''Those vows they wrote were cool.''

''Mmm,'' Fallon said again, and took another sip of wine.

''Touching.''

Her eyebrows rose. ''Touching?''

''Yeah. You know, the sentiments they expressed. Isn't a man permitted to use the word? You thought so, too.''

Fallon blinked. ''Were we talking about me?''

Cullen, who'd hours ago discarded his tuxedo jacket and bow tie, opened the top buttons of his shirt.

''You cried a little,'' he said softly. ''At the end.''

''Me? Cry at a wedding?'' Fallon turned toward him

and poked a finger into the middle of his chest. "Cullen. My darling little brother—"

"You're only a year older than I am, kid. Don't let it go to your head."

"The point is, I do not cry at weddings. Why would I? When you've been a bride nine trillion times—"

"A magazine-cover bride, six times, and don't look so surprised. Ma keeps count."

Fallon looked up at him. "Does she?"

"Damned right. And if you want to know the rest, she sends each of us a copy of every magazine that has you on the cover… As if we all didn't run to the nearest store and buy up all the copies ourselves."

Pleased beyond reason, Fallon smiled.

"That's nice."

"Nice? It's necessary. How do you think those magazines stay in circulation? If the O'Connells didn't buy 'em, who would?" He laughed, ducked away from the fist his sister teasingly aimed at his jaw. "But being a bride on a cover doesn't make you a bride in real life, babe. We both know that."

Fallon narrowed her eyes. "What's happening here? You think, now that Keir's gone down the aisle, we all should?"

Cullen shuddered. "Hell, no!"

"Good. Because I'm not the least bit interested in getting married."

"Fine with me. I'm just wondering why you were crying." His voice gentled. "You okay?"

"Of course I'm okay. Why wouldn't I be?"

"I don't know. That's why I'm asking. If some guy out there hurt you or something—"

"Oh, Cull," Fallon said softly. Her lips curved in a smile; she clasped her brother's forearms, lifted to her toes and kissed him on the cheek. "Thank you."

"Hey, did I or did I not beat up Billy Buchanan for you in fifth grade, when he wrote 'I Luv Amy' on that fence instead of 'I Luv Fallon' after he'd sworn to be your boyfriend forever?''

Fallon grinned. ''Probably because he couldn't spell Fallon, but yes, you did.''

''Well, any other SOB gives you a bad time, you tell me, okay?''

She stared at Cullen, wondering what he'd say if he knew that she didn't even date anymore, that one man too many had coveted her as a trophy to be won and ignored her as a woman who wanted to be loved for who she was, not what she was.

''Sis?''

Fallon smiled and looped her arm through his. ''Okay.''

They began walking up the hill, toward the turreted stone house illuminated by moonlight.

''It was just that it all seemed so—so right,'' she said after a minute, her voice soft and low. ''The flowers. The words. The music. The way Keir and Cassie looked at each other. I guess you're right. It was touching.''

''Sure.''

''Not that I want any of it for myself.''

''Your career,'' Cullen said, nodding as if he understood that there was no room in her life for anything else.

Except, how could he understand when she didn't? After years of hard work, her career was at its peak…and she wasn't enjoying it half as much as she'd expected.

She'd hit it big at seventeen, just walking along a New York street on a break between finishing high school and starting college. A man had come up to her, shoved his card at her, said, when she jerked back, that he wasn't a child molester or a lunatic, that he owned a modeling agency and if she wasn't a fool, she'd come in to talk with him.

Fallon had never been a fool. You didn't get to be valedictorian of your class or survive a childhood spent moving from place to place by being stupid. She'd checked out the name of the agency, called for an appointment and met with the man who now bore the distinction of having discovered her.

By the time she was eighteen, her face was everywhere. So was she. A week in Spain, another in Paris, long weekends in the Caribbean and on Florida's Gold Coast that very first year, and scores of places ever since.

Maybe that was why she'd been so emotional yesterday, at the wedding. Maybe it was knowing that Keir and Cassie were going to put down roots.

Maybe it was why she was staring out the jet's window again, wondering when she'd realized that one ocean was like another, one island like another, one man like another—

"Miss O'Connell?"

Fallon looked up. The cabin attendant was standing over her, smiling and offering the breakfast menu. She shook her head, declined everything but a small pot of coffee.

When it came, she raised her seat halfway and poured a cup.

You had to watch your weight when you modeled, more and more as the years sped by. The svelte figure you had at eighteen wasn't the same as the one you had at twenty-eight.

Twenty-eight, she thought, sipping at the hot black coffee. Pushing thirty. Not bad in this business. Her body was still all right; hours in the gym kept it that way, but she'd have to do some things to her face soon, if she wanted to keep going. Maybe get her eyelids done or her mouth plumped with collagen. Take a shot of Botox to keep wrinkles from between her brows.

She hated even the thought of doing something so artificial. As it was, there were times she looked in the mirror after someone had done her hair and her face, after someone else had chosen what she would wear, after still another person told her to look soulful or excited or whatever would sell cars or hand lotion, and wondered who she was.

Surgery, injections, little tucks and snips would only make the real Fallon more difficult to find.

Sometimes, she looked in the mirror and wondered what life would be like if she were a real person instead of a woman created by the camera.

Fallon grimaced and put down her cup.

For heaven's sake, what was wrong with her?

She was Fallon O'Connell, supermodel. Thousands of women would give anything to trade places with her, and every last one of them would tell her she was certifiably crazy not to be happy.

She had a wonderful, exciting life. And she knew, even if nobody else except her family did, that she was more than just a pretty face.

She smiled, remembering the way Sean and Cullen had greeted her at the Hartford airport a few days ago, enfolding her in rib-squeezing hugs, Sean saying he was glad to see she was still as homely as sin, Cullen adding yes, it was true, and wasn't it a terrible shame?

Fallon chuckled. Her family knew how to keep her grounded.

She pressed the seat button and sat up straight.

Enough of this silliness. She had to concentrate on the job ahead. It was an incredible assignment. She'd be the only model in the shoot, and she'd work with Maurice, her favorite photographer, and Andy, a genius of a makeup artist who'd always been able to make her look ethereal.

Carla—the *Bridal Dreams* editor who'd set up the whole thing—would be there, too, but that was it. Just their little group, and nobody else, not even the mansion's owner. That was a relief. She'd done shoots on private property before and sometimes the owners got so star-struck and excited, they got in the way.

Not this time.

This owner, Carla said, was an old man with a bad temper. God only knew what magic Carla had worked to convince him to let them use the site for the shoot. When Fallon had asked, Carla winked and said it was a secret. She'd probably used that same magic to get the old guy out of the way. Carla said she'd given him the option of staying around but he'd refused.

So there'd be just a handful of people, people Fallon already knew, and the ruins of an old castle, a view Carla swore went on forever, the sun, the sea, the beach…

And the volcano, smoldering in the distance.

She felt better, just imagining it.

She'd been to Sicily before, only for a couple of days. That had been work, too, but she'd been one of three models. The other girls had hated the island. They said it was too rugged, too old-world, too windswept, but Fallon had loved it.

Sicily was reality. Islands where the trees were lush, the land gently rolling, the people smiling and laid-back were fantasies.

A touch of reality was a breath of fresh air in a life where the end product was illusion.

The sound of the jet's engines changed. It was subtle, but she'd flown enough to recognize the different nuances in tone. The pilot was throttling back. Soon, he'd put down the flaps and lower the landing gear.

Fallon leaned toward the window. The sky was turning light; a slender red thread stretched across the horizon. They'd be over land any minute, touching down in Paris where she'd change planes for the last leg of her flight.

Perhaps, she thought with a little kick of excitement, perhaps Sicily was where she'd finally figure out who she was and what she was going to do with the rest of her life, because the truth was, the future was on her mind lately.

On her mind, a lot.

Fallon shut her eyes, blocked out the sound of the engines and the excited voice of the little boy across the aisle. She took a deep breath, held it, then exhaled slowly and deeply.

A couple of relaxation exercises, she'd be absolutely fine.

A few hours later, not even a day's worth of relaxation exercises would have helped calm her nerves.

What kind of place was this?

Was there supposed to be a deluge in Catania at this time of year? Was she supposed to be so wet and cold that she was shivering?

Plus, nobody spoke English. Well, nobody here at the cab stand. Nobody spoke Italian, either. Fallon did, a little. More than a little; she had a good ear and she'd picked up a considerable amount of the language when she lived in Milan for six weeks at the start of her career.

What people were talking here sounded like Italian, but it wasn't. It was a dialect, sort of what you heard in New York when you went into one of those fantastic little shops all the way downtown where they said "proh-voh-lone" when they meant "prah-vah-lohn-eh" or "scun-geel" when they meant "scun-gee-lee."

You thought you understood. And you did. Almost. But there was a huge difference between clarifying things by smiling and pointing at a chunk of cheese or a tray of octopus and trying to figure out how to ask if this was or was not the place to wait for a private car that was supposed to come for you.

Fallon shoved a wet hank of hair from her eyes.

Where the hell was her ride?

Her flight had come in on time. She'd collected her luggage, gone through customs, headed out the door absolutely according to Carla's directions…

And waited.

And waited.

And waited some more, without the protection of an

umbrella or a raincoat, just a thin cotton jacket over an even thinner T-shirt and cotton slacks.

Where was that miserable car?

She darted out from the wretched protection of an overhang and checked the road again, searching for a car that looked as if its driver might be searching for *her.*

Fiats and Alfa-Romeos went by. And taxis, lots of taxis, and, damn it, she'd have taken one if she knew where she was going but she didn't have the address. Why would she have needed it, when a car was picking her up?

Fallon dashed back to the wall, soaked to the skin, her hair dripping down her back and in her eyes, her clothes plastered to her body.

Maurice, the photographer, and Andy, the makeup guy, had flown over yesterday with Carla. She'd had to come a day late because of the wedding. No doubt the three of them were sitting in that castle, warm and dry, drinking *vino* while she stood here and drowned.

Okay. To hell with waiting for a driver who wasn't coming. She'd go into the terminal, find a phone, call the *Bridal Dreams* office…

And reach nobody. It was the beginning of the day here, which meant it was still the middle of the night in New York.

"Damn," she said under her breath, "damn, damn!"

A big black car pulled out of the line of traffic and turned toward the curb. Fallon held her breath. Was the driver looking for her? She couldn't see him; the windows were darkly tinted and the rain was coming down in sheets, but yes, the car was stopping, the driver was getting out, going around the car, opening the door…

Fallon raced to the car and tossed her suitcase inside.

The driver looked startled. *"Signorina. Uno momento!"*

"It's okay," she gasped, "you don't have to put the case in the trunk. Just let me get inside where it's dry."

"By all means," a deep, amused voice said. "Any port will do in a storm."

A man was sitting in the shadowed corner of the back seat, smiling at her.

Fallon's first thought was that he was gorgeous. Dark hair, heavily-lashed dark eyes, a classical Roman nose...

Her second was that this couldn't possibly be her car if someone was already inside it.

Her third was that she was out of the wet and the cold for the first time in almost half an hour.

She cleared her throat. "I don't suppose... Is there the slightest possibility someone sent you to meet me?"

The man grinned. "I'd love to say yes but, regretfully, I have to say that nobody sent me to meet you."

"Ah." Still crouched just inside the car, Fallon put her hand to her hair and shoved the sodden mass from her face. "Well, then, I'm sorry to have bothered you. I mean, I've been waiting for a car that was supposed to come for me, and—"

"How about fate?"

"Excuse me?"

"Would it be all right if I said fate sent me to meet you?"

Oh, yes. Definitely gorgeous, and with a smooth line.

"Unfortunately," she answered, with a quick smile, "fate's not going to take me where I'm going." Still smiling, she started scooting backward. "Again, my apologies for—"

"My driver can take you wherever you're going."

She blinked. Stefano knew he'd surprised her with his offer. Hell, he'd surprised himself, too.

What was he doing, telling a strange woman she could use his car to take her wherever it was she was going? On the other hand, she was a delectable stranger, even as wet as she was. Even? Stefano let his gaze drop to her breasts, their roundness, their tight little nipples perfectly outlined under her clinging shirt.

If anything, the rain heightened her beauty.

He felt a quick stir in his loins, a sudden surge of hunger that shocked him with its intensity. He hadn't felt this kind of desire since his breakup with Carla. Actually, not for weeks before that.

"That's very generous of you, *signore,* but I can't accept."

His eyes lifted to hers. Her face was a little flushed, as if she'd noticed the way he'd looked at her. She was shivering, which made sense considering how wet she was, and Stefano cursed himself for evaluating her sexually at such a moment.

"Of course you can. I'm getting out here and my driver has nowhere to go after he leaves me. He can take you to your hotel."

Fallon shook her head. "That's just it. I'm not going to a hotel. I—"

"The rain's coming in. Why don't you sit down, let Luigi shut the door and turn on some heat while we discuss this."

She hesitated. He knew she had to be weighing the pros and cons of the situation. Should a woman get into a car with a stranger or not?

He smiled.

"You're American."

"Yes."

"Well, so am I. That makes us kindred souls. What's the title of that old book? *Strangers in a Strange Land.*"

"Heinlein," she said, with a delighted smile, and that seemed to do it. The woman bounced onto the leather seat beside him, shoved her hair back from her face and held out her hand. "Fallon O'Connell," she said, but when he reached for her hand she laughed, drew it back, wiped the wetness on her trouser leg before holding it out again. "I'm soaked."

"So you are."

Stefano smiled as he clasped her hand in his. God, she

was beautiful! Who was she visiting in Sicily? A man? He felt an irrational surge of jealousy for some faceless stranger. Maybe she wasn't visiting a man. Maybe he ought to stay on the island instead of returning to New York and celebrate his newfound freedom.

"And your name is…?"

He laughed. "Sorry. I'm Stefano Lucchesi. It's very nice to meet you, Miss O'Connell."

"Fallon, please. It's nice to meet you, too, Mr.—"

"Stefano." He let go of her hand, though he really didn't want to, sat back and folded his arms. "Now that we've been formally introduced, tell me why you can't let my driver take you to your destination."

"You'll think I'm crazy."

"I doubt that."

"Well, you see, I don't know the address."

Stefano grinned. "A mystery vacation?"

She laughed. She had a great laugh, light and musical and real.

"I wish. I'm not on vacation at all."

"Ah. Don't tell me. You're the American sales rep for Lamborghini."

She laughed again, and he thought how nice it was to be able to make her eyes crinkle up that way.

"I'm here on assignment for a magazine, but the person who hired me didn't give me an address. It didn't seem necessary, because she said she'd have a car pick me up."

Stefano felt his smile tilt. "*She* said?"

"Yes."

He drew a deep breath. "I don't suppose you're a model, Miss O'Connell."

"It's Fallon, remember? And yes, I am. Did you just recognize me?"

She said it with a smile but there was disappointment in her eyes. Why? he wondered. Because he hadn't recognized her sooner? Yes, that would be the reason. He knew the kind of woman she was, aware of her looks, trading on them, assuming no man could resist her. And he, like a fool, had been busy proving her right.

Until now.

She was connected to Carla, a part of Carla's plan to violate his sanctuary. And he wanted nothing to do with her.

"No," he said curtly, "I didn't recognize you."

"Oh. Then, how—"

"There's talk all over the island of the idiots who are going to take foolish pictures for a useless magazine."

It was a lie. There'd been no talk. Carla had kept to the bargain; she'd been discreet and he'd surely told no one, but it was as good an excuse as any. He was angry, angrier than he had the right to be, and for no good reason. What Fallon O'Connell did for a living was her affair, not his.

Apparently, she thought so, too. Her smile vanished; that lovely face turned cool.

"I don't consider my occupation useless, Mr. Lucchesi."

"My apologies," he said in a way that made a mockery of the words. She knew it, too, because color swept into her cheeks.

"You don't know anything about my profession, mister! The pictures will be beautiful, and thousands of readers would tell you how much the articles in the magazine—"

"I'm sure they would," he said, cutting her short, "but then, there's no accounting for bad taste."

Just for a second, he thought she was going to slug him. The thought had a certain appeal. Her hand swinging in an arc, his reaching out to stop her, grabbing her by the shoulders, pulling her against him and crushing that lush mouth beneath his until her indignation became desire…

Damn it, was he crazy?

"Okay." Her voice was low and trembling with repressed anger. "That's enough."

She reached for the door; he caught her hand to stop her and felt a bolt of electricity shoot from her fingers to his before she jerked back.

"How you earn your living is your affair. The point is, I know the place you want." He leaned forward and tapped his driver's shoulder. "Luigi. The lady wants to go to the *castello*. Take her there."

"I'd rather walk than accept a favor from you."

"Don't be a fool. How can you go someplace if you don't know its location?"

"Just tell me where it is and we'll call it even."

"My driver will take you."

"Damn it, are you deaf? I don't want to spend another minute in this car!"

"It isn't the car, it's me."

Her eyes flashed. Soaked to the skin, as disheveled as a wet cat, she still had a presence about her.

"You've got that right!"

"In that case..." Stefano wrenched the door open, stepped into the road and slammed the door shut. "*Arrivederci,* Miss O'Connell. Luigi?" He slapped the side of the car. "*Andante.*"

Fallon O'Connell said something to him. He couldn't hear it but this close to the smoked glass window, he could see her mouth open in angry indignation.

Whatever it was, he suspected it wasn't polite.

She reached for the door and he slapped the car again. Luigi, ever obedient, discreetly activated the door locks and floored the gas pedal.

The car shot away from the curb.

Stefano strode into the terminal, got halfway through it and stopped. What the hell was he doing? He cursed under his breath, an eloquent, earthy string of Sicilian that would have made his grandfather proud as he took his cell phone from his pocket and called his pilot.

"Change of plans," he said briskly. "We're not going

anywhere today. In fact, you might as well take the next few days off. I'll be staying in Sicily for a while.''

Of course he'd stay, he thought grimly as he hurried back to the taxi stand. What had he been thinking, to risk leaving the *castello* while Carla and her people were there?

She had instructions. So did his house staff. None of the *Bridal Dreams* people were to be permitted past the door. Carla had been upset; where would she put her little crew? she'd said. She'd already told them they'd be staying in the castle.

Untell them, he'd said coldly.

For all he gave a damn, she could put them in sleeping bags on the rocky beach, but there was an inn a few miles away and that was where she'd arranged they'd spend the week.

He'd checked to make sure she'd really made the reservations, and he'd pushed up the installation of a full security system for the *castello* by a couple of months. He'd even gone a step further and arranged for around-the-clock security people to patrol the grounds.

''Taxi, *signore?*''

Stefano nodded, handed over a few bills and climbed into the cab.

''Il Castello Lucchesi,'' he said.

Still, how could he be sure his orders were followed unless he was there?

He'd been stupid to leave his home while strangers were on the property. Going back was the only way to safeguard his privacy.

An image flashed before him of the woman he'd just met, her eyes wide and mysterious, her mouth warm and sensual. For an instant, he thought he could smell her scent, an innocent breath of vanilla that only accentuated the lushness of her beauty.

Stefano's mouth thinned.

He wasn't doing this because of Fallon O'Connell. He was doing it because it was logical.

There was no other reason.

None at all.

CHAPTER THREE

A TRAVEL magazine would have dubbed the Lucchesi Estate magnificent.

The setting was spectacular. Tall cypresses flanked the ancient ruins that had once been a medieval castle. It backed against a cliff that fell away to the deep blue Mediterranean, and faced the slumbering volcano called Mount Etna.

On the same plateau, probably where the ancient outbuildings of the castle had once sprawled, stood a modern castle, a structure that was all cool smoked glass and native stone. There was a terrace behind it, a garden surrounding that, and off by itself, a free-form pool with an infinity edge that made it seem as if the water in the pool fell straight down the cliff, into the sea.

Beautiful, all of it…and after almost a week, Fallon hoped to God she'd never set eyes on the place again.

The sun was merciless, blazing down like golden fire from a sky so blue it seemed artificial. Shooting on the terrace hour after hour, with the sea at her back, meant she spent most of her time staring at the castle and all that dark glass. It was like looking at someone wearing mirrored sunglasses. Were they watching you, or was it your imagination? It was always impossible to tell.

Filming in the pool was better, but Maurice thought that setting too tame. He preferred the beach, and that was hell.

The beach was rocky, the stones hot and sharp beneath her bare feet, and even when Maurice motioned her into the surf, the water was tepid against her ankles and calves rather than cooling.

The last day of the shoot seemed endless. Maurice was barking out orders, as usual.

"Angle toward me! Get that arm back! Think sexy!"

Think sexy? All she could think was thirsty, but she moistened her lips, turned a half smile to the camera and clung to the thought that they'd be finished in just another few minutes.

She was hot; her feet were raw from the rocks and her skin was itchy under its layer of sunscreen. Andy had used waterproof makeup on her face and it felt like a mask, and the hairdresser—Carla had brought along more than the three people she'd promised—the hairdresser had sprayed so much gunk at her head that she felt like she was wearing a wig.

"Let's go, O'Connell! This time, run into the surf. Look like you're having a good time. Give me lots of splash."

The only thing she wanted to give him was a sock in the jaw. But she was a pro; she knew how to do her job. And she was trying to do it, she really was. It was just that she'd come here expecting to love this place.

Instead, she hated it.

"Smile. Yes. That's it. Another one, over your shoulder this time."

The sun, reflecting off the sea in sparkling flashes, was too bright. She had a headache from it by the end of each day. The beach was impossible to walk on, all those stones cutting into the tender soles of her feet.

"Okay, honey. Drape yourself over the big rock. You know what I want, babe. Lean back on your hands. Nice. Very nice. Bigger smile. Yeah, like that. Good, fine—except turn your head. Give me the look. You know the one. That's it. Nice. Very nice. Now you're cookin'."

Cooking was the word. This place could pass for hell's anteroom. Had it been this hot last time she was in Sicily?

''Go a little farther into the water. Good. Push your hair back. Use both hands—I want to see those tits lift! That's it. Perfect. Now wet your lips and smile.

''O'Connell? Turn around. Try one hand on your hip. Give me a pout. Let your lashes droop. Look at me. You're a bride, you're on your honeymoon, and you're looking at your groom with sex on the brain and nothing else. Pretend you're going to get out of the water soon, go up to that castle and jump his bones. Good. Better. We're getting there.''

Go up to that castle? No way. The closest she'd come to it was the day she'd arrived.

The driver had taken her through an imposing gate, past a couple of men with ice for eyes who looked as if they should have been wearing camo and combat boots instead of suits, past security cameras tucked high in the trees, toward a soaring edifice of stone and glass.

''Il castello,'' the driver said, his voice as solemn as if he were in one of the ancient churches they'd passed on the way.

That he said anything at all startled her. He hadn't spoken a word since they'd left the airport. He didn't understand English, he'd indicated with a lift of his shoulders, but it was a lie.

He'd understood every bloody word his arrogant feudal lord had spoken. It was only when Fallon demanded he let her out of the car that the man suddenly turned mute. She'd ended up shouting at him; she'd come close to reaching over the seat and pummeling his shoulders with frustration.

That wasn't going to happen again.

''How nice,'' she said coolly.

The truth was, nice didn't come close.

She'd been expecting a medieval structure, cold, gloomy and desolate. This was a soaring mansion that somehow bridged the distance between the past and the present. She craned her neck and stared as they drove past it, until the car came to a gliding stop.

Fallon looked around as the driver got out and opened her door.

They'd stopped beside—

A tent?

"Signorina."

Confused, she looked up at the man. "Are you sure we're in the right place?"

"Si."

She stepped from the car. It was a tent, all right. A big one, true, the kind she'd seen at garden parties in the Hamptons, but a tent just the same.

The driver reached in for her suitcase and at that moment the *Bridal Dreams* crew ran out of the tent to greet her. She hugged Andy and Maurice, exchanged air-kisses with Carla, shook hands with the others and asked the obvious question.

Why were they all hanging around in a tent when there was that big old house just a couple of hundred yards away?

Off-limits, Carla said with a patently false smile. "The owner's eccentric. He doesn't want us using it."

The tent would be their office and dressing room. She'd made catering arrangements for lunch and had a portable john installed in a little cove on the beach.

"It's as if we're camping in the wilderness," Carla said with a gaiety anyone could see was false.

"Don't tell me we're camping here at night, too," Fallon muttered, and Carla laughed and laughed.

"Of course not, darling. We all have rooms at an inn just up the coast. It's a charming little place."

The others, who'd already seen the inn, groaned so that Fallon knew "charming" was a happy euphemism for not enough hot water, lumpy mattresses and threadbare linens.

Carla was the only smart one. She went back to New York on the second day.

Of course, it made for problems, not having Carla on-site. The stylist or the designer's rep or somebody else was almost always clutching a cell phone, talking to New York, asking questions, getting things clarified.

Nobody could figure out why Carla had left. It certainly wasn't the most practical thing to have done but that second morning, Carla's cell phone had rung, she'd answered it, turned white, glanced up in the direction of the big house on the cliff and the next anyone knew, she was gone.

"Important business in New York," she'd said, but Fallon didn't buy it. It just didn't sound right.

Fallon sighed.

Thank goodness the week was almost over.

Tomorrow morning they'd all fly back to the States, and not a moment too soon. Why she'd ever imagined she'd enjoy being on this godforsaken island was a mystery. She'd had enough of the heat, the rocks, the house or mansion or *castello* or whatever it was called looming way up there on the cliff.

She didn't like this place. Nothing about it seemed right, starting on day one when she'd mistaken that big black car at the airport for the one that was supposed to meet her.

That car. That man. Stefano Lucchesi, with the dark and dangerous eyes, the slow smile, the husky, sexy voice.

Ridiculous, how an obnoxious stranger had lodged himself in her mind. She knew the reason: she had zero tolerance for men who thought they owned the world. She'd spent most of the past decade dealing with jerks like that. You damn near tripped over them in every capital on every continent, men who thought that beautiful women were useless and self-indulgent, and that they could be bought or, at least, coerced.

"O'Connell, are you deaf? I said to turn around. Thank you. It's nice to know you're still with us."

Modeling was a strange business. It was full of men

like Maurice, all ego and temperament, and ones like Andy, who were gentle and kind.

And on the periphery were the predators.

Handsome men. Wealthy, powerful men. Men who prowled the clubs where the models danced and drank and relaxed after a day's hard work, who wanted the pleasure that came of wearing stunning arm-candy.

It was, of course, a reciprocal arrangement. The predators got the arm-candy; the girls got the attention, the gifts, the publicity.

Not Fallon. Not since she'd tumbled, hard, for a so-called captain of industry when she was seventeen. She'd given him her heart and her virginity; he'd given her a diamond bracelet and promises, lots of them.

Only the diamond had stood the test of time.

She'd been cautious after that but still, four years later, she'd ended up in a replay of that first relationship. Her lover had been good-looking, rich, notoriously sexy…and he'd given her up when someone new came along.

''O'Connell? Babe, put your hands on your hips, okay? Great. Hold that…''

Her few liaisons since then had been with nice, down-to-earth guys. No I-Am-In-Command egos to deal with. No hunky powerhouses. Nobody to start her pulse pounding excitement at the sight of him, the way it had in that car at the airport when she saw Stefano Lucchesi, saw that beautiful fallen angel's face…

A tremor raced down her spine.

She was definitely glad this project was almost finished. What she needed was the noise and energy of New York. She could deal with the crowds, the traffic, the weather that was always either too hot, too cold or too wet a lot better than she could deal with this place.

She was thinking crazy things, plus her senses were playing tricks on her. For instance, she kept having this feeling someone was watching her.

She knew about the crazies who stalked celebrities. A

friend had suffered that kind of unwanted attention from a fan without a life. The experience, even viewed from the outside, was spooky and frightening.

This was different.

The first time, she'd been on the cliff posing for Maurice with her back to the sea. Suddenly a door in the castle opened and a man stepped into the garden.

Nothing unusual in that. A place like this would employ a gardener. Half a dozen of them, for all she knew.

He'd walked slowly to the low wall that surrounded the garden, tucked his hands into his pockets and just stood there. Watching her. Or maybe watching the mechanics of the shoot. That was what she'd told herself, when he'd remained motionless for the next five or six minutes. People always gathered to watch when you did a shoot on a street corner or at a resort.

Later the same afternoon, the *Bridal Dreams* bunch had all been down on the beach, Maurice photographing her in the bridal gown, some moody shot he'd print in blacks and grays, with her standing so that the lacy hem of the gown trailed in the water. She'd been posing, smiling, pouting, whatever felt right or whatever Maurice demanded…

And she'd felt it again. Eyes, watching her.

A figure stood on the cliff. A man. Tall, broad-shouldered, narrow-hipped, standing with his legs slightly apart, his arms folded across his chest and the wind blowing his dark hair back from his face. The distance was too great for her to make out his features.

The sight of him was intriguing. That hard-looking body. The jeans that fit him like a glove, the black T-shirt, black-lensed sunglasses.

Who was he? Why did the sight of him make her breath catch?

She knew he was watching her, just as she knew he wasn't a crazy, some guy who'd fallen in love with her photo and wanted to tell her that they came from neighboring galaxies. She knew it in the most scientific way possible.

Her instincts told her so.

Fallon rolled her eyes, just thinking it, and Maurice's voice pulled her into the present.

"I don't want smirks, I want pensive," he shouted.

She nodded, took some deep breaths and gave him pensive.

The man always stayed at a distance, watching her as if he wanted to absorb her into his skin. At the same time he wanted to turn his back and forget he'd ever seen her.

Another scientific deduction. Besides, even if it was true, it made no sense.

The evidence all pointed to his watching not her but the entire group. He was surely one of the security guards that patrolled the place, and if she hadn't noticed him right away, that was just because he was good at blending into the scenery.

And if her sun-baked brain gave him more depth than that, painted him as almost cruelly masculine and incredibly sexy, that was her fault, not his.

Fallon blew the hair back from her forehead. Without question, the heat was playing games with her mind.

"Maurice?" She swung toward the photographer, hands on her hips. "Listen, Maurice, enough is enough. I'm melting. My makeup's running, my scalp's crawling with sweat."

"You want me to tell you you still look gorgeous? 'Cause you do."

"Yeah, right. That's wonderful, but I've had it."

"Ten minutes more, that's all. Lift your chin like so."

"You said ten minutes an hour ago."

Maurice lifted his chin. Fallon left hers where it was.

"Maurice," she said firmly, "everybody else has gone. They're all sitting in the tent, out of the sun, drinking something cold and waiting for you so they can take the van back to the inn."

"Let them wait. I'm not finished. Look at me, O'Connell. Give me a little more attitude. You're a bride and your groom's watching you and you want to show him what you've got. Good. Fine."

Did she want to show the man who watched her what she had? She'd thought about him last night, lying in her narrow, lumpy bed. Imagined his face. Would his eyes be dark? His nose classically Roman? His mouth full, his jaw chiseled?

Would he look like the man at the airport?

The skin on the back of Fallon's neck tingled. He was up there, watching her again.

She knew it.

She looked back, shading her eyes, making no attempt to be discreet and yes, there he was, standing with his arms folded, his eyes hidden behind those omnipresent dark glasses.

A hot arrow of desire shot through her so quickly, so unexpectedly, that she felt her knees turn to water. She wanted—she wanted—

Out of here. That was what she wanted. Turning, she splashed through the shallows to the beach.

"O'Connell?"

Her sunglasses were on a canvas folding chair. She jabbed them on her nose and shoved her feet into a pair of rubber thongs.

"What's happening, babe?"

"The session's over, that's what's happening."

"Yeah, but the light's changing." Maurice hurried after her as she headed for the path that wound up the cliff. "Babe," he whined, "look at the sky. Clouds, see? And the water's getting choppy. Nice little waves coming in. Moody stuff. I thought we'd try something new—"

"I'll see you later," Fallon said, and started up the path. Maurice was a great photographer but he never knew when to stop.

She did, and it was now.

She was out of breath by the time she reached level ground. The stranger was gone, which annoyed her. What kind of man watched a woman without making an effort to meet her? Because yes, he was watching her. Not the others.

Her.

Fallon strode toward the tent, where the *Bridal Dreams* people were sprawled in a semi-circular arrangement of canvas chairs, their faces tilted up to the sun.

Andy looked up and called out to her. ''All done?''

She nodded. He grinned and gave her a thumbs-up. She grinned back, returned the gesture and opened the door of the ancient little red Fiat she'd rented from the innkeeper as soon as she'd realized how isolated this place was.

Her jeans and T-shirt were lying in the back seat. Fallon pulled them on over her bikini, grimacing a little at the feel of the hot cotton against her sticky skin.

She wanted a shower and a cold drink. She wanted to pack her things for tomorrow's flight home and then, maybe, drive up into the hills for one last look over the sea.

Most of all, she thought as she let out the clutch and floored the gas pedal, most of all, she never wanted to see this cliff and its *castello* again.

Stefano watched Fallon O'Connell walk toward the tent he'd permitted to be raised on his property.

She seemed to be in a hurry to leave.

Was he the reason? Yes. He probably was.

Stefano opened the concealed minifridge built into the wall behind his desk, took out a bottle of water and raised it to his lips.

The lady thought he was watching her. He'd realized that days ago. The way she stiffened and looked around her whenever he appeared was a dead giveaway.

It didn't surprise him. Women who looked like her assumed they had the eye of every man who saw them.

She was wrong. He wanted nothing to do with her.

Concern for his privacy had drawn him back, not a woman, and a damned good thing, too. Carla had violated their agreement before he'd even had time to board his plane. She'd brought in more people than she'd said she would, and his housekeeper told him that she'd sought access to the house the instant his back was turned.

Stefano settled into a leather armchair, put his feet up on a hassock and took another drink of cold water.

Of course, he'd sent Carla packing. He'd wanted to toss out the lot of them, her and her hedonistic *fashionistas,* too, but that dark threat she'd made hung over his head. Instead, he'd done the best he could, told his former mistress to get off his property before he had her thrown off.

Then he'd settled in to get through the week without going crazy from boredom, and that was the only reason he'd taken to observing the *Bridal Dreams* group.

Fallon had reached the disreputable-looking old car she'd picked up somewhere. Stefano frowned as she opened the door, pulled out jeans and a T-shirt and slipped them on. The shirt was oversize but the jeans clung to her legs. Such impossibly long legs, he thought with lazy appraisal.

Clothed, she was as magnificent as she'd been in the string bikini.

Okay. Maybe he paid more attention to her than to the others. What man wouldn't? She was stunning, the kind of woman who'd silence a room simply by entering it. A man would have to be blind not to enjoy looking at her.

Tomorrow, there'd be nothing to look at.

This unwanted intrusion in his life was over. This was the last day the photographic crew would be here. Fallon O'Connell was driving away right now. He couldn't help smiling at the way the little Fiat bucked. She'd probably let the clutch out too fast. She was driving too fast, too, leaving a plume of dust behind.

The photographer had joined the others near the tent.

Soon, they'd climb into their hired van and then—and then, he'd never see Fallon again.

Stefano got to his feet and paced to the window.

He'd never see any of these people again. That was what he'd meant.

The Fiat disappeared in the grove of trees that led to the gate. The van followed scant seconds later. Stefano raised the half-empty water bottle in mock salute.

Good riddance to the lot of them.

His world was his own again. No more unwanted voices, drifting from the beach. No more people tromping across the ruins or standing on the edge of the cliff, looking out at his sea and his volcano.

No more Fallon O'Connell, with that lush mouth he'd dreamed of tasting, those high breasts that surely would fill his senses with their perfumed heat, those incredible legs that he could imagine wrapped around his hips.

Stefano frowned and put down the bottle.

All right. So his disinterest was a lie. The truth was that he'd watched her like a damned hawk, felt his body turn hard for her, pretended he hadn't wanted to take her to bed when it was all he'd wanted from the second she scrambled into his car. He'd watched her pose for the camera, seen her feign expressions of excitement and lust, and known he could make her actually feel those things, make her eyes long for the sight of him, her soft voice cry out for him, for his possession…

Was he losing his mind?

Stefano strode out of his study, through the kitchen where his housekeeper looked up in surprise.

"Signore? Avete desiderato qualcosa?"

"No," he said, trying to sound polite, knowing he sounded anything but that. "Thank you, Anna. I don't want anything. *Grazie.* I'm going out riding. Don't bother making me supper."

Anna pursed her lips. She was a small, thin woman, Sicilian to the marrow of her bones, and the only thing she seemed to want more than to fatten him up was to turn him into a true *Siciliano* who could read everything in the rise and fall of insect voices or the wind blowing in from the sea.

"A storm is coming. There will be wind and rain."

"I'll be fine."

"In the dark, the roads will be treacherous."

Just what he needed. A second Italian grandmother.

"I'll probably be back long before then."

Anna gave a deep sigh. "As you wish, *Padrone.*"

As he wished? Stefano almost laughed as he went into the garage and shut the door behind him. He walked past the first three bays to the last, stroked a hand lightly over the gleaming black Harley that was his vehicle of choice wherever the roads were narrow and twisting.

If things were as he wished, Fallon O'Connell would either be waiting in his bed or he wouldn't be thinking about her at all.

He put on his helmet and his black leather jacket, pressed the button and waited while the door slid up. Then he straddled the bike and kick-started it to roaring life.

He knew where she was staying, knew he could go there and confront her, tell her that the hot flash of sexual awareness he'd seen in her eyes when they met pulsed within him, too.

But he wouldn't.

Wanting her was a weakness. She was a friend of Carla's, a citizen of Carla's gaudy world. Besides, wanting any woman was a weakness just now. Carla had left a bad taste in his mouth. Didn't people say that celibacy—temporary celibacy—was good for the soul?

God knew his soul could use all the help it could get.

Stefano snapped down the visor of his helmet and roared out of the garage. A long, hard ride would calm him down.

So would the knowledge that he would never lay eyes on Fallon O'Connell again.

An hour later, the island was wrapped in the black, wet, howling embrace of the storm Anna had predicted.

The wind was a wild thing, tearing at Stefano as he came around a tight curve on a narrow road. Another mile, maybe two, and he'd be—

What in hell was that?

The bright beam of his headlight pierced the darkness and picked out the shape of a small car coming toward him.

"Sweet Jesus," Stefano said, and braked, but it was too late. The driver of the car must have seen him, too, and braked as he had, but too hard. The car skidded and swerved across his path and he knew, with terrifying clarity, that it was heading directly for a gnarled tree, but it was the rest of what he saw in that sudden blaze of light that tore a cry from his throat.

The car was an old red Fiat. And the horrified face of the woman behind the wheel, her mouth drawn open in a scream Stefano could not hear, was Fallon's.

CHAPTER FOUR

TIRES squealed agonizingly as they fought for purchase on the wet road, but nothing could stop the forward momentum of the Fiat as it slid, with sickening inevitability, into the tree.

Stefano leaped off his motorcycle and ran toward the car.

"Fallon," he shouted, "Fallon!"

The night was silent except for the incessant drumming of the rain and the pounding of his own pulse.

His first thought was that she was okay. She'd managed to slow her speed considerably before the crash and the damage to the car seemed confined to a crumpled fender.

When he reached the car, he groaned aloud.

It was an old car, with no airbag to have cushioned Fallon from the force of the crash. The windshield on the driver's side was shattered. She lay slumped against the steering wheel, and tiny shards of glass glittered like stars in her dark hair.

Stefano grabbed the handle. The door wouldn't give.

"Come on," he shouted, "come on, damn it!"

Desperate, his breath sobbing in his throat, he pulled harder. It was useless. The door was either locked or jammed shut.

He cursed, ran around the car, slipping and sliding in the wet dirt, wrenched open the passenger door and climbed inside.

"Fallon?" he said as he reached for her.

She didn't respond.

Tearing off one glove, he slid his fingers to her wrist. Yes, thank God, he could feel the beat of her pulse.

She was alive.

His belly knotted when he saw that she hadn't fastened her seat belt. If only she'd worn the belt. If only it hadn't been raining. If only he hadn't come around the curve just then.

Stefano blanked all those "if onlys" from his head. All that mattered was what he did next. The accident, everything that led up to it, was part of the past and couldn't be changed.

He started to move her, then froze as his mind played back everything he'd ever read or heard about the folly of moving someone who'd been in a bad accident.

You could make a bad injury worse, cause paralysis or death.

Did those caveats apply when you were on a road in the middle of nowhere with the rain pouring down? He knew these roads and these mountains. The odds of someone coming along to offer help ranged from zero to none. There was a farmhouse perhaps ten miles away. With luck, it would have a telephone.

For the first time in his life, Stefano was immobilized by indecision. Should he move Fallon? Ride his bike to the farmhouse, hope there was a phone, call for an ambulance, then come back to be with her?

Gritting his teeth, praying to whatever deity might be listening, Stefano eased Fallon into his arms, then drew her carefully toward him. She moaned once but made no other sound.

He paused when he got her into the passenger seat. Holding her in the crook of first one arm and then the other, he shrugged free of his heavy leather jacket and wrapped it around her. Her head was still down but her breathing was steady.

"I've got you now, sweetheart," he whispered. "You're safe."

Still, no response.

Holding her to him, gently, his hands trembling, he tipped her head up.

Oh, God!

Her face. Her beautiful face!

Crimson streamed from a gash on her forehead that reached into her hairline, from another on her cheek, from yet a third that slashed wickedly across her chin. She had no other wounds that he could see, but those were enough. Knowing who she was, what she was, Stefano understood that what had happened on this night would forever change Fallon O'Connell's life.

His heart lurched.

"Fallon," he said softly, "can you hear me?"

She moaned again. Her lashes fluttered.

He leaned closer. "Fallon?"

Her eyes opened and she stared blindly at him.

"What—what happened?" she said in a weak voice.

"There's been an accident."

"An accident?"

"Yes." He searched for words that would reassure her. "You're going to be all right."

"I don't—I don't remember..."

"That's all right. You don't have to remember. Not just yet. Fallon?"

"Mmm?"

She was tumbling back into unconsciousness. Was it best to let that happen or to keep her awake? Damn it, why didn't he know? He'd sat through a first-aid course in college. Had he been asleep?

Stefano turned his face to the sky, let the rain beat down on him.

What did you do for someone who'd suffered head trauma?

"Fallon. Listen to me."

"I'm lis'ning."

"Tell me where you hurt."

"Sleepy."

"Yes. I know, but first tell me if you hurt anywhere. Your arms? Your legs?" He took a deep breath. "Your back?"

"Head," she whispered, and punctuated the word with a hiss of pain. "Head hurts."

She lifted her hand and raised it to her forehead. Stefano caught her wrist, afraid she might do more damage to her wounds and even more afraid the awful reality of what had happened might send her into shock.

"Listen to me, Fallon. I have to get help."

"Don'leave me."

He wound his fingers through hers. "Only for a little while," he said softly.

No reply. Her lashes drifted to her cheeks but, God, she wasn't sleeping. Not with her face so pale, her blood so dark.

Stefano lifted her hand to his lips and pressed his mouth to her knuckles. Then he got to his feet, wincing at the sudden pain that shot through his arm.

Pain in his arm? Was he hurt? He looked down at his forearm, saw an ugly gash oozing blood. He must have cut himself on something, glass from the windshield or torn metal on the car. Whatever had happened, it meant he probably wouldn't be able to carry her very far.

Not that carrying her to shelter was a real option. The rain was coming down so hard he half expected Noah and the ark to come floating by.

Okay. Maybe he didn't remember much about how to treat an accident victim, but it certainly didn't make sense to expose a woman who might be going into shock to the force of a cold rainstorm.

What then? Leave her here, alone? No. That was out of the question.

He looked at the Fiat. A crushed fender and a smashed windshield didn't necessarily preclude the engine from working.

There was only one way to find out.

Hands shaking, he fastened the seat belt around Fallon. Then he climbed over her, brushed glass off the driver's seat and got behind the wheel. Carefully, holding his breath, he turned the key.

The starter motor whined. The engine coughed once, twice. Then, with a shudder and the squeal of metal on metal, it started. It didn't sound as if it would last very long but all he needed was to coax ten miles or so out of it, if luck was with him.

He got the car into gear and backed it away from the tree, shifted gears again, made a tight, cautious U-turn and stopped.

The wound on his arm was throbbing; he could feel a cold sweat break out on his forehead and his teeth were starting to chatter. Shock, he figured, and only gave a damn because it might mean he had less time to get help for Fallon than he'd thought.

He looked at her.

She sat with her head lolling against the headrest, her face still pale, the blood starting to coagulate. Her battered flesh was starting to swell. Such perfection, so cruelly destroyed.

His throat constricted and he leaned closer and feathered his lips over hers.

Then he took a deep breath, put the car in gear again and began what he suspected might be the most important journey of his life.

Pain. Pain, sharp and throbbing. Harsh white light. A smell of something coldly antiseptic.

And voices. A woman's, brisk and demanding, speaking in Italian, followed by a man's, urgent and low-pitched, speaking American English.

"Signorina O'Connell. *Apra I vostri occhi.*"

"Fallon? Come on. Open your eyes."

Open her eyes? Could she do that? She wanted to; it

was awful to lie here this way, trapped in the dark. Was she asleep and dreaming? If she fought hard enough, could she compel her eyes to open?

"Fallon. Please. Look at me."

Sorry, she thought. *Sorry, but I can't.*

Her eyelids were weighted down.

Down, down, down.

Fallon tumbled back into darkness.

"Fallon."

Fallon sighed. It was that husky male voice again, calling her back.

"I know you can hear me, Fallon. I want you to open your eyes."

He was half-right, whoever he was. She could hear him, but opening her eyes was impossible.

"You can do it."

A hand, hard and warm, wrapped around hers.

"I know you can do it."

He was wrong. She couldn't do anything but lie here and sleep.

"Damn it, don't you want to get better? You won't, if you don't open your eyes. You have to wake up. You must wake up!"

"*Signore.* I know you're upset but please, you need some rest. *Il dottore* would like to check your arm again. I know you refused stitches earlier, but if you would just come with me—"

"Not until she's conscious."

"*Si,* so you said, but that might take hours." The woman's voice gentled. "Days, perhaps, *signore.*"

"Then I'll stay with her for days," the man said roughly. "I'll stay as long as it takes."

"You need to take care of your own injury, *signore.*"

"You need to take care of your own injury," Fallon said weakly, as she opened her eyes. "She's right."

The man and the woman swung toward her, staring at her as if they couldn't believe she'd spoken.

Well, why would they? She'd thought the words, but they hadn't come out sounding quite like that. Her speech was stiff and slurred.

That didn't seem to matter to the people standing beside her bed. Both of them said her name with excitement.

"Signorina O'Connell!"

"Fallon! Fallon, thank God."

Fallon looked from one face to the other. The woman was dressed in white and was obviously a nurse. The man—the man looked familiar. Dark hair. Dark eyes. A smile that softened an otherwise hard-looking mouth.

Who was he? Why couldn't she recall his name? It lay just at the tip of her tongue.

"It's good to have you with us again, *signorina,*" the nurse said. "How do you feel?"

It was a good question. How *did* she feel? Exhausted. Achy all over. Confused. But most of all, her head hurt. And her face. From the neck up, she was a throbbing mass of pain.

"Whappen?"

"Scusi?"

"She wants to know what happened."

The man reached for her hand and laced his fingers through hers. It felt good, letting him do that. He was strong; she could tell by just looking into his eyes, and with their fingers entwined, she could almost feel some of that strength flowing into her.

"There was an accident," he said softly.

"Accident?"

"Yes. A car accident."

A car accident? Fallon closed her eyes, tried to remember. She saw herself in a car, saw a winding, wet road, a bright light, a tree…

And then nothing.

"Fallon?"

She made the mistake of shaking her head to tell him she had no memory of it. Tiny hammer-blows of pain struck along her jaw, her forehead, scalp and eye socket. She hissed with the sharpness of it.

That sent the nurse into action.

''I shall get *il dottore,*'' she said, and hurried away.

A bell was ringing softly in the background; a mechanical-sounding voice was repeating a message over and over, requesting that a *Dottore* Something-or-other call his office.

Fallon looked into the man's eyes.

''Is this a hospital?''

The words didn't come out sounding like that. *Izissaspital?* was closer to what she said, but evidently he understood because he nodded.

''Yes.''

A hospital. Of course. What other place would be so dazzlingly bright? The walls, the ceiling; even the unadorned light fixture in the ceiling blazed down with a white glow so vivid it hurt the eyes.

''The doctor will be here in a moment.''

The nurse was back, politely trying to get past the man, but he didn't give an inch.

''*Signore, par favore,* if you would let go of the lady's hand for a moment... I promise, I'll give it right back.''

Color stained his high cheekbones. He let go of Fallon's hand and she felt a flutter of alarm. He was the only familiar thing—the only vaguely familiar thing—in this strange and painful world.

''Don'go,'' she whispered.

His expression softened. ''Don't worry, *cara.* I won't leave you.''

The nurse's cool fingers closed around her wrist.

''Her pulse is okay?'' the man said.

''Fine.''

''Her temperature? It's okay, too?''

''I'll know after I take it,'' the nurse said gently. ''Just be patient, *signore.*'' A moment passed. The nurse nodded, put a stethoscope to her ears, listened and nodded again. ''The *signorina's* vital signs are excellent. I'll go and inform the doctor.''

She stood up; the man brushed past her and sat down beside the bed. When he touched Fallon's hand, she twined her fingers through his.

''What can I do for her?'' he asked the nurse in a low voice.

''You have already done a great deal,'' the woman said quietly. ''Getting her here as quickly as you did...''

''Yes.'' His eyes went dark. ''I meant the rest.''

''You can be here, *signore.*'' She smiled at Fallon. ''That seems to mean a great deal to the lady, *si?*''

It did. He was her only comfort...and yet—and yet—Why did he seem familiar? Why couldn't she place him?

''I don't remember you,'' Fallon said woozily. ''But I have the feeling that I should.''

''The gentleman brought you here,'' the nurse said, before Stefano could speak. ''He is, how do you say, your Good Samaritan, yes?''

Fallon knew better than to nod her head this time. She knew better than to smile, either. Moving her mouth was too painful.

''Yes,'' she said softly, and looked at Stefano. ''Did you find me on the road?''

''Not exactly.''

His hand tightened on hers as the nurse padded quietly from the room. Stefano chewed on his lip. Nothing about this little scene was simple. Should he tell Fallon she was right to find his face familiar? Should he remind her of their initial meeting and how badly it had gone? Should he tell her he'd been watching her all week?

No. She was shaken and hurt, and things would get far worse before they got better, for she had yet to see her face in a mirror and realize the severity of her injuries.

But he could tell her what had happened on that wet road.

"You were driving your car," he said in a low voice. "I was riding my motorcycle. The road was narrow, the rain had just started and you came around a curve and skidded." He hesitated. "You didn't expect to see anyone else on that road and when you did—"

"Were you hurt, too?"

"Me? No. I'm fine." He cleared his throat. "Would you like some water?"

She nodded. He took a glass from the table beside the bed and carefully brought it to her lips. She tried to sit up, but he wouldn't let her.

"No, no. Don't move around. Not until the doctor checks you over. Here." He slid his arm around her shoulders, lifted her a bit and gently tucked the straw between her lips. "Drink a little. Easy. That's it. Good?"

Fallon nodded again and sank back against the pillows.

"How do you feel?"

"Awful," she said, and tried to smile but it didn't work. For one thing, it hurt. And the muscles in her face wouldn't cooperate. She lifted her hand, raised it toward her face. The man caught her wrist and stopped her.

"You have bandages," he said quickly. "It's probably best if you don't touch them."

"Bandages?"

"Yes. It'll be all right. You'll see."

"Bandages on my face? Am I cut?"

He could hear the underlying note of fear in her voice and knew he would have willingly done anything to take that fear away. How much to tell her? How soon?

"A little," he finally said.

Her eyes searched his. He saw the muscles in her throat move as she swallowed and he knew she had decided not to ask too many questions just yet.

God, he wanted to take her in his arms, hold her, soothe her as if she were a little girl needing his comfort.

"Tell me more about the accident."

"There's nothing more to tell," he said, clasping her hand again. "What matters is that you're alive and that you'll be walking out of here in no time."

Then, why wouldn't her Good Samaritan let her touch her face? Before he could stop her, Fallon snaked her other hand out from under the blanket and lifted. Her fingers danced over the bandages, then felt the puckered ridgelines of delicate silk stitches.

She felt her stomach tighten, then drop.

"More than bandages," she started to say in a shaky whisper, but just then the door opened and the nurse and a plump man in a white coat entered the room.

"Ah, *Signorina* O'Connell," he said in barely accented English, "how good to see you awake. I am Dr. Scalfani. How do you feel? Never mind. Not so good, I am sure, but we will make you feel much better, very soon. *Signore?* If you would wait in the hall..."

The man rose to his feet. "I'll be right outside," he said, leaning toward her and smiling. "Okay?"

Fallon gave his hand a last squeeze. "Tell me your name," she whispered.

"My name is Stefano. Stefano Lucchesi," Stefano said, and waited for her reaction, just as he'd waited for a reaction when she first opened her eyes and saw him.

There was none. Why would she recall his face, when she'd only met him the one time? Why would she recall his name, just because he'd introduced himself to her that day? He hadn't forgotten anything about her, but that didn't mean she'd had the same response to him.

"Signore?"

Stefano nodded. "Yes. Sorry. I'll wait outside."

The doctor poked and prodded, hummed to himself and spoke in rapid snatches of Italian to the nurse. Finally, he touched Fallon's face.

"I apologize," he said, "but I will be quick."

It hurt. Oh, it hurt, it hurt, it hurt.

"I know, *signorina,*" he said quietly. "You are in pain, yes?"

"My face..." She licked her lips, trying to find the right words yet afraid to say them. "Is there a lot of damage to my face?"

The doctor's gaze softened. "I don't know," he said bluntly. "It's too soon to tell what will heal and what will scar. I wish I could give you a more complete answer, but I can't."

Fallon looked past him, her eyes fixed on the empty white wall.

"I'm a model," she said in a low voice. "My face..."

"Yes. I understand. But being alive is the important thing, *signorina.* If not for the gentleman who brought you here, who knows what might have happened?"

Fallon nodded, even though it hurt.

"Yes," she said calmly, "who knows what might have happened?"

Without any warning, she began to weep.

The doctor patted her shoulder and murmured to the nurse. Fallon felt something warm slide through her veins.

Just before she sank into blackness, Stefano Lucchesi sat down on the chair beside her and reached for her hand. In a dizzying flash of light, she turned her gaze on him.

"I remember you," she said clearly, and then she fell into the darkness.

Another day slipped by. Fallon awakened, slept, awakened again.

And she was better.

Things hurt less; she wasn't groggy. The doctor examined her, hummed with pleasure and said she was on the road to recovery.

This time, she fell into a true sleep. When she awoke, the room was filled with daylight.

"Fallon. Welcome back. How do you feel?"

She turned her head and saw Stefano Lucchesi. Oh, yes.

She remembered him. He was as good-looking as the first time they'd met except now he looked exhausted; there was a heavy black stubble on his jaw and though she suspected he'd been beside her all the time, all she could think about was how he had mocked her for making her living as a model.

"What are you doing here?"

"I told you I'd stay with you, didn't I?"

"I don't want you with me, *signore.*"

His smile tilted. Until this moment, he hadn't been sure if what she'd said meant she really did remember him.

He knew the answer now.

"You recalled our first meeting," he said flatly.

"Yes." Fallon took a deep breath. "So, our paths have crossed twice, Signore Lucchesi."

"More than that," Stefano said. Why not get it out in the open? "You spent the week being photographed at my castle."

"At your..." She stared at him. "No wonder you knew exactly where I was going the day you told me how ridiculous it was that people should pay money to photograph me."

"I never said that."

"Incredible. First you insulted me, then you gave me a choice between crashing into a tree or killing you."

"That's not what happened."

He was right. She still couldn't recall the entire accident, but enough bits and pieces had come back so she knew it hadn't been his fault. Still, he deserved to feel guilty. The way he'd disparaged her occupation, and now this...

She knew it was wrong to put the two together, but it was almost as if fate had listened to his put-down of her and stepped in to lend a hand.

Why should she be the only one in pain?

"Your breakfast is here. Would you like to eat it?"

His voice was stiff but she had to give him credit; he

hadn't marched out the door. He might not feel guilty about the accident but he felt guilty about something, she thought grimly, and tried not to imagine how alone she'd have been if he'd left.

She looked at the tray table. Two white plastic drink containers and a small plastic cup stood on it.

"Juice," Stefano said. "Coffee, and what looks like cherry Jell-O. What would you like?"

"Nothing."

"You have to eat to get well."

"You should have told me you owned that castle."

"Yes, I should have. Does that make you feel better? Are we keeping score here? One for O'Connell, nothing for Lucchesi. Now stop being a fool and sit up and have some of this slop."

Fallon laughed. Not a good idea, considering that it hurt her entire face, but how could she not laugh at what he'd said?

And, if she wanted to be honest, how could she not admit that he'd scored points, too? If it weren't for Stefano Lucchesi, who knew how long it would have been before someone found her and brought her to the hospital?

"Maybe—maybe I'll try the coffee," she said after a few seconds. "If you'd ring for the nurse to lift the bed—"

Instead, he put his arm around her, eased her up against the pillows and brought the coffee to her lips.

"Easy. Don't drink too fast. How's that?"

"Awful," she said, but she sucked down half the contents of the container before falling back against the pillows.

"Thank you." There was no reason she couldn't be polite.

"You're welcome."

The silence stretched between them uncomfortably until Fallon cleared her throat.

"How long?"

"Since the accident? Two days."

"Two days." She moistened her lips. "Well, Mr. Lucchesi—"

"Stefano."

"It was—generous of you to spend so much time here, but I'm all right now, so—"

"You're going to be fine."

"Sure."

"I know things look bleak right now, but everything will work out." Stefano took her hand. "I swear it."

He spoke quietly and with such conviction that she turned her head and looked at him, wondering if she'd ever seen a stronger face, a more determined jaw.

She took a deep breath.

"I want to see my face," she said softly.

He blanched. "I don't think—"

"Please."

It was the "please," said in a shaky whisper, that did it. There was a mirror on the dresser. The nurse had pointed it out to him. "If the *signorina* should ask," she'd said, and he'd told himself that if Fallon did ask, he hoped he was a hundred miles away.

Stefano got the mirror and brought it to her. Her breasts rose and fell beneath the plain white hospital gown as she took a deep breath, and then she lifted the mirror and looked into it.

Stefano waited. Would she weep? Curse? For all he knew, she might faint. What hadn't been covered with bandages was now a canvas of black and purple and angry red.

Fallon didn't do anything he'd expected. Instead, she stared at herself while time dragged by, the only sign of what she was feeling visible in the tremor of the mirror, which finally fell from her hand to the bed.

She lay her head back and shut her eyes. Tears seeped from beneath the shelter of her lashes and tracked down her face like tiny diamonds.

It was Stefano who mouthed an obscenity as he reached to comfort her. She slapped away his hands and turned her face to the side.

"Go away."

"Fallon—"

"Are you deaf? I told you to get out."

"So you can wallow in self-pity?"

Her eyes flew open as she turned toward him. It had been a low blow and he knew it. She'd been brave and strong and he supposed she'd earned the right to some self-pity, if that was what she wanted, but he also knew that sympathy wasn't going to give her the courage to face whatever might come next, the weeks, maybe months, of healing; the decisions about possible further surgery and, most of all, the changes all this would bring to her life.

"Who the hell do you think you are?" she said, her voice quavering with anger. "You have no right—"

"The Chinese say that if you save a person's life, you become responsible for that person."

Her eyes flashed. "Then I guess we're both lucky that neither of us is Chinese."

"You survived a bad accident. Are you going to give up now?"

"That's my business."

"You're wrong. It's my business, too." He clasped her hands tightly in his. "There's some truth to what you said. You might not have had that accident if you hadn't come around that curve and seen me."

"Ah. Now I understand. You feel guilty. Well, don't. What happened was nobody's fault but mine. Okay? Now will you get the hell out of this room and leave me—"

Stefano silenced the bitter words by leaning over and brushing his lips over hers. She gave a soft gasp of surprise and he thought how sweet the whisper of her breath was before he drew back.

"I'm not leaving," he said in a low voice. "You might as well accept that."

Fallon stared at him. Of course he was leaving. She didn't want him here, didn't want anyone to see her like this, to be kind to her or gentle because if they were, she knew she'd break down, sob out all the terror and anguish in her heart…

But he was still there when she awakened hours later, and the next day, when she took her first steps, it was his arm she leaned on for support.

He was there until the day she was discharged and she told herself she wasn't looking for him all that morning, that she wasn't straining to hear the sound of his voice as she made phone calls, arranged for a taxi, for a hotel room in Catania where she would stay until she felt strong enough to face not just the long flight home but the shock and sympathy of her mother, her stepfather, her brothers and sisters and everyone who would have to see what she saw each time she looked in the mirror.

At her request, an aide bought her dark glasses and a wide-brimmed hat. Fallon put them on just before she stepped out the front door of the hospital for the first time in five days.

Oh, how blue the sky, how soft the air. She put back her head, drew a deep, deep breath.

"Fallon."

Startled, she looked toward the curb. A black Mercedes had pulled alongside it. Stefano was framed in the open door. He smiled, stepped from the car and came toward her.

"Stefano," she said, and when he held out his arms, she went straight into them.

CHAPTER FIVE

FALLON sat curled in a window seat at *Castello Lucchesi,* her arms wrapped around her drawn-up knees as she stared out over the sea.

She had been in Stefano's home for three days and she'd spent all of that time here, in one of the castle's guest suites.

A taut smile angled across her mouth as she thought back to that day more than two weeks ago when she'd come to Sicily anticipating the luxury of being housed in a castle, in a suite just like this, only to have Carla tell her that plans had changed.

"The owner is an unpleasant old man," she'd said. "He won't permit us inside his house."

Fallon sighed and lay her cheek against her raised knees.

Wrong on all counts. The castle's owner was gracious, even generous. He'd not only let her inside his home, he'd insisted she stay in it. He was young, surely no more than in his mid-thirties, vital, and so ruggedly handsome that any normal woman would surely feel her pulse quicken whenever she saw him.

But Fallon wasn't a normal woman anymore. She was a patchwork creature of bruises, stitches and swellings, and it would be a very long time before she'd react to a man again, or maybe it was closer to the truth that it would be a long time before a man reacted to her.

What man would want to touch a woman who looked the way she did?

Stefano had held her, even kissed her, but he'd been offering comfort. And, God, she was grateful for those soft touches, that light pressure of his lips against hers. He'd made her feel less alone, less grotesque.

Except, she wasn't going to take advantage of his kindness.

He'd brought her to her rooms that first day.

Fallon felt her face heat.

Brought her? He'd carried her, first up the wide stone steps outside the castle, then up the impressive stairwell that wound from the great entrance hall to the second floor.

"I can walk," she'd insisted, but her protest had only made him hold her more closely.

She'd heard the steady beat of his heart beneath her ear, felt the warmth of his body, and something had stirred deep inside her, an emotion as unwelcome in her new life as a hot flow of lava would be to this island.

She couldn't even think about herself as a sexual creature. Who would gaze into her battered face and want her? It was only that being in his arms felt so safe.

She had never felt as safe before.

When he'd shouldered open the door to the guest suite and sat her gently on the edge of a massive four-poster bed, she'd wanted to beg him not to let go of her. Instead, she'd drawn free of his arms.

"Thank you," she'd said politely. "You're being very kind."

"My motives aren't all that altruistic," he'd replied, and smiled, "*Castello Lucchesi* is brand-new. A new house needs a guest for luck. It's an old Sicilian saying."

"You're American," Fallon said, smiling a little in return. "And you just made that up."

Stefano grinned. "Maybe. But wait until you see the lunch Anna—my housekeeper—prepared. She's all excited about having someone besides me to cook for."

"Lunch?"

What would it be like to eat in a dining room instead of a hospital room, to have Stefano look at her across an expanse of linen and china? It had been simpler in the hospital. Dressed in a shapeless gown, perched on the edge of a narrow bed, she'd been a patient and he'd been a visitor. Now she was his guest, and the contrast between her battered face and the elegance of his home would be stark.

"Yes," he said, still smiling. "At one. You can sit outside afterward—there's a patio that looks onto the garden. Or I'll bring you back upstairs so you can take a nap, if you're tired. Dinner isn't until—"

"I really don't feel up to coming downstairs just yet," she said quickly. "Would your housekeeper mind bringing me my meals on a tray?"

"I should have thought of that. Tell you what. I'll ask her to set a table on the balcony just off your bedroom, and I'll join you here for meals until you feel up to—"

"No," she'd said quickly. "I mean, thank you, that's a kind offer, but I really don't feel up to company. You understand."

"Of course." He'd cleared his throat. "You're probably exhausted."

"I'm a little tired, yes."

"Tomorrow, then."

"Why don't I—why don't I ask... Anna? Is that right? Why don't I ask Anna to let you know when I'm feeling better."

His eyes had darkened in that way she knew meant he was displeased, but he'd said yes, certainly, he'd do as she preferred. Now two days had gone by and, true to his word, Stefano had left her alone.

Fallon sighed and sat up straight in the window seat.

The truth was, she was going crazy up here. The suite was handsome and spacious; there were magazines and books carefully arranged on a table in the sitting room and there was a TV set with satellite reception in the bedroom, but she didn't want to read or watch TV, she wanted to walk on the cliffs, explore the ruins, run on the beach.

Most of all, she wanted to see Stefano.

But she couldn't. Not when he didn't want to see her. If he did, he'd have come up here, knocked on the door and insisted she stop being a recluse.

Yes, she'd told him that was what she wanted, but she'd lied. Couldn't he figure that out? Didn't he *want* to figure it out? Was he just as happy she'd chosen solitude so that he didn't have to look at her, and wasn't that kind of paranoid thinking absolutely crazy?

The throaty growl of an engine below the window caught her attention. Fallon looked out just as a shiny black motorcycle and its rider wheeled into view from what she assumed was the garage. The rider stopped the bike to put on his helmet and, as he did, he looked up.

It was Stefano.

His eyes met hers. No smile. No wave. Just those dark eyes, burning into hers, and then his mouth twisted, he slammed down the visor, bent low over the bike and roared away.

Oh, God!

He'd seen her face for the first time in a couple of days, and she'd seen his reaction to it. As kind as he'd been, he hadn't been able to keep the truth from showing. It was how everyone would look at her from now on, with mingled expressions of pity and disgust and—

Fallon shot to her feet.

And, she really was going to go insane if she didn't get out of this silk-walled prison. She needed to leave this place and go where nobody knew her. It was what she should have done right away.

It took a while to figure out how to phone for a taxi but after a frustrating few minutes, she finally made the necessary arrangements. How long would Stefano be gone? She had no way of knowing; she only knew she had to be out of here before he returned.

The inn had sent over her luggage; Anna had put her things neatly into the closet. Now, hands shaking, Fallon tossed her suitcase on the bed, tore her clothing from the racks and shelves and dumped it inside. She was wearing a light cotton summer dress and sandals; they'd do for her taxi ride to a hotel. Any hotel. She'd ask the driver for a recommendation.

At last, she was finished packing.

Slowly, she eased the door open, listened for sounds and heard only the faint clatter of pots and pans rising from the kitchen.

Ridiculous, to steal out of the *castello* like a teenager breaking curfew, but she didn't want to answer questions. Not now. Once she was out of here, she'd phone Stefano, thank him for everything, explain that she'd had to get away, that she couldn't impose on him another minute.

Getting her suitcase down the stairs was hard work. She was weaker than she'd thought and by the time she got to the door that led out to the garden, she was light-headed and shaking. Still, she noticed how handsome the *castello* was. The huge expanses of glass were warm and inviting, and heightened the drama of ancient stone walls that spoke of power and isolation.

When the door swung shut behind her, Fallon dropped the suitcase, sank down on it and took half a dozen deep breaths. She felt woozy but there was no time to waste.

Stefano could come back any minute.

She waited until her heart stopped pounding, then rose to her feet. She'd arranged for the taxi to meet her near the gatehouse in an hour. There were still more than thirty minutes to spare.

Far above, a seabird cried out as it flew across the bright blue sky. Fallon looked up, shaded her eyes with her hand, followed the bird until it was barely visible over the water.

That was what she wanted to do. Go down to the sea, feel the warm Mediterranean sun on her skin, let the silken water lap over her toes.

If she moved quickly, she'd have just enough time.

Fallon slipped off her sandals and ran to the path that led down to the rocky beach. The sun was at its zenith; it beat down on her with an almost brutal force as she made her way down the cliff. She still felt light-headed, even a little dizzy, but the sense of freedom was intoxicating and when she reached the beach, she walked into the water, threw back her head, held open her arms and drew the warm, sweet air deep into her lungs as if it were a life force that could heal her, not her face but her heart, her soul…

''*Ma e pazzo!* Are you crazy?''

The familiar male voice was sharp with rage and accompanied by the sound of falling stone.

Fallon swung around and saw Stefano running down the last few feet of the steep path, his face distorted with anger. She took a quick step back, cried out as she stepped on something sharp, and fell just as he reached her.

''What the hell do you think you're doing?'' he roared, and lifted her into his arms.

''Put me down!''

''Put you down? Put you down?'' He strode onto the beach holding her, his breathing rapid, his eyes hot and dark. ''The place I should put you is over my knee! *Il sole siciliano ha cucinato la tua cervella!*''

''I don't know what you're saying!''

''The Sicilian sun has cooked your brain.''

''I'm so glad I asked. How could I have lived without hearing that charming sentiment?'' Fallon punched his shoulder. ''Now put me down!''

''Where? In the water, so you can drown your troubles?''

''Is that what you think—for God's sake, I wasn't—''

''Or maybe you'd like me to put you down here on the

path so that you can lose your footing and make a long, graceful swoon onto the rocks.''

''That's ridiculous! Do I strike you as the swooning type?''

''You didn't, until a couple of days ago.''

''Owning a castle has gone to your head. Do you think you're some—some feudal lord who can intimidate the serfs?'' He didn't answer, and that enraged her even more. ''Damn it,'' she said, punching him again, ''I told you, put—me—''

''Stop hitting me. One misstep and we'll both end up on those rocks.''

''Let go of me and I'll stop hitting... Hey! Hey, what are you doing?''

''Protecting myself,'' he said grimly, and dumped her over his shoulder.

''You jerk! You goon! You—you medieval son of a—''

Fallon gasped as they reached the top of the cliff and Stefano upended her again, this time dumping her on her feet.

''Just what were you thinking?'' he demanded, holding her by the shoulders, shaking her until her teeth rattled. ''Huh? Answer me, damn it! What's going on in that beautiful but empty head of yours?''

''My head is not empty!''

''No. I didn't think so until now.''

''And it's definitely not beautiful.'' She twisted out of his hands and glared at him. ''Only a blind man would say it was.''

''Is that what this is all about? Do you really think your life is over because you're going to have a couple of scars on your face?''

''A couple of...'' Fallon narrowed her eyes. ''You know what, Stefano? You're a fool!''

She turned and started for the *castello* and for the place where she'd left her suitcase but she'd only taken a few steps before he caught up to her, clasped her arm and spun her toward him.

"You could have been killed. Did you ever think of that?"

"For your information, I went up and down that cliff at least two dozen times the week I worked here. Or have you forgotten that I defiled your precious *castello* while you were—while you were wherever you were that week?"

"I was here, right in my own home, and I don't care how many times you climbed that path, you didn't do it when you'd just come out of a hospital."

"I'm fully recovered from the accident. And what do you mean, you were here? I saw you leaving at the airport the day I arrived."

A muscle knotted in Stefano's jaw. He let go of Fallon and folded his arms over his chest.

"There was a change of plans."

"What? You mean, all the time we were baking in the sun, sweltering under that tent, you were watching the peasants from your castle?"

"Letting you people wander through my home was not part of the arrangement."

"*You* people." Fallon folded her arms, too, and cocked her head. "Yes. I'd almost forgotten what you think of people like me."

"Damn it, how did we get off the subject? I leave you for an hour—sixty miserable minutes—and what do I find when I return? A crazy woman, only a couple of days out of a sick bed, wandering the cliffs."

"I was not in a sick bed. And I wasn't wandering. I was standing on the beach."

"You were knee-deep in the sea."

"I was in water barely over my ankles." Fallon lifted her chin. "And why am I explaining myself to you?"

"What if you'd fallen on the path? If a wave had knocked you down?"

"Oh, for heaven's sake, stop being so dramatic! I'm fine. See?" Fallon held out her arms and turned in a swift circle. "I didn't fall, didn't drown, didn't so much as stub my toe."

"Only because you're lucky. You lie around for two days and then, wham, you set off on a hike!"

"I have not been lying around for two days. If I wandered anywhere, it was around and around your guest suite like a lost soul."

"And whose fault is that?" Stefano's mouth thinned. "Staying locked in your rooms was your choice, not mine."

"*Signore* Lucchesi—"

"Don't call me that. I'm as American as you are."

"Are you? The American men I know wouldn't try to tell me what to do and when to do it."

The muscle in his jaw took another quick jump.

"In that case," he said silkily, "you've been dealing with the wrong ones."

"Oh, give me a break! Just because you have this—this lord of the manor complex—"

"You're pushing your luck," he said softly.

"Not half as far as you've pushed yours. What makes you think you have the right to tell me what to do?"

His eyes narrowed. "Shall I show you?"

His voice was soft as silk, yet she could sense the steel beneath it. Stefano had shown her such tenderness since she'd awakened in the hospital that she'd almost forgotten the man he really was, the man who'd insulted her that first day at the airport and denied Carla and the rest of them access to his castle.

"Fallon?"

She blinked. He'd closed the slight distance between them and now he stood only inches from her, so close that she could see that his eyes were a brown so dark they were almost black.

A curl of heat licked through her blood.

How would he prove his right to show a woman who held the power in a relationship with him? By taking her in his arms and proving his strength with his kisses, his caresses, his body?

The thought, so unexpected, so primitive, so unlike her, sent color shooting to her face. She stepped back, raised her chin and looked straight into his chocolate-colored eyes.

"You've been kind," she said calmly, though her heart was racing. "And generous. But if you think that gives you the right to make decisions for me, you're wrong."

"My apologies," he said stiffly. "Of course, you're free to do as you like."

"It's not that I'm ungrateful—"

"I don't want your gratitude."

"Well, you have it anyway." Fallon cleared her throat. "Actually—actually, I've been thinking…"

"And?"

"And, I've decided it's time I left."

His mouth twisted. "Ah. I suppose that explains the suitcase artfully hidden behind the flower bushes."

She felt color rush into her face. "I thought—I figured it was best to leave while you were gone."

"Because?" Stefano tucked his hands into the pockets of his jeans. "Did you think I'd bolt the doors and raise the drawbridge if you told me you wanted to leave?"

"Of course not. It just seemed—um, it seemed simpler that way." She looked at his face, the cool amusement etched across his mouth and in his eyes, and felt a rush of anger. "Damn it, don't laugh at me! All right. I thought you might try to convince me to stay."

"With what? A trip to the dungeon? Whips and chains?"

"I just wanted to avoid a scene, okay? I could imagine you trying to make me believe I was better off here, at *Castello Lucchesi,* than anywhere else."

He nodded, rocked back on his heels and gave her a look that said he found all this vaguely interesting.

"And how would I try to do that?"

"Well…well, you'd say—you'd say this was a perfect place to recuperate."

"Because it's peaceful? Because it's away from those who might stare at you?"

Her face grew hot. "You're blunt."

"I'm honest, and please don't tell me that's not a concern of yours."

"Why would I do that?" she snapped. The freshening wind snatched at her hair and blew it across her face. She scooped it back and tucked it behind her ear. "I mean, you seem to know everything about me."

"I thought I did."

"Which only goes to prove the size of your ego! You've only known me for a little more than a week—"

"I watched you."

She stared at him. "Excuse me?"

"I watched you." This time, it was his face that was suddenly striped with color. "When you were here with the others."

"You? You were the man who…? But why?"

"I'd never seen a shoot before. It was—interesting."

Fallon laughed. She could imagine him finding a photographic safari in Kenya interesting, but a fashion shoot?

"Try again," she said, and the color on his cheeks deepened.

"All right." His voice roughened. "The truth is, I didn't give a damn about the others, or what they were doing. I only saw you."

A little tremor danced up her spine.

"I knew someone was watching," she said softly. "I felt eyes on me. I saw someone… I thought it was one of the castle's security guards."

"Well, it wasn't. It was me."

"And—and why did you watch me?"

"Because you were beautiful," he said bluntly. "And serene, and filled with life...and yet, all the time, I felt you were searching for something."

His words, spoken so quietly, stunned her. How could he have made judgments about her without even speaking to her? And yet, he was right. Those qualities—her serenity, her vitality—were the very ones her agency often used to describe her.

As for the rest...he was right about that, too. She *was* searching for something. For someone. But none of those things applied to her anymore. They described the woman she'd been, not the one she'd be from now on.

Suddenly this talk, this argument, seemed pointless.

"You have a vivid imagination," she said carelessly. "Anyway, I might have been those things before but everything's different now." She turned away. "Thank you for all you've done, but it's time I left."

"It would be foolish to pretend some things about you aren't different," he said, clasping her wrist and trying to make her look at him. When she stood her ground, he stepped in front of her. "Fallon," he said softly, "look at me." Gently, he lifted her face to his. Tears glittered in her eyes and he fought back the desire to kiss them away.

"What's inside you, those qualities in your heart and soul, all the things that make you you, haven't changed." His gaze moved slowly over her face, lingering on her slightly parted lips before meeting her eyes again. "And you're still beautiful."

"No! I've seen myself in the mirror. You can't lie to me, Stefano. I know what I look like."

"You need time to heal. You know what the doctor said. It's impossible to judge what your cuts will be like until the swelling goes down and the stitches come out."

"Look at me," she said fiercely. "Go on, damn it! Take a long, hard look. Do you think what you see is going to vanish just because the stitches come out?"

"Do you really think scars can change the sweetness of your smile, the wisdom I see in your eyes? All you need is time to accept yourself."

"How can I accept someone I don't know?" The tremulous admission freed the tears she'd managed to choke back. They ran down her cheeks as she wound her fingers tightly through his. "Don't you understand? I'm not me anymore!"

"What's inside you is the same," Stefano insisted. "You're too bright to believe that the faces we show the world are our real selves."

"Two weeks ago, I'd have agreed with you. Something like that is easy to say when you look in the mirror and see someone you've always known but now I see—I see—"

Her voice broke. He mouthed an oath in Sicilian and drew her into his arms, held her tight against him until she sobbed and leaned into his body.

"I look at myself," she whispered, "and I see a stranger."

Stefano tucked her head under his chin. Her hair smelled of the salty sea and of the flowers that grew in the castle garden. He wanted to kiss her; he wanted to shake her. Instead, he held her close and rocked her in his arms.

"I know it can be difficult to see beyond what once was," he murmured. "When I first came here, to *Castello Lucchesi,* I saw only ruins. Lost dreams. Hopeless illusions. I couldn't understand why my grandfather had always talked of the *castello* as if the centuries hadn't changed it." He pulled back just enough so he could frame her face with his hands and look down into her eyes. "I decided he'd been filled with an old man's foolishness." He smiled, gently ran his thumb over her soft underlip. "Then I walked the cliffs. I listened to the wind whispering through the fallen stones. And I understood that what had made the castle great was still here, would always be here. I had only to look deep enough to see it."

Fallon drew a shuddering breath.

"What if you'd walked the cliffs, searched deep within yourself and—and found nothing?" The wind was as soft as her voice. "What if you'd discovered that what everyone thought was here had been just an illusion?"

Stefano's eyes dropped to her mouth again. One taste, that was all. One delicate savoring, and he gave in to need, bent his head and kissed her with such tenderness that she felt her heart stand still.

"I've seen a lot of things in my life. I know what is truth and what is illusion. The house I built here is an illusion. Its true beauty comes from the power of the stones that were once part of a real *castello*." A muscle knotted in his jaw. "Your true beauty comes from deep inside you. Nothing can change it."

Fallon swallowed past the lump in her throat. Oh, she wanted to believe him! Wanted to think that her face had never been anything but a mask…

"Stay here," Stefano said quietly. "Let me help you."

"You have a life to go back to. People who need you."

"I have a life I created and people who jump when I speak." He smiled, stroked dark strands of silky hair away from her cheeks. "They can jump just as well from four thousand miles away."

She laughed, really laughed, for the first time since the accident had stolen her from herself.

"Spoken like a true feudal lord."

"Is there anything you have to go back to that can't wait a few weeks? People who will worry about you?"

Fallon shook her head. She'd deliberately not contacted her family. Her mother had a weakened heart; her brothers and sisters had their own lives to deal with and besides, she didn't want the entire O'Connell clan rushing to her side, smothering her with well-meant love and sympathy. Not yet.

"A man?"

She looked up. Stefano's eyes were dark.

"No," she said. "There's no one."

"There is now," he said huskily and this time, when his gaze fell like a caress on her mouth, she cupped his jaw and drew his lips down to hers.

CHAPTER SIX

COULD a woman sink into a man's kiss?

Yes, Fallon thought, oh yes, she could.

She wanted to drown in the heat of Stefano's mouth, let her body melt into his. She wanted his hands on her breasts, his teeth on her skin, his mouth between her thighs.

She wanted all of that, now. Here, on the cliff overlooking the sea, with the scent of flowers mingling with the scent of saltwater. This man, this stranger, had become her friend. Her protector.

Now, he would be her lover. And she—she would become flame in his arms.

He groaned against her mouth, a sound of hot, unbridled passion. His body was hard against hers, his kisses soft and sweet even as he nipped her bottom lip between his teeth.

He wanted her as she wanted him; they'd been building to this from the moment they met and now—now it was time.

His hands lifted, cupped her breasts. His fingers skimmed over the light cotton that covered her yearning flesh and she hissed at the exquisite ache of desire that flashed from her nipples to her loins.

"Stefano," she whispered, and he said her name, took the kiss deeper until she was filled with him, with his taste. He trailed his hands down her body, bunched her skirt in one fist, slid his fingers under her fragile summer skirt, up and up her thighs, setting flashfires where he touched her.

Fallon moaned. She raised her leg and wound it high around his.

He was burning her. Melting her. Killing her with his touch, his kisses, his hands.

"Stefano," she said again, "please. Oh please..."

"Yes," he said, his mouth against her throat as her head fell back. "Yes," he said again and he cupped her between her thighs and she cried out, knowing he could feel exactly what he was doing to her, that her heat and wetness were kissing his palm.

This was what she'd longed for. Always, not just the past days or weeks but forever, from the start of time, from the first heartbeat of the universe...

And then, without warning, his arms dropped away from her. She was standing alone, shivering with the sudden chill of his rejection, and when she blinked her eyes open, she saw him looking at her as if he'd never seen her before.

"God," he said roughly, "what are we doing?"

Fallon's throat tightened with pain.

Stefano was staring at her through eyes that were dark, but not with passion. They were dark with shock. With pity. With distaste, and she knew, God, she knew that he'd suddenly realized what he was doing...and who he was doing it with.

How else would a man look at her now? Even this man, who had been so kind.

She wanted to weep. To curse. To slam her fists against his chest and hate him—but how could she, when she understood?

She was grotesque.

And now that she'd flung herself into Stefano's arms, she was something even worse.

She was pathetic.

"Forgive me," he said roughly. "I didn't mean…"

"No." Fallon could feel herself shaking. She wrapped her arms around herself and drew a deep, deep breath. "No," she repeated, "of course you didn't."

"Fallon." He held out his hand. She glanced at it, shook her head and took a quick step back.

"It's all right, Stefano. I understand."

"I'm sorry."

"Yes. So am I." She forced herself to look up, to meet his eyes as she searched for something to say before she fled. "It was—it was just something that happened. I mean, I didn't… I had no intention of…" God, oh God, she wanted to die! "It's been such a strange couple of weeks…"

"For me, too," he said quickly, grabbing the lifeline she'd tossed. "Otherwise, I'd never—"

"I know. Neither would I."

"I wouldn't have—have taken advantage of you that way."

She nodded. He was being a gentleman, taking the blame for her humiliating loss of control when they both knew that his kiss had been affectionate, that she was the one who'd dragged his head down to hers and turned the kiss into something hot and dangerous.

"We'll just—we'll forget this happened," she said, forcing a smile to her lips. "All right?"

He nodded, his eyes still locked to hers, the look of pity so obvious that she wanted to weep.

How would she ever be able to face him again?

"Well." She cleared her throat. "I, uh, I appreciate our talk."

"Our…? Oh. That."

"That. Yes. And—and you're right. I have to start facing the world again."

Stefano nodded. He didn't seem capable of saying anything sensible, and that made nodding his head like one of those damned plastic toys the safest bet.

How in hell could he have done this? Lost control, pawed a woman still weak from an accident that had changed her life? He'd meant only to reassure her, let her know that he cared for her, that he'd take care of her. Instead, he'd come on to her with all the subtlety of a bull moose in rut.

What kind of man made a move on a woman who kept telling him how grateful she was for all his kindness and understanding? Damn it, he didn't want her returning his kisses out of gratitude, he wanted her to respond to him because she wanted him, but how could she know what she wanted when the wounds to her soul were so new?

She'd come a long way but she was still fragile, still vulnerable. What son of a bitch would take advantage of her in that condition?

When she was healed, both outside and in, he'd take her in his arms again, tell her that he wanted to make love to her, to change that look of thankfulness in her eyes to a look of deepest passion…

"…not tonight."

He blinked, focused his eyes on Fallon and realized she was slowly backing toward the house.

"Sorry?"

"I said, I'll think about everything we discussed. You know. Your advice. And—and we'll talk again, but not—"

"Fine. We can talk in the morning." He smiled. Not an easy thing to do, when you'd made such an ass of yourself moments before. What in *hell* had he been thinking? "Join me for breakfast."

"Oh, no. I mean, Anna will bring my breakfast to my room, the way she always—"

"She won't."

Fallon lifted her eyebrows. "Excuse me?"

He'd spoken without thinking but now that he had, he knew it was the right thing to say.

"I'm going to tell her that you'll be taking your meals downstairs from now on. With me."

The look of horror on her face almost made him laugh. His elegant PA had once come to work wearing one brown shoe and one black one. When she'd realized it, Paula had looked the same way Fallon did now.

"That's not possible," she said quickly. "I mean—I mean, I'm not quite up to—"

"Is eight too early for breakfast?"

"If I were going to eat breakfast, eight would be fine, but I never—"

"Anna told me. Black coffee, right?"

Fallon cocked her head. "*Anna* told you?"

"Yes. Coffee for breakfast, a lettuce leaf for lunch—"

"She told you," she repeated, her tone gone icy, "as in, your housekeeper's been reporting my habits to you?"

Stefano shrugged his shoulders. "I wouldn't put it that way."

"No?" She folded her arms. Being angry at him for his smug arrogance was safer than standing here and wishing the ground would open up and swallow her. "Well, I would. And I repeat, I'd rather eat upstairs."

"And *I* repeat, you'll be taking your meals with me."

Fallon narrowed her eyes. What was that old saying about leopards not changing their spots? She'd pegged Stefano Lucchesi right on Day One. Too bad his angel of mercy disguise hadn't lasted.

"I don't take orders very well, *signore*. Perhaps we'd both be better off if I kept that appointment I made with a taxi."

His smile was slow and taunting. "Did you have an appointment, *signorina?* Strange, considering that I haven't seen or heard a car since we've been out here."

Now that she thought about it, neither had she. Fallon

frowned and looked at her watch. More than an hour had gone by since the cab was supposed to meet her at the gate…

Slowly, she lifted her head.

"Your guards turned my cab away," she said flatly.

"They have their orders. Nobody comes in, without my permission…"

"And nobody goes out. Is that the message?"

Stefano shrugged again, a casual lift of the shoulders that made her want to slap him.

"It's the only way I can ensure my privacy." He paused. "And yours…or do you really think no one's likely to discover that the woman who ran off the road on a rainy night and the woman who's a world-famous model are one and the same?"

She felt the color drain from her face. *"Paparazzi?"*

"Sicily is a hotbed of gossip and there've been some rumors. I assumed you wouldn't want to deal with them yet."

"No. No, I wouldn't. I haven't even notified my family."

"Do you want me to do it for you?"

"I'll do it when—when I'm ready."

"In that case," he said gently, "my orders to the guards will stand. Yes?"

"Yes," Fallon said, and it wasn't until hours later, after she was tossing and turning and trying, without success, to fall asleep, that she wondered if she hadn't been manipulated yet one more time by a man who was an expert at the game.

It seemed to come down to a choice between having Anna file reports with Stefano and letting the lord of the manor take mealtime notes himself.

Fallon opted for the latter. Besides, there was always the possibility he'd storm the guest suite and carry her downstairs if she didn't go willingly, and she wasn't about to end up in his arms again.

They had breakfast at eight, lunch at one, dinner at eight and stilted conversation accompanied each meal. During the day, Stefano went into his study; she walked along the cliffs, along the beach—*Let him just try and stop me,* she thought the first time she made the climb down—and in the evenings, she retreated to her sitting room and he…

She had no idea what he did in the evenings.

Most nights, she'd hear the roar of his Harley leaving at nine, then hear it again as he returned long hours later. He probably had a woman in some little hill town; a man like him wouldn't be without a woman for very long. She knew a lot about him now, thanks to a surreptitious trip to his study one evening after he'd gone out.

She knew she didn't belong there. Stefano never invited her inside, not that she expected him to. Not even Anna went past the heavy mahogany doors, but she was going crazy with boredom. There was only so much satellite TV you could watch before your brain turned to mush, she'd told herself as she stepped across the threshold.

Knowing she was in his *sanctum sanctorum* made her heart pound just a little, but the room wasn't what she'd expected. It wasn't Bluebeard's lair; it wasn't an opulent Playboy knockoff. It was just a room, handsomely paneled and carpeted, and furnished with leather chairs, a desk and an assortment of office equipment—a computer, a fax machine, a couple of printers—that explained how Stefano could stay away from New York and his office for weeks at a time.

And there were pictures on the walls.

Stefano, looking very young, grinning broadly as he stood beside a white-haired man with his same handsome features. The grandfather he'd talked about, she assumed.

Stefano, wearing a hard hat, smiling into the camera as

part of a group of half a dozen other hard-hatted men, all of them looking pleased with themselves against a familiar backdrop of sea and sky she recognized as the view right outside the castle.

There were magazines, too, and newspapers, and a quick flip through the stack verified what she'd already dredged out of her knowledge of New York's movers and shakers: Stefano Lucchesi was *the* Stefano Lucchesi, the one who'd created a corporation from the ground up and built a personal fortune that made the most jaded bankers drool.

Fallon took a last look around. Then she switched off the light and left the room. Everything she'd seen confirmed that Stefano was exactly as she'd pegged him. He had a decent streak—the way he'd treated her was proof of that—but, at heart, he was gorgeous, rich as Midas, and, she was certain, hell on women.

Not her, Fallon reminded herself as she went up the stairs. She was immune to that kind of man. She'd lost interest in them after she'd realized some men collected beautiful women the way others collected stamps…

And then she remembered that she didn't need immunity anymore, that she was no longer a woman a man like Stefano would look at more than once, and she went into her room, closed the door after her, went out on the balcony and stared out over the dark, dark sea.

On the fourth morning of their new arrangement, Stefano looked at her over the rim of his coffee cup.

"Are you ready?" he said.

"Ready for what?" Fallon said, startled.

"You have an appointment with the doctor."

Her heart fluttered. Did she? She'd pretty much managed to force all that out of her head. She wore dark glasses, even in the house; she let her hair fall over her face.

She caught Stefano frowning sometimes when he looked at her and she was never sure if it was because he thought she was trying too hard to hide herself or because he wished she'd do a better job of it.

In either case, she wasn't prepared for the bright lights of a hospital or even a trip out the gates of *Castello Lucchesi.*

"Did you forget?"

"Yes," she said politely, "I did. Do you have his number? I'll call and cancel."

Stefano pushed his plate away. "Why?"

"Why what?"

He looked up, his eyes narrowed. "Why would you cancel your appointment?"

"Well—well, I'm feeling fine. There's no need to—"

"Today's the day the stitches come out."

Her belly knotted. "The stitches..."

"Yes." His voice gentled. "It's a big day for you."

Fallon dropped her hands in her lap and curled them into fists.

"I'll go some other time."

"Nonsense," he said briskly, and shoved back his chair. "Tell you what. After you've seen the doctor, we'll celebrate by having lunch at a little restaurant I know. They do a cold seafood salad that's—"

"I'm not ready," she said in a small voice.

Stefano wanted to pull her from her chair, gather her into his arms, hold her and kiss her and tell her that he wasn't ready, either, not for the damned stitches to come out but for her to leave him once they were and she looked at herself and realized that she was scarred, yes, but that in some crazy way, she was more beautiful than ever...

"I'll be with you," he said softly, and she looked up and smiled at him in a way she hadn't done in days, not since he'd come close to ruining things by coming on to her too hard, too fast, too soon. "I'll be with you every step of the way,'' he said, and he rose to his feet, held out his hand, and felt his heart lift with joy when she hesitated and then put her hand in his.

Unfortunately, the doctor had other plans.

''No,'' he said firmly, when Stefano said he would stay in the examining room while the doctor took out the stitches. ''Take a walk, *signore.* Get a cup of *espresso.* The *signorina* and I want to talk.''

Whatever they'd talked about hadn't done much good. Stefano knew that the second the nurse said he could go back into the examining room. Fallon sat on a high stool, her body rigid, her face turned away from him.

The doctor took him by the arm and walked him into the hall.

''We were very lucky,'' the doctor told him. ''There was no infection, no distortion, no raised ridges of angry flesh.''

''But?''

The doctor sighed, took off his glasses and polished them on the hem of his white jacket.

''But, she refuses to deal with reality.''

''You can hardly blame her for that, Doctor. Did you know she was a model? That her face was her career?''

''Do you want to see her make a complete recovery, *Signore* Lucchesi? Or do you want to keep her dependent on you?''

''Be careful what you say to me, *Signore* Dottore,'' Stefano growled, but the doctor was unmoved by his warning.

''It's inadvertent, of course, but you're doing it all the same. The *signorina* is made of strong stuff but it would be simple for her to hide in a cocoon if you are too generous with your compassion.''

''I haven't done that! Did she tell you that she locked

herself away in her room? That I all but forced her to come downstairs and sit at my table for meals?''

''Has she gone anywhere else? To the store, to a café, even out for a drive?''

Stefano sagged back against the wall. ''What are you suggesting? That I shove her into public, demand she show her face to the world when I see how it hurts her even to look at herself?''

''What I suggest,'' the doctor said gently, ''is that you help her move forward.'' He put his hand lightly on Stefano's arm. ''The lady is healed on the outside—now, she must heal in a far more difficult place. Inside her heart, where the pain hurts the most.''

Going home, Fallon sat silently in the car, hidden behind dark glasses and a floppy-brimmed straw hat.

''Everything went very well,'' Stefano finally said.

She didn't answer.

''The doctor says—''

''I don't want to talk about it.'' She fell silent. Then she gave a bitter little laugh. ''The irony of it is that I'd been thinking and thinking, the last few months, about what else I'd like to do with my life.''

''And?''

''What do you mean, and? I didn't think I'd have to make the decision in an instant.''

''But you've given it some thought…?''

''How could I?'' she said sharply. ''Don't you get it? Everything's changed.''

The car pulled through the gates of the *castello* and glided to a stop at the front door. Stefano said something to his driver, got out and opened Fallon's door himself. She moved quickly past him and he went after her, put his hands on her shoulders and skimmed them down her arms, to her wrists.

More than anything he'd ever done, he wanted to help her. Part of it was for her but he knew that if he were honest, part of it, maybe the biggest part, was purely, selfishly, for himself.

He felt something he couldn't name for this woman. Hell, he wasn't ready to give it a name, or even look at it too closely, but it was there and he knew he didn't have a chance in hell of figuring out what it was until she was whole again.

"I understand," he said carefully, "that you won't get better until you accept what's happened to you."

She gave him a look that said he was crazy. "Do I have a choice?"

"*Cara.* There's a difference between acceptance and sufferance."

Her eyes narrowed on his. "Here we go. Philosophy 101, Sicilian style."

"I've told you repeatedly, I am not—"

"You are. I can hear what happens, that—that change in the cadence of your words, the way you suddenly have of sounding as if you're a font of old-world wisdom."

It wasn't true. He was trying to help her, she knew, but the only way he could do that would be to say, *You don't need those glasses or that hat. Yes, your face is scarred but I can see past those scars. I want you, anyway. I've always wanted you, even before I met you…*

She took a gulp of air.

Hadn't they said she'd suffered a mild concussion? Maybe that was why she was thinking such irrational thoughts. She didn't want Stefano, didn't need him, didn't need anyone to lean on. She never had and never would. Her mother had leaned all over her father and where had it gotten her? Dragged all around the country, that was where, while his wife and kids made the best of a bad situation.

Besides, she'd already embarrassed herself with this man.

No way in the world was it going to happen again.

"Never mind," she said. "It doesn't matter."

"Fallon. Look, I don't want to quarrel with you—"

"Then keep quiet."

"Can't we have a civil conversation?"

"No."

She was impossible! Fire and steel and silk, all in one package.

He didn't want to quarrel, he wanted to talk. No, he didn't want that, either. What he really wanted was to haul her into his arms, kiss her senseless, tell her that he'd already figured out what she would do with her life. She would spend it with him.

He swallowed hard.

What he had to do was be calm. Rational. Convince her to be the same way. They *would* talk, the way they'd managed to do for a little while the day he'd found her on the beach.

It was just that he wasn't good at reading women unless it involved simple things, like when they asked you if a dress made them look heavy. *No.* Or if this hairstyle was attractive. *Yes.* Or if he'd like to leave a change of clothes in the closet or a razor in the medicine cabinet, in which case he always knew what to say and how to say it so that his answer was as polite and painless as possible.

This situation was new to him. He needed to tell a woman the truth in a way that would help her, and how did a man do that?

"I'm just trying to point something out to you, Fallon."

She lifted her chin. He could see the warning in the gesture. *You're on thin ice,* she was saying.

"And that would be…?"

"Feeling sorry for yourself won't help."

Damn it! Of all the stupid things to say! He could see her turn rigid with anger.

"I didn't mean—"

"The hell you didn't!" Face white, she tore her hands free of his.

"So, you think I'm wallowing in self-pity."

"I didn't say that."

"You didn't have to. It's what you think."

"I don't." He hesitated. "But even if you were," he said, choosing his words with extravagant care, "feeling sorry for oneself would be natural, given the circumstances."

"This has nothing to do with *one*self," Fallon said, jabbing her thumb against her chest, "it is to do with *my*self! With me, not you and not some—some saint who'd probably look in the mirror and say oh, how wonderful, look what's happened to me!"

"Fallon. *Cara*..."

"Do not *'cara'* me!" She swung away from him, strode toward the house, then turned back. "Do you want to hear a funny story, Stefano? I've got a great one. The doctor was called away for a couple of minutes right before he took out my stitches. His nurse brought me a couple of magazines to leaf through, while I waited for him to come back. And I opened one of them and turned a few pages and you know what I saw?" Her mouth twisted. "Me. Me, looking like a human being instead of a freak."

Stefano fought the desire to drive back to the hospital, find the nurse and pry open her skull to see if she really had a brain inside it.

"I'm sorry that happened to you, but—"

"And then Dr. Frankenstein comes in and expects me to ooh and ahh over his wonderful job of cut and paste!"

"Fallon. Please—"

"I'm going home tomorrow."

"And do what? Lock yourself in your apartment?"

"What I do is my business!"

Fallon turned her back. Stefano grabbed her arm and spun her toward him.

"That's it," Stefano said grimly. *"Basta!"*

"At least we agree on something. *Basta,* indeed. Enough is exactly right. You are not my keeper, and don't bother giving me that speech about the Chinese and their inane proverbs."

"Have you looked in the mirror?" He caught her by the elbows and shook her. "Answer me! Have you looked?"

"I don't have to look. I see everything I need to in your face."

"What?"

She twisted out of his grasp, flew into the house and up the stairs, and all he could do was stand there and try to figure out what in hell had just happened.

CHAPTER SEVEN

FALLON dumped her suitcase on the bed, opened the closet and tore her clothes from the shelves and racks.

She should have left here that first time instead of letting Stefano talk her into staying on. She didn't belong here and he certainly didn't belong in her life.

The gall of the man! Who in hell did he think he was, telling her how she should feel and act?

Stefano Lucchesi lived by his own rules in his own private universe. People jumped when he spoke; wasn't that pretty much what he'd said? What he'd boasted, for heaven's sake? He'd probably never had to sweat for an honest day's pay in his pampered, self-centered life.

How could he possibly understand what it was like to have one of the most sought-after faces in the world one minute and the next—the next—

Fallon dumped an armful of shoes into the suitcase.

His world was secure. Hers was a blur, it had been turned upside down by a bored god with an eye for black comedy. She'd lost her career.

Far worse, she'd lost her sense of self.

All those articles in women's magazines about finding yourself… She'd always thought it the height of self-indulgence to waste energy gazing at your own navel, but now—but now—

Her mouth trembled.

Better to think about Stefano and how mistaken she'd been thinking he had a single bone of compassion in his body.

Did he see her as a charity case? What a fool she'd been to stay here.

Fallon stormed into the bathroom, grabbed the wicker trash basket from the corner and swept the vanity clean of all her makeup and creams and lotions. Half the stuff landed in the basket, the rest on the floor. Tins opened, shadows spilled.

Jasper Johns would have called the resultant mess a work of art.

She thought it fitting.

She didn't need all those stupid tools of her trade—her former trade—anymore. Who would care if she wore the right color lip gloss? Who'd give a damn what kind of mascara she used to darken her lashes?

A woman with a face that could scare little children didn't need makeup, she needed a paper bag.

What she definitely did *not* need were Readings from Oprah as served up by the Lord of the Manor.

Fallon slammed a fist against the marble vanity.

"Stefano Lucchesi," she muttered, "you are a smug, sanctimonious, self-serving, holier-than-thou son of a bitch!"

"Alliterative," she heard a deep voice behind her say in a thoughtful tone, "but untrue. My mother was a very nice woman."

Fallon whirled around. Stefano was lounging in the bathroom doorway, hands tucked casually into his pockets.

"What are you doing in my room?"

"As for sanctimonious, self-serving and—what was that other thing you called me?"

"I said, what—are—you—doing—in—my—room?"

"Holier-than-thou. That was it." Stefano sighed, leaned a shoulder against the doorjamb and crossed one moccasin-clad foot over the other. "Sounds good but it's repetitive, don't you think? Considering that someone who's sanctimonious is those other things, too."

Fallon glared at him. "How dare you barge in here?"

"I didn't barge, I knocked."

"With what? A feather?" she said, blowing the hair from her eyes and folding her arms over her chest. "I certainly didn't hear you."

"Well, you couldn't have. You were making too much noise, stamping your feet and breaking the place up."

Color streaked her cheeks. "I have never stamped my feet in my life. You have a vivid imagination."

Stefano raised one eyebrow and looked down at the tile floor. Fallon looked, too, and her color deepened.

"I was in a hurry. I dropped a few things."

"So it seems. I'll bet there's a king's fortune of magic elixirs there."

"What I do with my stuff is my business."

"I thought women loved all those silly little pots of nonsense."

"It's not nonsense."

"Then why throw them away?"

"I have no use for them anymore."

He gave her a long, indecipherable look. *Go on,* she thought grimly, *I dare you.* One more lecture on Facing Reality and she'd smack him… Or fall into his arms and weep.

Oh, God. Was she that close to tears? Was her mask ready to slip? Quickly, she bent down and began scooping up the scattered cosmetics. Stefano squatted beside her and grabbed her hand.

"Let me do that."

"I am perfectly capable of cleaning up after my own messes."

"I'm sure you are," he said calmly, "but there's nothing wrong with accepting a little help."

That wasn't a topic she wanted to pursue. Instead, Fallon gave him a scathing look, reached for the basket and began dumping makeup into it.

Stefano picked up a little container of eye shadow.

''Caramel Crème Sundae?''

''If you think it's your shade,'' Fallon said sweetly, ''be my guest.''

''And Wild Honey Mousse,'' he said, plucking a tube of lip gloss from the floor. He looked up, his eyes meeting hers. ''Why is it these things always sound like the menu in a bad French restaurant?''

''Give me that,'' Fallon demanded, snatching the gloss from him and tossing it into the trash. ''And go away. I told you, I don't need your help.''

''You need someone's,'' he said quietly. Before she could respond, he scooped up almost all the remaining containers and tossed them in the basket. ''I'm almost done.''

Glaring, Fallon sat back on her heels. He was right; he'd finished the job. He could pick up several of the little pots and tubes at one time. The stuff looked like sample sizes in his big hands.

Such capable, comforting hands.

Fallon shot to her feet. ''Thank you,'' she said stiffly.

''You're welcome.''

''And I'm sorry if I made so much noise it bothered you.''

''I didn't hear a thing until I was right outside the door.''

''Then why—''

''I came to apologize.''

She blinked. ''Apologize?''

''Right.''

Stefano brushed off his hands, then wiped them on the seat of his jeans. It was crazy, but the simplicity of the gesture was disarmingly boyish.

''I was an ass,'' he said.

''I beg your pardon?''

''You heard me. Telling you how I thought you should handle things was wrong.''

Fallon stared at him. Did he really think an apology would erase her memories of his arrogance?

"In fact," he said with a little smile, "I was a sanctimonious, self-serving, holier-than-thou ass."

She didn't want to smile, but how could she prevent her lips from curving just a little bit?

"Close, wasn't I?"

Stefano grinned. "Yeah, but close only counts in horseshoes and hand grenades." His smile tilted. "Seriously, I was dead wrong. What happened to you was hell. You're the only one who can possibly know the emotional cost involved."

He really did look sorry for what he'd said. All things considered—he'd stayed with her every moment in the hospital, brought her to his home to recover—she supposed she could bend a little and accept his apology.

Besides, she was leaving the *castello* soon. Surely, under those circumstances, it was simple good manners to forgive a man who was willing to admit he was a jerk.

"I didn't mean to hurt you," he said softly. "You must know that I'd never do that."

Their eyes met and held.

No, Fallon thought, he wouldn't. He'd meant well and if she were to be brutally honest, he'd given her advice she knew, in her heart, she needed to take. Wallowing in self-pity, hiding from the world, wasn't going to change the past any more than it would help move her into the future.

Stefano reached out a hand, as if to touch her. Then he pulled it back and cleared his throat.

"I'll leave you alone now. But if you change your mind, if you want company or someone to talk to..." He smiled. "Or if you'd like a target to throw things at, all you have to do is—"

"You were right."

She knew she'd blurted the words in one quick rush,

but how else could she have gotten them out of her mouth?

''What?''

Fallon swallowed hard. ''I said, you were right.'' She looked at the floor, at her feet, anywhere but at his face. ''I've been drowning in self-pity.''

''No,'' he said quickly. ''That's not true. I was wrong to imply it. I only meant—''

''Self-pity. And denial.'' Fallon took a deep breath and looked up. ''I keep thinking, if I hadn't been on that road, if it hadn't started to rain...'' She caught her bottom lip, worried it between her teeth. ''I know that thinking that way is a waste of time.''

''It isn't, when it's a part of healing. That's what I overlooked.''

She smiled a little. ''When I was little, I broke my arm riding my brother's bike. It was a dumb thing to do—the bike was much too big for me and I knew it. Afterward, when I found out I'd have to wear a cast for almost the entire summer, I moaned and groaned and finally my mother said, *Fallon, my girl, if you'd put half the energy into getting on with things as you're putting into regretting them, you'd be a whole lot happier.*''

Stefano grinned. ''Are you sure your mother isn't Italian? That's pretty much the same speech my grandmother made when I ran home crying because Mr. Rienzi caught me stealing a water pistol from his store and boxed my ears.''

''You? A thief?'' She smiled again. ''I'd never have believed it!''

''Hey, it was the price of initiation into the Mott Street Mohicans.''

''The Mott Street...?''

Fallon laughed. Really laughed, and the sound went straight through him, from the top of his head to the tips of his toes. So far, he could count on one hand the number of times he'd seen her laugh since the accident. What he wanted, more than anything, was to hear that sweet sound, see her eyes light, all the time.

"Uh-huh. What can I tell you? It was summer, we'd been playing cops and robbers and I'd already blown my allowance on candy and comic books. How can a cop catch a robber without a gun?"

"Plus, swiping a toy was a rite of passage?"

"I think getting your ears boxed and your backside warmed was the actual rite of passage."

They both smiled this time, and then Fallon's smile wavered.

"The thing is, my mother would probably have told me exactly what you did this afternoon. I need to look ahead, not back."

"I'm glad to hear you say that," Stefano said softly. He moved closer, reached out and tucked her hair behind her ear.

"I wasn't angry at you, I was angry at myself. You—you've been wonderful. Kind and generous and compassionate." Her lips curved in a smile. "Not alliterative, but true."

He smiled, too, and slipped his arms around her.

"You're a remarkable woman, Fallon O'Connell."

Fallon's eyes blurred with tears. "I'm not," she said, shaking her head as she leaned against him. "I'm a mope."

Stefano chuckled. "If you are, you're a beautiful mope."

"Please don't lie to me, Stefano. I know what I look like."

He bent his head and pressed a kiss into the silkiness of her dark hair.

"Then you know that your eyes are the color of the sea," he said softly, "that your mouth is as pink and soft as the petals of a rose." He framed her face with his hands and raised it to his. "And you know that the woman you really are is as whole as she was before that accident, and that she's more lovely than any man deserves.''

His words swept through her like sweet fire. She met his eyes, and when his gaze dropped to her mouth, she sighed his name and parted her lips as he kissed her.

His arms tightened around her, brought her tightly against his body so that she could feel the hardness of his erection. Desire quickened her heartbeat; she said his name again and wound her arms around his neck.

''Fallon,'' he whispered against her mouth, ''Fallon, *belissima.*''

He kissed her again, and she began to tremble, stunned with the intensity of her need. She'd never felt this way in the arms of a lover, never wanted to give this much, to take this much. The realization terrified her; she stiffened and pulled back.

''I can't. Stefano, I'm sorry. I—I—''

She could almost see him fighting for self-control. At last, he smiled and leaned his forehead against hers.

''Do you know that we've never been out on a date?''

''A date?''

''You know. I bring flowers, we go to a special place for supper, we drink champagne, dance in the moonlight...'' He smiled, reached behind his neck, caught her wrists and brought her hands between them, to his chest. ''A date, Fallon.''

Her heart gave a kick. She wasn't ready to face the world. Not yet. Oh, not yet!

''Bella signorina,'' he said solemnly. ''Would you do me the honor of coming out with me tonight?''

''Stefano.'' Fallon slicked the tip of her tongue across her bottom lip. ''I know it's the right thing to do. Going out in public, I mean, but—''

He brought her hands to his mouth, kissed first one and then the other.

''And I know the perfect place. A terrace in a beautiful garden, and just beyond it, a cliff that overlooks the sea.''

"Do you mean...here? At the *castello?*"

He kissed her, his mouth moving gently over hers. "The volcano has been restless all week. If we're lucky, she might light the darkness for us tonight."

Fallon smiled. "I'd be honored to have supper with you, *signore.*"

"Seven o'clock, then. I'll be waiting."

She lifted her face to his and when he kissed her this time, she thought that surely the earth must have moved under her feet.

At six, Fallon was standing beside her bed, staring unhappily at the clothing tossed across it.

She'd put everything away, hung the dresses and pants neatly on hangers, folded the shirts and shorts and stacked them on the shelves...and then she'd pulled all of it out again, outfit by outfit, held dresses and blouses and pants against herself as she stared into the mirror and said no, no, no.

Fallon sighed and sank down on the edge of the bed. She'd been on a lot of dates. She knew what to wear to a foreign film at a funky little theater in the Village and how to dress for late supper at the newest bistro. And this was only a dinner at home.

No, it wasn't. This was dinner at a castle, with a man who made her feel things she'd never felt before.

What was the dress code for that?

A summer dress and high heels? A long skirt with a halter top? Sweats and sneakers? She wanted to look right. To make Stefano's eyes light when he saw her. To somehow make him go on thinking she was still beautiful, still desirable...

A light knock sounded at the sitting room door. Fallon rose to her feet, smoothed back her hair and hurried to open it.

"Signorina? Sono Anna."

"Yes, Anna. I didn't ring for any—"

"Scusi," Anna said importantly and pushed a small cart laden with glass vases past Fallon and into the bedroom.

"Scusi," the impassive Luigi mumbled, following on Anna's heels, his arms filled with long, white florists' boxes.

"Excuse *me,*" Fallon said in bewilderment. "What is all this?"

"Fiori," Anna said. *"Fiori, tutti per voi."*

Sicilian or Italian, whichever it was, the meaning was clear. Flowers. Flowers, all for her.

"*All* of them?" Fallon said, waving her hands.

She watched, stunned, as Luigi opened the boxes and Anna emptied them of their beautiful contents. Yellow roses. Red roses. Black tulips, pale lavender orchids, white hyacinths, purple violets and blue pansies, even an assortment of wildflowers. Anna bustled from sitting room to bathroom to bedroom, filling the vases with water, then with flowers, and arranging them on every available surface.

At last, she smiled at Fallon and handed her a small ivory envelope. She made a shooing motion at Luigi, who dipped his head.

"Signorina," he said politely.

The door swung shut, and Fallon was alone.

She turned in a slow circle, staring at the flowers that filled the sitting room. She went into the bedroom and stared some more.

Then she opened the envelope, took out the note card and read it.

I wanted to send you flowers, but I didn't know which were your favorites.

Scrawled beneath the message was Stefano's signature.

Fallon picked up the yellow roses and buried her face in their soft petals. She'd never had a favorite flower but from now all of these would be.

Smiling even as her eyes filled with tears, she went to the bedroom closet and took out the only garment she'd left hanging in it. Her racing heart told her it was the one thing, the only thing that would complement this night.

CHAPTER EIGHT

BY SIX-FORTY, Stefano had paced his bedroom and sitting room so many times he was surprised he hadn't worn a hole in the carpet.

At six forty-five, he decided that if he checked his watch again he'd probably rip it off his wrist and hurl it at the wall. Better to check the mirror, run his hands through his hair…

Basta!

He was behaving like a schoolboy.

Briskly, he shut off the light and went down the stairs to the terrace.

Yes. This was better. He could breathe easier out here, where day was already giving way to night. The sky had taken on a delicate translucency; the sea seemed touched with tendrils of gold, and the omnipresent trails of molten lava that flowed down the face of Mount Etna were as bright as ribbons of fire.

Anna had set the terrace table with the *castello's* finest linens, flatware and china. A serving cart stood to the side, laden with covered platters and bowls; a bottle of Cristal champagne stood chilling in a bucket. Everything was ready for the evening.

Everything but him.

He was pacing again, this time back and forth along the terrace. He couldn't recall being so on edge before. He was cool under fire in business; it went without saying he was relaxed in his dealings with women.

People said *il lupo solo* had nerves of steel.

All true…but not tonight.

What if Fallon had changed her mind about accepting his apology?

What if she'd decided against joining him for dinner?

What if she laughed at all those flowers?

He'd never intended to send so many when he phoned the florist.

"I want a dozen yellow roses," he'd said, imagining the color against the ebony of her hair, and then he'd thought, but what if she doesn't like yellow roses?

So he'd ordered red ones, too. And black tulips, to show her that even in somberness there was beauty. And pansies, because Fallon was as down-to-earth as she was elegant, and orchids and hyacinths and now he could only wonder if she was upstairs laughing at him, or staring in the mirror, telling herself she'd made a mistake in agreeing to spend the evening with him at all.

Stefano checked his watch again. It was five after seven. If she didn't show up soon, he was going to take the steps two at a time, push open her door, tell her that he was going crazy and it was all her fault—

"Hello."

He swung toward the terrace doors and felt his heart stand still. Fallon was standing there, a smile trembling on her lips, and she was every dream a man could imagine come to life.

He'd dressed in a tux for the evening. He'd only wanted to create the right setting for her reentry into the world. It hadn't mattered to him what she wore, jeans or a gown.

She'd chosen to wear a gown, a long, slender length of silk that clung to her body, its color a green as deep and pure as her eyes. Her hair was loose, a straight fall of sable into which she'd tucked one delicate yellow rosebud.

"Hello," he said, although he had to clear his throat to get the word out, but maybe it was all right because her smile steadied and she started toward him on impossibly high stiletto heels. He tried not to think about her wearing those heels, that smile, the yellow rose and nothing else.

"I'm sorry I'm late."

Stefano shook his head, moved toward her and reached for her hand.

"*Mia bella,*" he said huskily, "how beautiful you are!"

Fallon put her hand in his. "So are you."

He laughed, grateful for the reprieve.

"I've been called many things, but 'beautiful' isn't one of them." He kissed her knuckles, her palm, then tucked her hand into the crook of his arm. "I'm glad you liked the yellow roses."

"All the flowers are wonderful. My rooms look like a garden."

His face felt warm. Was he blushing?

"Well," he said, "I didn't know which ones you'd prefer."

"All of them. It was the loveliest gift anyone's ever given me." She looked up and smiled again. "Thank you."

He looked into her eyes, at her mouth, and wanted to kiss her. Just a light kiss, a way of saying it had been his pleasure to send the flowers, but her scent teased his nostrils, a strand of her hair brushed his cheek, and he felt his body turn hard.

Now he understood why he'd been so edgy all afternoon, why he'd snapped at Anna when she'd asked a simple question about dessert, why he'd snapped at Luigi over an equally simple question about the car, why he'd gone down to the beach and swum far into the sea—farther than he knew was wise—before swimming back to shore.

He wanted Fallon.

That was what this night was all about.

He wanted her in a way he'd never wanted a woman before. He looked into her face, saw both the scars that marked it and the beauty that defined it, and imagined how it would feel to move over her and watch her eyes darken with pleasure as he filled her.

The truth was that this night was less about luring her back into the world than it was about luring her into his bed, and if that didn't qualify him to be the self-serving SOB she'd said he was, it came damned close.

"Stefano?"

He blinked at the soft tone of inquiry, brought his eyes back to focus on her.

"Is something wrong?"

Yes. Something was very wrong. She made him feel things he didn't understand. More than hunger. More than desire.

"No," he said, and cleared his throat, "but there will be, if we let Anna's meal get cold." He slid his arm around her waist, drew her against him and lowered his voice to a stage whisper. "She's thrilled you're dining with me tonight."

A wash of pale pink rose in Fallon's cheeks.

"So am I," she said softly, and the need Stefano felt for her pounded through his blood.

He opened the Cristal and poured it into Baccarat flutes. He served Anna's paper-thin smoked tuna, her *caponata,* the grilled lamb and what she said was a Sicilian specialty, *pasta con le sarde.*

The tuna was like silk, the *caponata* a heavenly mingling of tomato, aubergine and olives. The lamb was delicious and the pasta with fresh sardines dazzled Fallon's taste buds with hints of the sea and of the fennel that grew everywhere on Sicily.

But she managed only a bite of each.

How could she eat when her heart felt lodged in her throat? When Stefano was so gorgeous, so masculine, so funny, so wonderful?

It was a warm night and, after asking her if it was okay

with her, he'd discarded his tie, his jacket, undone the top couple of buttons of his shirt and rolled back his cuffs.

As handsome as he'd been in his tux, he was even more handsome this way. Dark and dangerous and sexy, she thought, and felt her pulse accelerate.

They talked of the New York they both loved, of Sicily, of places they'd seen in their travels. He told her about buying back the land that the *castello* was built on; when he described the elderly Sicilians who'd owned it, he lapsed into a really awful imitation of Marlon Brando doing Vito Corleone, and she burst into giggles.

Stefano's eyes darkened.

"I love the way you laugh," he said, and she thought how long it was since she'd felt so happy. Not just since the accident, she realized, but long before that.

She hadn't felt this filled with life in a very long time.

"Tell me about *Castello Lucchesi,*" she said. "About your grandfather."

He shrugged his shoulders, leaned back in his seat and sipped his wine.

"I loved him," he said simply. "He was tough and hard, like this island, and as giving and generous as its people."

"And you built the castle for him."

She said it so simply that he knew she understood.

"Yes. I built it for him. I only wish he'd lived long enough to see it."

Impulsively, she reached for his hand. His fingers closed tightly around hers.

"I'll tell you the story someday. For now, let's just say that revenge can become a way of life for some people." He smiled and squeezed her hand again. "Your turn. Tell me about you."

She said there wasn't much to tell, yet somehow, a quarter of an hour later, she was still talking, telling him about her family, the years spent growing up and moving from place to place while her father searched for ways to make the roll of the dice and the turn of a card pay off.

She told him things she'd never told anyone, how gawky she'd felt in high school when she shot up to five-ten and all the other girls, even her sisters, were inches shorter.

"Height impaired," Stefano said, straight-faced.

He grinned and so did she, and that made her laugh all over again and when she did, he thought how incredible it was to see her laugh so many times in one wonderful evening.

"Meg and Bree caught up, eventually," Fallon said, and suddenly she knew she couldn't manage the pretence much longer. She wanted to be in Stefano's arms, to feel his mouth on hers, and if he didn't touch her soon, she was going to make a fool of herself by throwing herself at a man who was interested in being kind, not in being her lover.

God, what was she thinking?

Fallon sat up straight, put down her fork and touched her mouth with her napkin.

"Well," she said briskly, "it's getting late."

Was it? Yes, Stefano thought in surprise, it must be. A while ago, he'd lit the tall white tapers that stood in the center of the table and the tiny lights strung among the trees in the garden had come on. To the west, the blackness of the night was broken only by the faint lights of scattered houses and by the rivers of fire that streaked the breast of the volcano.

Speakers, hidden in the garden, sent the softest possible music into the flower-scented night.

Beautiful, all of it, but not as beautiful as Fallon.

She was getting to her feet. He didn't want her to go. But she was probably tired. All this—the meal, though neither of them had eaten much; the wine; even the night air must have exhausted her…

Stefano stood up.

''Don't go.'' She looked at him, her eyes wide and shining, and he felt a fist close around his heart. ''You can't leave until we've had our dance. Remember? I asked you to have supper with me and to go dancing.''

''I know, but here…?''

''Here. Right here. Right now.'' His voice had taken on a note of command and then it softened. ''Please,'' he said, and opened his arms.

He saw the little lift of her breasts and knew she'd caught her breath. Would she turn him down? If she did, he'd be a gentleman and let her go.

The hell with that. He hadn't made a fortune by being a gentleman. If she said no, he'd pull her into his arms, bring her soft body against his, stroke his hands over her until she sighed and said yes to dancing with him, yes to making love with him, yes, yes, yes…

''Yes,'' Fallon whispered, and went into his arms.

He held her close. Put one hand at the base of her spine, curved the other around the nape of her neck, under the lush mantle of her hair. She was tall, taller than ever in those incredible shoes, and that was good because it meant when he brought her head against him, her face tucked just against his shoulder and he felt the warm sigh of her breath against his throat.

Stefano put his lips against her hair. He'd held her before but never like this, with her body pressed against the full length of his, her breasts soft against the hardness of his chest, her long legs molded to his.

He shut his eyes. The music was slow and soft and he began moving to it, holding her close, inhaling her fragrance, feeling himself grow aroused at the sway of her body against his. He wanted her so badly it was agony, feeling her against him, but he didn't want to push her into something she didn't want or wasn't ready for, and he almost laughed as he wondered what the world would think of *il lupo solo* right now, cautious and unsure for the first time in his life.

One kiss, he thought. One taste, and then Fallon whispered his name on a sigh. Stefano looked down into her face, saw eyes that were dark and filled with desire, a mouth that trembled in anticipation of his kiss, and he forgot everything but this woman and this night and what his heart told him they'd both wanted from the first time they'd met.

He bent his head, took her mouth. Her lips parted, opened to his, and he groaned, angled his head, slanted his mouth over hers again and feasted on her taste. She made a little sound, the breathless whisper a woman makes in the moment of her surrender, and he gave up thinking.

His hands skimmed over her, molding her breasts, toying with the tight, erect nipples. Fallon's head fell back and he nipped at her bared throat, kissed the hollow where her pulse raced as rapidly as his.

"Tell me what you want," he whispered, and she cupped his face, brought his mouth to hers.

She didn't answer. For a long, agonizing minute he thought he'd made a mistake, that he wanted her so badly he'd fooled himself into thinking she felt the same way.

Then a tremor went through her and she brought his mouth down to hers.

"You," she said fiercely. "Only you."

He bunched her gown in his hands, pushed it to her hips, thrust one leg between hers and almost lost himself when she cried out and moved against his thigh.

He cupped her bottom, groaned when he felt her warm, naked flesh. She was wearing a thong; the thought of how she must look in the wisp of silk almost drove him to his knees. He slid one hand between her thighs, cupped her mons, felt the heat and wetness of her against his palm and knew he was close to the edge.

Quickly, he scooped her into his arms. She kissed his throat as he carried her up the stairs; when he reached his bedroom, he shouldered the door open, kicked it shut behind him and took her to the bed, setting her down beside it, letting her slide down his body until her feet touched the floor.

"I don't want to hurt you. If it's too much, if you want me to stop—"

She put her hand over his mouth. "I'm not made of glass."

"I know. But—"

She kissed him, her mouth soft and warm. Then she stepped back, her eyes never leaving his, and reached behind her for the zipper that went down the back of her gown.

Stefano caught her shoulders.

"Let me do that," he said in a thick voice.

She lifted her hair and turned her back to him. Slowly, he drew down the zipper, kissing every inch of her spine as he uncovered it. Then he slid down the thin shoulder straps and, in a whisper of silken sibilance, the green silk floated to the floor.

He drew her back against him. She was almost naked now, braless, wearing only the thong and the stiletto heels. He shut his eyes, cupped her breasts, groaned as he felt her nipples thrust against his palms.

"Fallon," he said, and turned her toward him.

God, she was exquisite. High breasts, a slender waist, gently curved hips and legs that went on forever.

And her face, her beautiful, elegant face with its fine bones, chiseled features and on them, the cruel reminders of how close he'd come to losing her before he'd had the chance to know her any place but in his dreams.

"Don't look at me like that," she said, her voice shaking. "My face—"

He caught her wrists as she began lifting her hands, circled them with one hand and clamped them against his chest.

"I want all of you," he said fiercely. "Do you understand? I want everything you were, everything you are, everything you will be.'' He lowered his head toward her, holding her eyes with his. ''I'll give you everything I am, in return. Tell me you agree to that, *bellisima,* because it's the only way it can be for us.''

He waited, wondering if he'd pushed too far, demanded too much. Her eyes filled with tears and he thought he had, but before he could gather her close, tell her he would accept whatever she could give, she lifted her mouth to his and kissed him.

Stefano tore off his clothes and dug a small packet from the drawer in the night table. Then he lifted Fallon into his arms and came down with her in the center of the bed.

Slowly, he took off her shoes, pausing to kiss her delicately arched feet, her toes. He kissed her mouth, her breasts, her belly. She moaned and arched toward him and he peeled the thong away so that she lay before him naked, vulnerable, and he knew that he would never want another woman after this night.

He kissed her thighs, her labia, kissed the budding flower hidden there as she sobbed his name. She reached down to stop him but he caught her hands, held them at her sides, kissed and licked until she arched beneath him again and came.

He gathered her to him then, held her, soothed her, kissed her mouth and told her how wonderful she was.

''Stefano,'' she said, ''Stefano, please…''

''Yes, *cara,*'' he whispered, and he drew back, parted her thighs and on one long, hard thrust, sheathed himself deep inside her. Fallon cried out his name and he watched with fierce pleasure as another orgasm tore through her. Then she reached up and touched his face, and that gentle caress was his undoing.

Stefano groaned, let go and went with her.

Fallon awoke with a start.

An arm, heavy and possessive, lay curled around her waist; there was a leg draped over hers. Stefano's arm.

Stefano's leg. She was in his room, in his bed. Smiling, she let her head fall back against his shoulder. She must have fallen asleep in his arms.

Something rumbled in the distance. Thunder, she thought, and snuggled closer. Lightning, too; every now and then, it pierced the blackness of the bedroom. Maybe it would rain. She liked rain, and the thought of waking to it in Stefano's arms was…

"Mmm," Stefano said, and wrapped both arms around her.

Fallon touched her hand to his face. His jaw was soft with stubble; she gave a little laugh when he caught the tip of her finger gently between his teeth.

"Hey! That hurts."

"It doesn't."

"It could have."

"Well, it's what you get for waking me. Have you no pity for a man on the brink of collapse?"

She wiggled a little, felt the quick surge of his erection against her belly and reveled in the knowledge that she could do that to him with such ease. It made her feel reckless and bold.

"For a man on the brink of collapse, you seem pretty sturdy to me, *signore*."

"Mmm," he said again, and kissed her, his mouth sleep-warm and sweet against hers.

Fallon gave herself up to the kiss. Then she sighed and buried her face against his shoulder.

"It's going to rain," she said softly.

Stefano groaned. "Just what I need. An impossible weather report in the middle of the night."

"I thought it never rains on Sicily this time of year."

"That's why it's impossible."

"Then why do I hear thunder? There's lightning, too. Back home, that means—"

"You heard thunder? And saw lightning?"

"Yes. Can't you?"

He could, now. Hear the muffled roar, see the sudden sizzle of flame that lit the darkness.

Stefano chuckled, tunneled his fingers into Fallon's hair and kissed the tip of her nose.

"It's obvious you aren't Sicilian, sweetheart. If you were, you'd know that isn't a storm heading toward us."

"Of course it is."

"It's the volcano."

"What?" Fallon shot up in bed, automatically clutching the top sheet to her breasts. "You mean, it's erupting?"

"Etna's been erupting for years." Stefano reached for her. "Come back. I need you in my arms."

"But what's that hitting the windows?"

"Ash, mostly. Maybe some small bits of hardened lava."

Fallon gave a little shriek, forgot about blankets and modesty and ran to the window.

"I've never seen a volcano erupt!"

Stefano rolled his eyes and sat up. He had seen it before. Besides, what he really wanted to see right now was Fallon as he made love to her.

She swung toward him, her face lit by a sudden explosion of flame. Her hair was wild; her eyes were bright with excitement.

She looked like a goddess.

"Stefano, don't you want to come and see this? It's incredible!"

Yes, he thought, and felt his heart turn over, oh, yes, it was.

He reached for his discarded trousers, pulled them on, then jerked the blanket from the bed, went to the window and wrapped her in it.

"Oh," she said, blushing, and he laughed when he realized she'd forgotten she was wearing only her skin and thought that he was covering her because of it.

"Oh, indeed," he said.

He swung her into his arms, kissed her and strode toward the door.

"What are you doing? Stefano, where are we going?"

"You can see the fireworks better from the garden."

"Let me get dressed, then. We can't—"

"We can," he said firmly, and silenced her with another kiss.

It was a perfect night for watching the volcano. The sky was shot with stars and their cold white brilliance formed a backdrop for the hot crimson lava.

Stefano sat in a lounge chair hidden in a stand of flowering hedges, settled Fallon in his lap and pulled the blanket over them both. She leaned back against him, oohing and aahing at the light show.

"Look," she said, "oh, isn't it beautiful?"

"Beautiful," he agreed, even though he couldn't think about anything but the feel of Fallon's skin against his, the silken pressure of her breasts in his palms.

But she was right; the sight was spectacular and Etna was being a lady this night, filling the sky with fire, not danger, and after a while he caught Fallon's excitement, shifted her in his arms so that he could press his cheek against hers and watch the show.

After a while, Fallon gave a little hum of distress.

"What's the matter?"

"I just thought…what if Anna wakes up?"

"What if she does?"

"Well, she might come out here. To watch, like we are. And she might see—"

Stefano grinned. "See what? You, naked in my lap?"

"I'm not naked," she said primly, which was stupid, she knew, because she *was* naked under the blanket, and Stefano's hands were on her breasts.

Oh, the feel of his hands. The faint abrasion of his thumbs, the stroke of his fingertips…

"Where do you live in New York?"

"On Greene Street, in Soho."

"Lots of traffic in Soho."

"So?" She giggled at the unintended pun. "I mean, so what?"

Stefano bit lightly at her neck. "So, I'll bet the traffic doesn't wake you."

"Well, no. But—"

"It's the same thing. The volcano is part of life here. Anna's probably still snoring."

"What about Luigi?"

"What about him? He has an apartment above the garage and the only thing he's ever said about the volcano is that it's a pain in the…behind."

"Well, how about the security—"

Stefano said something in Sicilian, kissed Fallon to silence and told her the only person she had to worry about was him because the feel of her naked bottom shifting as she gestured toward the house and garage was having a predictable effect.

She went still in his arms. He was right. She could feel the ridge of his erection pressing against her.

Suddenly, the fire in the sky was nothing compared to the fire pooling low in her belly.

What had happened tonight had been beyond her wildest dreams. She hadn't planned on letting it happen but once Stefano had kissed her, had told her he wanted her, she couldn't have turned back for anything in the world.

And she wanted him again.

Slowly, deliberately, she turned in his arms until she was facing him. Her lashes dropped over her eyes; she parted her lips and licked them.

"What predictable effect, *signore?*" she murmured.

Stefano growled her name, cupped her face in his hands and took her mouth in a kiss so hot and hungry she moaned.

"You're a witch," he said huskily. "A beautiful, seductive witch."

She kissed him again, snaked the tip of her tongue into his mouth.

"You're playing with fire, *cara.*"

She knew she was, but what was the point in playing it safe? She wanted this moment, this man, wanted him now, here, while the sky burned with fire, and she put her mouth to his ear, bit the lobe...

Stefano shuddered, reached between them, told her what he was going to do to her in explicit language even as he freed himself and surged into her. Fallon cried out and flung her head back, rode him, drove them both higher and higher until their mutual release was as hot as the lava flowing down the mountain.

"Stefano," she sobbed as she collapsed against him, "I've never...it's never been like this before. Never, never..."

He held her, rocked her, stroked her and kissed her as she trembled in his arms. After a while, she quieted; she sighed and drifted into sleep. Still he sat holding her, his face turned to the volcano, and knew that its fiery display was far less powerful than the truth that scorched his heart, his mind, his soul.

He was in love with Fallon.

CHAPTER NINE

FALLON lay on a rattan recliner beside the pool, protected from the sun by a beach umbrella as she basked in the afternoon heat.

She had on a floppy-brimmed hat, sunglasses, a thong bikini and what felt like a ton of sunscreen. Bees buzzed softly in the flowering shrubs that shielded the pool from the house. The sound suited her drowsy mood.

Sighing, she opened one eye, looked up at the sun and decided it was time to turn onto her belly. It was probably the most work she'd done in the couple of hours since she'd come outside and left Stefano to catch up with work in his study, maybe even the most she'd done since they'd become lovers two weeks ago.

Stefano definitely spoiled her.

"I can do that," she'd told him a while ago when he knelt beside her and smoothed sunscreen lotion over her skin.

"I'll do it, *cara.* You know what the doctor said about the dangers of too much sun."

She'd made a face and rolled her eyes and protested that, honestly, he didn't have to fuss over her all the time.

What a lie!

The truth was, she loved having him fuss over her. There was something wonderful in your lover treating you as if you were precious to him.

No man had ever given her that feeling before.

Her lovers had given her expensive gifts, taken her to

clubs where lesser mortals waited behind velvet ropes, showed her off like a glittering trophy.

Stefano had given her flowers, taken her into the privacy of his home, and showed her off to nobody. Their relationship was private and meant for no eyes but their own.

"You're so good to me," she'd murmured as he stroked the lotion over her skin.

His hands had stilled. He turned her over and when she looked into his face, she saw that tight, almost predatory expression on it that she knew meant he wanted her.

"Stefano," she'd murmured, lifting her arms to him, and they'd made love while the breeze sighed and the bees hummed and the water lapped softly against the edge of the pool.

"I'll never have enough of you," he'd whispered afterward, as he lay with his face buried in her throat.

Her arms had tightened around him. She would never have enough of him, either, she'd thought, and struggled not to let the enormity of what she felt for Stefano Lucchesi spill from her lips.

She loved him. Loved him desperately, passionately, in all the June-moon, love-and-marriage ways she'd scoffed at. She'd known it for days. For weeks. And denied it, because the realization was so terrifying.

What if he didn't love her?

She tried not to think about it. She was on a hiatus from reality. So was he. He'd told her as much, lying here with her in his arms a while ago.

He'd made a joke of it, laughed and said his people were half-convinced he'd lost his mind because he'd never stayed away from his office anywhere near this long before.

Then his eyes had become dark.

"Sooner or later, *cara,*" he'd said, "we'll both have to go back to the real world."

Fallon felt a coldness creep over her despite the heat

of the Sicilian sun. She knew he was telling her that they'd cocooned themselves in a fantasy world.

He was right. She couldn't expect him to stay here forever. And she couldn't go on hiding much longer, either. The night of the accident, Stefano had phoned the inn where the photo crew was staying. He'd left a message with the manager in Fallon's name, simply saying she'd decided to tack on some vacation time and wouldn't be heading home with them.

Fallon smiled.

Even then, he'd been protective of her.

Once she'd left the hospital, she'd called her mother, told her she'd decided to take a few weeks' vacation. Mary Elizabeth bought the story but when she tried the same ruse on her agent, things hadn't gone as well. Jackie was a New Yorker, born and bred; smokescreens never stopped her.

"Bull," Jackie told her bluntly. "You don't do long vacations, O'Connell, and we both know it. What's going on?"

Nothing, Fallon had insisted. She was tired, that was all, and she needed a rest. After a while, Jackie said yeah, okay, when she was ready to tell her what was going on, she'd be ready to listen.

Fallon rolled onto her belly and rested her face on her arms.

Lying to Jackie had been an act of plain cowardice. It wasn't as if she was playing for time until her face healed enough for her to face the camera again. She'd *never* let herself be photographed again. Her scars would fade a little more with time but basically, what she saw in the mirror now was as good as it was going to get.

Modeling, Jackie, that whole life were already history.

But she wasn't ready to deal with peoples' reactions to her. Her mother's anguish. Her siblings' sympathy. The thinly veiled looks of horror from her business associates, the blood-in-the-water feeding frenzy of the tabloids.

She was safe from all of that here. And happy. Happier than she'd ever been in her life, despite the accident. She'd never known such peace and joy as she'd found in this quiet place with a man who'd been a stranger less than a month ago.

Now she understood what she'd seen in her brother's face the day of his wedding. Keir had stripped his soul bare for Cassie. That was what being in love was all about. Your lover could show you heaven with a kiss or send you to hell with a careless word. She'd never been in love but she'd seen what happened to others.

Crossing Fifty-seventh Street wearing a blindfold back home was less dangerous than falling in love.

She was careful not to say "I love you" to Stefano, though the words were always on her lips.

Maybe he'd say them first.

Maybe she'd awaken one morning in his arms and he'd tell her what she yearned to hear, that he adored her, wanted her, needed her…

"Hey."

Stefano's soft voice and warm breath were at her ear. Fallon turned over and smiled.

"Hey yourself." She snaked her arms around his neck and brought his mouth to hers. "Did you get a lot of work finished?"

"Uh-huh." Stefano sat down on the edge of the lounger and gathered her into his arms. He'd changed into a swimsuit and his skin carried the coolness of the high-ceilinged rooms inside the *castello*. "And you? Did you get a lot of resting done?"

Fallon grinned. "Any more resting and I'll turn into a sloth and start hanging, upside down, from the branches of the nearest tree." She ran her hands over his muscled chest. "Mmm. My own personal air conditioner. Very nice."

"I'm glad you approve." Smiling, he ran his hands

down her arms. "You're as toasty as a fire on a winter afternoon."

"Sicilian sun will do it, every time."

"You smell delicious, too," he said, nuzzling her hair aside and kissing her throat. "What are you wearing?"

Fallon batted her lashes. "An exclusive fragrance, *signore. Eau de Sunscreen.*"

"*Eau de Woman,*" Stefano said, laughing as he kissed her mouth again. His hands skimmed over her back, around her ribs and cupped her breasts. "You should take this suit off, *cara,* and get an all-over tan."

Fallon caught her breath as he rubbed his thumbs over her nipples.

"An all-over tan, huh?"

"Yes." Stefano reached behind her and undid the bra's clasp. "All in the interests of good health, of course."

"Of course. Your suggestion couldn't possibly have anything to do with—" her breath caught as he bent and kissed her naked flesh "—with getting me out of my clothes."

His laugh was low and incredibly sexy. "And it worked."

"Brilliantly," Fallon whispered as she lifted her hips so he could slip off the tiny thong that covered her. "Your turn," she said, and cupped the hardness of his arousal.

Seconds later, they were both naked and Stefano was deep inside her, and the scents and sighs of their love-making drifted languidly on the warm, sea-scented air.

Afterward, sated, they lay quietly in each other's arms.

"We should go in," Fallon said lazily.

"Mmm." Stefano gathered her closer. "Soon."

"I have to shower."

"Mmm."

She sighed, closed her eyes and snuggled against him. "Want to go for a walk on the beach?"

Stefano ran his hand up and down her back in long, soothing strokes.

"Too much effort."

She smiled, her lips curving against his throat. "How about me beating you at Scrabble again?"

"You only beat me because you refuse to let me use perfectly acceptable words."

"'Qat' and 'zuz' are not words, acceptable or otherwise."

Stefano laughed, rolled onto his back and drew her on top of him.

"You're just ticked off because I took you to the cleaners playing poker last night."

"The least you could have done was told me that was how you'd made your first stake," Fallon said, trying to sound indignant and failing. It was difficult to sound indignant when you were pressed, naked, against your lover's sexy body and his hands were gently cupping your bottom.

"I did tell you."

"Uh-huh. After I'd lost the game. You took advantage of me, Lucchesi."

Stefano worked at looking wounded. "How about some credit here? We could have been playing strip poker."

"As if I'd have agreed to that," Fallon said haughtily, and spoiled the act by nipping at his bottom lip. "Actually, that sounds like fun."

"Only because you owe me a hundred trillion *lire*."

They both grinned. Stefano thought, as he did a dozen times each day, how happy it made him to see her smile. Would she still be smiling after he told her what he had in mind?

"Actually," he said, clearing his throat, "I thought we'd try something different this evening."

Fallon folded her arms on his chest. "Strip Scrabble?"

He smiled, took a strand of her hair and wrapped it around his finger.

"That's tempting, *cara,* but I thought we'd drive into Catania for an early supper."

She became stiff in his arms. "What for?"

"I told you," he said patiently, "for an early supper. And I thought you might like to see the shops. There are some little galleries near the harbor—"

"I'm not in the mood for shopping."

"In that case, we'll just go in for supper. I made reservations at a little café on the water—"

"No, thank you."

Fallon tried to roll away from him. Stefano expected it and tightened his arms around her.

"Don't turn away from me, *cara.*"

"I'm getting up, that's all. The sun—"

"The café won't be crowded early on a weekday evening."

"How nice," she said politely.

"A quiet meal, some wine—"

"I said no."

"Fallon." He tilted her face to his. "You have to face the world sometime."

"And what a wonderful way of putting it that is."

Her tone was bitter but he wasn't going to let himself be drawn into an argument, not when he'd just spent an hour making calls to New York, dragging his top people out of late dinners and early beds, trying his damnedest to deal with a problem without flying back and handling it in person.

His attempts had been useless. He had to go back, and there wasn't a way in hell he'd do that before he settled things here.

"You can do this," he said softly. "And you won't be alone. I'll be with you."

She swung her legs off the recliner and this time, he let her go. She rose, grabbed an oversize towel from the table beside them and wrapped it around her body.

"I'm not going with you. I can't make it any clearer than that."

"You *are* going. I can't make it any clearer than that."

Her eyes flashed. "I don't take orders from you or anybody else."

Stefano sat up, reached for a towel and wrapped it around his hips. Hell, what a mess he was making of things.

"Let's start again," he said carefully. "I don't want to quarrel over this."

Fallon nodded. "No." Her voice was very low; he had to strain to hear it. "Neither do I."

"Good." He forced a smile to his lips as he stood up and cupped her shoulders. "*Cara.* Come to Catania and have supper with me. I know a little restaurant I'm sure you'll like."

"I'm sure I would, too," she said, her smile as false as his, "but I don't feel like having dinner out. *You* go. I'll have supper here."

Stefano glared at her. So much for trying again. He'd forgotten that she could be as stubborn as she was beautiful.

"Don't be ridiculous."

"I'm being practical. You must be going stir-crazy, never going anywhere, never seeing anyone, never doing anything except—"

"This isn't about me going out and you know it."

Fallon flashed a bright smile. "Really, I won't mind. A host doesn't have to feel housebound just because his guest—"

He cursed, not in Sicilian but in English as pithy as only a man raised in New York could. His fingers bit into her shoulders.

"That's crap. You're not my guest."

"All right. Maybe that's a little formal."

"And I'm sure as hell not your host. I'm the man who—"

Who what? He stared at her blankly. This was hardly the time to tell her he loved her. Declarations of love deserved the softness of moonlight and the scent of roses, not a sun hot enough to be lethal and the smell of chlorine.

Besides, he'd promised himself not to say anything until he was sure she was ready to hear it. In a handful of weeks, Fallon had dealt with a horrendous accident that had changed her life. He wanted to give her time to be whole again.

And he didn't want her to confuse her feelings for him with gratitude.

Now, he'd almost ruined everything, almost blurted out the most important message of his life with no finesse, no planning, no—

"The man who—?" she said softly. "Who what?"

He felt a muscle jump in his jaw. "Who can't imagine going anywhere without you. Come with me, sweetheart. It'll be all right, I promise."

It was the closest he'd come to saying he loved her. How could she turn him down? Fallon took a deep breath and went into his arms.

Once again, Stefano waited on the terrace. Once again, he paced it from end to end.

He'd paced his own bedroom, too, the one he now shared with Fallon, and the sitting room attached to it, staring at the bathroom door each time he walked by, wondering what she could be doing in there that could take so long and telling himself that it was none of his business.

He knew women. They had little rites of passage they followed before going out in public. Face, hair, nails. He didn't mind that. He was just afraid Fallon was frozen before the mirror, trying to hide a face that didn't need hiding.

He thought about knocking on the door and telling her

that. Then he thought better of it and that was when he headed downstairs to the terrace.

"Stefano?"

He swung around and saw the most beautiful woman in the world step through the door.

Fallon was wearing a short dress in some kind of gauzy material. It had little straps and a short skirt that showed off her legs. She'd pulled her hair back from the unscarred side of her face and let the rest of it dip over her temple and cheek in a delicate fall that softened the scars without hiding them.

It was a brave thing, a wonderful thing, and he felt a rush of love so fierce it terrified him. Thinking you were in love was one thing; knowing it, giving away your heart, was another and he knew, in that moment, that was exactly what he'd done.

What would the world think of *il lupo solo* now? he wondered, and the thought made him smile.

"Do I look all right?" Fallon lifted her hand to her hair, danced her fingers over the glossy black wing that kissed her cheek. "I figured, if we're going to do this, we might as well do it right."

"You look beautiful, *cara,*" he said, going to her and drawing her into his arms. "More beautiful than you can possibly know." He kissed her, a long, tender kiss that deepened as she rested her hands on his chest and responded to it. "Just keep that thought," he whispered. "Okay? *We're* doing this. Together."

She smiled as he took her hand in his.

"I'm scared silly," she said. "I couldn't do this without you."

He grinned and kissed her again. "I don't want you doing anything without me," he said, and he put his arm around her waist and walked her to the car.

Stefano was right.

There were some wonderful shops near the harbor.

Fallon dragged him into half a dozen of them, oohing and aahing over everything she saw.

She was self-conscious at first but after a while, she lost herself in the fun of the shopping expedition and she forgot to wonder whether anyone was staring at her or, worse still, looking at her with pity in their eyes.

"I have to buy presents for my family," she told Stefano. He knew their names by now and a little bit about them, and he trooped after her good-naturedly as she selected beribboned tambourines for Meg and Bree, good luck charms carved from lava for Cullen and Sean, and a beautiful terra-cotta bowl for her mother and stepfather.

Fallon paused in the last shop. Something caught her eye. It was the figure of a knight, dressed in armor. Was it a puppet?

"Those are marionettes, *signorina,*" the salesclerk said, leaning in and following her gaze. "All made by hand. Marionettes date far back in the history of the Sicilian people. Would you like to see them?"

Only one, Fallon thought, and looked at Stefano. He was leaning against a counter, arms filled with packages, ankles crossed, wearing the polite smile and glazed look of a man who'd long ago tuned out.

"Stefano." She touched his chest and he blinked and smiled into her eyes, and she thought, as she had thought a hundred times in the past hour, how much she adored him…

And how much she'd hoped that what he'd been going to say, this afternoon, was that he was the man who loved her.

"Yes, *cara.* Do you see something you like?"

"Why don't you wait for me outside? I know it's crowded in here."

He glanced at the door and the street like a man granted a reprieve.

"No," he said valiantly, "I'm fine."

"And so am I," she said softly. "I am. Really. I can do this myself."

He bent his head and gave her a long, sweet kiss. The salesclerk cleared her throat; Fallon blushed and Stefano grinned, then sauntered out the door. As soon as he was gone, Fallon pointed to the marionette dressed in a knight's regalia.

"That one," she said, and had it gift-wrapped for her very own knight, who had taken her to live in his castle.

The little café was as charming as Stefano had promised.

They sat at a table overlooking the water. Fallon took one look at the menu and gave up.

"You order," she told Stefano.

Their meal was delicious; the wine warm and strong.

"It's a little rough," Stefano said, "but it's local."

"It's real," Fallon said. "That's good. Things that are real are what matter most."

Stefano reached for her hand and brought it to his lips.

"You're an incredible woman," he said softly.

She shook her head. "I've taken all my strength from you. I'm glad you didn't let me stay home and feel sorry for myself."

"*Cara.* I didn't mean—"

He felt her hand tighten in his. Her face had paled and at the same moment he realized she'd forgotten about her scars, that she'd somehow pushed her hair back behind her ear, he realized she was staring past him.

He looked around, ready to take on the world…and saw a man and woman seated at the next table with a little girl, four or five years old. The child was staring at Fallon, her eyes rounded with fascination; the father had hold of her arm and was talking to her in a low, urgent whisper.

No, Stefano thought, *please, no…*

Too late.

"Mommy," the kid said in perfect American English, "Daddy, what happened to that lady's face?"

The woman paled. The man compressed his lips into an angry line.

"Hush," he said sharply.

Stefano's hand tightened on Fallon's and almost crushed it, but she reached down into a part of herself she hadn't known existed, took a deep breath and said, in a voice that carried as clearly as a bell, that it was all right, children were naturally honest.

"I had an accident," she added. Her eyes met Stefano's. "But I'm all better now."

Stefano dropped a handful of bills on the table. He put his arm around Fallon as they left the café and walked slowly through the warm night to his car. She wasn't quite as unaffected by what had happened as she'd seemed; he could feel her trembling.

"You were wonderful," he said softly.

She gave a tremulous laugh. "She was just a child. I didn't want her to be frightened."

They reached the car. Stefano had driven it himself; he closed the door after Fallon, got behind the wheel and reached for her hand.

"I repeat," he said softly, "you're an amazing woman, Fallon O'Connell."

Her heart was still thumping. Facing the little girl and everyone else in the café had been hard, but she was happy she'd done it.

She knew she couldn't have, without Stefano.

"You're pretty amazing yourself," she said with a little smile. She thought of the marionette and her smile broadened. "My knight in shining armor."

Stefano gathered her into his arms. "I'm no knight, *cara,* I'm only a man." He hesitated. "And, like any man, I've been avoiding telling you something unpleasant."

Her smile tilted. "What is it?"

He lifted her chin and brushed his lips over hers.

"I spent most of the morning on the phone with New York."

"And?"

"And, an important deal's gone sour. I'd hoped to work things out but—"

Fallon worked at holding her smile. "But, you have to fly back."

"Yes. There's no way around it. I wish there were."

She nodded. "I understand."

Stefano linked his hands in the small of her back. "I'd much rather stay here than go to New York. You know that."

She nodded again, wondering how long he'd be gone, imagining herself walking the beach like an old-time sea captain's wife, staring out to sea while she waited for her man to return.

It didn't sound appealing. She didn't want to be without Stefano, and she couldn't really see herself with nothing to do but wile away time until he returned.

"I'll count the days until—"

"No," he said softly.

"No?" she repeated, uncertainty in her voice.

"You can't wait here for me." Stefano took a breath, then expelled it. "I won't be able to get back to Sicily for months."

Fallon stared at him. People said your life flashed before your eyes when you were drowning, but it wasn't true. She was drowning now and all she could think of was that she had to get through these next moments without losing whatever remained of her pride.

"Oh. Well. Well..." She put her hands on his chest. "Well, I think—I think you misunderstood me. I meant—I meant, of course I'll miss you but we'll see each other again sometime, and—"

"*Cara.* Are you crazy?" His voice was gruff. "Why do you make everything so damned complicated?" He kissed her, hard, and when she tried to jerk her face away, he wouldn't let her. "Did you really think these few weeks together would be enough? I want you to come to

New York with me.'' He took a deep breath. ''Stop looking at me as if you don't understand what I'm saying, *cara.* I want you to live with me and share my life.'' His eyes darkened. ''If that isn't what you want, too, tell me now.''

What could she tell him that wouldn't lay her soul bare? Fallon made a sound that was half laugh, half sob, lifted her face to Stefano's and kissed him. With a growl, he took control of the kiss, taking it deep, putting his hands on her with an urgency that set her on fire. She made a little sound of surrender; he nipped at her lip and soothed the tiny wound with his tongue. She whimpered when he broke the kiss and leaned his forehead against hers.

''Another minute,'' he said with rough urgency, ''and I'll take you right here.''

His words, the images they conjured, made her breath catch. She whispered his name and lay her hand against him, shuddering at the powerful surge of his erection.

Stefano growled a word in Sicilian, curled his fingers around the nape of her neck and kissed her again. Then he took her hand, enclosed it in his around the gearshift lever, took her back to the *castello,* to his bed, to the world they had created together, and to a passion so intense it threatened to consume them both.

CHAPTER TEN

SOMETHING changed between them that night.

Their lovemaking, always passionate, took on added intensity. Their need for each other was insatiable.

They had to get up early, Stefano said; he'd arranged for his jet to be ready by 8:00 a.m. But they were on fire for each other and even when they drowsed off, Fallon lay close in Stefano's arms, their bodies still joined.

She awoke, again and again, to the incredible feel of his hands and mouth urging her to join in a celebration of their ardor.

"Is it too much for you, *cara?*" he whispered to her once, when she caught her breath.

"Never," she whispered back, "oh, never."

It was true. She couldn't get enough of him. She wanted his touch, his taste, his hard body demanding her compliance. The way he held her as they slept, his arm curved over her waist, his hand cupping her breast, were gestures of pure male possessiveness.

She belonged to him. And that was how she wanted it.

The realization amazed her. She'd never wanted to be owned by anybody. Watching her parents' relationship, the way her mother had always subjugated her needs to her father's, had been a bitter lesson.

But when Stefano held her to him, even as they slept, when he kissed her mouth, her breasts, the very heart of her femininity and whispered that she was his, she felt ecstasy, not fear.

He belonged to her in that same way.

It was why she told him to lie back, why she kissed his throat, his chest, his belly. It was the reason she took him in her mouth during that long night and thrilled to his groans of passion.

She'd never done this with another man, but Stefano was hers, she was his, and she wanted to become one with him as he had become one with her.

At dawn, warm and boneless as a cat, she lay quietly in his arms, her head on his shoulder.

"Do you realize I don't know anything about you?"

Stefano gave a soft, wicked chuckle that made her smile.

"You know what I mean."

He took her hand and brought it to his mouth. "What would you like to know?"

"Well, tell me about the *castello.* What happened to the old castle? Why did you build a new one?"

"It's a long, boring story."

Fallon rolled onto her belly, crossed her arms on his chest and propped her chin on her wrists.

"Tell me."

He stroked her hair, took her back through the centuries and described the pirates, warriors and rebels who'd tried to conquer this land. He told her about his grandfather and the promise he'd made to recover what the old man had lost.

"How did he lose it?"

Stefano smiled. "It's like the plot of a bad opera."

His grandfather's and grandmother's families were old enemies, their troubles going so far back that nobody was sure of the reasons. Somehow, his grandparents met and fell in love anyway. They eloped, and the long-simmering feud burst into flames. People had accidents, disappeared… Eventually, his grandfather decided the only way to protect his wife and children was to abandon his land and start over in America.

"Did he ever regret that decision?"

"Never. A man does what he must for love."

It was a romantic reply but then, the story was wonderfully romantic. Snuggling closer, Fallon asked Stefano to tell her more about himself.

To please her, he talked about things he'd never mentioned to anyone else. The loss of his parents. The initial shock of living with his grandparents. That first stroke of financial luck.

Genius, she said, not luck.

"Or maybe stupidity," he said, laughing, "I could have lost every dollar I'd won."

"But you didn't."

"No. I struck it rich." He rolled her beneath him. "Like I did when I found you."

She smiled. "Flattery will get you everywhere," she said in a teasing whisper.

Stefano gave her a deep, lingering kiss. "You realize," he said softly, "you've ruined my image."

Fallon looked up at him and stroked the dark hair back from his forehead.

"What image?"

"One of the tabloids dubbed me *Il lupo solo*. The lone wolf."

"Mmm." Fallon wound her arms around his neck. "Nice. I've always thought it would be exciting to pet a wolf."

That made him smile. "I'm glad to hear it."

"Why do they call you that?"

"Oh, it started when I was foolish enough to give an interview. The reporter began asking personal questions. I refused to answer them." His tone hardened. "I have a public persona because it's required of me, but my private life isn't for public scrutiny."

"I know how you feel. I've never had a private life. Well, not once I began modeling…"

"Don't," Stefano said quickly. "Please, don't think about the past. The future is what matters."

She nodded and closed her eyes as he began to kiss her. She *was* thinking about the future, but why tell him that? He'd have enough to deal with, now that they were going home. She knew she'd draw attention.

People would talk about her. Her scars didn't matter, Stefano said, but in Sicily, their world had excluded everyone but themselves.

It would be different in New York.

She thought of what had happened in the café. The child had been direct. People back home wouldn't be. They'd smile to her face and whisper behind her back.

"Cara."

Fallon opened her eyes and saw the consternation in Stefano's face. He ran his hand down her body, his touch as protective as it was tender.

"I'll be with you. I'll look after you."

"I know you will, but..." Fallon framed his face with her hands. "They'll be all over you, Stefano. The press, I mean. A man who values his privacy won't enjoy having cameras and microphones shoved in his face."

He smiled, but she could see the steely resolve in the set of his jaw.

"Don't worry about me. I can take care of myself."

She nodded, but she wasn't convinced. For the first time since he'd asked her to live with him when they reached New York, she wondered if she'd agreed too quickly. The tabloids would be drawn to her, not to him. If she moved back into her own apartment, if they saw each other on the quiet...

"Forget that," Stefano growled. "I'm not letting you go."

He saw the surprised look on her face, but reading her mind had been easy. She was afraid of what she'd face back home and wondering if she could avoid attention by staying under the radar.

He wasn't going to let her do that.

He needed her, wanted her in his life, and that realization still stunned him. He'd never needed anyone before. Now, knowing what it was like to be with her, he wasn't going to let Fallon slip away from him.

He'd never understood people who thrived on gossip but he knew damned well there were those who did. That anyone would be interested in telling stories about him always amazed him.

He could only imagine the dirty thrill the jackals would have in talking about Fallon.

Stefano tightened his arms around her.

He'd take care of everything. A couple of calls from his attorneys, the all-too-real threat of an expensive lawsuit, and the sleaze purveyors would back off.

Besides, he'd be with Fallon all the time.

She had nothing to fear.

He would protect her, he promised himself, and then he kissed her, and touched her, and he forgot everything but his growing love for the woman in his arms.

Stefano said he had an apartment on Fifth Avenue.

Fallon laughed when she saw it. Calling a four bedroom, six bathroom duplex with two fireplaces, a sauna and a wraparound terrace overlooking Central Park an "apartment" was like calling the *castello* a cottage.

It was beautiful, she told him, just beautiful.

"You think?" he said, in a way that suggested he'd been wary of her reaction.

"I know! It's incredible. And the view..."

"Yeah." His grin reminded her of a kid on Christmas morning. "That's the real reason I bought the place." He tossed his keys on a small table near the door. "I had a decorator do the rooms but, I don't know, sometimes I think it still needs something."

Fallon was miles ahead of him. Fresh flowers. Some small paintings—the ones she'd found in a French antique shop, for instance—above that couch. Her Chinese rug centered on the marble floor, and those masks she'd picked up in Bali on that wall.

"I have—" She cleared her throat. Funny. She'd been sleeping with this man for weeks; she knew every inch of his body just as he knew every inch of hers, yet suggesting bringing some of her things here and adding them to his seemed almost too personal. "I have some—some stuff," she said, trying to sound casual. "Things I collected in places I've been, and I thought..."

Thought what? Stefano was looking at her so strangely. Maybe she'd gone too far.

"You thought?" he said politely.

"Never mind. It was a silly idea. I mean, this place is so perfect..."

"Tell me what you thought," he said, gathering her into his arms.

"Well..." She played with his tie. "I thought you might like to see how some of my things looked—"

"Here?"

She nodded. Stefano tilted her face up and kissed her.

"They'll look wonderful."

"But you haven't even seen them."

"I don't have to. Give up your own place. Move all your things here. You don't need an apartment of your own anymore."

She longed to do it, but logic held her back. Had he really thought about how different life was going to be in New York?

"Let's take things one step at a time," she said carefully. "I mean... This isn't Sicily, Stefano. We had our own world then. Just you and me, and nobody else."

He silenced her with a kiss. "It's still just us. Nobody else matters."

"You've spent your life running from the press, Stefano. I've spent mine dealing with it. They're going to be merciless. They'll want to invade my privacy. *Your* privacy."

"I'll take care of the press," he said grimly.

Fallon touched the tip of her tongue to her top lip. "Maybe. But even if you do, people will talk. They'll have questions."

"Mr. Lucchesi?"

It was Stefano's housekeeper. She'd been good at disguising her reaction to Fallon's scars, but Fallon had seen the quick flash of recognition, then shock followed by a look of pity in the woman's eyes.

"Sir, Miss Allen is here."

A woman came briskly across the marble floor toward them.

"Stefano. I'm sorry to bother you so soon after your arrival, but—" Her voice faltered as she looked at Fallon. There it was again. Recognition. Shock. Pity, intermingled in a way that made Fallon's belly knot. "But some documents came in and they're urgent."

Stefano nodded and introduced Fallon to his PA, but the papers had distracted him and Fallon knew he'd missed the woman's reaction.

"You're going to be busy, Stefano," Fallon said politely. "Why don't I wait on the terrace?"

"Don't go." Stefano glanced up, slid his arm around her waist and drew her against him. "I'll only be a minute." He kissed her lightly and walked a few feet away.

Fallon thought his assistant's eyebrows would fly off her face.

"Um, don't I... Have we met before, Miss O'Connell?"

"You might have seen my picture," Fallon said calmly. "I am—I was—a model."

"Oh. Oh, of course. I knew... I mean, I recognized..."

They stared at each other in strained silence. *Yes,* Fallon wanted to say, *it's me. And yes, my face was cut. And yes, your boss wants me anyway...*

But she said nothing and, after a moment, Stefano rejoined them.

''Well,'' the PA said briskly, ''if you don't need me, sir... Oh. One other thing. You have that Animal Defense Fund dinner tonight.''

Stefano glanced at Fallon. ''Phone and make my apologies.''

''But they're honoring you with—''

''Tell them I'm sorry but something's come up.''

''No.'' Fallon spoke quietly, her words meant only for Stefano. ''Please, don't cancel on my account.''

''It's your first night home,'' he said softly. ''I'm not going to leave you.''

''But the dinner. The award—''

''They'll muddle through without me,'' he said, and smiled.

Fallon took a deep breath. When she was seven and Meg and Bree, Cullen, Sean and Keir could all swim like seals, she was still afraid to do more than dip one foot in the water. Her mother said she'd had a scare when she was little, something about wading into a lake and everybody thinking somebody else was watching her, and how she'd stepped into deep water, gone under and almost drowned.

''You'll get over the fear,'' Mary Elizabeth had said gently.

Fallon had. She'd done it by closing her eyes, holding her nose and jumping into the deep end of the pool at the chintzy motel where they'd been living.

Yes, she'd swallowed half the pool and yes, she might have drowned, but she hadn't. She'd survived, learned to swim, and learned a hard lesson.

When you were afraid, the best cure was to shut your eyes, hold your breath and jump.

''I'll go with you,'' she told Stefano.

''It isn't necessary. One step at a time, remember?''

''I want to go with you,'' Fallon said, and when she saw how his eyes lit with pleasure, she almost believed that she'd meant it.

After all, people were civilized. She could handle stares and Stefano could handle the rest. How bad could it be?

Bad.

Horrible, to put it bluntly.

Less than a month later, Sicily had receded so far into the distance that it might have been a dream.

To Fallon's surprise, reporters weren't the problem she'd anticipated. Word got out; they came around, but never more than once. She was certain Stefano had done something to keep them at bay. Only a couple of lines hit the gossip columns and, just to be on the safe side, she phoned her mother and told her she'd been in an accident, in case the news spread.

Mary was upset and wanted to fly to New York. Fallon lied, said her injuries were nothing much and promised to come home for a visit over Labor Day weekend. As luck would have it, the rest of her family were out of the country, on business or on vacation, so she didn't have to worry about fooling them.

On the surface, they seemed to have weathered the storm. They hadn't. The problem wasn't publicity.

It was Stefano, and what she was beginning to see in his eyes.

Not shock, of course. He was used to her scars.

What she saw was pity. That same gut-wrenching pity she saw in the eyes of others.

Her lover had a busy public life. A king might want privacy, but kingdoms weren't ruled from the shadows. The city slumbered in end-of-summer heat, which meant that life had moved east to the Hamptons.

Benefits, charity auctions, dinner parties. Invitations poured in and each time he received one, Stefano would tell her about it and say, with an air of studied casualness, *Do you want to go, sweetheart?* And she'd think "no" and say "yes," because she was determined not to change the way he lived.

Fallon had grown accustomed to the changes to her face and years of applying makeup had paid off. She could cover the scars so that they didn't show very much, at least from a distance.

Up close, things were different.

They'd go to whatever function it was and Stefano would hold her hand and introduce her to everyone in a way that made her importance to him clear.

People always said it was nice to meet her and wasn't the weather hot and humid, and all the while she'd see the usual sequence of shocked recognition, horror and pity on their faces and always, *always,* she knew they were trying to figure out why Stefano would have burdened himself with a woman who looked like her.

And then she'd look at Stefano and know *he* knew what she was thinking, and sometimes he'd murmur, *Shall we leave, sweetheart?* and whenever he did, she'd smile and say *No, of course not, this is fun…*

He pitied her. What else could that darkness in his gaze mean?

A woman wanted many things from her lover. Passion, tenderness, fidelity and yes, compassion, but pity? Never.

The worst of it was, she understood what had happened. In Sicily, her face had been the only reality. Stefano could look past it and see her for the woman she was. In all fairness, she knew that he still could.

But for how long?

The women in Stefano's circle had perfect faces, if not through genes and nature then by the skilled hands of a surgeon.

She heard snatches of female conversation, references to this plastic surgeon or that; once, she walked into a ladies' room and overheard two women in adjoining stalls discussing the miracles performed by a certain doctor. Their voices were loud enough, their comments deliberate enough so she half suspected the information was meant for her.

She did think about seeing a surgeon—someone in the States might have a different technique for dealing with her scars than the doctor in Italy—but she wasn't ready for that. She wanted to get used to this new face, this real face, before she made any decisions about changing it.

God help her, she wanted Stefano to tell her he loved her, and to tell it to her while she still looked like this.

At night, she lay in his arms, knowing he was as wide-awake as she, wondering what he was thinking. She wanted to ask him, but she was afraid to. If she was right and that was pity she saw in his eyes, if he could no longer see beyond her scars…

No. She wouldn't think that way.

Maybe she had too much time on her hands. She'd worked hard all her adult life. She'd never sat around for so long without doing something productive.

One morning, after Stefano left for a meeting, she dressed in a Chanel suit and a pair of Jimmy Choo stiletto heels and went to her agent's office. She'd already spoken to Jackie and told her about the accident, but they had yet to see each other.

It was tough, walking into the agency, striding past the photos of all the perfect faces that adorned the walls—photos that still included hers—and tougher still to see the flash of compassion in Jackie's eyes when Fallon whipped off her oversize dark glasses.

"I need a job," Fallon said bluntly.

Compassion didn't keep Jackie from being blunt.

"I can't use you anymore. Your face—"

"I know everything about this business, Jackie. Surely, somebody can use me for something."

Jackie tossed her pen aside and sat back. "I'm an agent, not an employment office."

"But you know people. You hear things."

Her agent tapped a finger against her lip. "Well, yeah. Matter of fact, I had lunch with Carla Kennedy yesterday. Wasn't your last assignment with her?"

"Does Carla have a job I could handle?"

"She's looking for an assistant." Jackie smiled. "A gopher. Go for this, go for that... You know the drill. Lie to people she doesn't want to deal with when they phone, make barely enough money to pay your bills..." Jackie's grin widened. "Though from what I hear, paying bills isn't your problem. You've got somebody to do that."

Fallon rose to her feet. "Thanks for the tip," she said politely. "And by the way, I haven't 'got' anyone to pay my bills. I made a lot of money, Jackie. You should know that. You got fifteen percent right off the top but what the government didn't take in taxes, I saved."

"I only meant—"

Fallon didn't want to hear the rest. She left the office, made her way through the cramped waiting room packed with hopeful girls from little towns nobody had ever heard of and taxied straight to the offices of *Bridal Dreams* magazine.

She gave her name to the receptionist and didn't flinch when the girl's eyes widened after a glance at her face.

Carla came bustling out to the desk to greet her.

"Sweetie," she said, "oh, you poor baby. I just heard the news the other day... Oh, my God, your poor face! Darling, what are you going to do? Have you seen a plastic surgeon?"

"No," Fallon said briskly. "I heard you're looking for an assistant."

"I can get some names for you. There's this incredible guy who took, I swear, ten years off Irene Whitmore's face—"

"*Are* you looking for an assistant, Carla?"

"Yeah, but why would you care?" Carla's smile seemed to tighten. "I also heard you're having a thing with Stefano Lucchesi. Is it true?"

"I really didn't come here to talk about myself," Fallon said pleasantly. "About that assistant's job..."

"What about it?" Carla blinked. "You mean... You?

You're interested in…?'' Her voice dropped to a purr. ''Don't tell me your boyfriend isn't paying your bills, darling. He has scads of money.''

''The job,'' Fallon said coolly. ''Is there one or isn't there?''

Carla led Fallon into her crowded office, motioned her to a chair while she perched on the edge of her desk, swinging one long leg over the other.

''It's not a job for a prima donna.''

''I didn't think it was.''

''Three hundred a week,'' Carla said brusquely, ''half an hour for lunch, no medical, dental or anything else. Still interested?''

Fallon had earned more than that in ten minutes, but the money didn't matter. Feeling useful—not having endless time to brood and think foolish thoughts—did.

''Yes,'' she said, and held out her hand. Carla ignored it.

''Does your boyfriend know you're going to be working for me?''

''I haven't told him yet.''

Carla seemed to find that amusing. ''You're hired,'' she said, and smiled like a cat anticipating a mouse fillet.

Fallon waited a week before telling Stefano.

She had the feeling he wouldn't like her news. She kept thinking back to her second day in Sicily, to Carla taking a call on her cell phone and then staring up at the *castello* as if she'd seen a ghost before taking off in a rush. And there were the lies Carla had told about the owner of the castle.

What was all that about?

Why hadn't she ever asked Stefano?

Something had gone wrong in the deal he'd made with Carla and *Bridal Dreams,* but that was another thing she only now wondered about.

Why would a man who cherished his privacy give permission to a magazine to film on his property?

Things had happened too quickly to ask questions in Sicily, and now they were happening the same way. There was a rift growing between her and Stefano. Not a big one: he still held her through the night and they still made love with that same intensity, but the lazy ease between them had been replaced by an almost cautious politeness.

She waited to tell him about her job until they were spending a rare evening at home.

"Stefano." He looked up from a magazine and Fallon took a deep breath. "I've taken a job."

He gave her a puzzled smile. "A job?"

She nodded. "Yes. Last week."

His smile tilted. "You took a job last week and you're only now telling me?"

A flush rose in her cheeks. He saw it and could have bitten his tongue off but then he thought, no, why shouldn't he be irritated? Fallon was changing; she'd become more quiet, more reserved, and now she'd found a job and never thought to mention it? Was she so unhappy, living here with him?

"I'm working at *Bridal Dreams* magazine as Carla Kennedy's assistant."

He blinked. Surely, he'd heard that wrong. "I beg your pardon?"

"I said—"

"You're working for Carla?"

"Yes."

"Why?"

"Because she needed an assistant and offered me the job. That's why."

"She phoned, out of the clear blue sky, and offered a job to you?"

"No. Of course not."

"You approached her."

"Damn it, why the inquisition? Yes. I approached her."

"And you did this without telling me?"

"Yes."

Stefano tossed aside the magazine. What the hell was going on? Was the woman who'd been content walking the cliffs with him so bored with her new life that she'd gone to work for his former mistress?

It sounded like the setup for a bad joke. The woman he loved, working for the woman he'd slept with and discarded.

But Fallon didn't know that. Carla, on the other hand, was probably laughing her head off.

"Well, you're not going to work for her anymore." He spoke coolly, which surprised him because what he wanted to do was shout. "Call her in the morning and tell her you quit."

"Excuse me?"

"There's no reason for you to work, Fallon. If you need money—"

Her color deepened. "This isn't about money."

"It's my fault," he said, in tones he meant to be conciliatory. "I should have opened an account in your—"

"I do not need money from you, Stefano."

"There's nothing wrong in needing—"

"Damn it, are you deaf?" Fallon shot to her feet. "I'm perfectly capable of supporting myself."

"Then why did you take a job with Carla Kennedy?"

"I like to work. I *need* to work."

He nodded, as if he understood, but he didn't. She needed to work? Why? She had him in her life now. She could redecorate this mausoleum of an apartment. She could come to his office and meet him for lunch. She could do anything she wanted, just as long as it included him.

Fallon had changed since Sicily.

She moped, she didn't laugh, she insisted on going to the endless rounds of charity benefits he'd simply sent checks to in the past, and he'd be damned if he knew the reason when all he saw in her eyes once they arrived at a party was sorrow each time some insensitive idiot couldn't keep his eyes off her beautiful, wounded face.

"What am I to you, Stefano?" Fallon said quietly. "Tell me."

His tongue felt glued to the roof of his mouth. My heart, he thought. My beloved. But how could he admit that until she was ready to hear it? Until she accepted herself as she was? Until she was whole?

"You're my responsibility," he said carefully. "I want to take care of you, Fallon. Surely, you know that."

She nodded. It wasn't the answer she'd prayed for, but at least it was honest.

"I do know it. But *you* must know that it's important I begin taking care of myself again."

Damn it, if he wasn't careful he was going to drive her away. Stefano swallowed his bewilderment and his anger. He reached for Fallon and took her in his arms.

"*Cara,*" he said softly. "This is a foolish thing to argue over."

He felt her relax against him. "Yes. It is."

"If you want to work, you should. But not for Carla."

"Why not?"

He took a deep breath. "She's a liar. She's not someone to be trusted."

"How do you know that?"

She was, as always, incisive and persistent. He admired her for that even as he tried to figure out what to say. How did a man tell the woman he loved that he'd had an affair with a woman she knew? A woman she saw every day? He knew Fallon didn't think he'd lived like a monk, but still…

A man broke such news cautiously, that was how. And caution meant not making such an admission to a woman who was already angry at you.

"Carla and I had an agreement for that shoot at the *castello* and she reneged on it."

"I've been meaning to ask you about that. How come you let *Bridal Dreams* take photographs there to begin with?"

Stefano managed a wry smile. "Carla made me an offer I couldn't refuse."

"What offer?"

"Must we discuss this now?" he said impatiently. He slid his hands up her arms, then down again to her wrists. "If you must work, I'd prefer you to find another job. Will you do that?" He smiled and tipped her chin up. "For me?"

Fallon sighed. Stefano had done so much for her. Surely, she could do this for him.

"Will you? Please?"

"Yes. If it's what you want, Stefano, I will."

She leaned against him, loving the feel of him, the strength of him, and all at once she knew that what she really wanted to talk about had nothing to do with Carla.

"Tell me something," she said in a low voice. "How would you feel if—if I saw a plastic surgeon?"

His expression didn't change but it didn't have to. A stillness came over him. He glanced at her scars, his gaze quick and guilty.

"The decision would be yours," he said carefully. "I wouldn't want to influence you."

Fallon nodded. She wanted to weep but she didn't. What should he have said? That he saw past her scars? That what he'd told her in Sicily held true in New York? That he wanted her for who she was, not for who she had been?

Somehow, she forced a smile.

"Thank you," she said, "for being honest."

"I would never lie to you," Stefano said.

It wasn't true and he knew it. He lied each day, by not telling her that he loved her.

He'd lied just now, by not telling her he didn't want her to go under the surgeon's knife.

He'd lied by not telling her about Carla.

I'm contemptible, he thought fiercely. *The only time I don't lie to her is when we make love.*

He crushed her mouth beneath his until she clung to him and moaned his name. Then he carried her into his bedroom, and sought to expiate his guilt by making love to her through the long night.

CHAPTER ELEVEN

THE next morning, Stefano disappeared into his study before breakfast. When he emerged, he said he had to fly out of town but that he'd be back in time for dinner.

"Just us," he said, taking Fallon in his arms. "We'll have a quiet evening. Is that okay with you?"

It was wonderful. She'd have bartered her soul for more like it.

"Yes," she said, "it's very okay."

Stefano leaned his forehead against hers. "I'm sorry I flew off the handle last night. We shouldn't have quarreled."

"It was my fault." Fallon looped her arms around his neck. "I should have told you about my job."

Stefano gathered her against him, holding her close.

"There are things I should tell you, too." He went on holding her, as if he never wanted to let her go. Then he lifted her face to his and kissed her, his mouth gentle and warm against hers. "We need to talk," he said softly.

Fallon nodded. "Tonight."

"Tonight," he echoed.

He kissed her again. There was something in the kiss that frightened her, a kind of finality, but before she could ask him about it, he let go of her, slung his jacket over his shoulder and went out the door.

Fallon stood alone in the marble-floored foyer for a long moment. It was silly, reading meaning into a kiss when what she needed to concentrate on were things that were in her hands.

Quitting her job, for example. Carla wouldn't be happy—she'd turned out to be a short-tempered boss who expected things to be done when she snapped her fingers, and Fallon was in the middle of organizing her files. Well, she'd stay on for a week, if Carla insisted. Stefano was a businessman; he'd surely understand that.

And then—and then there was what she'd decided about surgery. She'd raised the issue, not Stefano, but she'd seen his reaction. Still, she'd come to the conclusion that she wasn't going to do it. Not yet. Not until she was sure she was doing it for herself and not for him.

She loved him—oh, how she wished she felt free to tell him that—but something so drastic had to be for her, not for anyone else.

Fallon drew a deep breath, expelled it, gave herself a last check in the mirror and headed out the door.

The *Bridal Dreams* offices were in total confusion.

Something had gone wrong with distribution in the Midwest, the colors of the current cover were completely off, and the designer Carla intended to feature in the May issue had just revealed she was really a he and was tired of being in the closet.

Carla ran around barking orders and accusing everyone, including the kid who brought lunch from the corner deli, of trying to destroy her.

Under those circumstances, Fallon didn't have the heart to drop the news that she was quitting.

Things quieted down in late afternoon and she stuck her head around the half-open door to Carla's office.

"Carla? Do you have a minute?"

"Barely," Carla said irritably. "I hope you've come to tell me you finished with those files."

"Not yet. It's a major overhaul and—"

"I don't need excuses, Fallon. Just do your job and let me know when you're done."

Fallon shut the door behind her and came into the office. Carla looked up, surprised, as she sat down on the other side of the desk.

"I came to tell you I'm quitting. I'll finish the files," she added quickly, "but you'll have to find someone else."

Carla sat back, her eyes narrowing as they fixed on Fallon.

"I should have expected it. You think you're too good for what you're doing."

"It isn't that."

"Give me a break!" Carla smiled coldly. "You're accustomed to having everyone fussing over you and here you are, squatting in front of a dusty file cabinet or trailing around after me. As I said, I should have known."

"I'm quitting for personal reasons, Carla. They have nothing to do with you."

"What personal reasons?"

"I don't see any need to go into them." Fallon stood up. "I thought it only fair to give you notice. If you need me to stay through the end of next week—"

"It's your boyfriend."

"What?" Fallon felt her cheeks flush. "No. Stefano has nothing to do with—"

"He doesn't like you working for me."

"I told you, he has—"

"You can't lie worth a damn, O'Connell." Carla hunched forward, a thin smile on her face. "What's the problem? Does he think this is beneath you? Is he afraid people might think he isn't supporting you properly?"

"I'm not going to discuss my personal life," Fallon said coldly. She turned and reached for the door. "As I said, if you need me to stay until—"

"Or does he worry that the woman he slept with a couple of months ago and the woman he's sleeping with now are liable to compare notes?"

Fallon felt the blood drain from her head. Her hand

froze on the doorknob. Turn around, she told herself, turn around and face her.

"Men are funny," Carla purred. "Always worried we'll share their little idiosyncrasies. Not that we would, darling. After all, we both know what a fantastic lover Stefano is—though I must admit, I have wondered if he plays the same little games with you as he did with me. Taking your hands, for example. Putting them—"

"Stop it!" Fallon whirled toward the other woman. "Just stop it right now."

"Why? It's the twenty-first century, Fallon. Women are free to talk about sex if they..." She paused, and a knowing smile curved her mouth. "Oh, my," she said softly. "You didn't know. Stefano didn't tell you. Here you are, working as my little gopher, and you had no idea I knew your lover as well as you do. Better, probably, considering all the months he and I were together."

Fallon stared at that cold, lovely face, the hateful smile and the venom-filled eyes. She told herself she was being ridiculous. Stefano wasn't a monk. Of course there'd been women in his life. There'd been men in hers. What did it matter?

Except it did matter. He should have told her. Instead, he'd snapped and snarled and told her lies.

Hadn't it occurred to him that if she found out about Carla—*when* she found out—it would be humiliating to hear the news from anyone but him?

"Do sit down," Carla said pleasantly, "before you pass out."

"Don't be ridiculous!"

"Well, you're white as a sheet. Sit down, darling." Carla laughed. "I know getting coffee is your job, but I'll pour you a cup, if you need it."

Fallon sank into the chair. "I'm fine."

"He really didn't tell you?"

Fallon shook her head. "No."

"Ah." Carla folded her arms and leaned back. "Well,

I suppose we can hardly blame him. I mean, it all happened so quickly, me ending our relationship, him getting involved with you…"

"You ended it?"

"Oh, of course. And Stefano was furious. Well, we'd been together six months. I suppose he assumed… Anyway, women don't walk out on men like him. That's what he thinks, anyway." Carla's voice turned syrup-sweet. "Are you sure you want to hear this?"

"I don't care one way or the other," Fallon said, lying through her teeth.

"Well, anyway, it's all water under the bridge." Carla sighed. "I knew he was liable to do something crazy. I mean, when I told him we were finished, he was so upset… Oh, darling. I don't meant to imply that taking up with you was crazy, just that, well, there he was, being vindictive, saying he wouldn't let me use the inside of his castle because I'd hurt him, then phoning me the second day of the shoot to say he was going to find a way to make me change my mind about walking out on him…"

Carla kept talking but Fallon had stopped listening. The phone call. The second day of the shoot. Carla, white-faced, turning to stare at the *castello,* then offering a sorry excuse and rushing back to New York.

It made terrible sense.

Stefano had taken up with her on the rebound. And he'd taken her to the same bed Carla had slept in.

Fallon lurched to her feet. "I'm sorry, Carla, but I have to leave early."

"I've upset you."

Bitch! That was the whole purpose of the conversation. Did Carla think she'd been born yesterday?

"No," Fallon said, and forced a quick smile, "you haven't." She dug deep and managed to turn the smile into a just-between-us grin. "Men are impossible. Why Stefano would think it would bother me if he told me that you and he had—that you'd been involved, is beyond me."

"You're right," Carla said blandly. She hesitated, then leaned forward. "Darling? Do you want the name of that surgeon I mentioned? I mean, I'm sure your face isn't a problem for you but, well, knowing Stefano..."

"Yes?" Fallon said coldly. "Knowing him, what?"

"Nothing. It's just that he's such a perfectionist."

"My face isn't a problem for him," Fallon said, even more coldly. "If that's what you're suggesting."

"Perhaps not directly but, um, people talk. Well, no matter. Stefano's shown you such enormous compassion..."

"He has, yes." Fallon stared at the other woman, knowing that the best way to strike at her was to go for the jugular. "Perhaps that's why he never mentioned his relationship with you to me, Carla. I don't think it left much of an impression on him."

She made her exit on that note. It was pathetic, the saddest excuse for victory in the world, but it was all she could manage.

Swiftly, Fallon collected her suit jacket, her purse and headed for the street. Stefano had said he'd be back by early evening. And that they had to talk. Good. She wanted to talk, too.

About relationships.

About integrity.

Fallon stepped off the curb, ignored the traffic whizzing past her toes and, in the time-honored way New Yorkers hailed cabs, lifted her hand. A taxi swung out of traffic, horns blared, and the vehicle stopped beside her.

She climbed in, gave the driver Stefano's address, then tapped her foot all the way there.

Stefano unlocked the front door, dumped his keys and his briefcase on the table.

He called out his housekeeper's name, then remembered it was her day off.

Just as well.

He'd gotten back to the city earlier than expected and really didn't feel like bothering with anyone right now, not even his housekeeper.

What he wanted was to strip off his clothes, take a long, cold shower, put on shorts and a T-shirt, mix a pitcher of Margaritas—Fallon liked Margaritas, he thought, smiling—and put it in the refrigerator to chill while he did some serious thinking before she got home.

Stefano dropped his clothes on a chair in the dressing room.

He'd better do some serious thinking. He'd already made a couple of really bad errors. First and most important, he should have already told Fallon that he loved her. He was as sure as a man dared be that she loved him, too.

If there was any danger in telling her how he felt, he'd be damned if he could see it anymore.

Stefano turned on the shower, stepped inside and let the side and overhead sprays pelt his knotted muscles. He was tired; he hadn't slept much last night, lying in bed thinking about how life could turn things upside down.

How the woman you wanted to spend the rest of your life with could end up working for a woman you never wanted to see again.

Hell.

That had been his second mistake. He should have taken a deep breath, looked Fallon straight in the eye last night and said, *I don't want you working for Carla because I had an affair with her.*

Instead, he'd chickened out. Said nothing. Done nothing. Breathed a sigh of relief that Carla hadn't been the vindictive bitch he'd have figured her for, and kept his mouth shut because he hadn't been able to think of a way to tell Fallon the truth.

He'd had an affair with Carla and ended it because it

was time for it to end. Carla hadn't meant a damned thing to him except, at the end, trouble.

Stefano turned the water off and reached for a towel.

Well, he wasn't going to screw up anymore. As soon as Fallon came through the door, he'd sit her down and tell her everything, starting with the fact that he loved her.

He smiled and wrapped the towel low on his hips, but his smile faded as he thought of the third thing he had to tell Fallon.

It was the reason he'd flown to Boston.

He had a college buddy there, a guy who'd become a physician and headed up a department of one of the country's most prestigious hospitals. Jeff was a cardio-thoracic surgeon. He literally held people's hearts in his hand. He was the best, and Stefano had figured he'd know only the best.

If Fallon wanted restorative surgery on her scars, only the best would do.

"How bad are the scars?" Jeff had asked him.

"Not bad enough for her to go under the knife," he'd answered, and Jeff's eyebrows had risen.

"So it's like that, huh?"

"Like what?"

Jeff had grinned. "Like you finally found the right woman."

Stefano hadn't bothered denying it. "Yes. Damned right I did, and why she wants this surgery is beyond me."

"Does she want it for herself?" Jeff said.

It had been Stefano's turn to raise his eyebrows. "Of course. Who else would she want it for?"

Jeff shrugged. "You, maybe. I mean, if she thinks—"

"I love her just as she is. She knows that. Look, she was a model. I thought she'd gotten past looking in the mirror and only seeing those scars, but I was wrong."

"Yeah, that happens. Okay, my man. I'll give you the names of two guys in New York."

"The best?"

Jeff grinned. "The absolute best. As long as the lady wants this for herself—"

"Of course, I'm going to try and talk her out of it."

"No, you won't."

"Sure I will. She caught me off guard, bringing the subject up last night, but I'm certainly not going to let her undergo surgery if… What?"

"Listen, I understand. You love the lady. You want to take care of her. But this is her face, Stefano, her life and her choice. Be there with her when she goes to see these men, discuss the pros and cons with her if she wants, maybe offer your opinion on which guy to go with if she asks, but don't try talking her into, or out of, anything."

"This is one hell of a major decision, Jeff. I can't just let her—"

"Yeah, pal. You can."

Stefano reached for his discarded trousers, dug into the pockets and took out the slip of paper on which Jeff had written the names and numbers of the surgeons he'd recommended.

Okay. Jeff was the doctor; he was just a man so much in love that he could hardly see straight. He'd play this whatever way Fallon wanted, and—

The front door opened, then slammed shut.

Stefano frowned. "Fallon?"

Yes, it was Fallon. He could hear the tap of her heels coming up the stairs. Quickly, he ran his hands through his damp hair. She was early. He hadn't had time to make the Margaritas or chill two glasses…

"Stefano."

He swung toward the bedroom door. He'd only been gone a few hours but seeing her reminded him of how he'd missed her.

"*Cara…*"

Whoa. That look on her face. Cold eyes, rigid posture. Trouble was coming, with a capital *T*.

"What's wrong?"

Fallon tossed her purse in the direction of the dresser. It landed on the carpet instead, but she made no move to pick it up. Neither, after another look at her eyes, did Stefano.

"Wrong? Why should anything be wrong?"

"Well, I don't know. You look—you look—"

"What? Angry? Furious?" She crossed her arms and glared at him. "How do I look, Stefano?"

"Upset," he said warily.

"Good guess."

"Sweetheart." He cleared his throat. Something had gone wrong. *Carla,* he thought instantly, and started toward Fallon. "Does this have anything to do with—with what we talked about last night?"

"As I recall, we didn't talk about anything last night. Correction. I talked. You danced."

He paused a couple of feet away. "Danced?" he said, even more warily. "I don't understand."

"Oh, it's simple. I talked. I asked questions. You danced around them. Why should I quit my job? Why shouldn't I work for Carla? Because you wanted it that way, that was why."

Fallon could feel her pulse racing. All the way here, she'd imagined what she'd say to Stefano. She hadn't really sorted out the words but she'd reached one sure conclusion.

She wouldn't cry. Wouldn't tell him how humiliating it had been, learning about him and Carla the way she had. Wouldn't tell him that it killed her, *killed* her, to know he'd made love to Carla in that same bed in the *castello* where he'd made love to her, in the same bed here in his apartment, that Carla had walked out on him and her leaving had angered him so much that he'd become vengeful and taken another woman on the rebound.

"You son of a bitch," she said, and all her good intentions flew out the window. "Why didn't you tell me you'd been Carla's lover?"

"*Cara.* Sweetheart—"

"Do not 'cara' me. Do not 'sweetheart' me! Do you know what it was like, hearing about your affair from her?" Fallon rushed forward and slammed her hands against Stefano's chest. "How would you like it if you were at a meeting and the man you were doing business with leaned over, smirked and said, 'I used to sleep with Fallon O'Connell.'"

"I'd kill him," Stefano said darkly.

"Ha!"

She hit him again and Stefano caught her wrists.

"Listen," he said, "I know I should have told you."

"She walked out on you. That was why you wouldn't let us into that—that crypt you call a castle, why you spied on us while we worked. She walked out and you were miserably unhappy."

"I threw her out."

"So you claim."

"I threw her out, Fallon. I wouldn't let any of your crew into the *castello* because I'd never wanted to let Carla use it in the first place."

"Oh, please. As long as she was sleeping with you, you were happy to give her whatever she wanted, but when she broke up with you—"

Stefano's expression turned grim. "Is that what she says? It's a lie."

She wanted to believe him, oh, she wanted to, but he'd lied to her already. Why wouldn't he lie again?

"As for why I watched you work, I told you the reason." His hands tightened on her wrists. "I was watching *you.* Only you. That day at the airport changed everything. I saw you, I wanted you—"

"And you always get what you want. Isn't that how you view life?"

Stefano let go of her, spun on his heel and strode across the room. He muttered something his Sicilian grandmother would have erased with a mouthful of soap, then stalked toward Fallon again.

"I'm not going to fight with you," he said as calmly as he could. "I admit, I should have told you."

"Yes. You should have. If you lo— If you respected me, you'd have at least told me last night."

"You're right. I did a stupid thing." He hesitated. He had news that would make her happy, but how could he tell it to her when she was almost shaking with anger?

"Fallon."

"If you're going to try and sweet-talk your way out of this—"

"I'm not." He reached for her. She let him cup her shoulders but she wouldn't let him draw her to him. All right. He deserved what she was doing to him but that would all change in a minute. "Don't you want to know where I was today?"

"No."

So much for the easy lead-in. "I flew to Boston, to see an old friend."

"How nice for you. Did you sleep with her, too?"

"For God's sake, Fallon!" Stefano let go of her, took a steadying breath. "I'm trying to tell you something important. Something I know will make you happy."

That you love me, Fallon thought, so clearly, so distinctly, that for an instant she was afraid she'd spoken aloud. Because that was the only thing she wanted to hear, the only thing that could make what had happened today fade away.

That was what her anger was about, what everything was about. She needed to hear Stefano say, *I love you. I love you exactly as you are. I've never loved anyone else, never wanted anyone else, as I love you.*

"Sweetheart."

Her eyes met his. Something glittered in those deep brown depths, something she'd never seen there before. Her heart lurched. She felt as if she were going to do something really stupid, like faint or throw herself into his arms and say, *I know what you're going to tell me, Stefano, and I love you, too.*

"I have something for you," he said softly.

He reached into his pocket. Fallon's heart did an unsteady two-step. All her life, she'd thought stuff like marriage proposals and engagement rings were for other women. Now, she knew they were the most important things in the world, and what else could Stefano be taking from his pocket but a ring? What else would make him hold out his hand as if he were handing her the earth?

A piece of paper. That's what. A paper with a couple of names and phone numbers scrawled on it.

She took it, stared at it, then at him.

"I don't understand. What is this?"

He smiled, as if he were giving her not just the earth but the sun and the moon, too.

"The names of the two best plastic surgeons in New York. If anybody can make you look the way you once did, it's one of them."

He was smiling. He looked so happy. So smug. So certain he was handing her something that would solve all their problems.

"The way I once did?" she said in a papery whisper. "Like Fallon O'Connell, supermodel. Is that what you mean, Stefano?"

He nodded. She nodded, too. Then she tore the paper in half, dropped it at his feet as she walked out of the bedroom.

He called her name, shouted at her to come back, ran after her and reached for her, but she shrugged him off and kept on walking, out of his apartment and out of his life.

CHAPTER TWELVE

FALLON stepped from the elevator and almost ran through the lobby of Stefano's apartment building.

The doorman smiled and touched a finger to his hat. "Afternoon, Miss O'Connell. Do you want a—"

"No," Fallon said, and brushed past him.

Of course she wanted a taxi. She wanted a rocket to Mars, whatever would get her out of here fast, but if the doorman hailed a cab for her he'd be able to tell Stefano where she was going...

And she never wanted to see him again.

Never.

He'd ripped out her heart.

He'd let her traipse into Carla's office like a lamb going to slaughter and followed it up by making it crystal clear he was tired of playing the martyr. He wanted her to turn into Fallon O'Connell again, *the* Fallon O'Connell, and just in case the message wasn't clear enough, he'd gotten her the names of not one but two surgeons.

He'd probably expected her to throw herself into his arms with gratitude.

The stupid, insensitive, heartless son of a bitch!

All that nonsense about wanting her for herself, about seeing who she really was...

She reached the corner as the light turned red. Traffic ground through the clogged intersection; caught in the knot of impatient pedestrians on the sidewalk, Fallon choked back an angry sob.

She knew who she was. She was a woman with a

scarred face and a liar for a lover, and the sooner she took back control of her life—

''Fallon? Fallon!''

Fallon craned her neck and looked back. Stefano was running toward her. He looked upset and angry.

Angry? What did *he* have to be angry about?

The light was still red, cars were moving bumper to bumper, but she darted off the curb and dodged through them. Horns blared, drivers cursed.

Fallon didn't care.

All she wanted was to get away.

''Fallon,'' Stefano shouted, ''damn it, stop! Have you gone crazy?''

Maybe she *had* been crazy. Now, she was sane. She didn't want to see him, hear his lies, look into his eyes and know what a fool she'd been to have fallen in love with him.

Another intersection. Another red light—and an empty taxi, idling at the head of a long line of vehicles. Fallon dashed for the cab, pulled the door open and hurled herself inside.

''Drive,'' she gasped.

The cabbie shot her a look in the mirror. ''Where to?''

''Anywhere. Just get moving.''

She looked back. Stefano was halfway to the corner. He was panting, running hard, still shouting her name. People were staring at him, even blasé New Yorkers who'd long ago learned that the secret to survival was not to see anything you didn't want to see.

''Just go,'' she said urgently.

The light changed. The cabbie glanced in the mirror again.

''I don' wan' no trouble, miss.''

''No trouble. See that man? He's—he's my husband. I found him with another woman. I'll give you an extra twenty if he doesn't catch us.''

Stefano was almost at the cab. His face was red. "Fallon!" he yelled.

"Fifty dollars," she said desperately. "Fifty dollars to get me out of here."

The cabbie nodded, stepped on the gas and left Fifth Avenue and Stefano Lucchesi far behind.

Two blocks later, Fallon told the driver to take her to La Guardia airport.

Going to her apartment was out of the question. That was surely the first place Stefano would check. The airport was safer.

She was lucky. A flight to Vegas was about to board and yes, there was a seat left.

An hour into the flight, Fallon made three phone calls. One to her agent, one to Carla's office at *Bridal Dreams,* one to the concierge at her apartment building in Soho.

"Jackie?" she said, when her agent answered, "it's Fallon. In case you need me, I'll be in London for a week or so."

"Why would I need you?" Jackie asked in bewilderment, but Fallon had already broken the connection.

Next, she called Carla's office.

"In case Carla didn't mention it," Fallon told her secretary, "I quit."

The girl laughed. "So does anybody with half a brain. You want to pick up your check or should I mail it?"

"Actually, I'll be in San Francisco for a couple of weeks. I'll pick it up when I get back."

Setting up the final diversion was the simplest.

"Jason," she told the concierge in the building where she owned a condo, "it's Fallon O'Connell. I know, I know. Well, I've been—I've been away. And I'm going away again. Tokyo. Right. So if anyone should come looking for me… Thanks. That should do just fine."

She hung up the phone. The west coast, the Far East and the United Kingdom. Stefano would keep his minions busy for a while. By the time he figured out she really had no wish to see him again, his interest in finding her would have vanished.

The man was in the middle of a losing streak. Neither of his last two women had lasted very long, and both had walked out on him.

That, at least, was some satisfaction. But the truth was, sooner or later, he wouldn't even remember her.

Never mind.

Right now, she had to think about what she'd say to her mother when she reached Vegas.

Hi, Ma, here I am and oh, yes, my face is a mess, isn't it?

Hi, Ma, it's me and why would you think something was wrong just because I've turned up on your doorstep without so much as a toothbrush?

Fallon closed her eyes and leaned her head back. She'd offer a simple story. No details, no dramatics and above all, no tears.

Not one.

She thought it was an excellent plan until her mother opened the door to the O'Connell penthouse at the Desert Song Hotel and Casino, took one look at her and said, "Oh, Fallon. Oh, my darling girl..."

"Oh, Ma," Fallon sobbed, and flung herself into her mother's waiting arms.

A week later, Mary Elizabeth O'Connell Coyle and her husband, Dan, stood close together in their bedroom, whispering like children plotting.

"I don't know what to do with her," Mary said. "She's always been so logical, so focused. Now she stays in the guest room and hardly comes out."

"Well, the accident..."

"No, it's not that. What happened must have devastated her—God knows, it did me—but I can tell that she's come to grips with the scars. It's something else, an ache inside her that goes deeper than the wounds left by the accident.''

''I don't understand.''

''She mentioned a man's name when she came here last week. She said he was a particularly persistent reporter and if he phoned, I was to say I had no idea where she was.''

''Well, that makes sense. Those vermin would sell their own mothers for a buck.''

''No, this is different. She got this sad look when she mentioned him. He's no reporter, Daniel. Fallon wants to avoid him, but I'm sure it's for more personal reasons.''

''You think he hurt her?'' Dan narrowed his eyes. He had his own grown children but Mary's were almost as dear to him. ''Tell me his name. I'll find the bastard and teach him what it means to hurt a girl of ours.''

Mary smiled. Who'd ever have imagined, at this stage in her life, she'd find another wonderful man to love?

''I know you would,'' she said gently, ''but I really don't think that's the solution for this kind of hurt.''

''Well then, what is?''

''I don't know.'' Mary sighed. ''Fallon's always been so independent. Even when she was little. 'What's the matter?'. I'd say, if I found her looking upset, and she'd say, 'Nothing's the matter, Mother,' in a tone that made it clear she wanted me to mind my own business.''

''Stubborn.''

''Very.''

Dan grinned. ''I can't imagine where she'd get such a trait, Duchess. Can you?''

Mary laughed softly. Almost everyone who knew her referred to her as the duchess but few said it to her face. Her sons did, and now Daniel, and she loved the term of affection on his lips.

''I know. She's like me, more so than any of my daughters. But I feel useless.''

''Fallon's tough. She's got your genes. All she needs is a little time.''

''Ah, but time slips away so easily. You and I have lived long enough to know that.''

Dan sighed and drew his wife close. ''Well, I don't know what other options you have, dear. She's a grown woman.''

''You're right.'' Mary patted Dan's chest, then stepped back. ''Go on. I know you have a security meeting scheduled.''

''Will you be all right?''

''I'll be fine. Fallon and I will have coffee, and I'll see if I can get her to talk to me.''

''And if she won't?''

''Then I'll talk to her. See if I can get her Irish up. A little anger would be better than moping.''

Dan chuckled.

''What?'' Mary said.

''Felonious mopery. That's what we used to call it when I was on the job in New York, if you saw some guy just hanging around the streets, doing nothing. Felonious mopery.''

''Police talk for what ails my daughter,'' Mary said, and laughed. They smiled at each other. Then she smoothed down the collar of her husband's shirt. ''I have to do something about it, of course.''

''Of course. But what?''

Mary shrugged her shoulders. ''Something,'' she said in a quiet voice.

''Mary. Look at me.''

Daniel put his hand under his wife's chin and lifted her face to his.

''Go on,'' she said gently. ''Go to that meeting. I'll see you later.''

''Why do I get the feeling I ought to stay right here?''

''Because you still have the instincts of a policeman.

And those same instincts should tell you there are times it's better to know as little as possible about a situation.''

Daniel gave a deep sigh. ''I'll be in my office downstairs, Duchess, if you need me.''

Mary smiled. ''I'll remember that.''

She walked him to the front door and gave a sidelong glance to the guest room on her way back. The door was shut. It was always shut. After that one outburst when she'd arrived, Fallon hadn't said more than a dozen words; she stayed in her room except for meals, when she came to the table and poked at her food.

It was the housekeeper's afternoon off. Rather than call down for room service, Mary went into the kitchen, made fresh coffee and filled a serving tray with all the necessities for a civilized coffee break. At the guest-room door, she hesitated, then cleared her throat.

''Fallon?''

''Yes?''

''I've brought us some coffee.''

''Thank you, but I don't want any.''

''Jenny made some of those oatmeal scones you always loved.''

''I'll have one later.''

Time to play a mother's ace card, Mary thought, and sighed.

''I'm supposed to take an afternoon break, Fallon. The doctor says so, and I've gotten in the habit of coffee—decaf, of course—at about this hour, but if you don't want to join me—''

The door opened, as she'd known it would.

''Thank you, darling,'' Mary said, brushing past her daughter, determinedly ignoring the lifeless expression and drooping body language even though those things troubled her more than the scars. They spoke of a deeper wound that might be harder to heal.

''Would you like to go out on the terrace, Fallon? It's

hot, but it's a lovely clear day and the air will do us both good."

"First tell me why the doctor wants you to take a break in the afternoon. You said your last tests were fine."

"And they are." Mary nodded at the sliding doors. "Would you, darling? Thank you." The women stepped outside, both of them blinking in the sudden glare of the sun.

"If your tests were fine, why did he tell you to take a break?"

"Well, he did say that when I first got out of the hospital, but my heart's sound now." Mary put the tray on a round glass-topped table. "I just stretched the facts, that's all. How else was I going to get you to open your door?"

"Letting me think there was something wrong with you wasn't very nice, Mother."

"No," Mary said blithely, "it wasn't. It's awful when someone you love lets you worry needlessly, isn't it?"

"That's sneaky, Ma. And it's not the same thing at all. I'm not making you worry about me. You're doing it all on your own. I told you what happened. I drove into a tree and cut my face."

"That's not what's brought you here," Mary said as she filled their cups. "I know you like cream in your coffee but I'm never sure if you're dieting or not."

"No need to diet," Fallon said with forced gaiety, "now that I'm not modeling anymore."

"But your figure will still matter to you."

"I suppose. Is that what you want to talk about? My figure? My future? What I'm going to do with myself, now that I'm finished modeling?"

"Are you?" Mary said bluntly. "Finished modeling? What about makeup? Or surgery?"

Fallon's face turned white. "Don't tell me. You want to recommend a surgeon, too."

"No, I don't have any... Too?"

"Forget it, Mother."

"I only meant—"

"I know what you meant. You'd like to see me look like my old self again."

"I'd like to see you with some spirit again," Mary said, "and if all this moping is because of the scarring on your face, then I think you might want to consider doing something about it."

"I'm not moping."

"On the other hand," Mary went on, as if Fallon hadn't spoken, "the scars don't detract in the least from your looks."

"Ha!"

"Besides, I seem to recall that the last time we saw each other, you said something about being tired of the business and wanting a change."

"I did. I just didn't expect the decision to be taken out of my hands."

"Life's like that sometimes. Things happen, choices are made whether you want them or not." Mary held out the platter of scones. "Want one?"

"No, thank you."

The women sipped their coffee in silence. Then Mary put down her cup.

"The man you mentioned, the reporter—"

"What about him?"

"He has an Italian name. Did you meet him in Sicily?"

"You know, Ma, you have this infuriating habit of asking questions but not answering them."

"Do I?"

A smile flickered on Fallon's lips, then faded. "Yes."

"This Steven Lucchesi—"

"Stefano Lucchesi."

"Right. What magazine does he write for?"

Fallon hesitated. Had she said Stefano wrote for a magazine? The day she'd arrived was a blur. She remembered seeing Mary's face, seeing her open arms, knowing she had to protect herself from Stefano, should he somehow track her here…

"Fallon? Who does he write for?"

"He's—he's freelance."

"I see. Did you meet in Sicily?"

"Why would you think that?"

"Well, the Italian name…"

"He's an American. And yes, we met in Sicily." What did a few details matter? Her mood was rotten, her temper mean, and her mother wasn't going to leave her alone until she'd pried some answers out of her.

"Was he on assignment to get photos of you?"

"No. Not exactly."

"But he got some."

"Mother…"

"And he's driven you crazy since then."

Fallon's eyes flashed. Wonderful, Mary thought. It was her daughter's first real reaction to anything since that outburst of emotion when she'd arrived.

"Why are you asking all these questions, Ma? Has Stefano called?"

"Stefano?" Mary raised her eyebrows. "Interesting, that you're on a first name basis with a reporter you despise."

"Just remember, if he calls—"

"I don't know where you are."

"Exactly."

"Because he's a persistent reporter."

"Right."

"And not just a man who's trying to find a woman who ran away from him."

"Absolutely ri—" Fallon blinked. "What?"

"Dan thinks your Mr. Lucchesi mistreated you," Mary said casually. "But I said, a woman doesn't mope around the house—"

"Who said anything about running away? And I have not moped!"

"And cry in her sleep—"

"I most certainly do not cry in my—"

"Yes, you do. And a woman doesn't do those things over a man who's been cruel to her. Not a woman with O'Connell blood in her veins."

Fallon shot to her feet. "What on earth are you talking about?"

Mary looked at her daughter. "I don't know," she said calmly. "Not in any detail. I only know what I think, which is that you and this Mr. Lucchesi had a lovers' quarrel—"

"A lovers' quarrel?" Fallon slapped her hands on her hips. There was fire in her eyes and her chin was high. Mary wanted to grab her and hug her and welcome her back…but she knew better.

"Yes," she said, still calmly, "a lovers' spat, and you left him and now you regret it, and—"

"I do not regret a thing! Stefano Lucchesi is a self-centered, self-indulgent son of a bitch!" Fallon strode to the end of the terrace, turned sharply and strode back. "I never want to see him again."

"Because?"

"Because he's a liar and a cheat. Because he used me. Because—because—"

"Because you fell in love with him, and he fell in love with you, and neither one of you was smart enough to know when it was time to admit it."

Fallon felt her heart stand still. That wasn't her mother's voice. It wasn't Dan's. It was—it was—

She swung around. Stefano stood in the open door to the terrace, his hands on his hips, just as hers were; his eyes shooting sparks, just as hers were.

He looked awful. Disheveled, as if he'd been sleeping in his custom-made suit. As if he'd run his hands through his dark hair a hundred times. As if the stubble on his face hadn't seen a razor in a week…

And she, oh God, she loved him!

A whole week of telling herself she'd never loved him, that she'd confused gratitude with love, went sailing into the blue Las Vegas sky. A whole week of chastising herself for ever having returned to the States with him, turned into nonsense.

She loved him, this man who'd hurt her, she loved him...

And what was that he'd said? That he loved her?

"Yes," he said grimly, his eyes locked to hers so that she knew she'd spoken the words aloud, "I love you, though I'm damned if I know why I should. To walk out on me, just when I was about to tell you what you mean to me. To run from me and leave me with half a dozen blind alleys to search—"

"Three," Fallon said, her voice trembling.

"Tokyo. London. San Francisco." His eyes narrowed; he came toward her slowly, one step at a time. Dimly, Fallon saw her mother stand up, smile at her, touch Stefano's shoulder and slide the terrace door closed behind her. "Do you have any idea what a week in hell is?" Stefano grabbed her shoulders. "I sloshed around London in the rain for two days, drove the streets in San Francisco until I never wanted to see one again, got to Japan just in time for a damned typhoon—"

"A couple of lessons in humility never hurt anybody."

"Is that what this was all about? Did you think I needed to be humbled?" His hands tightened on her. "I love you. Didn't that mean anything to you?"

"You don't love me," she said, and tried to pull free. He wouldn't let her. Instead, he jerked her to her toes.

"Don't tell me what I do or don't do, damn it! Your mother's the same piece of work you are. I phoned, I said I was crazy in love with you and if she knew where you were, she had to tell me, and she said, 'you don't love my daughter or you wouldn't have broken her heart.'" His voice roughened. "And I said, Mrs. O'Connell—"

"Coyle," Fallon said numbly, while her brain tried to process what was happening. "My mother's name is—"

"I said, Mrs. O'Connell, I didn't break your daughter's heart, she broke mine. There I was, about to do something I'd sworn I'd never do, get down on one knee and say, 'Fallon, I love you. I adore you. I need you more than I need breath. Will you marry me?' and instead of giving me the chance to say all that, your daughter tore my heart in pieces and dropped it on the floor."

"I tore up a slip of paper," Fallon said, her voice trembling, "because you wanted Fallon O'Connell, supermodel, instead of the Fallon O'Connell who lives inside me."

"That's crap!"

"You want me to have surgery on my face."

"I want you to smile again, damn it."

"That's it. Make it sound as if the surgery was for me, not for—"

Stefano kissed her to silence. His mouth was hard against hers and why wouldn't it be? he thought furiously. He wanted to shake her, to turn her over his knee, to make her know that he'd almost lost his mind when he'd thought he'd lost her.

Maybe he had. She wasn't kissing him back, wasn't doing anything…

And then, slowly, her lips softened against his. Her hands rose and clutched his shirt. She made a soft, sweet little sound that he'd been afraid he'd never hear her make again.

His kiss gentled and he gathered her in his arms. At last, he took his mouth from hers.

"I love you," he said gruffly. "Can you imagine what it did to me when I saw the shadows in your eyes? I realized you were hurting inside, that I was being selfish, that if it weren't for me you'd have contacted a surgeon—and then you confirmed it all, the night before you ran away."

"Confirmed what?" Fallon said in confusion.

"Don't you remember? You asked me how I'd feel, if you had surgery." He cupped her face in his hands. "That was when I knew it was time to stop lying to myself and pretending that my love for you was enough to heal you. You have to do what's right for you, not for me."

"Oh, Stefano. All this time, I thought..." She touched his cheek. "But the names of those doctors—"

"The friend in Boston I told you about is a doctor. He gave me their names. If you want surgery, then I want you to have the best. And I'll be with you, every step of the way."

Fallon gave a watery little laugh. "*You* want the surgery because you think *I* want it?"

"I told you, I've been selfish—"

"You?" She shook her head and wound her arms around his neck. "You're the most generous man in the world, Stefano. I thought you wanted me to have surgery. That you couldn't look at me without pitying me, and I don't want pity from you, I want—"

"What, sweetheart? What do you want? My heart? My soul? My life? They're all yours. I wanted to wait and tell you these things when you were whole. I was afraid if I rushed things, I'd take advantage of you."

Fallon laughed. She rose on her toes and pressed her mouth to his.

"I love you," she said. "I've always loved you, don't you know that?"

Stefano kissed her again and again, until she was clinging to him. Then he leaned his forehead against hers.

"I should have told you about Carla," he said in a low voice. "But I couldn't figure out a way to tell the woman I loved that I'd slept with a woman she knew, much less the woman she was working for. Not when things suddenly seemed precarious. You'd stopped smiling, stopped looking at me with something special glowing in your eyes."

Fallon nodded. He'd made mistakes, but so had she.

All that mattered was that they loved each other and that they'd found each other again.

"Fallon. Sweetheart, will you be my wife?"

She smiled. The look on Stefano's face was one she'd thought she'd never see again.

"Yes," she said softly. "Oh, yes, my love, I will."

He drew her close and kissed her.

On the other side of the glass doors, Mary Elizabeth O'Connell Coyle put her hand to her lips. Eyes damp, she drew the blinds, picked up the phone and dialed Special Guest Services.

"This is Mary O'Connell Coyle," she said. "Susan, you know that lovely wedding you did for Daniel and me? What if I wanted to plan one that was just a little bit bigger..."

EPILOGUE

MEGAN O'CONNELL gazed at herself in the mirrored wall of the guest suite bedroom at *Castello Lucchesi,* stroked a hand down the long skirt of her pale yellow maid-of-honor gown, and sighed.

"Lovely," she said in a dreamy voice.

Briana, standing beside her in an identical gown, smoothed back an auburn curl and looked at her sister's reflection.

"Such modesty," she said sweetly.

"I was talking about the gown."

"Oh," Bree said.

The sisters' eyes met. Meg stuck out her tongue. Bree grinned and stuck hers out, too.

"In that case, I'll have to agree. The gowns are gorgeous."

"And what a cool idea Fallon had," Meg said, "asking us both to be her maid of honor."

"And me to be her bridesmaid," Cassie Bercovic O'Connell said. She stepped toward the mirror. "Especially now."

All three women dropped their gaze to Cassie's round belly. Their eyes met in the glass and they started to giggle.

"I look like an elephant," Cassie said.

"Hey."

The women turned. Keir, Sean and Cullen stood in the open doorway, tall and handsome in black tuxes.

"I resent that." Keir smiled at his wife. "You look," he said softly, "like an incredibly beautiful woman."

Cassie laughed as she went to him. "An incredibly pregnant, incredibly beautiful woman, you mean."

"You're all beautiful," Cullen said gallantly, which earned him a round of female applause.

"He's right," Meg said, "we are. Us in pale yellow, Cassie in pale green, Ma downstairs in sapphire—"

"And Fallon in to-die-for white satin." Bree sighed dramatically. "She almost makes being a bride seem like a good idea."

Megan shuddered. "Bite your tongue!"

"Well, of course I didn't mean it was a good idea for you or me. It's just that Fallon's so happy. Oh, and you, too, Cassie… Damn. I'm putting both feet in my mouth, aren't I?"

"Yeah," Cullen said amiably, "but you usually do."

"Go on, ruin that nice stuff you said a couple of minutes ago."

"Well, you paid me to say—*oof!* Hell, Bree. Elbows like that would be considered lethal weapons in some states."

"I'm just glad you didn't see what an awful bunch of men you were getting as brothers-in-law before you told Keir you'd marry him," Meg told Cassie. "Or we might have lost you before we got you!"

"Yes," Cassie said with affection, "they're reprobates of the first order."

"And now we'll have another male on the O'Connell team," Sean said. "Well, he's a Lucchesi, but you know what I mean."

"He's a good guy," Keir said. "He's crazy about Fallon."

"And he knows how to win a battle without spilling blood," Cullen added. "I mean, I'm sure Ma had her heart set on making this wedding at the Desert Song."

"She did. But your sister and I explained that the *castello* means everything to us."

The O'Connell clan turned as one. Stefano stood in the doorway, wearing a tux, looking as serious and as nervous as they all figured a man was supposed to be on his wedding day.

"I just want to tell you… I love Fallon with all my heart. I know how you cherish her and I promise you, I'll cherish her, too."

There was a moment of silence. Then Stefano's soon-to-be sisters-in-law sniffed and reached for the lace hankies they'd conveniently tucked into their gowns. His new brothers-in-law cleared their throats. And Mary Elizabeth, looking as regal as a duchess, beamed at her growing family as she sailed into the room.

"For the record, once I saw this magnificent castle, I wanted the wedding here, too." Mary looked at Stefano. "It's time," she said softly.

"Yes," he said, and the smile that lit his face made the women weep all over again.

Fallon and her bridegroom took their vows on the terrace, beneath a bower woven from a dazzling array of flowers.

It was better to stick with one or two varieties, the wedding planner had told them, but Stefano and Fallon smiled and said they wanted roses and tulips, orchids and hyacinths, violets and pansies and wildflowers.

The breeze was gentle and warm, scented by the sea and the flowers as it whispered over the assembled guests.

Stefano held Fallon's hand throughout the ceremony. His eyes never left his bride's face. Her scars were still there, but they were invisible to her, to him, to anyone who knew her.

They'd written the vows themselves, so the words had special meaning. And, though nobody knew it, they'd already planned another ceremony only for the family at the

Desert Song. But this ceremony, this place, would always be their very own.

The last words of the ancient ritual that binds man and woman through all eternity sighed away on the breeze.

"Stefano," the justice said, "you may kiss your bride."

Stefano smiled and gathered his wife into his arms. "*Cara,*" he whispered, "*Ti amo.*"

Fallon smiled, too. "*Mo ghrá,*" she whispered back, "*gráim thú.*"

Sean shifted closer to Cullen. "What in heck was that?"

Cullen cleared his throat. "Fine Irishman you are, bro. It was Gaelic. She called him her heart and said she loved him."

"Wow." Sean smiled. "Serious stuff."

"Very."

Cullen watched his sister kiss her new husband. He looked at his mother and his stepfather, holding hands like a pair of kids. His dark blue gaze moved to Keir, who stood with his arm around Cassie. Keir's hand was on his wife's hip but his fingers were splayed possessively over her rounded belly.

Cullen's throat tightened. The world seemed to tilt. He remembered a woman. A night. A memory that was little more than a whisper in the matrix of time.

"Cullen?" Sean leaned in. "You okay?"

"Sure." Cullen cleared his throat. "Warm out here, that's all."

"What you need is a glass of champagne."

The string quartet began playing the recessional. Stefano and Fallon turned toward their guests, who rose to their feet, smiling and applauding. The O'Connell brothers shook hands, kissed the women in their family and Sean, always ready for a party, reached behind a flower arrangement and held a magnum of Cristal aloft.

"Ta-da!"

The O'Connells cheered. Sean popped the cork, Keir produced glasses, and the pale golden wine began to flow.

"This'll cure whatever ails you," he told Cullen.

"Sounds like a plan," Cullen replied, and the world turned right side up again.

CLAIMING HIS LOVE-CHILD

SANDRA MARTON

CHAPTER ONE

July, the coast of Sicily

MEMORIES of the woman and the long, hot night she'd spent in his arms were demons that haunted Cullen O'Connell's waking and sleeping hours.

He didn't like it. What was she doing in his head? The sex had been great. Okay, incredible, but sex was all it was. She was bright and beautiful, but he hardly knew her. Outside the context of the night they'd spent together, she meant nothing to him.

Cullen had no reason to think about her, especially now.

He was in Italy to celebrate his sister's marriage with the rest of his family. The past few days had been great. Whether they were partying or just sitting around talking, Cullen had never found better company than his brothers. Add his three sisters to the mix, things only got better. Toss in his mother and stepfather for good measure, you had a gathering of the O'Connell clan that would put any other party to shame.

As for the setting—most people would call it idyllic. *Castello* Lucchesi stood on a cliff overlooking the Mediterranean with Mount Etna, trailing ribbons of fire, as a backdrop.

The perfect setting for the perfect party. Cullen's mouth thinned. Then, why was he so restless? Why was he thinking about a woman he barely knew? Why this increasing desire to head home to Boston?

Too much togetherness?

Maybe.

Cullen sighed, undid the jet studs at the collar and cuffs of his frilled white shirt, rolled the sleeves back on his tanned, muscled forearms and stared out over the sea. He'd already discarded the jacket of his tux, left it draped over one of the little white folding chairs in the garden of the *castello.*

It had never happened before. Well, there was a first time for everything.

Maybe it was the occasion making him feel edgy. This was the third O'Connell wedding in two years. First his mother's, then his brother Keir's, and now his sister Fallon had tied the knot.

Or the noose, Cullen thought as he went up the winding steps that led to the crenellated watchtower overlooking the castle and the Mediterranean.

What was it about weddings that made women weep and men want to run for the hills?

At least this one had been unusual. The high cliff, the blue sea, the magnificent castle…

Cullen smiled.

And that game of touch football yesterday, on the beach below the castle. The Shirts—Megan, Briana and Fallon—had come within one touchdown of trouncing the skins—Sean and Cullen, with Keir and Fallon's groom, Stefano, spelling each other.

Meg had protested. "No fair. That's four to three."

"It isn't," Cullen had insisted. "The four of us don't play at the same time. And you're a fine one to talk about what's fair, considering that you darned near fractured three of my ribs with that elbow of yours."

"Yeah," Bree said, poking out her chin, "but that only means you've always got a fresh player with unbroken ribs on the field."

"Well, you've got a cheering section building your morale," Cullen had retaliated.

They'd all looked at Keir's pregnant wife, Cassie, sitting

on the sidelines. Cassie had grinned, pumped both fists in the air and yelled, *Yea,* which was exactly the distraction Meg needed to shout "Fumble," scoop up the ball and charge across the goal line.

"Cheater!" Cullen had yelled, and his sisters said, yeah, right, and so what? All was fair in love, war and football.

Somehow they'd all ended up in the pool, laughing and ducking each other under the water. Well, all except Stefano and Fallon, who'd wandered off alone, gazing into each other's eyes. And Keir and Cassie had stayed on the sidelines, too, with Keir hovering over his wife as if she were made of crystal.

Cullen leaned out of the tower's embrasure, which still bore the warmth of the sun that was only now starting to lower in the sky.

The last few days had been fun. The evenings, too. Lots of good food and *vino,* and plenty of time for Stefano to get to know them and them to get to know him. It had all been great…except for those unwanted flashes of memory. The X-rated images, captured forever in his head.

Marissa, whispering his name. Clinging to him. Moving beneath him, taking him deep, so deep, inside her…

"Hell," Cullen muttered. It was pretty sad when a grown man could turn himself on by thinking back to something that had happened two months ago.

Exhaustion could explain it. He'd flown in Friday, straight from a week of twelve-hour days spent between his office and the courtroom. Combine that with jet lag, a Sicilian heat so oppressive you could almost feel it melting your bones, toss in worry about Fallon's accident and the scars left on her lovely face, and he had every right to be a basket case.

At least he wasn't worried about Fallon anymore. His sister was so happy, so beautiful, so cherished by her new husband that it was a joy to see.

As for all this stuff about a woman he hardly knew… There was no point in trying to figure it out. What he needed was a breather. A real one. A true break in routine. The case back home was done with; he had nothing urgent on his agenda. He could change his flight, go to Nantucket instead of Boston, provision his boat, take her out to sea for a few days. Or fly to his cabin in Vail. The Rockies were spectacular in the summer; he'd always meant to do some hiking but he hadn't found the time. Well, he'd find it now, pick up some stuff and backpack.

Or he could go to Madrid. Or London. He hadn't been there in a while. He could go to Maui, or the Virgin Islands.

He could go to Berkeley.

Cullen blinked. Berkeley, California? His alma mater, the place where he'd taken his law degree? It was an okay place but it wasn't exactly one of the world's premier vacation spots.

Yes, but Marissa Perez was there.

Back to square one. Man, he definitely needed a change! Sure, she was in Berkeley. So what? He'd spent a couple of evenings with her. Okay. A weekend.

And he'd spent one night, or most of it, with her in his bed.

Maybe the best thing was to let the images come instead of fighting them. Lessen their impact by letting them wash over him, like a wave hitting the beach far below the tower.

Simply put, Marissa Perez had been spectacular in the sack.

He'd never had a better time in bed, and that was saying a lot. Only a foolish man lied to himself and Cullen had never been a fool. It was simple honesty to admit he was a man who had a knack for getting it on with the opposite sex. Truth was, that knack had brought him more than his fair share of women who were beautiful and exciting and bright and great between the sheets.

For all of that, he'd never enjoyed sex with any of them as much as he had with Marissa.

Cullen scowled and turned his back to the sea.

Out of bed had been another story.

Oh, the lady was beautiful. Exciting. And bright. But she was as prickly as the cactus plants that grew on the sides of these Sicilian roads, as sullen as Mount Etna looming over the sea. She made him uncomfortable, for God's sake, and why would a man put up with a woman who did that?

Hold a door open for her, she gave you a look that said she was perfectly capable of opening it herself. Start to pull out her chair at a restaurant, she grabbed it first. Try to talk to her about anything but the law and the topic you were going to present over Alumni Weekend and she took you straight back to it, reminded you, though politely, that she was here only because she'd been chosen to be your liaison during your couple of days on campus.

Cullen's mouth hardened.

The lady had an attitude. She'd done her best to make it clear dealing with him was a chore she hadn't wanted but despite or maybe because of it, there'd been an almost instantaneous flash of heat between them, right from the minute she picked him up at the airport. Then, on Saturday night, she'd been making some stiff little good-night speech in the car outside his hotel when all at once the rush of words had stopped, she'd looked at him and he'd reached for her…

And changed things by taking her to bed.

No more haughty intellectual talk about torts and precedents. No more stiff insistence on proving her independence. Not during that long, hot night together. She'd said other words, instead, gone pliant in his arms, uttered soft cries of pleasure as he touched her, tasted her, filled her…

"Got to tell you, bro, a man looks like that, his thoughts are probably X-rated."

Cullen looked down. Sean was climbing the watchtower steps. He took a deep breath, forced those last images from his mind and smiled at his kid brother.

"Pathetic," he said lazily, "that all you can think of is sex."

"The point is, what were *you* thinking of, Cull? From the expression on your face, she must be amazing."

"She is," Cullen said, deadpan. "I was admiring the volcano."

"Etna?" Sean nodded. "Quite a lady, all right, but I'm not buying it. Only a geologist would get that glint in his eye over a volcano."

"Vulcanologist, and is that why you came up here? To take notes on the volcano?"

"I came to escape our sisters. Meg and Bree are back to sobbing into their handkerchiefs, and now Ma and Cassie have joined in."

"Well," Cullen said, grinning, "what do you expect? They're women."

"I'll drink to that."

"So would I, but it would mean we'd have to go back to the terrace."

"No, it wouldn't."

Sean winked and pulled a pair of sweating green bottles from his rear trouser pockets. Cullen clapped a hand to his heart.

"No," he said dramatically. "It can't be!"

"It can."

"Beer? Honest-to-God beer?"

"Better. Ale. Irish ale. Here. Take yours before I change my mind and drink them both."

Cullen took the bottle Sean held out. "I take back everything I ever said about you. Well, maybe not everything, but a man who can find Irish ale at a Sicilian wedding can't be all bad."

The brothers smiled at each other and took long, satisfying drinks of the cold ale. After a minute, Sean cleared his throat.

"Anything on your mind? Anything you want to talk about, I mean? You've been kind of quiet."

Cullen looked at his brother. *Yes,* he thought. *I want to talk about why in hell I should still be thinking about a woman I slept with one time, weeks and weeks ago...*

"You bet," he said, with a quick smile. "Let's talk about how you snagged this ale, and what it'll take to get us two more bottles."

Sean laughed, as Cullen had hoped he would. The conversation turned to other things, like how weird it was to see Keir hovering over his pregnant wife.

"Who'd have believed it?" Sean said. "Big brother, talking about babies... Is that what happens when a man marries? He turns into somebody else?"

"*If* he marries, you mean. Hell, how'd we end up on such a depressing topic? Marriage. Children." Cullen shuddered. "Let's go see about the ale," he said, and just that easily, Marissa Perez went back to being nothing more important than a memory.

HOURS later, in a jet halfway over the Atlantic, Cullen looked at the flight attendant hovering over him in the darkened comfort of the first-class cabin.

"No coffee for me, thanks," he told her.

"No supper? No dessert? Would you like something else, Mr. O'Connell?"

Cullen shook his head. "I spent the weekend at a wedding in Sicily."

The flight attendant grinned. "Ah. That explains it. How about some ice water?"

"That would be perfect."

Truth was, he didn't want the water, either, but she meant well and he had the feeling saying "yes" to something was the only way he'd convince her to leave him alone. She brought the glass, he took a perfunctory sip, then put it aside, switched off the overhead light, put his seat all the way back and closed his eyes.

Whatever had been bothering him had faded away. Talking to Sean had done it, or maybe all that goofing around in the garden. Everyone except Keir and Cassie, their mother and stepfather had ended up in the pool again. Well, Stefano and Fallon hadn't been there, either, but nobody had expected them to be. After that, they'd all changed to dry clothes, the mood had mellowed and they'd sat around in the encroaching darkness, talking quietly, reminiscing about the past.

One by one, the O'Connells had finally drifted off to bed. All but Cullen, who, it turned out, was the only one of them who'd made arrangements to fly home that night instead of the next day.

On the way to the airport, he'd thought about the ideas that had floated through his mind earlier. Going to Nantucket instead of straight home, or to Colorado, or someplace in Europe…

Why would he do that?

Whatever had been bugging him was long gone. He'd climbed out of the back seat of Stefano's limousine feeling relaxed and lazy, gone to the first-class check-in line, had time for a coffee prior to boarding.

He still felt relaxed. He liked flying at night. The black sky outside the cabin, the gray shadows inside, the sense that you were in a cocoon halfway between the stars and the earth.

That was how he'd felt that night after he'd taken Marissa to bed. Holding her in his arms, feeling her warm and soft against him until she'd suddenly stiffened, started to pull away.

"I have to go," she'd said, but he'd drawn her close again, kissed her, touched her until she moaned his name and then he'd been moving above her, inside her, holding back, not letting go because she wasn't letting go, because he had the feeling she'd never flown free before and the first time it happened, it was damn well going to be with him…

"Damn," he said softly.

Cullen's eyes flew open. He put his seat up, folded his arms and glowered into the darkness.

So much for feeling nice and relaxed.

This was stupid. Worse than stupid. It was senseless. Why was Marissa in his head? He hadn't seen her since that night. She'd left his bed while he was sleeping, hadn't shown up to take him to the airport, hadn't answered her phone when he called. Not that morning, not any of the times he'd tried to reach her after he was home again.

He always got her answering machine.

You've reached Marissa Perez. Please leave a brief message and I'll get back to you as soon as possible.

His last message had been brief, all right, even curt.

"It's Cullen O'Connell," he'd said. "You want to talk to me, you have my number."

She'd hadn't phoned. Not once. Her silence spoke for itself. They'd slept together, it had been fun, and that was that. No return visits, no instant replays. End of story.

Fine with him. The trouble with most women was that you couldn't get rid of them even after you explained, politely, that it was over.

Cullen? It's Amy. I know what you said, but I was thinking…

Cullen? It's Jill. About what we decided the other night…

Marissa Perez took an admirable approach to sex. A man's approach. She took what she wanted and shut the door on what she didn't. That didn't bother him. It didn't bother him at all.

Why would it?

For all he gave a damn, she could have slept with a dozen men since that night with him. After all, he'd had several women in his life since that weekend. Okay, he hadn't taken any of them to bed, but so what? He'd been working his tail off. Besides, a short break from sex was a good thing. It only heightened the pleasure in the future.

Tomorrow, he'd phone the blonde he'd met at that cocktail party last week. Or the attorney from Dunham and

Busch with the red hair and the big smile. She'd come on to him like crazy.

Definitely, he'd celebrate his homecoming with a woman who'd be happy to take his calls and happy to see him. And he'd sleep with her, make love until crazy thoughts about Marissa Perez were purged from his mind. Surely, his memories of that night were skewed.

Cullen muttered a couple of raw words under his breath as he sat up and switched on his overhead light. To hell with what time it was in New York. The blonde from last week was a party animal. This hour of the night, she was probably just coming in the door.

He dug his address book and his cell phone from his pocket, tapped in her number. She answered after two rings, her voice husky with sleep.

''H'lo,'' she said. ''Whoever you are, you'd better be somebody I really want to talk to.''

He smiled, turned his face to the window and the night sky. ''It's Cullen O'Connell. We met last—''

''Cullen.'' The sleep-roughened voice took on a purr. ''I'd started to think you weren't going to phone.''

''I had things to clear up. You know how it is.''

''No,'' she said, and gave a soft laugh, ''I don't know how it is. I guess you'll just have to show me.''

Cullen felt the tension drain away. ''My pleasure,'' he said, imagining her as she must look right then, sleep-tousled and sexy. ''How about tonight? I'll pick you up at eight.''

''I already have a date for tonight.''

''Break it.''

She laughed again and this time the sound was so full of promise that he felt a heaviness in his groin.

''Are you always this sure of yourself?''

He thought of Marissa, of how she'd slipped from his bed, how she'd ignored his phone calls…

''Eight o'clock,'' he repeated.

"You're an arrogant SOB, Mr. O'Connell. Luckily for you, that's a trait I like in a man."

"Eight," Cullen said, and disconnected.

He put away his cell phone, sat back and thought about the evening ahead. Dinner at that French place. Drinks and dancing at the new club in SoHo. And then he'd take the blonde home, take her to bed, and exorcise the ghost of Marissa Perez forever.

CHAPTER TWO

September: Boston, Massachusetts

THE end of summer always came faster than seemed possible.

One minute the city was sweltering in the heat and the Red Sox were packing in the ever-faithful at Fenway Park. Next thing you knew, gray snow was piled on the curbs, the World Series was only a memory and the Sox hadn't even made it to the playoffs.

Cullen stepped out of the shower, toweled off and pulled on a pair of old denim shorts.

Not that any of that had happened yet.

It was Labor Day weekend, the unofficial end of summer with the real start of fall still almost three weeks away. Cold weather was in the future, and so was the possibility, however remote, that Boston could rise from the ashes and at least win the division championship.

Cullen strolled into the kitchen and turned on the TV in time to catch the tail end of the local news. The Sox had lost a tight game yesterday; nobody had much hope they'd do any better today, said the dour-faced sportscaster.

"Wonderful," Cullen muttered as he opened the refrigerator, took out a bottle of water and uncapped it.

The sports guy gave way to the weatherman. Hot and humid, the weatherman said, with his usual in-your-face good cheer. Saturday, 10:00 a.m. and the sun was blazing from a cloudless sky, the temperature was pushing ninety with no break in sight from now through Monday.

''A perfect holiday weekend,'' the weather guru said as if he'd personally arranged it.

Cullen scowled and hit the off button on the remote.

''What's so perfect about it?'' he growled. It was just another weekend, longer than most, hotter than most. Long, hot, and…

And, what was he doing here?

Nobody, but nobody, stayed in town Labor Day weekend. Driving home from his office yesterday, traffic going out of the city had been bumper to bumper. He'd felt like the only person not heading off for one last taste of summer.

He should have been among them. He'd intended to be.

Cullen lifted the bottle to his lips and drank some water. He'd certainly had enough choices.

Las Vegas, for the usual O'Connell end of summer blast. Connecticut, for the barbecue Keir and Cassie were throwing because Cassie was too pregnant for the long flight to Vegas. He had invitations to house parties in the Hamptons, on the Cape, on Martha's Vineyard and half a dozen other places, and there was always the lure of three days at Nantucket.

Instead, he was here in hot and muggy Boston for no good reason except he wasn't in the mood to go anywhere.

Well, except, maybe Berkeley…

Berkeley? Spend Labor Day weekend on one of the campuses of the University of California?

Cullen snorted, finished off the water and dumped the empty bottle in the sink.

Back to square one. Wasn't that the same insane thought he'd had flying home from Fallon's wedding in July? It made no more sense now then it had made then. You thought about the West Coast, you thought about San Francisco. Or Malibu. Maybe a couple of days at Big Sur.

But Berkeley? What for? Nothing but college kids and grad students, protesters and protests, do-gooders and doomsayers. Maybe that vitality was part of why he'd loved the place as a law student, but those years were a decade behind him. He was older. He'd changed. His idea of a great party involved more than take-out pizza and jugs of cheap wine. And, except for a couple of his law school profs, he didn't have friends there anymore.

Okay. There was Marissa Perez. But he could hardly call her a friend. An acquaintance, was what she'd been. Truth was, he didn't ''know'' her at all, except in the biblical sense of the word, and even if his sisters sometimes gleefully teased him about being a male chauvinist, he had to admit that sleeping with a woman wasn't the same as knowing her.

Especially if she crept out of your bed before dawn and left you feeling as if you were the only one who'd just spent a night you'd never forget.

Damn it, this was crazy. Why waste time thinking about a woman he'd seen once and would probably never see again? He was starting to behave like one of the attorneys at his firm. Jack was a dedicated fisherman, always talking about the big one that had gotten away. That's what this was starting to sound like. The sad story of Cullen O'Connell and The Woman Who Got Away.

Cullen opened the fridge again. It was empty except for another couple of bottles of water, a half-full container of orange juice and a lump of something that he figured had once been cheese. He made a face, picked up the lump with two fingers and dumped it into the trash.

So much for having breakfast in.

Maybe that was just as well. He'd pull on a T-shirt, put on sneakers, go down to the deli on the corner and get himself something to eat. Solve two problems at once, so to speak; silence his growling belly and do something useful, something that would end all this pointless rehashing of the weekend he'd spent with the Perez woman.

Yeah. He'd do that. Later.

Cullen opened the terrace door and stepped into the

morning heat. The little garden below was quiet. Even the birds seemed to have gone elsewhere.

First he'd try thinking about that weekend in detail, concentrating not just on what had happened in bed but on all of it. A dose of cool logic would surely put an end to this nonsense. Sighing, he sank down in a canvas sling back chair, closed his eyes and turned his face to the sun.

His old Tort Law prof, Ian Hutchins, had invited him to fly out and speak to the Law Students' Association. Cullen hadn't much wanted to do it; he had a full caseload and what little free time he could scrounge, he'd been spending on Nantucket, working on his boat. But he liked Hutchins a lot, respected him, so he'd accepted.

A week before Speaker's Weekend, Hutchins had phoned to make last-minute updates to their arrangements.

"I've asked my best student to be your liaison while you're here," he'd said. "Shuttle you around, answer questions—well, you remember how that works, Cullen. You were liaison for us several times while you were a student here."

Cullen remembered it clearly. People called it a plum assignment and, in some ways, it was. The liaison networked with the speaker and drove him or her around in a car owned by the university, which invariably meant it was in a lot better shape than the student's.

Still, it was almost always a pain-in-the-ass job. Pick up the speaker at the airport, drive him or her here, then there, laugh at inane jokes about what it had been like when the speaker was a student on campus. When Ian added that Cullen's liaison would be a woman, he almost groaned.

"Her name," Ian said, "is Marissa Perez. She's a straight-A scholarship student with a brilliant mind. I'm sure you'll enjoy her company."

"I'm sure I will," Cullen had said politely.

What else could he say? Not the truth, that he'd met enough brilliant female scholarship students to know what to expect. Perez would be tall and skinny with a mass of unkempt hair and thick glasses. She'd wear a shapeless black suit and clunky black shoes. And she'd either be so determined to impress him that she'd never shut up or she'd be so awestruck at being in his presence that she'd be tongue-tied.

Wrong on all counts.

The woman standing at the arrivals gate that Friday evening, holding a discreet sign with his name printed on it, was nothing like the woman he'd anticipated. Tall, yes. Lots of hair, yes. And yes, she was wearing a black suit and black shoes.

That was where the resemblance ended.

The mass of hair was a gleaming mass of ebony waves. She'd pinned it up, or tried to, but strands kept escaping, framing a face that was classically beautiful. Gray eyes, chiseled cheekbones, a lush mouth.

Perfect. And when his gaze dropped lower, the package only got better.

Yes, she was tall. But not skinny. Definitely not skinny. The businesslike cut of the black suit couldn't disguise the soft curves of her body. Her breasts were high, her waist slender, her hips sweetly rounded, and not even the ugliest pair of sensible black shoes he'd ever seen could dim the elegance of legs so long he found himself fantasizing about how she'd look wearing nothing but a thong and thigh-high black stockings.

Cullen felt a hot tightening in his belly and a faint sense of regret. The lady was a babe but she might as well have been a bow-wow. There were unwritten rules you followed on these weekends. He did, anyway.

He never hit on the students he met, any more than he mixed business with pleasure in his professional life back home.

Still, as he walked toward her, he liked knowing he'd spend the next couple of days being shuttled around by a woman so easy on the eyes.

''Miss Perez?'' he said, his hand extended.

"*Ms.* Perez," she replied politely.

She held out her hand in return. He took it and the brush of skin against skin rocked him to his toes. ZTS, he told himself. The old O'Connell brothers' explanation for what happened when a man met a stunning woman. Zipper Think Syndrome. He looked at the lovely face turned up to his, saw her eyes flash and had the satisfaction of knowing she'd felt the female equivalent of the same thing.

Maybe not. Maybe he'd just imagined it, because an instant later, her expression was as bland as when he'd first spotted her.

"Welcome to Berkeley, Mr. O'Connell."

After that, it was all business. She drove him to his hotel, made polite but impersonal small talk through a standard hotel meal in a crowded dining room, shook his hand at the elevator in the lobby and said good-night.

The next morning, she picked him up at eight, chauffeured him from place to place all day and never once said anything more personal than "Would you like to have lunch now?" She was courteous and pleasant, but when he opened the restaurant door for her—something he saw irritated her—and their hands brushed, it happened again.

The rush of heat. The shock of it. And now he saw it register on her face long enough for him to know damned well it really had happened, though by the time they were seated, she was once again wearing that coolly polite mask.

He watched her order a salad and iced coffee, told the waitress he'd have the same thing, and contemplated what it would take to get that mask to slip.

Minutes later, he had the answer.

When he'd had the dubious honor of shuttling Big Names from place to place, he'd boned up on their most recent cases and on things in the news that he'd figured might interest them.

His Ms. Perez had done the same thing. He could tell from the always-positive, always-polite references she made during the course of the morning. She'd read up on his own work and reached conclusions about his stance on the work of others.

What would happen if he rocked her boat? Their salads arrived and he decided to find out.

''So,'' he said, with studied nonchalance, ''have you been following Sullivan versus Horowitz in Chicago?''

She looked up. ''The women suing that manufacturing company for sexual discrimination? Yes. It's fascinating.''

Cullen nodded. ''What's fascinating is it's obvious the jury's going to find for the plaintiffs. How the defense could allow seven women on a jury hearing a case that involves trumped-up charges of corporate discrimination I'll never—''

Score one. Those gray eyes widened with surprise.

''Trumped up? I don't understand, Mr. O'Connell.'' Maybe it was score two, or had she simply forgotten to reciprocate on the first name thing?

''It's Cullen. And what don't you understand, Ms. Perez?''

''You said the charges were—''

''They're crap,'' he said pleasantly. ''Shall I be more specific? It's nonsense that a company shouldn't have the right to hire and fire for reasonable cause. The manager of that department should never have loaded it with so many women. Not that I have anything against women, you understand.''

He smiled. She didn't. Score three.

''Don't you,'' she said coldly, and put down her fork. Oh yeah. Definitely, the mask was starting to slip.

''The only reason you believe all that claptrap about affirmative action,'' he said lazily, ''is because you're going to benefit from it. No offense intended, of course.''

That had brought a wash of color into her cheeks. It was a stunning contrast—the brush of apricot against her golden skin—and he'd sat there, enjoying the view as much as he was enjoying the knowledge that she was at war with herself.

Was she going to ''yes'' the honored guest to death, or tell him she thought he was an asshole?

''Hey,'' he said, pushing a little harder, ''you're female, you're Hispanic... Life's going to be good to you, Ms. Perez.''

That did it. To his delight, what won was the truth.

''I am a lawyer, like you, or I will be once I pass the bar. And I am an American, also like you. If life is good to me, it'll be because I've worked hard.'' Ice clung to each syllable. ''But that's something you wouldn't understand, Mr. O'Connell, since you never had to do a day of it in your entire, born-with-a-silver-spoon life.''

Whoa. The mask hadn't just slipped, it had fallen off. There was real, honest-to-God, fire-breathing life inside his well-mannered, gorgeous gofer.

She sat back, breathing hard. He sat forward, smiling.

''Nice,'' he said. ''Very nice.''

''I'll phone Professor Hutchins. He'll arrange for someone else to drive you around for the rest of the time you're here.''

''Did you hear me, Ms. Perez? That was a great performance.''

''It was the truth.''

''Sorry. Wrong choice of words. Mine was the performance. Yours was the real thing. Honest. Emotional. Wouldn't do in a courtroom, letting it all hang out like that, but a really good lawyer should have at least a couple of convictions he or she won't compromise on.''

She glared at him. ''What are you talking about?''

''I told you. Integrity, Ms. Perez. And fire in the belly. You have both. For a while, I wasn't sure you did.''

He picked up his glass of iced coffee and took a long sip. God, he loved the look on her face. Anger. Confusion. Any other place, any other time he'd have used that old cliché, told her she was even more lovely when she was angry, but this wasn't a date, this was what passed for a business meeting in the woolly wilds of academic jurisprudence.

Besides, she'd probably slug him if he said something so trite.

"I don't… What do you mean, you were performing?"

"Monroe versus Allen, Ms. Perez. One of my first big corporate cases—or didn't your research on me go back that far?"

She opened her mouth, shut it again. He could almost see her mind whirring away, sorting facts out of a mental file.

"Mr. O'Connell." She took a breath. "Was this some kind of test?"

Cullen grinned. "You could call it that, yeah, and before you pick up that glass and toss the contents at me, how about considering that you've just had a taste of what you may someday face in the real world? You want to blow up when stuff like that's tossed at you, do it here. Out there, you'll be more effective if you keep what burns inside you. Discretion is always the better part of valor. Opposing attorneys, good ones, search for the weak spot. If they can find it, they use it." He smiled and raised his glass of iced coffee toward her. "Am I forgiven, Ms. Perez?"

She'd hesitated. Then she'd picked up her glass and touched it to his. "It's Marissa," she'd said, and for the first time, she'd flashed a real smile.

Cullen got to his feet, slid open the terrace door and went back into the coolness of the living room.

The rest of the afternoon had passed quickly. They'd talked about law, about law school, about everything under the sun except what happened each time they accidentally touched each other. She'd dropped him at his hotel at five, come back for him at six, driven him to the dinner at which he'd made a speech he figured had gone over well because there'd been smiles, laughter, applause and even rapt concentration.

All he'd been able to concentrate on was Marissa, seated,

as a matter of courtesy, at a table near the dais. No black suit and clunky shoes tonight. She'd worn a long silk gown in a shade of pale rose that made her eyes look like platinum stars; her hair was loose and drawn softly back from her face.

The dress was demure. She wore no makeup that he could see. And yet she was the sexiest woman imaginable, perhaps because she wasn't only beautiful and desirable but because he knew what a fine mind was at work behind that lovely face.

Even though he figured it might kill him, he did the right thing.

He never so much as touched her elbow or her hand during the after-dinner reception and when she drove him back to his hotel for the last time, he sat squarely on his side of the car and kept his eyes on the road instead of on the curve of her thigh visible under the clinging silk of her gown.

"Thank you for everything," he said politely, once they reached the parking lot.

"You're welcome," she said, just as politely, and then, so quickly it still stunned him, everything changed.

To this day, he didn't know what had happened, only that what began as a simple handshake changed into a fevered meeting of mouths and bodies.

"Don't go," he'd whispered, and Marissa had trembled in his arms as she opened her mouth to the searing heat of his.

They'd gone to his room through the back entrance of the hotel because they couldn't stop touching each other and when he undressed her, when he took her to bed…

"Oh man," Cullen muttered, and he stripped off his shorts and headed for the shower again.

THIS time, after he toweled off, he shaved, put on a pair of khakis and a black T-shirt and reached for the telephone.

He needed a change of scene. That was a no-brainer. It

was a little late to make weekend escape plans—the roads would still be crowded—but he knew all the back ways to reach the airport at Nantucket. Yeah. Maybe the best choice was the closest choice.

His cottage, and his boat.

Cullen punched in the number of the couple who took care of the cottage. The woman answered; he asked how she was, how her husband was, how the weather was…and then he heard himself tell her he'd just phoned to touch bases and no, he wouldn't be coming out for the weekend and he hoped they'd have terrific weather and enjoy the three days, et cetera, et cetera, et cetera.

He hit the disconnect button, ran his hand over his face. Okay. Obviously, he wasn't in the mood for a weekend of sailing. Well, what *was* he in the mood for? Something other than rattling around here, that was for sure.

Who to call next? Keir, to ask what time the barbecue was on? His mother, to tell her he'd be home after all? Or should he head for one of those other parties, maybe that one in Malibu? That was a better idea. His family would take one look at him, ask questions he couldn't answer.

Hell.

Cullen grabbed his address book. He'd call the redhead he'd dated a couple of times the past month. She was pretty and lots of fun, and if he hadn't called her in a week or two, it was because he was busy.

He hadn't taken her to bed, either.

How come?

Perhaps this was the weekend to remedy that oversight. The lady had made it very clear she was more than ready to join him in the horizontal rumba.

Cullen smiled, thumbed open the address book, flipped to the page that had her number on it…

"Crap!"

He slammed the book shut, took a quick walk around the room and tried to figure out what in hell was going on.

No sailboat. No gorgeous redhead. What *did* he want to do with the weekend?

The answer came without any hesitation and he acted on it that same way, not fighting it anymore, just grabbing the address book and telephone again, punching in a series of digits before he could change his mind.

"Flyaway Charters," a cheery voice said. "How may we help you?"

"You can tell me how fast you can get me to Berkeley," Cullen said. "Yeah, that's right. Berkeley, California."

CHAPTER THREE

BY THE time the chartered Learjet landed in California, Cullen had come to the conclusion he was crazy.

He'd flown 3,000 miles in six hours, gone from East coast time to Pacific coast time—something that always left him feeling vaguely disoriented—and now, as he stepped onto the tarmac, he was engulfed by air so hot and humid it made the weather he'd left behind seem like an arctic paradise.

And for what?

What in hell was he doing?

He'd never chased after a woman in his life. Well, not since the seventh grade, when he'd made a fool of himself over Trudy Gershwin, but seventh grade was long gone. He wasn't a kid. Neither was Marissa Perez. She was history and so was the night they'd spent in bed.

History? Cullen slung the strap of his carry-on bag over his shoulder as he walked toward the terminal. That night was barely a blip in the fabric of his life. Who gave a damn why she'd slept with him, then vanished and refused to take his calls?

Trouble was, he'd reached that conclusion somewhere over the pastures and fields of the Midwest, a few hours and fifteen hundred miles too late. He'd come within a breath of telling the pilot to turn the jet around.

He'd thought about phoning his brothers. One or the other would give him good advice.

Hey, bro, Sean or Keir would say, *you know what your problem is? You've got a bad case of ZTS.*

Yes, he'd thought, I do. He'd smiled, even reached for the phone…and then he'd realized that first he'd have to tell the whole story, the weekend in California, making a fool of himself with Marissa, the infuriating months since then.

Besides, this wasn't ZTS. He wasn't thinking with his gonads, he simply wanted answers. Closure. The word of the day.

So he'd sat back, finished the flight and now, as he stepped into the welcome chill of the terminal, Cullen told himself he was glad he had.

Closure. Right. That's what he wanted, what he was entitled to, and, by God, he wasn't going home without it.

He found the rental car counter easily enough, managed a "hello" he hoped was civil and slapped the confirmation number of his reservation on the counter.

"Good afternoon, Mr. O'Connell," the clerk said, her smile as bright as if she were about to hand him a winning lottery ticket instead of the keys to…

A four-door sedan? Cullen blinked as he read the paper she slid in front of him.

"There's some mistake here, miss. I reserved a convertible."

The blinding smile dimmed just a little. "I know. But this is a holiday weekend."

"And?"

"And, it's all we have left."

He knew she meant he was lucky to get anything with an engine and four wheels. She was right, too, and really, what did the type of car he drove matter? He wasn't here for a good time; he was on a safari to Egoville because, yeah, the simple truth was this was all about ego. His. The Perez babe had dented it, and he was here to set things right.

Man, acknowledging that nasty truth really put the icing on the cake.

Cullen glared, muttered something about inefficiency as

he signed the papers and scooped up the keys. He started to stalk away but after a couple of steps, he rolled his eyes and turned back toward the counter.

"Sorry," he said in a clipped tone. "I'm in a bad mood, but I didn't mean to take it out on you."

The clerk's smile softened. "It's the weather, sir. Everybody's edgy. What we need is a good soaking rain."

Cullen nodded. What *he* needed was a good soaking for his head. If he'd done that in the first place, he'd still be back home. Since it was too late for that, he settled for buying an extra-large container of coffee, black, at a stand near the exit door. Maybe part of the problem was that he was still operating on East coast time. Pumping some caffeine through his system might help.

It didn't.

The coffee tasted as if somebody had washed their socks in it. He dumped it in a trash bin after one sip. And the sedan was a color that could only be called bilious-green. Five minutes on the freeway toward Berkeley and Cullen knew it also had all the vitality of a sick sloth.

Not a good beginning for a trip he probably shouldn't have made.

Cullen fell in behind an ancient truck whose sole reason for existence was to make green sedans feel like Ferraris.

Beggars couldn't be choosers.

His hands tightened on the steering wheel.

And that was the one thing he wouldn't do with Perez. Beg. No way. He'd confront her, get in her face if that's what it took, and he wouldn't let her off the hook until she explained herself, but he wouldn't let her think he was pleading for answers…

Even if he was.

Damn it, he was entitled to answers! A woman didn't give a man the brush-off after a night like the one they'd spent. All that heat. Her little cries. The way she'd responded to him, the way she'd touched him, as if every caress was a first-time exploration. And the look on her face, the way her eyes had blurred when he took her up over the edge…

Had it all been a game? Lies, deceit, whatever a woman might call pretending she was feeling something in a man's arms when she really wasn't?

Cullen hit the horn, cursed, swung into the passing lane and chugged along beside the wheezing truck until he finally overtook it.

Whether she liked it or not, Marissa Perez was going to talk to him.

He had her address—she'd never given it to him but he'd found it easily by using her phone number to do a reverse search on the Internet. Another exit…yes, there it was.

Cullen took the ramp and wound through half a dozen streets in a neighborhood he remembered from his own graduate days. It was still the same: a little shabby around the edges but, all in all, safe and pleasant. He'd wondered what kind of area she lived in, whether it was okay or dangerous or what.

He hadn't liked imagining her in a rundown house on a dark street. Not that it was any of his concern.

"What the hell's with you, O'Connell?" he muttered, digging her address from his pocket. "You thinking of turning into the Good Fairy?"

Her building was on the corner. Cullen parked, trotted up the steps to a wide stoop and checked the names below the buzzers in the cramped entry. No Perez. He checked again, frowned, then pressed the button marked Building Manager.

"Yes?"

A tinny voice came over the speaker. Cullen leaned in.

"I'm looking for Marissa Perez's apartment."

"She don't live here."

He glanced at the slip of paper in his hand. "Isn't this 345 Spring Street?"

"She used to live here, but she moved."

"Moved where? Do you have her new address?"

"I got no idea."

"But she must have left a forwarding—"

Click. Cullen was talking to the air. "Damn," he muttered, heading back to his car while he took his cell phone from his pocket. He hadn't intended to call. Why give her advance notice of his visit? Now, he had no choice.

And no success, either.

"The number you have reached, 555-1157, is no longer in service."

He tried again, got the same message. What was going on here? Cullen called the operator and asked for a phone number for Marissa Perez.

There was none. Not a public listing, anyway.

Annoyed, he tossed the cell phone aside. There wasn't a way in the world he could shake loose a privately listed number from the phone company. Back home, maybe, he could pull some strings, but not here.

Someone had to have her number or her address. The bursar's office, the dean's office…

Or her advisor. Ian Hutchins.

Cullen sat back and drummed his fingertips on the steering wheel. The offices would be closed for the weekend. Ian was the logical choice, but he'd want to know why Cullen was trying to get in touch with Marissa.

He was digging himself in deeper and deeper.

A sane man would turn around and head for home but then, a sane man wouldn't have come out here in the first place.

He started the car. It lurched forward. The engine bitched when he tried to coax more speed from it, but it finally gave a couple of hiccups and complied.

Even the car knew he wasn't in a mood to be screwed with, he thought grimly.

He only hoped the Perez babe could read him just as quickly.

THE Hutchinses lived in a big Victorian on a tree-lined street in North Oakland.

Music, and the sound of voices and laughter, spilled from the yard behind the house. The air was pungent with the mingled aromas of smoking charcoal, lager beer and grilling beef.

Cullen climbed the porch steps, took a deep breath and rang the bell. After a minute, Hutchins's wife, Sylvia, opened the door.

"Hello," she said, her lips curving into a cautious smile that suddenly turned genuine. "Cullen O'Connell! What a nice surprise."

"Hello, Sylvia. Sorry to barge in without notice, but—"

"Don't be silly!" Laughing, she took his arm and drew him inside the foyer. "I was afraid you were the fire marshal. Ian's grilling steaks."

Cullen chuckled. "The Hutchins method of incineration. Nothing's changed, huh?"

"Not a thing," Sylvia said cheerfully. "Come inside, Cullen. I had no idea you were in town. Ian never said a word."

"He doesn't know. And I apologize again for not phoning first. You have guests."

"We have half the Bay area, you mean. You know these barbecues of Ian's—students, faculty, friends, every person he's ever met on the street. Besides, why would you call first? You're always welcome. Let me get you a drink and introduce you around."

"Actually, I just need a couple of minutes of Ian's time."

"Oh, come on. There are a couple of unattached women here—Ian's third-and fourth-year students—I'm sure would love to meet you."

"Is Marissa Perez one of them?" *Holy hell.* How had that slipped out? Cullen felt his face burn. "I met her that last time I was out here. She drove me around all weekend."

Sylvia arched an eyebrow. ''Marissa? No, she's not here. Come to think of it, I haven't seen her in a while.'' She winked. ''I'm sure we can find a replacement.''

''Sylvia,'' Cullen said quietly, ''if you'd just tell Ian I'm here… I need to ask him something and then I'll be on my way.''

''Ah. You're really not in a party mood, are you?'' Smiling, she patted his hand. ''I'll get Ian. Why don't you wait in his study?''

Cullen bent and kissed her cheek. ''Thanks.''

The professor's study was a small room off the foyer. Cullen had always liked it. An old sofa covered in flowered chintz faced a small fireplace; an antique cherry desk stood in a corner. The walls were hung with family photos, and an ancient Oriental rug lent a mellow touch to the hardwood floor.

The place felt familiar and comforting. And when Ian Hutchins crossed the threshold with a beer in either hand, Cullen smiled.

''As always,'' he said, taking a glass from Hutchins, ''the perfect host.''

''It's not the fatted calf—I've got that laid out on the barbecue—but I figured you might be thirsty.'' The men shook hands, then sat down. ''If I'd known you were going to be in town—''

''It was a last minute decision.''

''And Sylvia tells me you can't stay for our party.''

''No. I'm sorry, I can't. I'm just passing through and I wondered…'' *Get to it, O'Connell.* ''Remember when I was here to give that speech?''

''Of course. We had a lot of excellent feedback. Matter of fact, I was going to give you a call, see if you'd be interested in—''

''The woman who was my liaison. Marissa Perez.''

Hutchins cocked his head. ''Yes?''

''I'm trying to get in touch with her.'' Cullen cleared his

throat. "Turns out she's moved. I thought you might have her new address."

"May I ask why you're trying to contact Ms. Perez, Cullen?"

Cullen stared at the older man, then rose to his feet. He put his untouched glass of beer on a table and tucked his hands into the pockets of his trousers.

"It's a personal matter."

"Personal."

"Ms. Perez and I had a misunderstanding, and I'd like to clear the air."

"How personal? What sort of misunderstanding?"

Cullen's mouth narrowed. "Excuse me?"

"I said—"

"I heard what you said, Ian. And, frankly, I don't see that it's any of your business."

Hutchins put down his glass, too, and got to his feet. "Easy, Cullen. I'm not trying to pry, but, well, I owe a certain amount of confidentiality to my students. I'm sure you understand that."

"Hell, I'm not asking you to tell me her social security number!" *Easy,* Cullen told himself. *Just take it nice and slow.* "Look, I want to talk to her, that's all. If you're not comfortable giving me her address, then give me her phone number. Her new one's unlisted."

Hutchins sighed. "Is it? Well, I'm not surprised. All in all, Marissa seems to have done her best to sever all her university relationships."

"Why? What's going on? Did she transfer out?"

"Worse. She quit. And I'm worried about her."

"What do you mean, she quit? You said she was one of your best students. Why would she quit?"

"She wasn't *one* of my best, she was *the* best. I don't know why she withdrew from school. She began behaving strangely, is all I know, and made what I think are some poor decisions, but..." Hutchins took a deep breath, then slowly expelled it. "That's why I was questioning you,

Cullen. I figured, if you and she had become friends, perhaps it would be all right to share my concerns with you.''

''Ian, you've known me for years. You know you can count on me to be discreet.''

Hutchins nodded. ''Very well, then. Here's the situation. Marissa's walked away from a promising future. I know that sounds melodramatic but it's true. She was to edit *Law Review* next year and after graduation, she was slated to clerk for Judge Landers.'' He spread his hands. ''She's turned her back on all of it.''

''Why? What happened to her? Drugs? Alcohol?'' Cullen could hear the roughness in his own voice. He cleared his throat and flashed a quick smile. ''We can't afford to let the smart ones get away, Ian. There must be a reason.''

''I'm sure there is, but she wouldn't discuss it. I tried to talk to her the first time I realized something was wrong. She flunked one of my exams.'' Hutchins gave a sharp laugh. ''Understand, she never so much as gave a wrong answer until then. Anyway, I called her in for a chat. I asked if she had a problem she wanted to discuss with me. She said she didn't.''

''And?''

''And, because I was her advisor, I began hearing from her other instructors. The same thing was happening in their classes. She was failing tests, not turning in papers, not participating in discussions. They all asked if I knew the reason.''

''So, you spoke with Marissa again…''

''Of course. She told me she'd had to take on a heavier work schedule at some restaurant. The Chiliburger, I think she said, over on Telegraph. I offered to see about some additional scholarship money but she said no, she had expenses that would extend beyond the school year.'' Hutchins frowned. ''She looked awful, Cullen. Tired. Peaked, if you'll pardon such an old-fashioned word. I asked her if she was sick. She said she wasn't.'' Hutchins shrugged. ''Next thing I knew, she'd dropped out of school.

I phoned her, got the same message I assume you got. I even went to her apartment, but she'd cleared out.''

''Did you go to this place where she works? The Chiliburger?''

''No. This is America,'' Ian said with a little smile. ''People are entitled to lead their lives as they wish. Marissa had made it clear she didn't want to discuss her problems. I'm her advisor, not her father. There's a certain line I don't have the right to cross.''

Cullen could feel a muscle knotting and unknotting in his jaw. Hutchins was right. Marissa Perez was entitled to lead her life as she saw fit. If she wanted to sleep with a stranger and then ignore him, she could. If she wanted to drop out of law school and walk away from a future others would kill for, she could do that, too.

And he could do what he had to do. Find her, and find out what in hell was going on.

''You're right,'' Cullen said as the men walked slowly to the front door. ''You did everything you could.''

''You're going to talk with her? Assuming you can find her, that is?''

Cullen laughed. ''I have a feeling finding her won't be hard. Getting her to talk to me might be a different story.''

CULLEN knew exactly where to find the Chiliburger. It was, as burger joints went, an institution.

He had eaten countless fries and burgers within the confines of its greasy walls; he'd studied in its vinyl booths, at wooden tables scarred with the incised initials of at least four decades' worth of students.

He drove to the restaurant, lucked out on a parking space and strolled inside. A blast of heavy-metal music made him wince. Even the stuff pouring from the jukebox was the same. So was the aroma of fried onions, chili and beer.

He scanned the room. It was crowded. No surprise there, either. Holiday or not, there were always some students who remained in town. It was coming up on supper time, and they'd gather at places like this for a cheap meal and some laughs.

He spotted a vacant booth way in the back, went to it and slid across the red imitation leather seat. The table was still littered with plates and glasses; he pushed them aside and reached for the stained menu propped between the ketchup bottle and the salt and pepper shakers.

As far as he could tell, only one waitress was working the tables, a heavyset blonde of indeterminate age.

No Marissa.

After a while, the blonde appeared at his elbow and shifted a wad of gum from one side of her mouth to the other.

''You know what you want or you need more time?''

''A Coke, please.''

''That's it?''

Cullen smiled. What she meant was, *You're going to take up space at one of my tables and that's all you're going to spend?*

''And a burger. The house special, medium-well.'' He shoved the menu back into its hiding place, considered asking Blondie about Marissa and decided this wasn't the right time. ''No rush.''

''No rush is right. I got all these tables to handle by myself.''

''Nobody else on with you tonight?''

''Oh, there's somebody on with me.'' Blondie rolled her eyes. ''She just isn't here yet, is all.''

Cullen tried not to show his sudden interest. ''She's late?''

''She's always late,'' Blondie said. ''Last couple months, anyway. You want guacamole or mayo on that burger?''

''You pick it. How come?''

''How come what?''

''How come the other waitress started showing up late?''

Blondie shrugged. ''How would I know? Only thing I'm

sure of is that it's a pain in the butt, trying to cover for her so the boss doesn't realize she's not here."

"Then why do it?"

The waitress's expression softened and she leaned toward him. "'Cause she's a nice kid. Always did her fair share until now."

"And that changed?"

"It sure did. She says she's just been feeling under the weather." The blonde shifted her gum. "You ask me," she said slyly, "the trouble with her is that she's—"

"She's what?"

Something in his tone must have given him away. Blondie drew back. "What's with all these questions?"

"I'm just making conversation, that's all."

"Well, you got questions about Marissa Perez, ask her direct. She just came in. I'll put your order in, but it'll be her takes care of— Mister? Mister, what's the problem?"

What was the problem? Cullen didn't know where to begin. Marissa was coming from behind the counter that ran the length of one side of the room, but this wasn't the Marissa he'd spent countless nights dreaming about.

Her face was devoid of color; there were rings under her eyes. Her hair, which he remembered as being as lustrous as a crow's wing, was dull and lifeless.

Something was terribly wrong with her.

He shot to his feet.

She saw him as he did.

She paled—though how she could get paler than she already was, he thought grimly, was hard to comprehend. He saw her lips form his name as she took a step back.

"Marissa," he said, but he knew she couldn't hear him, not over the din of music and loud voices.

She stared at him. Her lips formed his name. For a second, he thought she was going to pass out. He mouthed an oath, took a step toward her, but she pasted a bloodless smile to her lips and started toward him.

‘‘Cullen,’’ she said in a thin voice, ‘‘what a nice surprise.’’

It didn’t take a genius to know that her smile was a lie. She was surprised, all right, but nice? No way. She was about as glad to see him as a lone gazelle would be to see a lion.

‘‘Yeah,’’ he said coldly, ‘‘what a nice surprise.’’ His hand closed around her wrist. ‘‘You look terrible.’’

‘‘Are you always so free with compliments?’’

‘‘Cut the crap.’’ Why was he so angry? So what if she looked like death warmed over? It wasn’t his business, he told himself, even as his eyes narrowed and drilled into hers. ‘‘Is that why you didn’t call me? Have you been sick?’’

‘‘I didn’t call you because I didn’t want to call you. I know that must come as a shock, Cullen, but—’’

‘‘Is that the reason you left school?’’

Her face colored. ‘‘Who told you that?’’

‘‘You were the best student Ian Hutchins had, and you quit. You moved out of your apartment, you’re working your tail off in a joint like this and you look like hell. I want to know why.’’

‘‘Just who do you think you are, Mr. O’Connell? I don’t owe any explanations to you or anybody. My life is my—’’

‘‘I’m making it my business. Last time we saw each other, you had the world by the tail. I want to know what happened.’’

‘‘But you’re not going to find out. I told you, I don’t have to— Hey. Hey, what do you think you’re doing?’’

Cullen was tugging her toward the door. Marissa tried to dig in her heels, but he paid no attention.

‘‘Stop it!’’ she said in a frantic whisper. ‘‘Are you crazy? You’ll cost me my job!’’

‘‘Tell her you’re taking a break to talk to an old friend,’’ he growled when Blondie hurried toward them.

‘‘Marissa? You okay? You want me to call the cops?’’

And turn this bad dream into a full-fledged nightmare?

"No," Marissa said quickly, "No, I'm fine. I'm just—I'm taking a break..."

The next thing she knew, she was tucked in the passenger seat of Cullen's car and they were pulling away from the curb and into traffic.

CHAPTER FOUR

MARISSA swung toward Cullen.

"Are you insane?" Her voice rose until it was a shriek. "Take me back! Turn this car around and take me—"

"Buckle your seat belt."

"You son of a bitch! Did you hear what I said?" She lunged toward him and slammed her fist into his shoulder. "Take-me-back!"

Cullen took one hand from the steering wheel and wrapped it around hers.

"You want to hit me, wait until we stop moving. For now, keep your hands to yourself. And put on that belt."

She stared at him. His profile looked as if it had been chiseled from stone. He was driving fast, weaving in and out of traffic, and she knew she had about as much chance of getting him to take her back to the Chiliburger as she had of changing what happened the weekend they'd met.

You couldn't turn back time.

Marissa lay a hand protectively over her belly. Then she clipped the ends of her seat belt together.

Given the chance, she wasn't even sure she would turn it back. At first, oh God, at first, she'd have given anything to erase that night but now—now, things had changed. She'd faced what had happened, gone from hating the changes in her life to hating only herself for her weakness and stupidity, for making the same mistakes her mother had made…

No.

She took a deep breath.

She wasn't going there. All that was behind her and, anyway, it had nothing to do with the man sitting beside her except in the most fundamental way. Besides, why was she wasting time on this nonsense? She had more immediate concerns. Her job. She'd come in late again, and two minutes later, Cullen had dragged her away. Would Tony take her back? He would. He *had* to. She'd beg. She'd grovel, if that was what it took. She needed the money desperately.

How would a man like Cullen O'Connell, born to wealth and power, ever understand that?

She'd tell Tony that Cullen was an old boyfriend. That he'd just gotten in from out of town. She'd laugh, make it seem as if it was all about being macho. That was true enough. Cullen did have a macho quality. Tony thought he had one, too, but it wasn't the same. Cullen's was the kind some women found attractive.

All right. *She'd* found it attractive, but that didn't give him the right to swagger into her life and take over. As for telling him why she'd quit school, changed all her plans…that wasn't going to happen.

The only way to handle him would be to play on that machismo. Make him think she saw his high-handed interference as gallantry, and that she appreciated it even if it had been misplaced.

Marissa cleared her throat.

"Look, I appreciate your concern, but—"

"What street?"

"What?"

"I said, what street do you live on? I'm taking you home."

"No," she said quickly, "you're not. You're taking me back to the Chiliburger."

"You want to give me your address, or you want to drive in circles until we run out of gas?" He looked at her as they stopped at a red light. "Your choice, lady."

Lady. The way he said it turned the word into something vaguely impolite. So much for finding a way to handle him.

"I don't think you understand," she said, trying to stay calm. "I need that job."

"You have a bachelor's degree and three years of law school." He smiled sardonically as he stepped on the gas. "Oh yeah. Right. I'll just bet you sure as hell need a job serving burgers and fries."

"How readily you jump to conclusions, Mr. O'Connell. I have a degree in political science. Do you see anybody clamoring for my services? As for three years of law school... 'Sorry, Miss Perez,'" she said in a high-pitched voice, "'but we really don't have any openings in our office for paralegals.'" She looked at Cullen, eyes flashing dangerously. "Translation. 'Are you kidding? Why would our attorneys want to work with a clerk who probably thinks she knows everything?'"

"Okay. So getting a good job would be tough."

Marissa sank back in her seat and folded her arms. "Something like that," she said tonelessly.

"What about your scholarship money?"

"What scholarship money?"

"Ian Hutchins says—"

"I *had* a scholarship. You have to attend school full-time to keep it."

"And?"

Look how he'd drawn her into this discussion! Marissa blew back the hair that had fallen over her forehead.

"And," she said coolly, "this conversation is over."

They sat in silence for a few seconds. Then Cullen looked at her.

"I'm still waiting. Where do you live?"

"None of your business. How many times do I have to tell you that? Take me back to the Chiliburger."

"Yeah, I'll bet your boss would like that. What's he do, work you twelve hours a day?"

"Tony agreed to give me extra hours, yes."

"What a prince," Cullen said sarcastically. "Hasn't he noticed you look like you're going to fall on your face any minute?"

Marissa almost laughed. Tony probably had no idea what she looked like. She was a waitress, a commodity about as invisible in a place like the Chiliburger as the film of old grease on the griddle.

But she wasn't going to tell that to Cullen. She wasn't going to tell him anything. She'd made that decision months ago.

She could take care of herself. She always had...except for that night. How could it have happened? Hadn't she learned anything, growing up?

Some girls' mothers taught them to cook or sew.

Hers had taught her the truth about men, and life.

The day she got her first period, her mother handed her a box of tampons and a bucket of advice.

"You're a woman now, Mari," she'd said. "Men will look at you, but don't you let 'em come near you. They're all like the son of a bitch planted you inside me, gruntin' between your legs, then zippin' up their pants and walkin' away. The rest is your problem. You remember that, girl. Nothin' lasts, especially if you're dumb enough to hope it will."

She always had remembered, until Cullen. How come? Was it because her mother had omitted one salient bit of advice, that when a man took your breath away, he took away your ability to think?

That's what had happened to her. Cullen had taken her breath away. One look, and she'd been lost. He was so ruggedly handsome, so funny, so smart...and each time their hands accidentally brushed, it seemed as if a bolt of electricity sizzled straight through her bones.

No matter. She wasn't her mother, despite what had happened. *She* wouldn't confront a man who was little more than a stranger with a truth he wouldn't want to hear. She wouldn't beg him to believe her. She knew how things would go if a woman named Perez tried to tell a man like Cullen O'Connell that he'd played a role in a sad little tragedy that was really of her own making.

Her fault, all of it.

She should have been strong enough to ignore the hot attraction between them instead of melting into his kiss. And when he'd asked if she had protection just before he undressed her, she should have remembered that though she took the pill to regulate her period, she'd been off it the start of the month because she had the flu.

Marissa closed her eyes.

Oh yes, she should have remembered…but how could she, when she'd wanted him so badly? When the taste of his mouth, the touch of his hands, drove her wild? Lost. She'd been lost—

"…that address but hey, what's the point? There are worse things than spending the night driving around the Bay."

Marissa opened her eyes. They were heading for the water and the bridge across it, getting farther and farther from the Chiliburger. For all she knew, Tony had already lined up someone to replace her.

"This is ridiculous," she said sharply. "Don't you ever give up?"

"No," Cullen said, just as sharply, "I don't."

There was a warning in his words, but she decided to ignore it. If she played along, he'd go away.

Back to Plan A, and letting Mr. Macho think he'd won.

"All right. Drive me home, if that's what it takes to get you out of my face."

"A charming image."

"I'm not interested in charm, Mr. O'Connell. I just want to get rid of you. Make a U-turn, then take a right at the first light."

He nodded and did as she'd told him. Marissa let out a pent-up breath. Just a little while longer and she'd be back at the Chiliburger. Except for her latenesses the past few weeks, she was a damned good waitress. Tony would take her back. He had to.

She needed her job. How else would she be able to put away enough money to have her baby?

The baby she would love, as her mother had never loved her.

The baby Cullen O'Connell had fathered.

CULLEN couldn't believe where her directions took him.

He slowed the car and stared out the window. The houses that lined the street looked as if they were only a couple of weeks away from being condemned. A bunch of kids wearing what he figured were gang colors lounged against a graffiti-scarred brick wall; a scrawny dog pawed through a spilled bag of rotting garbage near the curb.

"This is where you live?"

"You can stop in the middle of the block."

Well, that was definitely the answer to his question. "This isn't exactly a garden spot."

"Oh, but that's the reason I chose it. I didn't want to be bothered by photographers from Showplace Homes."

Marissa's tone was as cool as his. She was still pale but the angle of her jaw told him she'd regained some of her composure. So would he, as soon as he dropped her off. He still wasn't sure why he'd carried her out of that miserable dive. So what if something had gone wrong in her life?

She was right. It wasn't his problem.

Still, he might be able to help her. He'd helped other students. Ian called him once in a while, asking if he had any contacts who could offer a job to a recent graduate, or if he knew anybody who was taking on interns for the summer. He could do as much for Marissa. All he had to do was get her to talk to him, tell him what the trouble was.

Cullen frowned as he pulled to the curb in front of a four-story building that looked little better than the rest on the street.

On the other hand, she didn't want help. She didn't want anything from him. And that was fine. Two people, one spring night. It wasn't exactly a memory to tuck into a journal.

Okay. He'd sit here, wait until she went inside, let her sashay across from the gang-bangers and the pile of rags stirring in a nearby doorway.

Sure he would.

Cullen reached for the door. No man would let a woman walk alone on a street like this.

"I'll see you inside."

"That's not necessary."

"Yeah, it is. Those kids don't look much like Boy Scouts."

"No! Really?"

She fluttered her lashes with such innocence that he had to laugh. For a moment, the tension between them eased. Her lips curved in the start of a smile and he remembered how soft her mouth was, how sweet it tasted. Their eyes met; she was remembering, too.

Then, why hadn't she returned his calls?

He sprang from the car and made it to the sidewalk just as she stepped onto it.

"I'm walking you in," he said grimly. "And if you give me a hard time about it, we'll have a repeat of our exit from the Chiliburger."

She shot him a look of pure venom. He ignored it and walked her to the broken concrete steps that led to her front door. He started to ask for her keys, but why would you need keys when there was a hole where the lock should have been?

"I can't believe you live in a place like this," he said curtly.

Her response was just as curt. "I can't believe you think it's any of your business."

Right again, he thought. Nothing about her was his business. Nothing…except the answers he'd come for and had yet to get. He caught her by the shoulders as she pushed open the door.

''Just tell me one thing,'' he said roughly. ''Why didn't you answer my calls?''

Two spots of color stained her pale cheeks, but her response was swift. Only a tremor in her voice told him he'd caught her off guard.

''I didn't see much point in it. We both knew we weren't going to see each other again.''

''You knew that, huh?'' His tone was harsh. ''Then, how come I didn't?''

''It was a logical conclusion. You live in the east, I live here. The odds on us getting together were—''

''So, what was that night? Just a casual roll in the hay?'' She flinched, but he wasn't about to stop now, not when he'd been carrying all this anger inside him for so long. ''Is that your style? Go to bed with a guy and forget about him the next morning?''

The crimson in her cheeks suffused her entire face. He felt her arm jerk and he knew she was going to slug him, but before she could, he clamped his hand around her wrist.

''You get the hell out of my life!''

''Answer my question first.''

''I'm not answering anything.'' Fury danced in her eyes. ''Get away from me or I'll scream.''

Cullen laughed. ''And that's going to bring the good citizens of this fine neighborhood running, right?'' His face turned hard; he let go of her and slapped his hand against the door. ''Trust me, Ms. Perez. I'm as eager to see the last of you as you are to see the last of me. We get to your apartment, I'm out of here.''

Marissa stared at him. Then she turned on her heel, marched into a narrow vestibule perfumed by cabbage, cheap wine and urine, and started up the stairs.

Two floors. Three. She never paused for breath until they reached the fourth-floor landing. Then she turned to him. Her face was pale again, her breathing rapid.

Cullen felt a twinge of alarm.

''Are you okay?''

''I'm fine. And this is where we part company.''

''Maybe you should see a doctor.''

''Maybe you should give the advice bit a rest.''

Her tone was flippant, but it didn't fool him. Something was wrong. Very wrong. Cullen narrowed his eyes on her face.

''Ian thinks you might be sick. Are you?''

''My health isn't—''

''My business. Yeah, I know.'' He looked past her, at the scarred and dented door that led to her apartment, and something tightened deep inside him. What was she doing here? He wanted answers. Better ones than he'd gotten so far. ''That was a steep climb. How about a cup of coffee before you send me on my way?''

''How about you just go?''

His mouth thinned. Marissa Perez was really getting to him. He thought about hauling her into his arms and kissing her. Maybe then she'd drop this disguise of cool disinterest.

No. He wouldn't do that. He wouldn't give her an excuse to tell him he was a fool when he knew it already.

''I'll settle for a glass of iced water.''

She folded her arms. He could see the ''no'' forming on her lips, but something unexpected changed her mind. A door creaked open; a woman in a dingy slip peered at them.

''Oh,'' she said brightly, ''sorry. I thought it was someone for me.''

The door swung shut, but not quite all the way. Clearly, they had an audience.

Marissa muttered something, then dug in her pocket for her keys. When her door swung open, she jerked her chin and Cullen stepped past her. As soon as they were inside, she slammed the door and confronted him.

''All right,'' she snapped, her hands on her hips, her face turned up to his. ''What's it going to take to get rid of you? What do you want?''

"I told you. Some water. I'm winded."

Marissa's eyes narrowed. Did Cullen O'Connell think she was stupid? He wasn't even breathing hard. Four flights of steps were nothing to him. She still remembered how hard his body was, that six-pack abdomen, those knotted muscles in his shoulders and arms.

He was up to something, but what? Was he here at Professor Hutchins's request to try and find out why she'd left school? That would really be a laugh. As if she'd tell Cullen, of all people, what had happened to her. That she was carrying his child. Lesson one, learned at her mother's knee: getting a woman pregnant didn't mean a man was a father.

She swung away from him, hurried into the kitchen and returned with a glass of water. He was standing where she'd left him, staring at the peeling walls, the sagging furniture, the worn linoleum.

"Here's your water." He didn't respond and she shoved the glass at him. "I'd appreciate it if you'd drink up and leave."

"Why?"

His voice was sharp, his eyes narrowed as they focused on hers, and she knew his one-word question didn't have a thing to do with what she'd said.

It was safer to pretend it had.

"Because I have things to do, that's why."

"Damn it, Marissa!" He put down the glass. He'd had it with being circumspect, with telling himself whatever was going on here was none of his business. He'd come for closure and found a dozen new questions instead, and he wasn't going home until he had answers. "Forget the games," he said, clasping her shoulders. "I want to know what you're doing in a dump like this."

He felt a tremor race through her body, but her eyes were steady on his.

"I live here. If it's not to you're liking, that's just too—"

"Hutchins says you've given up everything. *Law Re-*

view. The clerkship.'' His mouth twisted. ''Your last year of school. And for what? So you can live in a place that's about ready to be torn down? Work yourself to death at a joint like the Chiliburger?'' She winced as his fingers bit into her flesh. ''Tell me the truth, damn it. Are you sick? Do you need money? Tell me. I'll help you.''

''I don't need your help. And I resent your interference. This is my life. I can live it any way I—''

Cullen cursed, hauled her to her toes and covered her mouth with his. It was what he'd dreamed about, all these months; what he wanted even now, when she'd done everything possible to fuel his anger.

''No,'' she gasped, and pulled away, but he took her face in his hands, knotted one hand in her hair and kissed her again and again until, all at once, she gave a little sob of surrender, sank against him, opened her mouth to his and wrapped her arms around his neck.

Here it was again. That incredible heat. Desire, erupting like a volcano that had been slumbering under a cover of clouds. He wanted her as he'd wanted her that night, as he'd never wanted another woman.

''Marissa,'' he whispered. She sighed his name against his lips and he deepened the kiss, tasting the sweetness he'd never forgotten, drinking it in as if it might assuage his endless thirst for her.

His hand stroked down the length of her spine, traced the delicate vertebrae, slid under her loose shirt and found the ripeness of her breast. Her breath sighed into his mouth as he cupped it, swept the tips of his fingers over the tightly furled nipple.

''Marissa,'' he said again, and she rose on her toes, pressed herself against him as he moved his hand lower, spread his fingers over her belly.

Her gently rounded belly.

Rounded, as his sister-in-law's had been the day he'd driven to the vineyard she and Keir owned, early in Cassie's pregnancy.

Want to say hello to your nephew? Cassie had asked him, and she'd taken his hand, spread it over her stomach…

Cullen went still. He lifted his head, stared down at Marissa, saw her pinched face, her shadowed eyes.

"My God," he said hoarsely. "You're not sick. You're pregnant."

Marissa cried out and pushed free of his arms.

God, what had she done? She'd lost herself, lost the ability to think. The same thing had happened that night she'd slept with this man. She'd forgotten everything then. Her morals. The code she lived by.

Only this was far worse. What she'd forgotten this time was the secret she could never share with him.

"Go away," she whispered shakily.

"Not until I have an answer!" Cullen grabbed her and shook her. "Are you pregnant?"

"No. I'm not. I'm not!"

"Don't lie to me, damn it! That's why you quit school." He let go of her, afraid of what he'd say, what he'd do. She'd given up everything for, what, a moment's foolishness with some man who didn't care enough about her to hang around and take care of her?

When?

When had it happened? His hands closed into fists. Was that why she'd left his bed that night? Because another man was waiting for her? Had she belonged to someone else, even then?

"Who is he?" he said, his words soft and cold. "And where is he? Why is he letting you go through this alone?"

Marissa sank her teeth into her bottom lip. She turned away from Cullen's accusing face. Despite the blistering heat trapped in the airless confines of her ugly apartment, she was shivering.

"Go away," she whispered.

Cullen's hands closed on her shoulders and he swung her toward him. "I'm right, aren't I? He's letting you face this alone. Does he even know what's happened to you? That you've given up the law, that you're sick—''

''I'm not sick,'' she said fiercely. ''I'm pregnant! And I don't need anyone's help! I'm doing just fine on my own.''

''Did he abandon you?''

''Abandon…?'' Marissa made a sound that was not quite a laugh. How could a man abandon you after a one-night stand? Her mother had always referred to what had happened in her own life as an affair, but Marissa was a realist. One night didn't make for anything but sex. ''No. The man who—the man I slept with doesn't know about this.''

''Why the hell not?''

''I told you. Because I can handle it myself.'' She shook free of his hands. ''For the last time, Cullen. This doesn't concern you.''

Cullen opened his mouth, then closed it. She was right again. It didn't. She was pregnant, she was going to ruin her life, but so what? He had no stake in any of it.

Except for one thing.

''You're right. What you do isn't my affair.'' His voice roughened. ''I just have one last question.''

''Don't you get it? I'm not answering any more questions.''

''Did you go to him that night?'' A muscle knotted in his jaw. ''Was that the reason you left my bed? So you could be with him?''

The accusation sliced through her like a knife. She didn't think, she reacted. Her hand flew through the air; she slapped his face with all the strength and despair so long constricting her heart.

The sound reverberated through the silent room; Cullen's head snapped back but it didn't stop him from snarling a curse, grabbing her wrist and yanking her hand behind her back.

''Answer me. Did you sleep with him that same night?''

''No!''

''First me. Then him. The man who was waiting for you.

Your lover. You left me so you could go to him, your body still warm from mine, your mouth still swollen with my kisses—''

''I don't have a lover. I *never* had a lover. I've never been with a man in my life except—''

She moaned, clamped her lips together. But it was too late. God, too late!

Silence. Endless seconds of it, ticking into the airless room. Marissa turned away and shut her eyes. After an eternity, Cullen spoke in a hoarse whisper.

''Are you telling me the child in your womb is mine?''

It still wasn't too late to lie. She could say she'd misspoken or he'd misunderstood.

''Marissa.'' Cullen turned her toward him. ''Marissa. Look at me.''

She shook her head. He put his hand under her chin and raised her face until their eyes met.

''I want the truth.'' His voice was flat. ''Now, or in a courtroom. Your choice. Am I the man who made you pregnant?''

She knew the warning was real. Cullen wasn't a man who'd make an idle threat. Her stomach was churning. This was exactly the kind of confrontation she'd dreaded.

Still, it had happened. And now that it had, what difference could it possibly make? Once he knew the truth, he'd stop all the fancy talk about some man letting her face this alone. That was okay, too, because once he understood that she wanted nothing from him, he'd be out of her life forever.

''Answer me,'' Cullen snapped. ''Is this child mine?''

Marissa took a deep breath. And said yes.

CHAPTER FIVE

ONE of the best things about growing up an O'Connell was having brothers and sisters who knew you almost as well as you knew yourself.

Forget "almost," Cullen thought as he sat across from his brother, Sean, in a Boston steakhouse. Truth was, his family, especially Keir and Sean, knew him about as well as he knew himself.

Maybe better.

That was a good thing when you were, say, sitting at a bar, eyeing women, rating them on the O'Connell scale. The old Zipper Think Syndrome. Not that Keir played the game with them anymore but there was a time a woman would walk through the door, stroll past them and they'd all look at each other and know precisely where the lady placed for each of them on the ZTS scale.

Yeah, but there were other times when the last thing a man wanted was to have someone else, even his brother, *especially* his brother, inside his head.

Cullen picked up his glass of ale.

Right now, Sean was doing his best to read his mind. Cullen could tell by the glint in his brother's eye. So far, the kid hadn't come up with anything—how could he, when the facts were so incredible? But Sean had definitely tuned in to both his mood, which was low, and his disposition, which bordered on ugly.

Now, Sean was trying his damnedest to improve things, telling a story that involved him, a Greek shipowner, an Italian prince, and a Hollywood sex goddess. Sean had the

Gaelic gift for gab and a terrific sense of humor, meaning the story was probably funny as hell and definitely intriguing.

Assuming a man was in the right mood.

Cullen wasn't.

How could he be? His life would never be the same again. He was still trying to come to grips with what had happened. The truth of it was, he doubted that he ever could.

Marissa Perez was pregnant.

No. That made it sound as if she'd gotten that way by herself. Well, she hadn't. Like the old saying went, it took two.

He'd made Marissa pregnant. Pregnant! How in hell had he let such a thing happen? He'd been with a lot of women and he always used a condom unless it was a long-term relationship and he knew his lover well, knew she was using her own means of birth control. Things like that were just plain common sense.

Cullen took a long, cool mouthful of ale.

Where had his common sense gone that night? One look at Marissa and his hormones had sent his brain scuttling for shelter. That was no excuse, not unless you were seventeen and led around by your—

"...so the prince said, okay, O'Connell. You agree to one last hand. I'll put up my Maserati." Sean grinned. "Guess what I said?"

Cullen looked at his brother. He hadn't the foggiest notion what he was talking about. What now? Maybe a smile and a shrug of the shoulders would work.

"No idea," he said brightly.

Good choice. Sean nodded and began talking again. Cullen let his thoughts slip back to Marissa.

He'd never fallen into bed with a woman that fast, either. One minute he'd been reminding himself that he didn't think much of profs or alumni who got involved with grad students because it was far too easy for that kind of thing to happen and the next…

The next, she'd been in his arms.

Somewhere between the parking lot and his hotel room, he'd asked her if she was on the pill. Something like that, anyway; as he recalled, his brain cells had still been working then.

Yes, she'd said, and he'd thought, he'd thought…

He hadn't thought anything. He was too far gone. They both were, their mouths fused, their bodies on fire, his heart racing as he'd stripped off her clothes, tasted her sweetly rounded breasts, parted her golden thighs…

"Cull? You okay?"

Cullen blinked. Sean was watching him, pale blue eyes fixed on his face like lasers.

"Sure. I'm fine."

"Because for a second there, you looked—"

"I said I'm fine, kid." Cullen cleared his throat and made a show of peering around the restaurant. "Where's our waiter? We need another round."

Sean nodded. "Good idea."

"So," Cullen said brightly, "the prince bet his car, and—"

"What I said was, he *offered* to bet his car." Sean's gaze narrowed. "You haven't heard a thing I said, bro."

"Of course I did. This guy you were playing wanted to bet his, uh, his Porsche."

"It was a Maserati."

"Right. His Maserati. And you said—"

"And I said…?"

Great. They'd made this dinner appointment weeks before, when Sean phoned to say he'd be passing through Boston. Now, it was turning into a pop quiz.

He should have canceled it when he had the chance, but canceling would have raised a bucket of questions. Now it looked as if keeping the engagement was going to do the same thing.

"C'mon, man," Sean said lazily. "You get it right, I'll pick up the check. What did I say?"

Cullen flipped a mental coin and went for broke. "You said 'no.'"

"Like I said, you haven't been listening. You might as well be on another planet, for all the attention you're paying."

"My apologies. I didn't know your ego was on the line here."

"Take it easy, Cullen. Something's the matter. I want to know what it is."

"Nothing. Just some stuff at work..."

"Try again."

"What do I have to do? Go back to when we were kids, say 'Cross my heart, hope to die' before you believe me?"

"I wouldn't buy that, either. Face it, Cull. Bluffing doesn't work between us. I can read you like a book."

"Read this, then. Nothing's wrong."

"Right. That's why you came in here looking as if it was even money the world's going to end tomorrow morning."

Cullen gave a quick laugh. "Not that soon," he said, "but soon enough."

"If I have to, I'll put you in a hammerlock that'll wreck your shoulder for a week, same as when we were kids."

"Memory playing tricks on you, is it? It was the other way around."

Sean flashed a smile. "It was, until I stomped on your toe. Ma damn near murdered us both, remember? You limping, me cradling my arm... Cull. Talk to me, man. Whatever it is, it can't be that bad."

Cullen felt a muscle knot in his jaw. "Trust me," he said, after a few seconds, "it can."

"What'd you do?" Sean smiled again. "Don't tell me. You lost a case."

"I wish." Cullen took a deep breath, then raised his eyes to his brother's. "I made a woman pregnant."

Sean's face turned white. "What?"

Cullen stared at his brother. Then he swiveled around in his seat. "Damn it, where's that waiter?"

Without a word, Sean rose from the booth, marched to the bar in the front of the restaurant and returned two minutes later with a bottle of Wild Turkey and two glasses.

"They don't let you pour your own here," Cullen said aimlessly.

"They do now," Sean growled as he filled their glasses. He took a long swallow of his drink, then motioned to the one he'd put in front of Cullen. "Drink that. Then tell me I heard you right."

Cullen nodded and tossed down half his drink. He shuddered, wiped the back of his hand across his mouth and looked at his brother.

"A woman's carrying a baby, and I'm the man who did it."

"You're sure?"

Cullen nodded. "Yes."

"'Cause sometimes you can't be sure, you know? Just because a woman says—"

"I'm sure," Cullen said grimly. "You remember how Cassie looked the first few months she was pregnant? Pale, hollow-eyed, sick to her stomach in the mornings and exhausted all the rest of the day? Same symptoms here. Plus a belly that's gone from flat to—"

"For God's sake, I'm not asking if you're sure she's knocked up, I'm asking if you're sure the kid is yours."

"I'm almost positive."

"*Almost* positive? What's that supposed to mean? She tells you, 'I'm going to be a mama, and you're the papa,' and you believed her?"

"It wasn't like that."

"Did you do a paternity test?"

"Yes." Cullen remembered the look on Marissa's face when he'd demanded the test, how she'd said it wasn't necessary because she wanted absolutely nothing from him, how he'd said it wasn't up to her, nothing was up to her anymore. ''I should have the results tomorrow.''

''And then you'll know for sure?''

''Right. Then, I'll know.''

''But for now, you assume you're the one who knocked the lady up because…?''

''Because I was there, and it happened.''

Sean sat back. ''When did she tell you?''

Cullen took a long swallow of bourbon. ''Two weekends ago. Labor Day.'' He finished his bourbon and reached for the bottle. ''Happy Labor Day,'' he said solemnly, ''and isn't that one hell of a bad pun?''

''How'd it happen? Hell, don't laugh. You know what I mean.''

''I wish I knew. I was—I was caught up in the moment.''

''Too caught up to reach for a rubber?''

''Listen, kid, you asked me a question. You want an answer or not?'' Cullen's mouth twisted. ''I'm sorry. It was a reasonable thing to ask. I'm on edge, is all.''

''She wasn't using anything? The pill?''

''She said she was, but she forgot she'd been off it for a few days… What?''

''Listen to yourself, Cullen. You were caught up in the moment. She said she was on the pill but she wasn't.'' Sean's eyes narrowed. ''The lady sounds like she's running a scam on you.''

Cullen felt his jaw tighten. ''I don't think so.''

''Well, I would. How long have you been sleeping with her?''

''I met her when I went out to Berkeley this past spring.''

''And?''

''And what?''

''And, she's been seeing nobody but you all this time? She flies here, you fly there? You're the only guy who's been with her, what, the last three months?''

''Four months. We were only together that weekend. That night.''

His brother's eyebrows rose. "You picked her up?"

"I didn't pick her up. She is—she *was* a third-year law student. My gofer for the weekend."

"Forgive me," Sean said sarcastically. "You *met* this babe—"

The knot in Cullen's jaw tightened again. "There's no need to refer to her that way."

He reached for the bottle of whiskey. Sean grabbed it first, capped it and shoved it aside.

"You don't need any more of this stuff. You're flying high without it. What's with you? You're the hot-shot attorney. Somebody in that fancy school you went to must have taught you how to recognize a scam when it comes up and bites you in the ass."

"You know what?" Cullen said softly. "I think we ought to end this discussion."

"Why? Don't you want to acknowledge the truth?" Sean leaned in, his eyes snapping with anger. "Face it. You met a clever babe, you fu—"

"Watch your mouth," Cullen said, his voice dangerously soft, his eyes suddenly cold.

Sean shook his head in disgust. "The lady's good, I'll give her that. She sure as hell must have screwed your brains out because now she says you knocked her up and—"

Cullen grabbed his brother by the front of his shirt and half-dragged him across the table.

"I told you to watch your mouth. You need me to back that up with something more than words?"

"Let go," Sean said quietly. "Or we're both going to regret what happens next."

The brothers stared at each other, the silence broken only by the rasp of their breaths. Then Cullen let go and sat back.

"Hell," he muttered. "I'm sorry."

"It's okay."

"It's just…Marissa wasn't even going to tell me what

had happened. If I hadn't looked her up…'' Cullen shook his head. ''I don't understand the woman. She has no money, she had to quit school, she's working her tail off at a restaurant that looks like a health inspector's nightmare, she moved into a place gave me the creeps just to look at, and she insists she doesn't want anything from me.''

''Maybe. Maybe not. Maybe she's just smart enough to figure she's better off playing it that way.'' Sean's mouth thinned. ''Go on, get that look on your face again. I don't give a damn. I just want to be sure you know what might be coming down before it's too late.'' He paused. ''I take it the lady's going through with the pregnancy.''

''Yes.''

''And what about you? Assuming it's yours, is that what you want? A kid walking around, carrying your genes?''

''You mean, would I want her to—'' Cullen's mouth tightened. ''Hell, no. It's one thing to talk about things in the abstract. I'm still all for choice, but this is different. Besides, the decision's not really mine to make.'' He fell silent, stared into his empty glass and then raised his eyes to Sean's. ''I always figured, another few years, I'd find the right woman, settle down, have a family…''

''And now?''

''And now… Well, if the child is mine—''

''I'm relieved to hear you say 'if.'''

''If it is, I'll do the right thing.''

''Meaning?''

''I'll pay for its support. And for Marissa's.''

Sean let out a long breath. ''Thank God for small favors. For a second there, I thought you were saying you'd marry this woman.''

''Marry her? No way. We hardly know each other. I live here, she lives there. Why would I marry her?''

''Who knows? An overdeveloped sense of morality, maybe. Concern for how she'd raise the kid.'' Sean grinned in an attempt to ease the tension. ''I'm glad to know you're not really crazy. It's one thing to take responsibility for your actions and another to jump into the deep end of the pool."

"Meaning?"

"Meaning, you can accept responsibility for paternity, if the test proves positive, without becoming a husband and father."

"No," Cullen said, "there's no danger of me doing that."

Sean heaved a sigh of relief. "I'm glad to hear it. Keep me posted, okay? And if you need a sounding board..."

"I'll call you."

A moment passed. Then Sean cleared his throat. "Hey," he said briskly, "did I tell you about this Swedish blonde I met in Monte Carlo?"

Cullen grinned. "How come they're always Scandinavian blondes?"

"What can I tell you? A man's got to adhere to a standard."

The brothers laughed and this time, when Sean told his story, Cullen did his best to pay attention. Even so, his thoughts kept wandering to what Sean had said about his taking responsibility without becoming a husband and father.

Court-ordered or self-imposed, responsibility without emotional involvement was the usual outcome of situations like the one Cullen was in.

The part of him that was a coolheaded lawyer had already started laying the foundation for such a plan. He would have his name on the child's birth certificate. He'd arrange for money to cover not just basic expenses but those that would ensure the child a good life.

There was only one problem.

Sean had said he could do the right thing without becoming a husband and father, but Sean was wrong. Wrong about part of it, anyway.

Cullen couldn't avoid being a father.

The day he'd planted his seed in Marissa's womb, a father was precisely what he'd become.

MARISSA shut the door of her apartment on the FedEx man, leaned back against it and stared at the envelope he'd just delivered.

She'd have known what it contained even if the return address hadn't said Bio Tech Labs in big blue and red letters. Nobody sent her official-looking packages. Not since she'd withdrawn from the university and surrendered the scholarship that had paid her room, board and tuition.

She swallowed past the lump in her throat. Here it was. The DNA-based paternity test report. Why was she so nervous? She knew what it would say.

Yes, but now Cullen would know it, too. He hadn't believed her when she'd told him he'd fathered her baby. Not that she could really blame him. Why would a man accept the word of a woman who fell into bed with him without knowing much more than his name?

Still, she couldn't come up with a reason why it should have mattered to him. He owed her nothing; she'd made that clear once he'd recovered from the shock of learning what their—their encounter had achieved. She *wanted* nothing. She'd made that clear, too.

"I assume you intend to go through with the pregnancy," he'd said.

She'd looked at him as if he were crazy. Did he think she'd given up everything she'd worked so hard for so she could get rid of the baby in her womb?

"Yes," she'd said calmly, "I do."

That was when he'd told her he'd want to see proof of his paternity.

"What for?" she'd said, and he'd looked at her as if this time she were the crazy one.

"So I can make the appropriate arrangements," he'd told her.

Marissa crossed the tiny living room, into the kitchen,

put the unopened envelope on the table and filled a kettle with water.

That was when she'd realized he intended to do something about his role in what had happened. Write her a check, ask her in turn to sign a document releasing him from all future obligation.

She put the kettle on the stove, turned on the burner and wondered if that put her a step ahead of her mother. Yes, she thought bitterly, it probably did. Cullen would at least acknowledge his participation in the creation of her child. Her son—she knew it was a boy, thanks to last week's amniocentesis that had also provided the DNA for Bio Tech Labs to sequence—her son wouldn't have a real father any more than she'd had, but at least she could tell him, when he was old enough, that his biological father had tried to do the right thing.

Not that she'd accept his help.

She wasn't going to do anything as demeaning as sign a paper like the one Cullen would undoubtedly produce. She didn't want anything from him. It was his problem if he couldn't accept that as the truth. She had a paycheck again—it had taken a couple of days, but Tony had finally agreed to let her come back. Even if he hadn't, she would never take a penny from Cullen.

Signing away her child's right to know his father, accepting money for such an agreement, would only make her feel dirtier than she already did.

"About me, baby," Marissa said softly, touching her palm lightly to her belly, "not about you."

Never that. From the moment she'd made the decision to go through with her pregnancy, she'd felt a connection to her child. Her son, she thought, and smiled. She would love him as she had not been loved, do whatever it took to make his life a happy one—

The kettle shrilled. At least, she thought it did but when she looked at it, it wasn't even steaming.

The doorbell.

That was a surprise. First the FedEx man and now, who? The superintendent, come to fix the toilet tank that had been running for days? Her downstairs neighbor, come to complain about the noise the continual flow of water was causing?

Marissa sighed, smoothed back her hair, undid all the locks but the chain, opened the door a crack…and felt her heart skid into her throat.

"Cullen?"

What a stupid question. Of course it was Cullen. You couldn't mistake him for anybody else. His height. His wide shoulders. Those deep blue eyes.

That hard, narrowed mouth that had once touched hers with such incredible passion…

"What are you doing here, Cullen?"

"Open the door, Marissa."

"We said all we needed to say last time."

"You want to discuss the child you're carrying through the door, that's fine. Why don't you give me a minute so I can ring your neighbor's bell? I'm sure she doesn't want to miss any of this."

Marissa tore off the chain and flung the door open. Cullen brushed past her. He was dressed formally, in a gray suit, white shirt and navy tie, and he was carrying a sleek leather briefcase.

The attorney, properly attired to do the bidding of his client, she thought bitterly, and lifted her chin.

"You're wrong, Cullen. We don't have anything to discuss."

"Shut the door."

Eyes flashing, she closed it with a bang. "Any other orders?"

"We *do* have things to talk about, Marissa. Private things that don't concern anyone but us."

Us. There was no "us." Just for a moment, weeks ago, when she'd first realized she was pregnant, she'd let herself dream of an "us"….

The kettle shrieked. Marissa spun toward the kitchen. She heard his footsteps following her across the worn linoleum. She didn't want to look at him, didn't want to see his face when he offered her money, and she bought time by busying herself with taking down a mug, putting a tea bag in it and filling it with water. When she finally turned around, Cullen was looking at the unopened envelope on the table.

''I see you got the DNA report.''

She shrugged.

His eyes met hers. ''You haven't opened it.''

''I don't have to. I already know what it says.''

''And now, thanks to a call to the lab, so do I.''

''Surprised?'' she said, trying for a cool tone but managing instead, she realized with dismay, to sound tremulous. ''Did you actually think I'd lie about something like this?''

''I'm a partner in a large law firm,'' he said quietly. ''I've seen a lot of things I wouldn't have believed.''

He was right. She knew it. After a second, she drew a long breath, then let it out.

''Why have you come here?''

Cullen pulled a chair out from the table. ''Sit down.''

Her home, such as it was, and he was inviting her to sit down. Marissa lifted her chin.

''I'd rather stand, thank you.''

''This is going to take a while,'' he said, and put the briefcase on the table where it looked incongruous enough to almost merit laughter, the softly expensive black leather lying on the scarred pine wood.

''I don't think so.'' Marissa put down the mug of tea and stuffed her hands into the pockets of her sweatpants. They were almost the only things she still owned that fit her. ''Actually, I know why you've come.''

His eyebrows rose. ''You do?''

''Yes.'' She cleared her throat. Why did this feel so much like moot court? How could you sleep with a man, hold nothing back when he made love to you, and end up standing in a kitchen facing him as if you were not just strangers but adversaries? "Yes, I do. You want to do what you believe is the right thing."

A muscle knotted in his cheek. "Yes. I do."

"So you're going to offer me money."

Cullen folded his arms. "Go on."

"And you're going to ask me to sign documents that say I've accepted such and such a sum, blah blah blah, for which I release you from all future obligation, blah blah blah."

"That's a lot of blah," he said.

He made it sound like a small joke but it wasn't, not with that streak of ice in his tone. A feeling of apprehension tiptoed down her spine like the cold footprints of some tiny animal, but she wouldn't let that stop her. She was only a year away from her law degree and then she'd be qualified to take the Bar exam. Did he think she wouldn't have figured all this out without his sitting her down and explaining it to her?

"Of course," she said coolly, "you and I both know that anything I sign isn't worth the paper it's printed on."

"That's correct."

"I could go to a judge virtually anytime and tell him I'd made a mistake, settling for whatever you're going to offer me. That I needed more money, or that I hadn't had adequate representation."

"Correct again."

Marissa narrowed her eyes. "I'm telling you all this so you won't be too distressed when I also tell you I'm not going to sign anything."

"Indeed," he said. Actually, he almost purred it. Again, she felt that a sense of disquiet. Silly, to feel it. What could he do but accept her decision?

"I'm also not going to accept anything you've come to give me, Cullen. I told you, I don't want anything from you."

"What about my name on my son's birth certificate? Do you want that?'

She stared at him. What had happened to his references to "the child"? When had this baby become Cullen O'Connell's son?

"Answer me," he said sharply, taking a step toward her. "You have all these plans, Marissa. Where do my wishes fit in?"

"I—I'll name you on the birth certificate, if that's what you want. There's no reason for my baby to be a—a—"

"Bastard," Cullen said coldly. "That's the word you're looking for. There's no reason for him to be raised in poverty, either."

"Poverty isn't a disease!"

"Don't you think this child deserves a good start in life? Good schools? A home that isn't located in a war zone? Do you think he should grow up with a mother who's working in a dive and still can hardly make ends meet? I'm assuming you managed to get back your career-building job at the Chiliburger."

He smiled thinly; it reminded her of a wolf's snarl. She knew better than to tell him he was right.

"I have a plan," she said stiffly.

"Really."

He was mocking her. She knew she should ignore it, that he could wound only her pride, but pride was all she had left.

"I won't wait tables forever. Once I get on my feet financially, I'm going to finish the credits for my degree."

"And when will that happen? Five years from now? Ten?"

"What matters is that it will happen."

"Oh, sure," he said coldly. "But until then, what's going to happen to my son?"

"You keep saying that as if my baby belongs to you."

Again, that thin, wolfish smile. Cullen moved quickly; the next thing she knew he was holding her wrist clamped behind her back. ''That baby belongs to me as much as he does to you.''

''No! He doesn't! Damn you, Cullen—''

''Why do you hate me? You're pregnant, but that's your doing as much as mine.''

''Let go. Let go!''

''You sure as hell didn't hate me the night we made love.''

''It wasn't love. It was—it was immoral. It was wrong. It was—''

''It was what we both wanted, and you know it.''

She tried to turn her face away from his, away from the icy glare of his angry eyes, and he clasped her chin and forced her to look at him.

''You burned for me that night, Marissa. You couldn't get enough of my hands on you, my mouth on you—''

Marissa spat a Spanish word at him. Cullen knew what it meant. Like his brothers, he'd dealt with Mexican workers on the grounds of the Desert Song in Las Vegas. They'd taught him their language, the best and the worst of it, and what she'd said was surely the worst.

''Liar,'' he said roughly, and he caught her mouth with his.

She fought him again, as hard as she had the last time. Sank her teeth into his lip, beat against his chest, but he went on kissing her, kissing her…

And felt the instant of her surrender. Her mouth softened under his; her sigh whispered against his lips.

Now, his fevered body told him. Lift her in your arms, take her to the bedroom, bury yourself in her again as you did that first time…

Cullen jerked back.

His hand fell to his side; he dragged air into his burning lungs and watched as Marissa's eyes flew open, as she staggered back against the table. They stared at each other in the taut silence of the hot afternoon and then she swung away from him.

"All right." Her voice was a croak. "Give me whatever you want me to sign. I'll take the check, too, just so you can have a clear conscience, but I promise you, I'll rip it in half just as soon as—"

"No."

Cullen's voice was like the snap of a whip. Marissa turned and stared at him.

"But you said—"

"*You* said. Never tell a man you know what he said before he says it. Nine times out of ten, you'll be wrong—and the tenth time, he'll do just the opposite to spite you."

She watched him, her eyes searching his for a hint of the true meaning of his words. Something awful, she knew; she could feel it in her bones.

"Then, why did you come here today?"

He smiled, and she knew she would remember the chill of that smile forever.

"I came to tell you what happens next," he said softly.

"What—what happens next?"

Cullen nodded. He'd thought about this a thousand times after his dinner with Sean, gone through the plan, gone over it, refined it…

And finally admitted that what he and Sean had agreed upon wasn't the right solution.

Like it or not, the child growing in Marissa Perez's womb was his.

Like it or not, he was responsible not just for its conception but for its life.

Like it or not, by late last night, he could think of only one appropriate plan of action.

"What happens next," he said slowly, his eyes on Marissa's face, "is that you're going to become my wife."

CHAPTER SIX

CULLEN was asking her to be his wife.

His wife!

Was he really suggesting she marry him? It was so preposterous she wanted to laugh...but the hardness in his eyes made it clear he wasn't joking.

"Well?" he said. "No reaction? That's not like you, Marissa. You always have something to say."

He was so smug. So sure of himself. Did he expect her to drop at his feet in gratitude? Was she supposed to applaud his sacrifice? Tie herself to a man who didn't want her, so he could salve his conscience?

He was in for the shock of his life.

She smiled. Casually, even graciously, as if she'd expected his proposal all along.

"Thank you," she said politely. "But I'm not interested."

"Not interested." His smile thinned. "*You're* not interested."

"That's right. It's a generous offer, but—"

"It's not generous, and it's not an offer. It's a logical argument for marriage. My son isn't going to be born a bastard."

She knew he was using the word to intimidate her, but she wasn't about to be intimidated. She could, and would, stand up to the Cullen O'Connells of this world.

"That's an outdated concept," she said calmly.

"In your world, perhaps. Not in mine."

"Ah. Yes, of course. That rarified air you breathe makes

everything different. I keep forgetting that. I already said I'll put your name on his birth certificate since it means so much to you.''

''Since it means so much to me?'' Cullen narrowed his eyes. ''What about what it'll mean to my son, when he's old enough to ask questions? Don't you think he'd want to know his father's name?''

He was right. Why not admit it? But before she could, Cullen was lecturing her again.

''Didn't it occur to you he'd have questions when he's older? What did you intend to tell him, when he began asking about his father?''

What, indeed? She'd been so busy thinking about how to get through the next months, she hadn't had time to think about what would happen years down the road. All she knew was that she wouldn't repeat her mother's endless litany of anger and accusation.

''I didn't think about—''

''No,'' Cullen snapped. ''I'm sure you didn't''

''I'll tell him something,'' Marissa said stubbornly. ''There's plenty of time to decide.''

Cullen's eyes locked on hers. ''You won't have to make those decisions because he won't ask those questions. He'll know I'm his father, right from the start.''

''You can't be serious about marriage. We don't know anything about each other.''

''We knew enough about each other to make a child. Remember?''

Remember? Sometimes she lay awake nights, wondering if she'd ever be able to forget.

''Children aren't stupid, Cullen. My son—''

''Our son,'' he said coldly.

''The point is, it will only confuse him if you pop in and out of his life. I know you think you want that now, but given time—''

''Did I say anything about popping in and out of his life?''

''Surely you weren't talking about a real marriage.''

''Two people living together. Having dinner at the same table at night. Raising their child together. If that's what you mean by a real marriage, you're damned right it's what I'm talking about.''

''It wouldn't work. How could it?'' she said desperately. ''I don't want—''

''I don't give a damn what you want. I'm talking about doing what's best for our child.''

Cullen swung away, shrugged off his jacket and tossed it on the back of a chair, followed that by undoing his tie, his shirt collar and his cuffs. She knew her horrid box of an apartment was hot as the anteroom to Hades, but even in her anger, seeing the strong, tanned column of his throat and his hair-dusted, well-muscled forearms made her remember things she didn't want to remember.

Marissa turned her back, dumped her mug in the sink and walked into the living room. It was, if anything, hotter than the kitchen and the mismatched old furniture made it feel like a trap.

Cullen had followed her in and she could feel his presence behind her. Big. Commanding. Almost overwhelming, and she let herself imagine, just for a moment, what it would be like to be his wife, before she turned and confronted him.

''Look,'' she said briskly, ''I appreciate what you're trying to do, but it's not necessary.''

''I don't think you have any idea what it is I'm *going* to do, Marissa.''

She caught the difference between his choice of words and hers. Ignore it, she told herself fiercely. He was just trying to shake her.

''Cullen. Really, I don't—''

''This isn't about you.'' His tone was whip-sharp. ''It's not about me. It's about our child.''

He put his hand over her belly. She caught her breath,

stunned at the image of Cullen cradling the small, helpless life inside her that flashed into her mind.

"There's not a way in the world," he said, "I'd let my son be raised like this."

"Like what?" Marissa moved away from his touch, struggling for composure. "Are you telling me I'm not fit to raise my own child?"

"Our child. And I'm not talking about your fitness to be a parent, I'm talking about the kind of life you can afford to give him."

"He'll have the best I can manage. Poverty doesn't necessarily limit someone," she said, trying not to wince at the absolute hypocrisy of her own words. It was true that poverty didn't have to limit your dreams, but the truth was that being poor was horrible. Only a fool would deliberately choose such a life.

Why was she saying these things? In her heart, she knew Cullen was doing the right thing. He wanted to accept full responsibility for his child. How could she fault that? How could she turn it down? *Why* was she turning it down?

Why? Because she'd gotten herself into this mess. She didn't need anyone to get her out of it. She didn't need Cullen O'Connell, didn't want him…

Liar, a voice inside her whispered slyly. *Liar, liar, liar!*

Her body flushed with heat; her eyes met Cullen's. He was watching her as if he knew what was going through her mind. She let out a shaky breath and turned away. She had to get him out of here before she said something, did something, she'd regret.

"Thank you for your offer," she said politely, "but marrying you is out of the question. We have nothing more to discuss. Please do us both a favor and go away."

"You'd like that, wouldn't you?" Cullen grabbed her shoulder. "If I just got out of your life? If you could pretend you'd never slept with me?"

Marissa gave a bitter laugh. "It's too late for that."

"Yes. It is," Cullen said through his teeth. "But it's not too late for some answers."

"You've had all the answers I'm going to give. I don't want to marry you. That's the end of it."

"Like hell it is!" He spun her toward him, his face dark with anger. "Why didn't you call and tell me you were pregnant?"

"What a good idea," she said coldly. "I can hear the conversation now. 'Hi. This is Marissa Perez. Remember me? I'm the woman you—'"

"Don't give me that crap. You knew I'd remember you. I phoned you a dozen times after that weekend and you never returned my calls."

"I lead a busy life. That's why I have an answering machine."

"Oh, right. You have an answering machine." A thin sneer curved Cullen's mouth. "Do you ever bother checking it for messages?"

Marissa stared at him. What would he say if he knew she'd listened to his messages over and over? That there'd been times she'd played them just to hear his voice?

But she'd known what he wanted, why he'd he called. She wasn't stupid.

She'd been pathetically easy.

Living with that knowledge was bad enough; phoning him, letting him know she hadn't forgotten him, would have been worse. Flying across the country for the weekend was nothing to a man like him. He'd have come to see her, she'd have tumbled into bed with him again and lost what little self-respect she had left.

The only humiliation greater than that would have been calling to tell him she was pregnant.

"Well? I'm still waiting for you to tell me why you didn't answer my calls."

"Wrong," she said. "You asked me to explain why I didn't tell you I was pregnant. Just for the sake of argument, let's suppose I had. What would you have said to me?''

''The same thing I'm saying now. That this child is as much my responsibility as yours.''

''Aren't you leaving something out?'' She heard the tremor in her voice and vowed she wouldn't let him see her weep. ''First you'd have said, 'Pregnant, Marissa? Why tell me? Who else have you been with?' And then you'd have demanded a DNA test.''

Cullen's eyes narrowed. ''You're damned right, I would. A woman tells a man she's been with once that she's having his child and he's not supposed to ask questions?''

No, she thought, *oh no, because if the night meant as much to you as it did to me…*

The thought, its implications, turned her legs to water. She jerked free of his hands and sat down in a straight-backed chair near the window.

''All right,'' she said calmly, ''I'm willing to admit you have the right to some interest in my baby.''

Cullen smiled tightly. ''How generous.''

''And that he can benefit from some connection with his father.''

''Another crumb. Go on.''

Marissa knotted her hands together in her lap. ''I'm willing to acknowledge you as my child's father. But I don't want your money. And I certainly don't want some—some sham marriage to assuage your guilt.''

''Is that what you think this is all about? Guilt?''

''No,'' she said sweetly, ''of course not. I think you just suddenly developed a desperate yearning for fatherhood.'' She sprang to her feet. ''Of course it's guilt,'' she snapped. ''What else would you call it?''

''Responsibility,'' he said coldly. ''For my actions. Or is that a concept that's beyond your comprehension?''

She wanted to laugh. To cry. To ball up her fist and hit him for his insufferable arrogance. She looked around at the awful place she'd taken to save money for her baby and finally permitted herself a bark of joyless laughter.

"When I found out I was pregnant," she said, "I considered my options. Abortion. Adoption. The intelligent, responsible solutions that sound so wise until you find yourself with a life inside you. And I knew that neither was the right choice for me."

"Ah." Cullen's voice was even more frigid. "So you decided on martyrdom instead."

"You son of a bitch! Is that what you think? That I gave everything for some—some misbegotten martyr's complex?" Her voice broke. Angry tears burned her eyes and she turned away. "Go home, Cullen," she whispered. "You've done your bit. Now, please, just go away."

There was a long silence. She heard his footsteps behind her, felt the light pressure of his hands on her shoulders. He tried to turn her to him but Marissa stood fast.

"You love this baby," Cullen said quietly.

She didn't answer. She didn't have to. Her answer was visible in the sacrifices she'd willingly made so she could keep the child. Why hadn't he understood that until now?

"Marissa. If you love him," he said quietly, "then you must want the best for him. So do I. A good home. Good schools. Most of all, two parents who'll be there for him. Are those such terrible things to want a kid to have?" Gently, inexorably, he turned her to face him. Her eyes were shiny with tears and he felt something tight start to unknot inside him. "Marriage is the right thing. In your heart, you know that's true."

"It wouldn't work."

"Why not?"

"Because—because, how could it?"

He smiled. It was such an illogical answer from a woman he knew prided herself for her logic.

"We'd make it work. We're two intelligent people. We'll find a way."

She shook her head. "We're strangers."

"No. We spent a night together." His voice dropped to a husky whisper. He hadn't meant to remind her of that but holding her like this, his fingers spread over the delicate bones in her shoulders, her face turned up to his, her eyes full of questions, Cullen felt the memory sweep over him. His gaze dropped to her mouth. "A night I've never forgotten."

Color striped her cheeks. "You can't possibly think sex is enough to build a marriage on," she whispered.

"Marriages have been built on less."

"Yes, but—"

There was only one way to silence her, and Cullen took it. He trapped her face in his hands and took her mouth with his. She made a little sound of surprise and tried to pull back; he took her bottom lip between his teeth and nipped the full, sweet flesh. God, the taste of her. Strawberries, he thought, sweet summer strawberries on a sun-drenched hill, and as he thought it, Marissa whimpered, leaned into him and opened her mouth to his. Cullen groaned, gathered her tight in his arms and kissed her with all the pent-up hunger of the last months.

She whispered a soft word in Spanish, moved closer, moved against him. She felt soft. Warm. Incredibly female, her breasts and body lush as they prepared for the birth of his child.

Mine, he thought fiercely. *All of this, mine.*

An eternity passed before Cullen lifted his head. When he did, Marissa was trembling in his arms, her breathing ragged. She looked small and shaken and all he wanted was to draw her to him again and comfort her.

"Marissa." He ran his hand along the side of her face, threaded his fingers into her silky curls and stroked them back from her flushed cheek. "How long will it take you to pack?"

"Pack?"

"Your things. Whatever you can't part with. Leave everything else and we'll buy whatever you want in Boston."

She stiffened in his embrace, put her hands against his chest. He didn't want to, but he dropped his arms to his sides.

"I'm not marrying you. I keep telling you that. Why won't you listen? I don't need your help. I don't need anyone's help." She stepped back and stood facing him, small white teeth bared like those of a cornered animal. "Go away, Cullen. You offered what you saw as the right thing and I turned you down. Surely, that's enough to make you feel good about yourself."

"You have a hell of a poor opinion of me."

"I don't have any opinion of you. I just want you to leave."

Cullen walked to the sofa, opened his briefcase and took out what she recognized as a legal document.

"Here," he said, and thrust it at her.

She took the paper from him but her gaze never left his. "What is it?"

"You're a third-year law student. Read it and find out."

She didn't move, didn't stop looking at him while the silence and the heat built in the small room. At last, she started reading.

He watched her, saw her face begin to drain of color. After a couple of minutes, Cullen walked to the window, drew up a shade so ancient it threatened to disintegrate in his hands and looked out on the street.

How would she react to what he'd handed her? With relief, a cold voice inside him said. With outrage, another voice whispered.

Truth was, he didn't know. She'd made an impassioned speech about wanting her baby but predicting her reactions to anything was turning out to be as impossible as predicting the ultimate path of a tornado.

After his talk with Sean the other night, he'd drafted the documents that would ensure a monthly stipend for the child in Marissa's womb, straight through to a university degree. As Sean had pointed out, that was all that was required of him ethically. Hell, it was more, considering the amount of money he'd decided to provide.

Except, that simple word—*father*—kept haunting him. He was going to be a father. He hadn't planned it, hadn't wanted it, not now. Someday in the future, sure. That's what a man did, wasn't it? Find the right woman, settle down to a pleasant if uneventful married life, have kids…

Fate, and one night of unthinking passion, had changed all that.

A tiny life floated serenely in Marissa's womb. A life he'd sired, and even though the timetable was off, that newcomer deserved all the things Cullen had intended a child of his would have. The things he'd told Marissa. A good home and good schools. Two parents. And other things almost as important. A dog. A cat. A tank full of guppies, if that was what the kid wanted. Electric trains and a bike, and Christmas mornings filled with joy.

Most of all, his child would have what Cullen had never had. A father who loved him enough to put him first and to put everything else, including his own pleasures, second.

It was the right way. The only way. Once he'd admitted that, he'd known that putting his name on a birth certificate and funding a bank account would never be sufficient.

Late last night, he'd drawn up a new document. Even then, he hadn't really been sure he'd use it. At dawn, exhausted, he'd tucked both sets of papers into his briefcase and stumbled to bed, telling himself he'd make his choice on the flight to California.

Instead, he'd made it only moments ago. For better or for worse, what he'd handed Marissa was a prenuptial agreement.

Cullen looked at her. She was still reading the document but he knew she was almost at the end by the look on her face. Well, he hadn't expected her to be thrilled by all it spelled out. He'd set out her choices. It was up to her to react to them.

Marissa looked up. The document he'd drafted hung limply from her hand.

"This is a contract," she said slowly.

"All those classes on contract law weren't wasted, were they?"

"Don't joke with me, damn it! You've drawn up a prenup!"

"Exactly."

"Marriage," she said, spitting out the word like an obscenity.

"Marriage," he said calmly. "That's what I've been talking about for the past hour."

"Forget it!" She stepped away from him, her color high. "Here's what I've been telling *you* for the last hour, Mr. O'Connell. I will not marry you. Never. Do you understand? As for the rest of this—this piece of garbage..." Eyes locked to his, she tore the document he'd given her in half, then in half again. The ripped paper fluttered to the worn carpet like white ribbons. "You know what you can do with it."

"Did you read it carefully?"

"You mean, the part that says we'll review the situation every two years?" Marissa laughed. "A loophole so you can institute divorce proceedings, when you've had enough."

"I'm not planning on divorce, Marissa. It's simply a safeguard for us both."

"It's an admission this will never work."

"I'm not going to argue the point," Cullen said calmly. "Besides, I was referring to the clause that sets out my financial commitment to you. It says—"

"I know what it says. You'll provide me with...what was the phrase? 'The appropriate financial support due a spouse.'"

Cullen felt his face heat. The words had a nasty sound, stated so baldly.

''It also says,'' he said quickly, ''that I'll pay your tuition at Harvard Law.''

''Just think,'' Marissa said coolly. ''All I cost you that night we went to bed was dinner. Heck, not even that. The law club picked up the tab.''

''Damn it,'' Cullen snarled, closing the distance between them, clasping her elbows and hoisting her to her toes. ''What's the matter with you?''

''What's the matter with *you?*'' she shot back. ''Do you think I'm still the same silly girl who foolishly tumbled into bed that night with you?''

''We made love that night. And we made a baby. There's nothing foolish in that.''

No, she thought, there wasn't. Creating a life was serious business.

''What am I asking that's so impossible, Marissa? I want you to marry me. Be my wife. Help me make things right for our son.''

Oh, how easy he made it all sound! Marriage, and a perfect life for their baby…

''We already agreed, we'd start ahead of some couples.''

She hadn't agreed to anything, but that didn't seem to matter, especially when she knew, in her heart, her case was weak. What kind of woman would deny her baby the advantages Cullen was offering?

''Other people aren't strangers,'' she said wearily. ''They have shared hopes and concerns.''

''We have shared hopes and concerns.''

She laughed, or tried to. ''Sure we do. I'll bet you're always hoping you'll be able to pay the rent when it comes due, and concerned what will happen if you don't.''

''You're proving my point about the logic of marrying me,'' Cullen said quietly, ''but that's not what I mean. I'm talking about things that matter. Like our love for the law. And I'll bet we share an interest in more than that.''

''For instance.''

He thought for a minute. ''Music.''

"I like Mozart."

He sighed. "I like stuff that came a little later."

"How much later?"

"Say..." A little smile flickered at the corners of his mouth. "Say, the late 1970s?"

Upset as she was, it was hard not to smile, too, but she didn't. Instead, she shook her head.

"Look, Cullen, I know you mean well, but—"

"How about boats? Do you like to sail?"

"As in, on the water?"

Cullen laughed. "Yeah. As in, on the water."

Marissa shuddered. "More water than can fit in a bathtub makes me nervous. Face it, okay? We come from different worlds. Even if—*if,* mind you, I were to consider marr—"

"Don't consider it," he said gruffly. "Just do it."

She started to speak but he stopped her with a gentle kiss, a soft brush of his lips against hers. Maybe it was that gentleness that was her undoing. There'd been so little that was gentle in her life...

"Marissa," Cullen whispered, and she let herself sink into the kiss. Into the hard comfort of his body, the warmth of his encircling arms, let herself imagine having this man, this strong, determined, sexy man, to lean on.

The thought dazzled her. Frightened her. She'd never lean on anybody, or be foolish enough to put her trust in a man.

"You see?" Cullen said huskily. "We can make this work."

"With sex, you mean. But—"

"But what?" He cupped her face and his eyes blazed into hers. "Is it wrong for a man to want his wife in his bed?"

"Yes. When they don't know each other. When their marriage is an expedient mockery. When—when they should never have—"

He kissed her again, harder this time, and as the kiss deepened, the earth seemed to drop out from beneath her.

Marissa moaned and clung to Cullen's shoulders. Wrong, she thought dizzily, oh, this was wrong. She was giving in to a base need again, admitting to the terrifying emotions that could only be her undoing.

"Cullen," she gasped, "Cullen, I think—"

"Stop thinking," he said fiercely. "Just feel. Just do it. Marry me."

How could she? And yet, how could she not? All this time that she'd been telling Cullen he was crazy to even suggest marriage, she knew she was being selfish. She had a child to think of. A life dependent on her that hadn't asked to come into this world.

"If I did," she heard herself say, "if I did, you'd have to agree to no sex."

"And give up the only thing besides the law that we have in common?"

He said it seriously but she knew he was laughing at her, and it made her all the more determined. Her breathing quickened. She'd always been good at chess. Wasn't that what this was? A game of chess...and she'd just checkmated him. She'd given Cullen a reason to withdraw his marriage offer. Surely, he was too virile a man to accept a sexless marriage.

"I can see right through you," he said softly.

"Excuse me?"

"You tie on a stipulation you assume I won't accept, and the onus is off you. We don't get married, but it's my doing, not yours."

Her laugh sounded false even to her own ears. "That's nonsense!"

"I don't think so. I think it's exactly what you're hoping will happen."

"Well, I don't care what you think." Marissa stepped out of his arms. "Your choice, Cullen. Take it or leave it."

Cullen narrowed his gaze on Marissa's determined, lovely face. He thought about telling her there wasn't a way in hell he'd accept her terms for very long, or pointing out that she was kidding herself if she thought she could live with them, either. For reasons that were beyond him, she couldn't seem to accept the truth, that she was the most sensual, sexual woman he'd ever known.

"Well?" she said. "What's your answer?"

He gave her a smile she couldn't read. Then he rolled his sleeves up another inch, took a quick look around him, and said she had better start packing.

Her heart thumped against her ribs. "Does that mean you accept my terms?"

"It means," he said calmly, "you have an hour before we walk out of this place and never come back to it."

"An hour? That's impossible."

"Nothing's impossible," he said, his eyes never leaving hers, "if you want it badly enough."

Were the softly spoken words a threat? Marissa couldn't tell, and she wasn't about to ask.

"Marissa?"

She looked up at him. A little smile curved his lips, but his eyes were cold. Whose chess game was in danger now, she wondered. His...or hers?

"An hour," she said briskly, and hoped he couldn't see that she was trembling as she went into the bedroom, opened the closet and took down her suitcase.

CHAPTER SEVEN

HOW could life get so complicated so fast? A man wanted to do what was right and ended up stepping into quicksand.

Two weeks had passed. Fourteen days. Three hundred and thirty-six hours. If you thought about it as blocks of time on a calendar, it wasn't much at all.

But when you'd lived through those hours, those days, those weeks, it was like viewing eternity from the inside out. How could time move so slowly?

Cullen stood on the terrace of his town house, overlooking the garden, a cup of coffee slowly going cold in his hand. Fall was trying to make a showing, but it wasn't succeeding. Though the leaves were starting to turn red and gold, the temperature was still as high as in midsummer.

That was too bad. He liked autumn. The brilliant blaze of foliage, the cool evenings… But this year's weather patterns seemed confused.

Like him.

Confused? No. Hell, no. He wasn't confused. Why would he be? Marissa despised him. She despised this place. She refused to speak to him, refused to look at him, refused, even, to acknowledge his presence.

There wasn't a damned thing confusing about that.

Cullen took a sip of coffee and made a face. The coffee was as cold as the mood inside the house but the coffee, at least, he could put aside.

Not so Marissa. She was his wife.

His untouched, unsmiling, Sphinx-silent wife.

Divorce would solve the problem. Half the people he

knew were divorced or separated. Giving up on marriage after only a couple of weeks wouldn't even make most of them blink. One of his firm's associates had just handled the breakup of a couple whose try at marital bliss had lasted exactly nine days.

Not that he'd expected bliss. He'd married for a purpose. Bliss had nothing to do with it. It was just that he'd had it with his wife treating him like he was a monster.

Even his housekeeper had taken to glaring at him. Concepcion came in at eight three mornings a week. As luck would have it, he'd had a deposition scheduled the day after Marissa's arrival, and God only knew how his Ice Bride had introduced herself.

Judging by the way Concepcion looked at him now, Marissa had probably told her she was being held captive in a modern-day version of Bluebeard's castle.

Was this what a man got for doing the right thing?

Cullen scowled, folded his arms and turned his back to the view.

He *had* done the right thing. That was one conviction that hadn't changed. So what if the woman who'd once looked at him with passion smoldering in her eyes now practically spat at him when their eyes met? What Marissa felt for him, what he felt for her, was secondary to the reason for their marriage—the child she carried.

His wife loathed him, Cullen thought grimly. Was it because he'd taken her out of her wonderful life in a Berkeley slum? Because she wasn't on her feet twelve hours a day in that ptomaine palace? Did she miss climbing four flights of stairs to a three-room sweatbox filled with furniture the Salvation Army would have rejected?

Oh yeah. He'd certainly given her reason to loathe him.

Add in law school, and anyone could see that he'd really treated her badly. If she ever got around to talking to him, he'd tell her he'd already done some checking. There was still time for her to apply to Harvard Law, but he'd be damned if he'd tell her that.

Let her approach him. Let her say something. Anything. Damn it, if she hated him, let her say so.

Let her say anything, he thought, and his scowl deepened.

The truth was, Marissa didn't talk, didn't look at him, didn't seem to be living on the same planet. As for emotion…the last time she'd shown him any was in her apartment. She'd stopped talking as soon as she'd agreed to become his wife. By the time they'd reached the airport, her sitting beside him like a mannequin in a wax museum, he'd started to wonder if doing the right thing was all it was cracked up to be.

That was why he'd decided to make a fast stop at Vegas, the center of quickie weddings, before heading for home. He'd intended to ask a judge he knew to tie the knot once they were in Boston, but Marissa's stony face, her expression of utter contempt had made him change his plans. Better to say "I do" in front of a stranger than an acquaintance who'd wonder what in hell was going on.

"You want any special kind of ceremony?" he'd asked Marissa at the airport.

No, she'd said. Just no. Not a smile, not a question, just that one cold word.

So he'd rented a car, driven down the Strip and pulled in at the first place he saw. The chapel had a ten-foot-tall statue of Elvis outside, complete with sideburns and blue suede shoes. Inside, the walls were covered with red satin hearts.

For one crazy minute, he'd considered turning around and dragging Marissa out of there, telling her nobody's marriage should start in a place as phony as this.

But sanity had prevailed, the same as when he'd thought about phoning the Desert Song and telling his mother he was in town. What would he have said? *Hi, Ma, guess what? I'm getting hitched and by the way, you'll be a grandma in five months?*

Right. That was just what a mother wanted to hear.

For now, Mary didn't know about Marissa. Nobody in his family did. Not yet. Well, Sean, but Sean didn't know the rest of it. That he was married…

Married. Was there a stranger-sounding word in the English language?

Standing in that red-silk chapel, facing a woman showing all the enthusiasm of a condemned prisoner on the gibbet, he'd ground his teeth together, barked out such a snappish "I do" that the J.P. had given him a look.

Marissa had whispered hers. That had really gotten the justice of the peace's attention.

"Are you all right, Ms. Perez?" he'd asked, his gaze dropping not so discreetly to Marissa's swollen belly.

"I'm fine," she'd replied. "Let's just get on with it, please."

The J.P. had made a joke of it after pronouncing them husband and wife.

"It's always nice to see a bride who's eager to tie the knot," he'd said.

Cullen had laughed politely, the J.P. had done the same, but Marissa had gone on looking like a corpse warmed over. In the end, nobody had fooled anybody. Marissa Perez had become Marissa O'Connell, and the occasion had not been a joyous one.

A muscle knotted in Cullen's jaw. He lifted the cup of coffee to his lips, grimaced and drank it down.

Did she think *he* was happy about this marriage? Oh, yeah. What man wouldn't be happy to have a wife who stayed in her rooms when he was around? Who refused to join him for meals? Who treated him as if she had never sighed in his arms, begged for his kisses, moaned his name when he spread her thighs and buried himself inside her?

The cup, squeezed far too tightly, shattered in Cullen's hand. He cursed, looked down at the white porcelain shards lying at his feet. Why was he thinking about the past? The future was all that mattered. The future, and the child in Marissa's womb.

Cullen slid open the terrace door, walked to the kitchen and took a dustpan and broom from the utility closet.

He was a civilized man, and his marriage was a civilized arrangement. That was what he'd promised himself during the long flight home from Nevada with Marissa never looking at him, never speaking a word, as if that swift flare of desire just a couple of hours before, in her apartment, had never happened.

It had infuriated him. What kind of game was she playing?

He'd made himself a vow.

He wouldn't touch her. He didn't want her in his bed if he had to battle past a show of contempt before he could get her to admit she wanted him. Sex had gotten them into this arrangement, but the well-being of a child was what would maintain it.

Out on the terrace again, Cullen was sweeping up the pieces of the cup when he noticed a smear of crimson on the broom handle and drops of crimson on the terrace floor. He'd gashed himself on the damned cup and never realized it. He headed back inside to get a bandage and saw that he'd left a trail of tiny blood drops across the pearl-gray Berber carpet.

That was all Concepcion needed. If he didn't get the mess cleaned up before she came back from the supermarket, she'd probably—

"You're bleeding!"

Cullen jerked around. Marissa was standing at the top of the wide marble step that led into the living room from the foyer. Her face was the same color as the marble.

"Marissa?"

She opened her mouth, shut it and swayed unsteadily on her feet. Cullen dropped the dustpan and broom and ran to her.

"Marissa," he said, scooping her into his arms, "what is it?"

"I'm all right," she whispered, but he could see that she wasn't.

"*¡Madre de Dios!* Is it the baby?"

Cullen looked up and saw Concepcion standing in the foyer, her black eyes wide with shock.

"I don't know. My wife just collapsed."

"I didn't collapse," Marissa said shakily. "Really. Just put me down. I'm fine."

Cullen and the housekeeper both ignored her.

"Sit the *señora* on the sofa. Put her head down. *Sí,* like that." Concepcion clasped her hands over her bosom. "She must be losing the child. The blood..."

"It's mine, not hers." Cullen squatted beside his wife and clasped her hands. "Marissa. Talk to me."

"I told you, I'm fine. I just felt dizzy for a minute."

"*¿Señora? ¿Se sucede qué? ¿Es el bebé?*"

Marissa shook her head. "*El bebé está muy bien. Acabo de sentirme mareado. La sangre...*"

"*Ah. Sí. La sangre.*"

Cullen's head swiveled from one woman to the other. How come it hadn't occurred to him that these two might share a language?

And how come Marissa had more of a relationship with his housekeeper than with him?

Damn it to hell, how come he didn't know the first thing about his own wife?

"What?" he demanded. "What's she saying?"

"It was the sight of the blood. It made her feel faint."

Cullen looked at his hand. The bleeding had stopped but there were spots on the carpet and there was some on his jeans. Based on how his housekeeper was glaring at him, she probably figured he'd taken to using small children and bunny rabbits for pagan sacrifice.

"It's nothing," he told Marissa, "just a little cut. A cut," he repeated, for the housekeeper's benefit.

Concepcion nodded. "I will take care of it."

"That's okay. I'll do it."

"I will do it, *señor.*"

"I said..." Hell. He sounded like a petulant ten year old. "Thank you, Concepcion. But for now, would you get us a cold compress?"

"I don't need one," Marissa said. She looked at him. "I'm fine. Really."

She didn't look fine, Cullen thought. She looked almost the way she had in Berkeley. Pale. Shadowed eyes. A mouth that trembled. Hadn't two weeks of rest and good nourishment done her any good?

"A cold compress will make you feel better."

She shook her head, sat up straight and carefully drew her hands from his. It didn't take a shrink to see that she was drawing back into herself.

She didn't want any help from anyone, especially him.

Concepcion clomped into the room with an ice pack, handed it to him and clomped out again to collect the fallen groceries. She disappeared into the kitchen and Marissa started to rise to her feet.

Cullen caught her hand and kept her beside him.

"Take it easy for a couple of minutes."

"I told you, I'm—"

"Fine. Right. Indulge me a little, okay? Let me put this ice pack on the back of your neck while you sit here."

He could tell that she was warring with herself. Should she leave to prove she didn't need to take his advice? A couple of seconds went by. Then she sighed, probably in resignation, and some of the rigidity ebbed from her posture.

"Give me the ice."

"I'll take care of it. You just lean forward. That's it."

She bent her head. Cullen swept her hair from the nape of her neck. The skin looked soft. Tender. He wondered what she'd do if he pressed his mouth to it instead of the ice.

"Ridiculous, isn't it?" she said. "A grown woman passing out at the sight of blood?"

He smiled, laid the ice pack gently against the exposed skin beneath her hair.

''We were on a picnic one time and a spider fell into my sister Megan's soup. She screeched like a banshee, her eyes rolled up into her head and she fell facedown into the bowl.''

Marissa made a sound he figured someone would make when they tried not to laugh. ''She must have been very young.''

''She was twenty.''

She did laugh this time. For some reason he couldn't fathom, that made him feel good.

''Okay, she was five. But it was a memorable performance.'' Cullen kept the ice in place and sat down on the step next to Marissa. ''I'm sorry you had a scare.'' His mouth curved in a smile. ''On the other hand, it was worth a little loss of blood to know you care.''

''I don't...'' Her cheeks reddened. ''It had nothing to do with you.''

''Ah. I should have known. I could have fallen at your feet, a Vorple blade in my heart, and you wouldn't have blinked.''

She stared at him. ''A Vorple what?''

''A Vorple blade.'' Cullen grinned and brandished an imaginary sword snatched from an imaginary scabbard at his hip. ''Like Darth Vader's light saber, only ten times more deadly.''

Marissa bit back another laugh. Laughing with this man would be a mistake. Anything that meant she was letting her guard down would be a mistake.

The entire flight to Boston two weeks ago, all she'd been able to think was that she was up in the air in more ways than one. Cullen O'Connell had come along, kicked the ground out from under her feet, forced her to admit that what he kept calling the right thing was exactly that.

And she was terrified.

Of course, she could never let him know that.

Was this how Dorothy had felt, swept up by that Kansas tornado and dropped down in the land of Oz? This absolute disorientation? This dizzying sense of fear? Except, in the mythical land of Oz, Dorothy had a tin man, a scarecrow and a lion to comfort her.

Marissa had nobody. Nobody but the man sitting next to her right now, his thigh brushing hers, his hand enfolding hers…

But she didn't have him. He'd done his duty, as he saw it. Married her. Brought her east. Installed her in his home…

In a guest room in his home.

Separate rooms. Separate lives. He'd rushed off the very first morning she was here, left her a stiffly worded note about having a deposition, as if he'd needed an excuse to explain what she'd understood all along.

She was his wife, but she wasn't ever going to be part of his life. And that was fine. That was how she wanted it. It was the only way she wanted it, and if he'd tried to arrange things differently, tried to make her share his life…

His bed.

If he'd tried that, she'd have made it crystal clear she'd meant what she said, that there wouldn't be any sex in this relationship. Why would she want to have sex with him? She'd been carried away that one night but she wasn't ever going to be carried away like that again. Wasn't going to lose control of herself again.

Not ever.

She wasn't going to feel his mouth on hers, his hands on her breasts. She wasn't going to feel the strength of his arms holding her close, or fall asleep with her head cradled on his shoulder, or awaken in the night to the whisper of his breath on her skin, his caress urgent, her response matching that urgency because she wanted him, needed him…

She'd never need anybody.

She sat up. Cullen took the ice pack away. "Feeling better?"

"Yes. Much. Thank you for your help."

He looked at her, but he didn't move away. Well, she'd move away from him. *Get up,* she told herself. *Marissa, get up…*

Cullen took her hand. "I'll bet you don't have any brothers."

"No. I don't."

"Because if you did, you'd be so used to the sight of gore that it wouldn't mean a thing."

"Really," she said, trying to sound bored but not carrying it off very well. From Vorple blades to brothers and gore, in less than a breath. The man had a gift. What was it the Irish called it? The gift of gab. That's what he had. It was one of the things she'd found charming, the night they'd met. The night he'd made her forget who she was, what she was, made her forget the whole world.

She began to stand up again. Cullen tugged her down beside him again.

"How about sisters? You have any of those?"

"I was an only child," she said stiffly.

"Lucky you."

"Not so lucky," she said, before she could censor herself. "I mean—it must be pleasant, having siblings."

Cullen chuckled. "Siblings, huh? Well, that's certainly better than some of the names I've called 'em. My brothers, especially."

"How many brothers do you have?" Not that it mattered. Nothing about his life mattered, except with regard to the baby inside her, but it was impossible not to ask.

"Two. And three sisters, every last one into what you might call blood sports."

Marissa raised her eyebrows. "Blood sports?"

"Sure. Football, baseball, soccer. It wasn't easy, growing up an O'Connell. My mother was always surprised the local emergency room didn't bolt the doors when they saw us coming.''

A peal of laughter burst from her throat. She hadn't meant it to happen, but she couldn't prevent it. The image of a harried woman followed by a small herd of children with scabby knees approaching a door barred by desperate nurses was just too much.

''There,'' Cullen said softly, ''you see? You do know how to laugh. I'd begun to wonder.''

''Cullen, really—''

''I mean, who knows? Girl grew up without a bunch of pain-in-the-butt sisters and brothers around, maybe she'd led such a sheltered life she didn't do much laughing as a kid.''

A sheltered life. If he only knew how funny that was. But he wouldn't. She never talked about her childhood. She didn't even like thinking about it. The past was the past. The future was all that mattered. That had been her credo from the time she was old enough to understand that not everyone lived the way she and her mother did.

''Hey.''

She looked at Cullen. He'd moved closer to her; his smile was intimate. She felt her heartbeat quicken. When he looked at her like this—when he was close to her like this—

''Why such a serious face?''

Because I think—I think—

''Marissa.''

His gaze on her lips felt like a caress.

''Marissa.'' He cupped her cheek, stroked his thumb lightly over her mouth. ''Are you so unhappy here?''

She couldn't meet his eyes. She looked down, saw the hand he'd injured lying, palm up, in his lap. The cut had stopped bleeding, as he'd said, but it looked raw and angry. What she'd told him about her childhood phobia was true enough; she hated the sight of blood and had ever since she'd seen a lifeless man, his shirt stained crimson, lying in the doorway of the apartment house where she lived.

But as Cullen's thumb moved across her lip, she knew that wasn't why she'd been so upset before.

She'd been upset because she'd thought he was hurt. Cullen. Her husband.

"Marissa," he whispered, and when she looked up through her lashes, he bent his head slowly toward hers…

"¿Esta usted seguro usted tiene todo razón, señora?"

Cullen turned quickly and saw his housekeeper in the doorway that led to the dining room, hands balled on her plump hips, her round bronzed face knotted with concern. He stared at her in amazement. Concepcion was a woman of few words and she never spoke before she was spoken to. He'd grown accustomed to her reticence; he'd long ago given up trying to get her to say more than yes, no or what shall I leave for your dinner?

Now, in the span of, what, half an hour, she'd said more than she'd said in the three years he'd known her. And she'd interrupted a conversation. Hell, she'd interrupted something far more important, a moment he'd hardly dare imagine might happen.

"What do you want?" He knew his tone was sharp, but he couldn't help it. It didn't help when Marissa drew away from him and rose to her feet.

"Gracias, Concepcion. Estoy muy bien."

"Este no es el viejo pai, en donde los bebé nacen sin ciudado."

"Sí. Lo sé."

"Entonces usted debe hablar a su marido sobre qué está sucdediendo."

"¡Éste es ninguno de su negocio!"

"Usted dice tan, pero estoy libre hablar mi mente."

"Are you deaf?" Marissa slipped into angry-sounded English. "I said—"

"Whoa."

Cullen stepped between the women, looked from one to

the other and tried a quick smile to calm things down. It was as useless as ice cubes on a griddle.

"What's going on here?"

Marissa flushed. "It's nothing."

"Give me a break, sweetheart. Concepcion's angry. At you?"

"No. Not at me, exactly." Silence. Then Marissa cleared her throat. "She's from Mexico."

"And?"

"And, I'm half Mexican. My mother was born in Guadalajara."

Cullen decided to ignore the what-do-you-think-of-that belligerence in her tone. He'd tackle that later, after he figured out why a domestic firefight had broken out.

"And?"

"And, since we share a language and, she assumes, a heritage, she thinks she knows what's best for me."

He'd take on that one later, too. God, this was like pulling teeth. *"And?"* Cullen said impatiently.

"She says—"

"The *señora* is pregnant," Concepcion announced.

"And?" Cullen said. "And" seemed to be the only word left in his vocabulary. "Of course she's pregnant. I know that."

"Do you, *señor?*"

"Concepcion!" Marissa's eyes all but shot fire. "That's enough."

"The *señora* needs someone to care for her." The housekeeper glared at Cullen. "You think it is enough you make her your wife, but you do nothing else. You leave her alone all day, you permit her to weep, you don't talk to her—"

"Weep?" Cullen said, staring at Marissa.

Marissa snapped out a sharp command. Concepcion flushed, turned on her heel and marched away.

"I'm sorry," Marissa murmured. "Please don't blame her. She told me she has a daughter my age, back in Mexico. Evidently, she's feeling maternal toward me."

''Weep?'' he said again.

Marissa's chin rose. ''What does it matter?''

Cullen grabbed Marissa by the shoulders. ''Are you crazy? The housekeeper knows that my wife's been crying, but I don't? Of course it matters! Why were you crying?''

''I told you, it doesn't matter.''

His mouth thinned. ''Because of me. Because of the marriage I demanded.''

''No. You were right. Marriage was the right thing. I'll get used to my new life.''

Her voice trembled when she said it. Her new life. The life he'd dragged her into. The life he'd done nothing to make welcoming.

God, he was a fool!

Cullen ground out a single, short expletive between his teeth.

''Wait here,'' he growled, and strode from the room.

''No! Cullen...''

But he marched in the other direction from the kitchen. Concepcion, at least, was safe from his ire.

Marissa sighed. Her shoulders slumped and she sank down on the steps again.

What a mistake she'd made, letting the woman hear her crying that first day. She hadn't intended it to happen; it just had. She'd awakened in this strange place, for a moment so disoriented that she'd thought she was in a bad dream.

Then she'd remembered. Cullen's visit to her apartment. His demands. Her concession to them. The horrid wedding ceremony that had united her to a man who didn't want her but was determined to do the moral thing, the anguish of the flight here with him sitting beside her knotted with tension. This enormous town house with its icily perfect décor.

And Cullen holding her elbow, hurrying her up the stairs to a guest room and abandoning her there because he clearly couldn't wait to be rid of her.

All that night, she lay in a bed that wasn't hers, in a

room that wasn't hers, waiting for the door to open. Waiting for her husband to come to her. To take her in his arms and kiss her and make her see that this marriage could work.

She'd told herself she didn't want him to kiss her. To touch her. It was a lie. When he touched her, oh, when he touched her, everything changed. Her fear, her humiliation at what he made her feel, all disappeared.

Maybe she needed to tell him that, she'd thought, and in those long hours of that endless night, that was what she'd decided to do. She wasn't a coward. She wasn't spineless. Come morning, their first morning as husband and wife, she would tell Cullen she'd thought things over and he was right.

If this marriage had any chance at all, they'd have to behave as if it were real.

She slept a little, awoke early, showered, dried her hair, brushed it until it hung down her back in dark, flowing waves. Then she took a pair of drawstring-waisted silk trousers from her suitcase and topped them with an oversize black cotton T-shirt. At last, she took a deep, deep breath and stepped out into the hall.

Stepped out into her new life…

Alone.

A woman in the kitchen introduced herself curtly as Concepcion, stared at Marissa's belly so hard that Marissa blushed, and handed her a note from Cullen. It was as abrupt as the housekeeper's greeting. He had a meeting he couldn't cancel and he'd see her for dinner.

A meeting he didn't want to cancel and a wife he regretted marrying, was more like it. Even a man who'd done what he called the right thing could come to his senses.

Marissa had crushed the note in her hand.

"The *señor* says you are his wife."

Marissa nodded. "*Sí,*" she'd said automatically, memories of her mother triggered by that familiar accent, "*soy su esposa.*"

Concepcion's face had softened. "You are Mexican?"

Marissa had lifted her eyes to the housekeeper's. "I am nothing," she'd whispered, and the tears had come.

If only she hadn't cried. If only she'd remained strong. She'd never broken down before. Never. Not in the face of her mother's bitterness. Not when the doctor at the clinic had confirmed that she was pregnant. Not when she'd gone to the bursar's office and signed the papers that said she was leaving school, leaving everything she'd ever dreamed of.

Even now, she was weeping. Angrily, she wiped her knuckles over her eyes. Stupid, stupid, stupid. Why had she cried on the first morning of her marriage? Why was she crying now? Why did what Cullen did or didn't do matter?

"Let's go."

Marissa looked up. Cullen was standing over her. He'd shaved away his early-morning stubble.

"Go?" she said blankly. "Go where?"

He reached down, took her hands, lifted her gently to her feet. And he smiled. Oh God, he smiled, and what happened to her foolish, foolish heart when he did was enough to make tears sting her eyes again.

"Out. First to the doctor, then to shop."

"But I'm fine. Really. That fainting spell—"

"A pregnant woman needs to see an obstetrician. I don't know why it took me so long to realize that."

"It's okay. I thought of it. I made some calls… There's a free clinic on—"

"A clinic?"

"Yes. It's not around here, but—"

"I called Ben Silverman. He's one of my partners. He said the obstetrician his wife used is terrific, so I phoned and made an appointment. They were really busy but I said it was important and the receptionist said, well, they'd just had a cancellation and… What?"

"Is this the first you mentioned, uh, the baby and me to anyone?"

Cullen thought about his conversation with Sean, but that didn't count. As far as his brother knew, he'd decided to offer financial support to Marissa and her baby, not marry her.

"Yeah." Color striped his cheeks. "Can you forgive me?" he said softly.

Bewildered, Marissa shook her head. "There's nothing to forgive."

"Of course there is," he said. He sounded angry. With surprise, she realized his anger was for himself. "I coerced you into this marriage and then—then, I chickened out."

"I don't understand."

"Those sisters I mentioned? Bree's into touchy-feely stuff. I think she'd call it, disassociation." Cullen's jaw tightened. "You made it clear you wanted no part of me. And instead of finding ways to make you see I could make you happy, I accepted that and didn't try to change it. I took the out you gave me, and I backed away." He lowered his head to hers, brushed his mouth over hers, did it again and again until he felt her lips soften and cling lightly to his. "Marissa. This is as new to me as it is to you. I'm every bit as scared but, damn it, we'll find a way to make it work."

"I don't—"

"I know. I don't know, either. The only thing I'm sure of is that we have to give it a try."

She sighed. He was right. "For the baby," she said quietly.

"For him. And for us. The thought of you weeping, of you feeling so alone, breaks my heart." Cullen tunneled his fingers into her hair, tilted her face up to his. "As for the practicalities of this new life… How could I have been such a fool? It's not enough to give you a roof over your head. You need a doctor. Clothing. Whatever it is makes women look in the mirror and smile."

"No. I have—"

"Don't argue with me," he said firmly. "We're going to the doctor. Then we're going shopping. You got that?"

"The doctor, yes. But not the rest. I don't need anything."

Cullen smiled. He hated himself for his stupidity. His insensitivity. His cowardice. But he loved hearing the way Marissa was talking. The way she was lifting that chin and looking right at him.

Yes. Oh yes. Tucked away inside, his bright, beautiful, stubborn Marissa had only been waiting to emerge.

She was still talking, telling him why she wouldn't spend his money. He decided not to waste energy arguing. It was easier and far, far more satisfying to silence this woman the only way that seemed to work.

He kissed her, felt her tremble as he did.

Then Cullen put his arm around his wife's shoulders and led her into the world.

CHAPTER EIGHT

IF SOMEBODY had asked Cullen to name ten of his favorite pastimes, sitting in the crowded waiting room of a doctor's office wouldn't have made the list.

Thankfully, he hadn't spent much time in places like that. Immunization shots before a post-Princeton, pre-Berkeley, around-the-world backpacking trip. A banged-up knee, courtesy of a losing argument with a recalcitrant halyard on his boat. A dislocated shoulder, a badge of honor he'd acquired during an our-office-against-yours, no-holds-barred racquetball tournament.

What he remembered from those infrequent stops in doctors' waiting rooms were outdated magazines, elevator music, and somebody always sitting right beside him, coughing like a character in the final act of a bad opera.

This visit wasn't like that.

Ben had recommended an obstetrician in the Back Bay area. Cullen lucked out and got a parking spot on the first try.

"That's a small miracle," he said, hoping to lighten the atmosphere, but it didn't work. Marissa didn't respond. She opened her door and got out before he could open it for her.

The doctor's office was in a redbrick version of Boston's most estimable dowagers: dignified, well-maintained, attractive enough to remind you that it must have been a beauty among beauties in its youth. Boxes of flowers hung at the windowsills; the black wooden door sported a brass door-knocker for show and a discreet buzzer for actual use.

''Looks pretty good,'' Cullen said, still trying for the right tone.

Marissa still didn't say anything. He wasn't surprised. She hadn't spoken a word all the way here. He was pretty sure he understood the reason. Understood it? Hell, he felt it, same as she did.

The wedding ceremony, though legal, had been pure Las Vegas. As such, it had seemed unreal.

This wasn't. There was nothing unreal about Cullen O'Connell and wife, parents-to-be, visiting an obstetrician together.

For a heartbeat, Cullen thought about turning tail and running.

What stopped him wasn't anything as grand as Doing What Was Right. It was simply the look on Marissa's face. She was as terrified as he was. Maybe more. She was the one carrying a child neither of them had planned, the one who'd been torn from her world…

Cullen cleared his throat. ''Let's do it,'' he said.

He took her hand, half expecting her to pull away. To his amazement, she threaded her fingers through his. He looked down. The top of her head came just to his shoulder. She was so small. So helpless…

So beautiful and determined, even now, her chin up, her eyes straight ahead.

''Marissa.''

She looked at him. From somewhere deep inside, Cullen dredged up a smile.

''It's going to be fine,'' he said.

She nodded. Still no words, but a nod was an improvement over silence.

Cullen took a breath, pressed the buzzer, opened the door… And stepped onto an alien planet.

Women. The waiting room was crammed with them. They sat side by side by side on a pair of black leather sofas, perched on the ladder-backed chairs ranged along two walls; one leaned against the receptionist's desk.

Nothing but women, Cullen thought dazedly, and they all had one thing in common.

Each sported a huge belly.

Cullen froze. He was just getting used to having a pregnant wife. This seemed dangerously close to more than a man could handle.

Marissa spoke her first words in an hour. ''You can wait outside, if you like,'' she murmured, as if she'd read his mind.

Cullen swallowed hard. ''No,'' he said briskly, ''why would I want to do that?''

Why, indeed?

DR. STERN wasn't.

Stern, that was.

That was Cullen's first thought. Stern had a ruddy face, a booming voice and a big smile. He was middle-aged, a big guy who looked like he'd played football in his college days. When it was time for Marissa's appointment, he came to the waiting room door himself.

''Mrs. O'Connell?''

For a second, neither Cullen nor Marissa moved. Then Marissa jerked to her feet. *Mrs. O'Connell?* Cullen thought in amazement. Nobody had called her that yet, not in his presence.

''I'm Dr. Stern. Come in, please. You, too, Mr. O'Connell.''

Me, too?

''We don't bite, Mr. O'Connell,'' Stern assured him.

The other women in the waiting room smiled appreciatively. Cullen felt his face redden.

''It's my wife who has the appointment,'' he said, wincing at the stupidity of the words as Stern let the door swing shut behind them.

It turned out Stern was more than pleasant. He was kind, as well.

''Of course,'' he said gently. ''But whenever possible, I like to meet the husband. After all, this is your baby, too.''

My baby, too, Cullen thought. *My baby, too…*

''Yes,'' he said, and cleared his throat. ''Yes, it is.''

The doctor led them into a small office paneled in light wood. Framed diplomas and certificates hung on one wall; the other was crammed with snapshots of newborns.

''My alumni,'' Stern said cheerfully, waving to the pictures.

Cullen stared at all those small, screwed-up faces. The knot in his gut took another turn. It was probably a Gordian knot by now. This was the real thing. Babies-in-the-flesh, not in the belly.

Could he handle this? Marriage, and now fatherhood?

''Cute little kids, huh?''

Cullen stared at the doctor's smiling face. ''Yeah,'' he said hoarsely. ''Cute.''

''So.'' Stern motioned them to chairs, settled in behind his desk, folded his hands on his stomach and smiled at Marissa. ''Mrs. O'Connell. Or may I call you Marissa? Good. Tell me about yourself, Marissa. I understand you've only recently moved east. I assume you've been under someone else's care?''

The doctor asked questions. Marissa's medical history, which was uneventful. Questions about her family history. Her mother. Her father, which elicited a tense, ''I don't know anything about my father.''

It caught Cullen by surprise, though he didn't show it. But it explained a lot. A woman who'd never known her old man might very well expect the same treatment from the guy who'd made her pregnant.

What kind of SOB would turn his back on a woman? On a helpless baby? He wanted to pull his wife from her chair, hold her in his arms…

''…since you didn't bring any records with you, we'll put in a request to your prior physician and ask him to forward the data to my office. With your permission, of course.''

Marissa nodded. ''It might take a while,'' she said softly. ''I mean, the doctors I saw before... It was a public clinic, and they were always very crowded.''

Stern's eyebrows lifted. ''Oh?''

Cullen felt a muscle jump in his jaw. There was a world of meaning in that ''oh.''

''Well, I've known clinics that do a fine job. It's just, well, you're right. It might take a while to get data from them.'' Stern looked from Marissa to Cullen. ''I'm assuming they did an ultrasound?''

''Yes.''

''And the baby was fine?''

''Yes. An ultrasound...and an amniocentesis.''

''Why? Did they see a problem in the ultrasound?''

Marissa could hear the sudden change in Dr. Stern's tone, the sharpening of those twinkling eyes behind the wire-rimmed glasses. She knew what she should say. *They did it because my husband wanted a paternity test...* But the words were so ugly that she couldn't get them past her lips.

Suddenly, Cullen reached for her hand, his fingers squeezing hers in reassurance.

''It was just procedural,'' he said smoothly. ''There were no problems, Doctor.''

Stern nodded. Then he leaned across his desk.

''I'm sure you're right. But in view of the fact that it's apparently going to take a while to get those records...would either of you object to my doing another ultrasound? We can do it right now. And, as you undoubtedly already know, it's perfectly harmless to the baby and mother.''

Cullen looked at his wife. ''Marissa?'' he said quietly.

She turned to him. ''It's expensive,'' she whispered, her face heating. ''The technician at the clinic said—''

''Do it,'' Cullen told Stern.

''Excellent.'' Stern rose to his feet. ''Tell you what, Mr. O'Connell. I'll have a look at your wife. And when we're ready for the ultrasound, I'll have my nurse come and collect you.''

''Me?'' Cullen said stupidly.

''Certainly.'' The doctor grinned. ''I'm sure you'll want a second look at that baby of yours.''

''Oh, but—'' *But what? I never had a first look? I didn't even know the baby existed until a few weeks ago?* ''Of course,'' Cullen said smoothly. ''That'll be—it'll be great.''

TIME crawled by.

The nurse popped in with a couple of magazines.

''Thought these might keep you busy,'' she said cheerfully, and shut the door before Cullen could answer.

Busy? Reading *Beautiful Babies* and the *Parenting News*? He opened one magazine, saw all those pictures of all those tiny infants looking helpless and totally dependent.

Sweet Jesus.

Sweat broke out on his forehead. He closed the magazine, closed his eyes, too.

What in hell was he doing here? How come he hadn't thought ahead? Why hadn't he figured agreeing to be a father to this child meant sitting in a doctor's office surrounded by pictures of rug rats?

Surrounded by pictures, and waiting to see pictures of his own. Fuzzy images of an unidentifiable something.

Hey, he'd seen those programs on the Discovery channel. A woman lying on a table. A tech standing beside her. A photo on a TV screen, and an oily voice explaining the unexplainable.

This is a baby in its mother's uterus. Do you see its head? Its heart? Its hands?

No, no, and no. Leaning forward, eyes focused on the TV set, all any sensible viewer could see was a featureless blob…

"Mr. O'Connell?" Thc chcerful nurse was back.

"Yeah." Cullen sprang to his feet. The magazine slipped, unnoticed, to the floor. "Look, I know you must be very busy. I mean, fitting my wife in like this— So, I'll just go into the waiting room and—"

"Doctor's ready for you, sir."

Cullen nodded. No way out, he thought, and walked down a hall that was surely a mile long, stepped into a small room, saw Marissa lying on a table, just like he'd expected, saw the smooth curve of her belly, saw a TV screen…

And saw his son, peacefully adrift within his wife's sheltering womb. Saw his boy's ten tiny fingers and ten tiny toes. Saw his big, dark eyes and damned well felt them grab his heart with a feeling so intense he felt tears burn his eyes.

Cullen sank into the chair beside his wife and reached for her hand.

He wanted to say something clever. Something meaningful, that they'd both remember forever.

But Marissa squeezed his hand, gave him a wobbly smile, and all he could do was lean down and kiss her mouth.

"Our son," he said, his voice as scratchy as if his throat were coated with dust.

And for the very first time since his sixth birthday, when his mother had said, yes, he could keep the puppy he'd found abandoned in a weedy lot near the miserable place they'd been living, Cullen O'Connell unashamedly wept.

CULLEN left the doctor's office carrying a wicker basket laden with little sample boxes and bottles of oils, soaps, lotions and creams. Brochures were stuffed in his pockets on every subject from childbirth to the hospital where the baby would be born. A schedule for Lamaze classes was tucked in his appointment book.

Marissa watched him balance the basket in the crook of

one arm as he popped the Porsche's trunk. The basket was small to start with but it looked positively Lilliputian, cradled against her husband's hard, masculine body.

Her husband.

The word sent a little shiver of pleasure along her spine. Strange, but until today she hadn't really let herself think of him that way. He'd been Cullen, or the man she lived with, or the man she'd married.

Now, in the blink of an eye, she found herself thinking of him by another name.

Her husband.

''Okay,'' he said, as he shut the trunk lid. ''All safely stowed away.'' He looked at her and grinned. ''It's gonna take us hours to go through it.''

She smiled. ''Uh-huh.''

''We'll probably need an interpreter, too.''

''You think?''

''I know.'' He helped her into the car, then went around to the driver's side and got behind the wheel. ''For instance, there's a coupon right on the top for something called a Onesie.'' He looked at her as he turned the ignition key and flashed a quick smile. ''You have any idea what in heck a Onesie is?''

''A little undershirt and diaper thingy,'' Marissa said, laughing when Cullen arched his eyebrows. ''Honest, that's what it is. I looked at baby clothes before— I looked at them in Berkeley.''

''Ah. Well, I suspect I'm going to be on new territory here.'' Cullen checked his mirror and pulled away from the curb. ''What I know about babies you could cram into a nutshell and still have space left for a hanging judge's heart.''

''No nieces or nephews in your family?''

''Not yet. Getting close, though. Keir—my older brother—Keir and his wife are expecting any day now.''

''Oh.''

Marissa fell silent. Cullen looked at her. He cleared his

throat. ''You'll have to mcct them soon. My family, I mean.''

''Have you—have you told them about us?''

''No. Not yet. I keep waiting for the right time.''

''I understand.'' Marissa shot him a tight smile. ''It's not easy to tell the people who love you that you had to marry a woman because—''

Cullen yanked the wheel hard to the right and stopped at the curb.

''I didn't have to marry you,'' he said gruffly. ''I chose to, the same as you chose to marry me.''

''Because it was the right thing,'' she said softly, and looked at him.

Their eyes met, hers searching his for an answer to a question she hadn't asked. And yet, somehow, he thought he might know the answer as well as the question.

The moment slipped by. Then Cullen started the car again and merged into traffic.

''Yes,'' he said, even more gruffly. ''It was.''

Marissa nodded and folded her hands together in her lap. ''So,'' she said, after another few seconds of silence, ''what did you think?''

''About the ultrasound?'' Cullen puffed out a breath. ''It's the most incredible thing I've ever seen. He was sucking his thumb. Did you see that?''

She smiled. ''The tech said maybe that's what he was doing.''

''He was,'' Cullen said positively. ''And then he turned his head. Looked straight at me.'' He grinned. ''Absolutely incredible. I just never expected it to be like that. So clear. So—so—''

''Incredible,'' Marissa said, and they smiled at each other until his smile faded and died.

''Can you forgive me?''

''For what?''

''For not being there for you from the beginning.''

''That was my doing, not yours.''

"No more talking about that. We made mistakes, but we're past them." He paused. "Aren't we?"

Marissa nodded. He was right. The time for reliving the past was over. And yes, today had been incredible…

Especially the way her husband had looked at her when he came into the ultrasound screening room.

She loved having him look at her that way, as if what had happened was what he'd wanted all along. As if they'd met and fallen in love the way people did in storybooks, married because they couldn't live without each other, planned this new life because it was the best possible celebration of their love.

Never mind. He was right. They could make this marriage work. And oh, she wanted it to work. Wanted it, wanted it…

"You know what I'm thinking?" Cullen said.

Marissa looked at him. "What?"

"We have to celebrate. Go out to lunch. Someplace special. But we'll have to pass on champagne. The doctor said no alcohol, no caffeine, no—"

"I haven't had any of those things since I learned I was pregnant."

"Yeah." Cullen's smile tilted. "But this is all new to me."

It was new to her, too, sharing the pregnancy with someone. For months, she'd kept it a secret, ashamed to let her professors know, afraid to let her boss know. Now, all at once, she was sharing it with Cullen.

With her husband.

Marissa's heart skittered into her throat. She felt close to tears. Silly, of course. Theirs was a practical arrangement, nothing more. Why would she want to weep? Hormones, that was the reason, all that pregnancy-related estrogen pumping through her body like a river in full flood.

"What do you feel like having? Lobster? A salad? I know this little place down near the harbor—"

Hormones or not, she was living a dream. This man

who'd filled her thoughts for so long was hers. They were really married. Crazy as it seemed, she hadn't actually let it hit her until today.

"Marissa? Sweetheart, you're not listening to me. Aren't you hungry?" He turned a worried face toward her. "You're not feeling sick, are you?"

"No, no. I'm fine."

"In that case, we'll head for the harbor. I'm starved. And you need to eat. You heard what the doctor said."

"He said I'm fine."

"He said you could stand to gain some weight."

"He only said that after *you* said you thought I was too thin."

"Look, I know you don't like being told what to do, but—"

No. She didn't. At least, she never had before. But this was different. Cullen wasn't telling her what to do so much as he was telling her that she mattered to him.

She liked that. She loved it. She might not take his advice but there was something special in knowing a man cared enough about you to be concerned for your welfare…

Except, Cullen was concerned about the baby. About his son, not about her. She wanted only the best for their child, too, but—but she wanted her husband to think about her as a woman, not only as the mother of his baby.

Marissa's throat constricted.

What was happening to her? For two weeks she'd avoided any contact with Cullen. She'd been filled with anger over the turn her life had taken, even though part of her knew that accepting the marriage he'd forced on her was the only logical choice.

Now, just because Cullen had held her hand during the ultrasound exam, because he'd had tears in his eyes watching their child move inside her, she was on the verge of becoming a woman who was soft and stupid when it came to men. A woman she'd sworn she'd never be.

No. That wouldn't happen.

Marissa sat up straight. "You're right," she said coolly. "I don't like being told what to do."

Cullen reached for her hand. She tried to jerk it back, but his fingers closed around hers.

"Okay. How's this sound? You're not too thin. You just need a couple of pounds to make you even more beautiful."

"Give it up, Cullen," Marissa snapped. "I don't need to eat more than I already do, and I'm far from beautiful. If anything, I look like a beached whale."

Cullen chuckled. What was wrong with the man? Didn't he know when he was being dismissed?

Ahead, a traffic light went from green to red. He pulled to a stop, brought her hand to his mouth and pressed a kiss to it.

"A beautiful whale."

Oh, the feel of his mouth against her skin. Did he know what his caress did to her? That she could feel herself melting? That it made her want to throw herself into his arms?

She wouldn't. She couldn't. It was dangerous to feel this way. She'd always known that and yet, look what she'd done that fateful night? Lost control, turned into her mother's daughter, and lost everything she'd planned.

It wasn't that she didn't love her baby. She did, with all her heart. She was even willing to admit that Cullen was a decent man, but this marriage had nothing to do with feelings. It had to do with his sense of honor, his sense of responsibility...and her vulnerability.

Their relationship would be reviewed every two years. And whenever her husband lost his enthusiasm for matrimony or for her, she'd be gone like yesterday's garbage. Only a fool would forget that little detail, and she was never going to be a fool with this man again.

Marissa tugged her hand from Cullen's and smoothed down her skirt. "It must be wonderful," she said without looking at him, "being able to rely on all that blarney."

"No blarney, sweetheart, just the truth. What could be lovelier than the sight of my wife, ripe with our child?"

His wife. Their child. It sounded so wonderful. So perfect. If only—if only—

''I know just the place for lunch,'' he said softly.

''I'm not hungry.''

''Well, I am.'' He shot her a smile. ''Come on. Loosen up. I told you, I want to take you somewhere special to celebrate.''

''And I want to go back to the town house.''

Cullen looked over at his wife's unyielding profile. That chin was up, cocked at an angle he knew meant trouble. What in hell had happened? It had to be hormones. He recalled Keir rolling his eyes and saying Cassie was driving him crazy, sugar-sweet one minute, acerbic and unreasonable the next.

Okay. He wouldn't leap to the bait. If Marissa wanted a quarrel, she wouldn't get one from him.

''Tell you what,'' he said, as the light went green. ''We'll drive out of town. I know this little place on the coast—''

''I'll tell *you* what,'' Marissa replied. ''We'll drive back to your town house.''

Cullen's mouth narrowed. Take it easy, he told himself. Just take it nice and easy…

To hell with nice and easy.

''*The* town house,'' he said coldly. ''*My* town house. Has it occurred to you that it's *our* town house? Our home?''

''No. It hasn't. And it isn't. Does that answer your question?''

Cullen's hands tightened on the wheel. Was it impossible for Marissa to spend more than a few minutes in his company without regretting it?

''You don't see anything to celebrate today?''

''My son is healthy. That's celebration enough for me.''

''*Our* son,'' Cullen said grimly. ''Why do you keep forgetting that?''

''How can I forget? You won't let me.''

''That's it,'' he snarled. ''I've had enough.'' And in a

decision made in a heartbeat, he swung onto a highway entrance ramp that would take them out of the city, put his foot down on the gas pedal and started the eighty mile drive to Hyannis, and the plane that would take them to his house on Nantucket Island.

CHAPTER NINE

ALMOST an hour later, the sign flashed by so quickly Marissa almost missed it.

Cape Cod.

Was that where they were going? And if so, why?

She had no idea.

Cullen hadn't said a word since leaving Boston. She'd wasted five minutes insisting he tell her what in hell he thought he was doing before she'd realized she was not only wasting her breath, she was playing into his hands. Her demand for answers was just what he wanted. So she'd clamped her lips together and sat back in stony silence.

He'd stopped only once, at a gas station outside the city. He'd filled the tank, made a show of taking the keys from the ignition and marched into the station's convenience store.

A damn good thing he'd taken the keys, she'd thought coldly, because his suspicion was right. She'd have driven off and left him.

He returned carrying two containers of coffee and two wrapped sandwiches.

''Decaf,'' he'd said, putting one container and one sandwich on the console beside her.

So, yes. Correction. He *had* spoken during the past hour, but just that one word, as if to remind her of what she already knew, that she was pregnant and carrying his child and because of that, she was in his control.

Of course, she'd ignored all of it. Him, the coffee and the sandwich. He'd pretty much done the same thing, making a face and putting aside his sandwich after just one bite…

Even that one bite was more than she'd had.

Her stomach was growling, though it seemed ridiculous to feel something as commonplace as hunger when you were being carried off to God only knew where by a man who thought a couple of smiles and a handful of "sweethearts" would turn you to clay in his hands.

Another sign zipped by. *Hyannis.* The name seemed vaguely familiar. Didn't some president have a home in Hyannis a long time ago? Ford. Johnson. Kennedy. That was it. Kennedy.

Not that she cared.

She wasn't much in the mood for visiting historical sights, Marissa thought coldly, and sat even straighter in her seat.

Damn it, why didn't he say anything? Another minute and she'd ask, even though she hated giving him the satisfaction.

There went sign number three. *Barnstable Airport.*

Airport?

Okay. That did it. Being taken on a car ride to nowhere was bad enough, but if Cullen thought she was getting on a plane and heading into the blue without knowing their destination, he was crazy.

"All right," she said, swinging toward him. "That's it. I've never been a fan of mystery tours, Cullen. What are we doing here?"

"Think hard enough," he said, pulling into a parking space, "and I'll bet you'll figure it out."

"Do you expect me to get on a plane with you?"

"You see?" His voice was cool as he opened his door, came around the car and opened hers. "I knew you'd come up with the answer."

He held out his hand. Marissa didn't move.

"If you think I'm getting on a jet without knowing where—"

"It's not a jet, it's a prop job. And I told you where we're going. Out to lunch."

"We already had lunch."

"We did not." Cullen glanced at his watch. "Get out of the car, please, Marissa. We're wasting time."

"No."

"You're behaving like a child."

"I'm behaving like an adult in charge of her own life. I'm not getting out of this car."

"One," Cullen said calmly.

"This is ridiculous! You have no right—"

"Two."

"Do you really think you can force me into—"

"Three," he said, reaching across her to the seat belt lock. Marissa slapped at his hands but he ignored her, undid the belt and pulled it back. "Let's go."

"I told you and told you, I am not—"

Her words ended in a shriek as Cullen lifted her into his arms and pushed the door shut with his hip.

"Damn you, O'Connell!"

"Probably," he said calmly. "It's up to you, lady. Do you walk, or do I carry you?" He jerked his head to the side. "We seem to specialize in having audiences. What this one sees or not is your choice."

Marissa glared at him, then shifted her gaze to a small building with *Michael's Air Taxi* painted on its side. A couple of men were standing near the door, watching them with interest.

Fine, she thought. Let them watch. Let them see that Cullen O'Connell was a bullying idiot.

"Well? Are you going to behave?"

Her reply was a string of Spanish words, delivered too rapidly for him to understand, and accompanied by fists pounding against his shoulder.

Cullen grunted. "Whatever," he said, and marched toward the building.

She slammed another fist into his shoulder and spat out

something about him having the intelligence of a dim-witted gorilla.

Creative, he thought grimly, and probably true. This had been a class-A stupid idea.

The more miles the Porsche ate up during the drive from Boston to the Cape, the clearer that truth had become. He'd never brought anyone here, to this one place in the world that mattered to him. He'd grown up in falling-down cottages beside weed-infested lakes, in apartments that were almost duplicates of the one where he'd found Marissa. After his old man finally hit it big, he'd lived in the anonymity of the huge owner's suite at the Desert Song Hotel.

His town house in Boston was almost as big, surely as handsome, and absolutely as anonymous.

The place they'd fly to, if Marissa ever shut up, was the only place he'd ever thought of as home.

Then, why was he bringing her there? She hated his town house, hated Boston, hated him.

Cullen strode the last few yards toward the air taxi office. Marissa had fallen dangerously silent, but that didn't keep the two guys standing outside the building from grinning like hyenas.

"Afternoon," one of them said pleasantly.

The other gave Cullen a mock salute and opened the door.

Cullen grunted his thanks and stepped inside. Mike, who owned the place and had surely observed every bit of the little performance through the window, raised his eyebrows.

"Nice to see you again, Mr. O'Connell," he said conversationally. "Flying to the island today, are you?"

Cullen eased Marissa to her feet but kept one arm tightly wrapped around her waist. Her silence was, he suspected, ominous. She wasn't a woman to give up so easily. If trying to beat his shoulders to pulp and calling down what he suspected was the wrath of the Aztec gods of her ancestors on his head hadn't accomplished what she wanted, he figured her best effort was yet to come.

''Yeah,'' he growled, ''nice to see you, too. You have two seats available on the next flight?''

Mike scratched his ear. ''Reckon so.''

''Fine. We'll take them.''

''He means, he'll take one of the seats,'' Marissa said.

Here we go, Cullen thought, looking at his wife. Oh yes, something was coming. She lifted her chin any higher, she wouldn't be able to see over it.

''Two,'' he said quietly.

''One,'' Marissa repeated. ''Just one seat to wherever it is you're going, Mike.''

''Nantucket, unless Mr. O'Connell here's changed his usual flight destination.''

''Frankly,'' Marissa said pleasantly, ''I don't care if Mr. O'Connell is flying to Nantucket, whatever that is—''

''It's an island,'' the air taxi owner said helpfully. '''Bout 30 miles south of here.''

''I don't care if he flies to Nantucket or Naples. All I know is that I'm not going with him.''

Cullen stretched his lips into a smile.

''Meet my wife.''

''I am not his wife. I mean, I am, but I'm not…'' Marissa drew a labored breath. ''Do you fly to Boston?''

''Well,'' Mike said with caution, ''we don't, no. But over in the terminal—''

''Excuse us a minute, would you, Mike?'' Cullen clamped a hand around Marissa's wrist and drew her into a corner. ''We're not going back to Boston,'' he said coldly. ''We're going to Nantucket.''

''You can go where you like. I'm going to Boston.''

''Really,'' Cullen said, turning the word into a sarcastic statement. ''And how are you going to do that? You don't have a credit card, and don't bother lying because I checked. You canceled your credit cards when you quit school, which is why I opened new accounts for you, but you ignored the cards I left for you the other morning.''

"I'll pay cash. Remember? That dirty green stuff people like you don't like to touch."

"I like that dirty green stuff just fine," Cullen said coldly, "but you haven't got enough to buy lunch, much less an airplane ticket."

"You don't know that."

Her chin was still angled in the air but there was a quaver of uncertainty in her voice. It made him feel like the son of a bitch he undoubtedly was, but it was too late to stop now.

"I do," he said, and told her the fare. Actually, he made up a number, but so what? His wife wasn't going back to Boston. She wasn't going anyplace. Not yet. He didn't have any idea why he'd dragged her here but she was here, and, damn it all, she wasn't going to leave until he'd figured out the reason. "See what I mean? Like it or not, you're stuck with me and my island."

STUCK? Trapped, was more like it, but what choice did she have?

None, Marissa thought bitterly, as the black SUV that had been waiting at the Nantucket airstrip bounced along a narrow road.

At least it turned out Cullen had been talking figuratively when he referred to "his island." This wasn't a private island, thank God. There were other homes, a town, roads. She'd feared they were going to be put down on a rock in the middle of the Atlantic, but obviously Nantucket was a civilized place.

A place the man she'd married knew well.

He was driving the SUV, shifting gears, taking lefts and rights in a way that told her he'd spent a lot of time in this place.

"Get in," he'd said brusquely, and when she hadn't moved quickly enough to satisfy his lordship, he'd lifted her up again, put her in her seat and started to buckle her in. She'd balked at that, slapping his hands away as she had when he'd reached across her to open her seat belt at the parking lot near the air taxi office.

Opening that belt, his hand had brushed over her breasts. She wasn't going to let that happen again.

She knew the act hadn't been deliberate. She knew, too, that her breasts were far more sensitive than usual, thanks to her pregnancy. Still, that swift whisper of Cullen's fingers over her nipples had made the muscles low in her belly clench like a fist.

Hormones. A simple chemical reaction. He was the closest thing she'd ever known to a tyrant but even if her head knew that, her body didn't. Cullen was a good-looking man. All right. He was a gorgeous hunk, and she reacted to him even though she despised him.

All it proved was that she was no better than other women who were at the mercy of their libidos. She was equally vulnerable, equally stupid, but she was ahead of the game for knowing it.

Not that she had anything to worry about.

Marissa shot Cullen another quick look.

No. She had nothing to fear on that account. She had no idea why he'd brought her to this place but it certainly had nothing to do with seduction.

No sex. That had been her stipulation to his contract terms. And he hadn't touched her. Two weeks of marriage, and nothing. They slept in separate beds in separate rooms. She was happy for that. Of course she was. She wouldn't have let him touch her. If he'd come to her in the dark of night, when she lay in the silence thinking about him, if he'd come to her then, said her name, sat on the bed next to her and lifted her into his arms, she'd have—she'd have stopped him.

Absolutely, she'd have stopped him.

Marissa swallowed past the sudden dryness in her throat. She remembered what he'd done, all those months ago. His hands on her. His mouth on her. Why would she want any of that? She was a decent woman. Just because she'd slipped once…

Slipped big time, she thought, and lightly pressed a hand to her belly.

No, she didn't want Cullen. What she wanted was the baby sleeping in her womb. Cullen wanted him, too. That was the only reason he'd married her. She had to remember that. Otherwise…

Otherwise, her husband could break her heart because—because—

Her breath caught. Don't go there, she told herself frantically. Not now, not ever.

The SUV jerked to a stop. "There's the house," Cullen said.

Marissa blinked and stared blindly at his face, his features lit by the gold of the late-afternoon sun. A smile curved his mouth, his beautiful mouth. She recalled the feel of it on her skin, and suddenly she knew that she should have returned to Boston even if she'd had to walk.

"Where?" she said, grateful now for the interruption, willing to talk, to do anything but let her mind lead her to a place she would not, could not go. "I don't see—"

And then she did.

It was an old, gray-shingled house, weathered by the wind, and stood on a rise of sun-bleached grasses. Before it, pale golden sand stretched toward a deep blue sea.

"Oh," she said, without thinking, "oh, Cullen, it's beautiful."

Cullen looked at her. She was leaning forward, face shining, eyes fixed on the cottage he'd restored with his own hands, and he let out a breath he hadn't known he was holding.

"Yeah," he said gruffly. "I think so, too."

He turned into the long driveway, slowed the car to a crawl and took this last bit of the trip slowly, as he always did. It was his way of shedding the attorney's skin he wore in Boston.

Now, he drove slowly for an even more important reason.

He wanted to give Marissa time to see his home. Her home. To absorb the silence, broken only by the sighing of the wind. To feel the seclusion of his untouched five acres of moors and beyond, the endless sea.

His jaw tightened.

And wasn't that pathetic? She'd said the house was beautiful, but so what? He'd seen photos of the moon that were beautiful. That didn't mean he wanted to spend a weekend there.

He had no neighbors. No TV. No phone, except for his cell, and his secretary knew she'd damn well better call him only in the event of an emergency.

Once he reached this place, he was isolated. He liked it that way. Marissa wouldn't. Hell, she'd come prepared to hate it, the same way she obviously still hated him. This morning's respite hadn't meant a thing.

Stupid. Stupid to have dragged her here.

Cullen gritted his teeth and gave the SUV more juice. Okay. He'd pause at the house just long enough for her to have time to rest. The doctor had given her a clean bill of health but driving a pregnant woman from one end of Massachusetts to the other probably wasn't the smartest thing he'd ever done. After that, he'd apologize for his actions, turn the SUV around, drive straight to the airport—

"A rabbit," Marissa said, in tones of such delight that Cullen looked at her.

She was smiling. Smiling!

He felt an answering smile curve his lips.

"You like rabbits?"

Brilliant, O'Connell. A totally brilliant conversational gambit…but his wife seemed to think it was.

"Oh, yes. There was a little park, when I was growing up…"

"Yeah?"

''Nothing. I just, I mean, I used to see rabbits there sometimes.''

Cullen nodded. ''Well, there are lots of rabbits on these moors.''

''Moors?'' She looked at him, still smiling. ''You mean, like in *Wuthering Heights*?''

He had no idea what was in *Wuthering Heights,* but he wasn't about to disagree.

''Right. That's what they call the meadows on this island. Moors.'' He cleared his throat. ''We have deer, too.'' Her smile broadened. ''And seals and sea turtles sometimes turn up on the beach,'' he said, feeling like a daddy putting his kid's gifts under the tree on Christmas eve.

''I've never— I mean, in Berkeley—''

''Uh-huh. Not much wildlife in Boston, either, or in Vegas.''

''Vegas?''

''Las Vegas. Where I grew up…''

Damn. He was babbling. But that look on his wife's face. That softness in her voice. She'd smiled like this, sounded like this, only two times since they'd met. This morning, while they'd watched the ultrasound pictures of their son…and a lifetime ago, that night they'd made love.

He pulled into the garage that was attached to the house, turned off the engine and waited.

Something was happening. He could feel it. Something inside him. He was close, so close to knowing why he'd insisted on bringing Marissa here, what he wanted from this place, from her…

''Marissa?''

''Yes?''

''Marissa, look at me.''

A second passed. Then she did as he'd asked but in that intervening bit of time, everything had changed. The set of her mouth, the look in her eyes… She was looking at him as if he were a stranger next to her on a train.

''Yes?''

Cullen felt his smile fade. ''Nothing,'' he said curtly, and the mystery of why he'd come here with Marissa closed around him again like fog rolling in from the sea.

HE'D phoned the couple who watched the place for him from the gas station, asked them to lay in some supplies, so there was steak and salad for supper, eggs and bacon for breakfast.

But he hadn't thought beyond that.

He kept clothes here—jeans, shirts, hiking boots, sneakers—but there wasn't a thing a woman could wear.

He'd never brought a woman here.

His wife was the first. He thought about telling her that as she stood in the center of the living room, her arms wrapped around herself, but decided against it. Why tell her something that wouldn't matter a damn to her? He didn't really know why it should matter to him.

Instead, he lit a match to the kindling and logs on the hearth of the big stone fireplace that dominated the room.

''Bedrooms are upstairs,'' he said briskly, as he rose to his feet and turned to her. ''There's a bathroom up there, too, and a powder room just off the kitchen, if you want to freshen up.''

''Which bedroom?''

''Sorry?''

''Which bedroom is mine?''

She asked the question in the tone you'd use with a bellman who'd shown you to a suite of rooms in a hotel.

''Either one,'' he said tightly.

''Perhaps I should have phrased it more clearly. Which room is yours?''

''The one that overlooks the beach.''

''Fine.'' Her smile was quick and polite. ''I'll take the other one.''

He nodded. ''Yeah,'' he said, and before he let himself say anything else, he swung back to the fireplace, put one foot on the stepped-up hearth, and glared into the flames.

An hour later, he knocked on her door.

"I have some stuff that might fit you. Jeans of mine, a couple of shirts."

He waited for an answer. There was none. Mouth thinning, he draped the clothing over the balcony railing outside the door.

"Dinner in fifteen minutes," he said.

That, at least, drew a response.

"I'm not hungry."

"You haven't eaten since breakfast."

"I said—"

"I heard what you said. You're eating for two now. Either you come down in fifteen minutes or I'll come up and get you."

Marissa glared at the closed door. It wasn't bad enough Cullen had her trapped in Boston. Now he had her trapped here, in a house in the middle of nowhere, a house not half the size of his town house, meaning they'd probably trip over each other for however long he insisted on keeping her here.

And wasn't it a pity? Because this house was a wonderful place.

Wonderful, she thought, and turned blindly to the window and the sea of beach grass. How many women had Cullen brought here? Made love to, before the fireplace or in the enormous bed in the master bedroom she'd looked into as she came up the stairs? There was a skylight over the bed. You could probably lie in his arms at night and count the stars.

Count the times he took you up to those stars, held you there, trembling on the brink of release.

Marissa sank down on the edge of the bed.

Why had he brought her here? She couldn't think of any reason that made sense. Surely not to count the stars, or lie in his arms, or laugh and hold hands and walk the empty beaches.

Did he think he could seduce her? Get her into his bed,

as he'd at first promised, when he'd told her he wanted her to marry him?

She turned and looked at herself in the mirror. No, she thought, no, there wasn't anything to worry about when it came to that. What man would want a woman who looked like this? If a man loved his woman, that would be different. He'd see the changes in her body as beautiful, but this marriage wasn't about love, it was about expediency and doing what was right and—

"Time's up." Cullen banged his fist against the door.

Not yet, Marissa thought. But sooner or later, it would be. Two years. And for all she knew, he wouldn't even wait that long to get rid of her.

Tears blurred her vision. She wiped them away, got to her feet, took a deep breath, and went to the door.

THEY ate on a small table set before the fireplace. The meal, Marissa thought, was probably delicious.

Cullen had grilled steaks on the hearth; he'd baked potatoes in the ashes and put together a salad.

Unfortunately, she couldn't taste any of it.

She put food in her mouth, chewed it and swallowed because she had a child's welfare to consider. Nourishment was important.

So was conversation, but neither of them made any.

It wasn't that she didn't have things she ached to say. Silly things, like, *Did you ever notice that the wind sighs like a lover's lament when it blows through the grass?* or *What a beautiful table this is,* or—or *I'd love to trace that little indentation between your mouth and your chin with my finger…*

"…would you?"

Marissa blinked. At first, she thought she'd spoken aloud, but then she realized Cullen was talking about the glass he was holding out to her.

"Marissa? Would you like something to drink?"

She stared at the glass while her heartbeat returned to normal. Then she managed a polite smile.

"Thank you, but I can't have any alcohol. The baby—"

"It's flavored mineral water." He gave her a quick smile. "Strawberry. I think I gave Peggy Denton a shock when I asked her to buy some and put it in the refrigerator."

Her fingers closed around the stem of the glass. "Peggy Denton?"

"Peggy and her husband, Tom, keep track of things here for me. I try to get up at least a couple of times a month but it's good to know somebody's keeping an eye on the place."

"Oh." *Come on, Marissa. You can do better than "oh."* "Yes. I'm sure it must be a worry to have a second home."

"It's a joy," Cullen said. "Having this place, I mean. And I don't think of it as my second home, I think of it as my only home. The Boston place is just—what's the phrase? It's just where I hang my hat."

"Well, I can understand that. This place is lovely."

"I'm glad you like it."

"I'm sure everyone who sees it likes it."

She looked up, met his gaze and blushed. What a pathetic ploy! And for what reason? Why should it matter to her if he'd brought a hundred women to his house?

"No one's seen it," he said quietly. "Just you."

"I don't understand."

"Yeah. You do." His eyes seemed to burn through her. "You were trying to figure out how many other women I've brought here."

"You flatter yourself," she said coolly. "Why would I care?"

"I don't know." His voice was low, almost a whisper. "I've got some ideas, but only you have the answer."

"I really don't know what you mean. Who you've invited here isn't my—"

She gasped as he leaned over the table and caught her by the wrist.

''Don't you think it's time we stopped the subterfuge?''

Marissa pushed back her chair. She tried to rise, but he wouldn't let her. She could feel her heart racing in the hollow of her throat. What kind of admission was he trying to wring from her? Whatever it was, she knew better than to give it.

''Let go of me, Cullen.''

Cullen got to his feet, tugged Marissa from her chair and pulled her into the heat and hardness of his body.

''We spent one night together,'' he said roughly. ''That's all—but I never forgot it.''

''Did you hear what I said?'' She slammed her hands against his shoulders. ''Let go!''

''Answers first, damn you! Tell me that night didn't mean a thing to you and I'll turn around and give your precious solitude back to you.''

''It didn't.''

''I don't believe you.''

''Great! You say you want answers but what you really mean is that you want answers that suit you!''

''What I want is the truth—or don't you know what the truth is anymore?'' His hands clasped her shoulders; his eyes burned into hers. ''You drove me out of my head that night. I'd never felt that way with a woman before.''

''Stop it!'' Marissa slapped her hands over her ears. ''I don't want to hear—''

Cullen grabbed her hands, brought them to his chest.

''I thought about you all the time. I dreamed about you. Do you know what it was like to find out that what happened between us hadn't meant a damned thing to you?''

''Stop it! Stop it!''

''How could you have trembled in my arms, cried out my name, taken me so deep inside you that I couldn't tell where I ended and you began, if it meant nothing?'' Cullen tunneled his fingers into Marissa's hair, forced her to look at him. "Tell me, damn you, or—or—"

"Or what?"

Her whisper hung in the air. He looked into her silver eyes, at her trembling mouth and the telltale pulse pounding in her throat, and knew he could take her now, that he was right, her anger was only a cover for what she wanted.

Him.

She wanted him as much as he wanted her... But he wouldn't take her like this.

Not in rage. Not in denial of whatever was driving them both. His wife would come to him willingly. Open her arms to him. Sigh his name, as she had the night they'd conceived their child, or this would only be sex...

And he—he wanted more than that.

Hell, what was happening to him? He felt as if he were standing on the brink of a precipice that waited to swallow him in darkness.

Cullen lifted his hands from her shoulders and stepped back.

"It's late," he said gruffly. "Go to bed."

"Cullen," Marissa murmured, tasting tears on her lips.

"Do us both a favor, okay?" He turned away, clasped the edge of the mantle with both hands and bowed his head. "Get out of here."

Marissa stared at the stranger who was her husband. Then she turned and fled.

CHAPTER TEN

AN IVORY swath of moonlight danced on a black sea. Stars glittered with cold brilliance against the night's ebony canopy and streamed through the skylight over Cullen's bed.

It was a view that had the power to make him see his home as a clipper ship sailing across a vast, wind-blown sea of marsh grass.

Tonight, for the first time since he'd added the skylight to the house, Cullen took no pleasure in it.

All he could think of was Marissa and the disaster that was their marriage.

He knew he should be exhausted from the long day and longer evening, but even though his body cried out for sleep, his mind wouldn't stop whirling.

Why had he brought her here?

Why had he thought it would change anything?

Most of all, why had he imagined he could make this marriage work?

Cullen rolled over on his belly and punched his pillow into shape.

He could tell by the angle of the moon that it was very late, the time that came in the deepest part of the night when small creatures scuttled about on the moors and the brush of the wind made the old house sigh.

He could hear the booming who-who-who-hooo of a hunting owl. The creak of a floorboard and the steady beat of the ocean's heart as it flung itself against the shore.

What he wanted to hear was the whisper of his wife's breath as she slept in his arms.

That was the reason he couldn't sleep. Each time he closed his eyes, he imagined how it would be to have her here, beside him. To feel her lying close against him.

But none of that would happen. Marissa lay in the next room, separated from him by far more than a wall. Was she awake? Was she waiting?

Cullen sat up and ran his hands through his hair.

If she was waiting, it was only to leave this place. To leave this marriage.

To leave him.

He snarled an oath, got to his feet and pulled on his jeans. What a hell of a mess he'd gotten himself into. Married to a woman who couldn't stand him, and for what? He should have listened to Sean. He should have given his child his name, his financial support, and if he'd wanted to carry things further, he could have been a long-distance father. Lots of men were and no, it wasn't a perfect way to raise a kid, but it could have worked.

Maybe it still could.

Cullen looked at the clock on the night table. It was almost three-thirty. The middle of the night, back in Boston. The start of the day for those whose lives were still governed by the sea on this dot of land off the coast of Massachusetts. The commercial fishing boats would be leaving the harbor soon, followed not long after by boats that took sport fishermen out to sea.

And he'd still be trapped here, in a house with a woman who despised him, wondering what in hell he was going to do with her.

With his life.

A chilly breeze fluttered the vertical blinds, blew over his bare skin. Cullen shuddered and closed the window. The house was cold, even though he'd made sure to turn up the heat because of Marissa.

Was she warm enough? Had she paid any attention at all when he'd knocked at her door and told her there were extra blankets in the closet?

Maybe he should knock on her door again. Ask her if she was okay. Maybe…

Maybe he was an idiot.

His wife wasn't a child. She could figure things out for herself. If she wanted another blanket, she'd find one. Just because they were separated by only a wall didn't mean he had to think about her constantly. Back in Boston, the master suite and the guest suite were on different levels of the town house, which meant she was never in his thoughts at night…

Who was he kidding? In Boston, he lay awake for hours, wondering what would happen if he went to her room, opened her door, went to her bed.

And because he knew what would happen, that Marissa would greet him with all the warmth of a princess greeting the ogre who held her captive, he always ended up standing under the merciless spray of an ice-cold shower.

What could be more pathetic than that?

This. What he was doing now. Pacing his room, lost in erotic fantasies and damning himself for bringing her here.

Enough.

Cullen dug a turtleneck sweater from a drawer, pulled it on, zipped up his jeans and stuck his feet into a pair of well-worn mocs. Once in the hallway, he went by Marissa's door without glancing at it, turned up the thermostat at the head of the stairs and then made his way down to the kitchen.

The icy breath of the old stone floor bit straight through his moccasins. He thought about going back upstairs for wool socks but he'd have to pass Marissa's room again and he didn't want to do that.

No special reason for it, just—just that he didn't want to take the chance on disturbing her.

Maybe a hot drink would chase away the chill.

There was just enough light in the kitchen for him to take down a heavy white mug and fill it with some of the coffee he'd brewed after dinner. He'd made herbal tea for Marissa but, of course, she'd refused to drink it.

Why would she want to drink his tea when she didn't want his baby?

No, he thought as he put the mug in the microwave oven, that wasn't true. She wanted the baby. She just didn't want to think of it as his.

Numbers flashed on the timer pad; Cullen opened the door before the buzzer could sound. He wrapped his hands around the mug of coffee, took a sip, felt its warmth slip through his blood.

He felt better already.

Sipping at the hot liquid, he walked slowly into the living room and stood by the window.

It would be dawn soon. The moon had set; the stars were getting dim. Clouds were rolling in over the ocean. Great. The day was probably going to be gray, raw and wet. Just right to match his mood.

If Marissa wasn't up by six, he'd knock on her door. No point in dragging things out. The sooner they left this place, the better.

Cullen started toward the stairs, thought about walking past that closed door again and turned back. There was no point in going to his room now. He might as well settle in down here and wait for daybreak.

He headed for the sunroom. It was his favorite room in the house.

He'd added it at the same time he'd added the skylight. Like the skylight, he'd thought long and hard before doing it. The house, severe of line and elegant in its simplicity, was almost 200 years old and had been built by a whaling captain in the days when whaling was a sad industry in these waters.

He hadn't wanted to spoil the lines of the house, but he had wanted to open it so it could look out on the sea and the sky. A crazy thought, maybe, though when he'd voiced it to an architect, the guy had looked at him, smiled and said yeah, he could see how that made sense.

It wasn't historically accurate to put a sunroom on a house like this but the architect had been careful with the design, making the room's proportions fit the house. The sunroom had a planked floor, glass walls and a glass roof. Cullen had furnished it simply. A small sofa, a couple of chairs, a coffee table, and the room's centerpiece, an antique telescope.

On a morning like this, he might be lucky enough to spot a whale breaching. That might improve his mood.

The door to the sunroom was closed, though he didn't recall shutting it. He turned the door knob, stepped inside…

And walked straight into his soft, sweet-smelling wife.

Marissa gave a thin scream. He danced back. The coffee, still hot as blazes from the microwave, sloshed onto his fingers.

Cullen said something a gentleman wasn't supposed to say, especially around a lady.

Marissa clutched what looked like his shirt around her. "Did you ever hear of knocking?"

"Did you ever hear of turning on a light?"

"What's that got to do with you scaring me out of my skin?"

"About as much as you giving me a third-degree burn. If you'd put a light on, I'd have seen you."

"If you weren't sneaking around in the dark, you'd have seen me." She paused. "How'd I burn you?"

"Coffee," Cullen said brusquely. "And I wasn't sneaking around in the…" He frowned. "Are you okay?"

"You mean, did I survive being run over by a truck?"

He sighed. "I didn't meant to scare you."

"And I didn't mean to burn you." Marissa paused. "Where?"

"Never mind. It's nothing."

She switched on a table lamp. She was wearing one of the shirts he'd left on the railing. She had it buttoned from top to bottom. The soft cotton bulged out gently over her belly and hung to mid-thigh.

How could a man's shirt on a pregnant woman's body look sexy?

God, she was beautiful.

"Where?" she demanded again.

Cullen blinked. "What?"

"Oh, for pity's sake! Where's the burn?"

Right here, he thought. Inside me.

"My fingers. But it's nothing."

Marissa grabbed his hand and examined it as carefully as a miner panning for gold.

"There's nothing there."

He nodded. "That's what I said."

"You said..." She huffed out a breath. "Fine. In that case, good—"

Cullen wove his fingers through hers as she started to brush past him. "Where are you going?"

"Upstairs. To bed. Where else would a person go in the middle of the night?"

"I don't know," he said lazily. "Maybe down to the sunroom, because she can't sleep." His hand tightened on hers. "Or because he can't sleep, either. Interesting, don't you think? That two people with insomnia should be prowling the house in the middle of the night?"

Color stole into Marissa's face. "I always have trouble falling asleep when I'm overtired."

"Hell." The smile that had begun angling across his lips disappeared. "Of course you're overtired. It's my fault."

"It has nothing to do with you."

"Sure it does. I'm the one dragged you all over Massachusetts today."

"There's nothing tiring about sitting in a car or a plane when someone else does all the work," she said stiffly.

"There is, if you're pregnant."

"I'm just tired, that's all. I—I didn't sleep very well last night."

"No. Me, either." Cullen's gaze narrowed on her face. "Your eyes are red."

"Are they?" She gave a little shrug and drew her hand free of his. "Well, as I said, I'm—"

"Tired. Yeah, I know, but..." His brows drew together. "Have you been crying?"

She jerked back, as if he were the one who'd burned her this time.

"Of course not! Why would I—"

"You were." He reached out a hand. She jerked back again but not quickly enough. His thumb brushed gently over her lashes and came away damp with what surely were tears. "Marissa. Are you sick?"

"I'm fine. I'd be even better if you'd let me get past you and—"

His hand closed on her shoulder. The sight of her swollen eyes frightened him. She hadn't wept, not once since their marriage. Angry tears, yes. But these weren't angry tears, they were tears of sorrow.

"Why were you crying?"

"I just told you, I wasn't."

"Don't lie to me," he said harshly. "You were, and I want to know the reason."

Their eyes met. She sank her teeth lightly into her bottom lip before tearing her gaze from his.

"I'm pregnant," she said coolly. "Pregnant women cry a lot."

"Over...?"

"Over nothing. Over everything." She turned away and gave a little laugh. "You want the truth? I heard an owl hoot. And a second later, I heard this terrible little cry..."

Her voice broke. Cullen sighed, clasped her shoulders and turned her toward him.

"The owl has to live," he said quietly.

Marissa nodded. "I know. I do, really. But—but I thought, what if it's that rabbit we saw this afternoon? One minute, so full of life. And the next—the next—"

"When I was a kid," he said cupping her face in his hands, "maybe eight or nine, I went fishing with my father. It was a big event, getting to spend the day with the old man. He was hardly ever home and when he was, he wasn't the kind of guy played much with his kids, so I don't know how I ended up with him that day. Maybe Sean and Keir were sick. Maybe the girls were off somewhere with Ma. Anyway, Pa took me fishing. And—"

"And," Marissa said, "you had a wonderful time."

The way she made the words sound told him she was hoping for a fairy-tale ending. He knew it was important to her, though he didn't know why, but there hadn't been many fairy-tale endings where he and his old man were concerned.

So he smiled, brushed his mouth over hers and realized, only after he'd done it, that he'd felt the sweet softening of her lips under his as he'd kissed her.

"We had a terrible time. Nothing I did came out right. He showed me how to bait my hook, and I still got it wrong. When I cast, I kept on snagging the line. I moved around in the boat when I should have kept still and kept still when I should have been moving."

Marissa's eyes filled. "That's so sad!"

"It's just the way it was, sweetheart." Cullen tucked a curl behind her ear. "But on the way home, my father suddenly pulled into a parking lot outside this store that sold the best ice cream in town. He bought me a strawberry cone—my favorite. A double dip, with sprinkles. I didn't even have to ask for the sprinkles. He just knew I wanted them."

"See?" She gave him a watery smile. "You had a good time after all."

Gently, he brushed his thumbs under her eyes and wiped away her tears. "Yeah. But I was too young to get the real message of that day. It didn't hit me until years later."

Marissa raised her eyebrows. "The real message?"

Cullen nodded. "Life's impossible to predict. Sometimes

what starts badly ends well.'' He lifted her face to his. ''Just as circumstances put me in that boat with my father, circumstance forced us into a marriage neither of us was ready for, but what happens next is what we make of it.'' He bent to her and kissed her again, felt her lips cling softly to his. ''Marissa? We can make this work, if we try.''

She stared up at him. ''I don't—I don't...'' Her voice broke. ''I wish things were different, Cullen. I wish—''

''We can make them different,'' he said, looking deep into her eyes. ''I know we can.''

She was crying openly now, the tears spilling down her cheeks, and his throat tightened. He didn't want to make her cry. He'd never wanted that. All he'd wanted, from the start, was to do the right thing...

The right thing, Cullen thought, and covered his wife's mouth with his.

He meant the kiss to be tender. An apology for making her cry. A promise that he would try to make their marriage work. But his name sighed from her lips to his, her body softened as he drew her close, and he was lost.

''Cullen,'' she whispered, and she lifted her hands, flattened her palms against his chest, opened her mouth to his.

She tasted like the first sweet drops of rain, pattering against the glass roof of the sunroom. Like the delicate flowers that bloomed on the moor grasses in summer. His heart began to race; his body hardened.

''Marissa,'' he said, his voice rough, the warning in it implicit.

She answered by rising on her toes and winding her arms around his neck.

Cullen groaned, angled his mouth over Marissa's and deepened the kiss.

''Yes,'' she whispered, and moved against him...and almost drove him to his knees.

There was no mistaking the message.

She wanted him, just as she'd wanted him that night. As he'd wanted her all these months.

Cullen pressed his lips to his wife's throat. Her head fell back as he touched the tip of his tongue to the hollow of it where her pulse matched the race of his.

One by one, he undid the buttons that went from collar to hem down the front of her shirt, his mouth following after his fingers as he kissed her throat, her collarbones, the elegant valley between her breasts.

When the final button was undone, he cradled her breasts in his hands, exulting in their new, luxuriant weight. He dipped his head, licked the aroused tips, drew first one and then the other into his mouth, loving their remembered taste and Marissa's soft moans of pleasure.

Cullen lifted his head, watched his wife's face as he feathered his fingertips over her nipples. Her eyes were dark, almost blind with rapture. Her lips were parted, her breathing swift and shallow.

"Do you like it when I do this?" he said thickly.

"Yes," she whispered, "oh, yes, yes, yes..."

Her soft admission sharpened the need that burned, hot and fierce, in his blood. He'd wanted Marissa the night they'd slept together, more than he'd ever wanted another woman, but not like this. Never like this. Desire pounded through him with each beat of his heart. For sex, yes. For possession of her body, yes. But for more, much more than that.

It was desire for Marissa that filled him. For her, for her alone.

He wanted to tell her that, but how could he speak when she was easing her hands under his sweater? When she was moving against him in an ancient rhythm that had not changed in thousands and thousands of years?

Cullen slid his hands down his wife's back, loving the silken glide of her skin against his callused palms. He cupped her bottom, lifted her, brought her tight against the heat and hardness of his erection.

"The baby," she whispered, and he felt a moment of terror.

"Am I hurting him?"

Marissa gave a throaty little laugh. "No. Oh, no. We can't hurt him this way. I only meant... My body's not the same, Cullen. I don't look like—like the woman you made love to that night."

No. She didn't. He already knew that. He'd tasted the ripe sweetness of her breasts, felt the roundness of her belly pressing against him.

"I know that," he said, and slowly drew the shirt from her shoulders. She tried to grab it, but it slid free of her hands and dropped to the floor.

"Cullen," she said with an embarrassed little laugh, lifting her arms and covering herself.

"I want to see you," he said softly.

He took Marissa's hands, brought them to his mouth, kissed the palms, gently eased them to her sides and looked at his wife. His beautiful wife.

His exquisite Marissa.

Her breasts were full and lush, the nipples dark as the sweetest cherries. Her belly was rounded, filled with the child they'd created together. And her face...her face was filled with desire. With joy.

With something it almost took his breath away to see.

"I—I gained weight," she said hesitantly.

He smiled. "I should hope so."

"I mean—I mean, I look—I look—"

"You look like my wife," Cullen said, as he swung her into his arms and carried her through the dark house and up the stairs to his bed.

CHAPTER ELEVEN

MARISSA clung to Cullen's neck, her face nestled in the hollow of his throat, as he carried her into his bedroom.

She was naked; he was still dressed. The rough textures of his clothes against her sensitive skin seemed to heighten her soft vulnerability, his hard masculinity. How could such a simple difference be so erotic?

He laid her down in the center of his bed and came down above her, his hands pressed to the mattress on either side of her body. He kissed her slowly, urging her to open to him, to let him taste her, to taste him in return.

And yes, oh, yes, Marissa returned those kisses. She loved the feel of his teeth sinking gently into her lower lip, the thrust of his tongue. On a soft moan, she reached up to draw him down to her.

Instead, he sat back, brought her hands to his lips, kissed the palms, sucked the tip of one index finger into the warmth of his mouth. Then, his eyes never leaving hers, Cullen pulled his sweater over his head and shucked off his jeans.

The room was lit with the pale luminescence of dawn. Marissa looked at the man who had been her lover for one night and who was now her husband.

He was beautiful, just as she'd remembered. How many nights had his image tormented her? His saint-and-sinner face, all hard planes and elegant angles. His shoulders, wide and taut with muscle. His powerful, lightly furred chest, tightly defined abdomen, narrow hips…

Her gaze skittered past his navel. A rush of heat surged

through her body, from her breasts to her loins. He was erect, fully aroused.

''Marissa,'' he whispered, and she raised her eyes to his and opened her arms.

Cullen came down beside his wife and kissed her, tunneling his fingers through her hair, pressing her back into the yielding softness of the big bed. She sighed against his mouth, said his name in a sweet whisper.

He cupped her breasts, kissed them, sucked on them. Moaning, she arched her back, lifting herself, and he accepted the offering, worshiping with hands and mouth this woman he had so long wanted. Gently, he ran his hand over the rounded contours of her belly, bent his head and pressed kisses over the taut skin, parted her thighs and cupped her hot, secret center. She cried out and he thought he'd go over the edge just from the sound of her voice, from the way she writhed beneath him, from the wetness of her.

God, she was so wet! For him. Only for him.

He kissed her deeply, stroked her deeply, and she gave a sharp, keening cry that tore through his heart.

''Marissa,'' he said thickly, and when he touched her this time, it was with his mouth.

She jumped at the first stroke of his tongue against her engorged flesh.

''No,'' she said, ''Cullen...''

She reached down to stop him, but somehow, somehow her hands tangled in his hair and instead of pushing him away, she held him closer, held his mouth on her, and all at once she came apart, came against his kisses, his wild, wonderful kisses. Colors exploded behind her closed eyelids; a river of flame swept through her veins, and then Cullen moved up her body, entered her, filled her, slipped his hands beneath her and urged her on and on and on while she clung to his shoulders...

And when he cried out and spilled himself into her, Marissa echoed his cry and tumbled off the edge of the world, safe at long last in her husband's arms.

THEY slept, curled in a lover's embrace.

Cullen woke first, to the sound of rain, the pale light of morning, and to the wonder of his wife, her body tight against his as she lay sleeping in the curve of his arm.

Carefully, he eased onto his side, still holding her close. Marissa murmured in her sleep, shifted easily with him and he gathered her closer, loving the feel of her breasts against his chest, her belly against his belly.

He slid his hand down her back, stroking his fingers lightly over her skin, cupping one buttock and lifting her into him. She sighed, wound her arm around him as she slept.

A hand seemed to reach inside his chest and tighten around his heart.

My wife, he thought. His beautiful, brave, defiant, incredible wife.

God, he was so happy! He'd never felt so happy be—

Marissa jabbed him with her elbow.

"Hey," he whispered. "Sweetheart? Are you awa—"

Another jab. Sharper this time, but how could it be her elbow? She was lying with one arm wrapped him and the other wrapped around her pillow.

Jab. Jab, jab, jab…

Oh, man! Cullen's eyes widened. His wife wasn't poking him in the gut.

His son was.

Carefully, he drew away just enough so he could push down the blankets. Something—a tiny elbow, maybe, or a little knee—made a ripple in the smooth skin of Marissa's belly.

Holy Hannah.

A grin spread over Cullen's face. "Hey, pal," he said softly.

Another poke. A delicate undulation. Then nothing. Cullen waited, caught his lip between his teeth, finally laid his hand lightly over his wife's tummy. A second passed, and then he felt it. A wave of motion. A feathery brush against his palm.

His baby was moving within his wife's womb.

Cullen felt his throat constrict.

Before he met Marissa, he'd thought he owned the world. If Aladdin's lamp had suddenly appeared and he'd rubbed it and a genie burst from the spout and said, *Cullen O'Connell, you have one wish,* he'd have said, without even stopping to think, *Tell you what, Mr. Genie. I don't need a thing. I already have everything I could possibly want.*

How wrong he'd been.

These were the things a man needed. A child to love. A woman in his arms. A woman he—a woman he—

"Mmm."

Marissa was waking up. He watched as she opened her eyes and focused on his face. A slow, shy smile curved her lips. How could a smile make a man feel so good?

"Good morning," he said softly. She smiled again and he bent his head and kissed her.

"I didn't mean to wake you," he whispered against her mouth. He stroked her stomach. "But I was getting acquainted with our son."

She looked at where his hand lay. His gaze followed hers.

"He made the introduction," Cullen said, and grinned. "Kicked me. Hard."

Marissa gave a soft laugh. How lovely it was to wake up, safe and warm, in the circle of your husband's arm, and to have the added bonus of hearing him sound as pleased as if their unborn child had already scored his first goal.

"He's been doing a lot of that lately," she said, reaching up and brushing a dark strand of hair from Cullen's brow.

"It's okay? I mean, he's supposed to jump around like that?"

"Uh-huh."

''He's not hurting you?''

She grinned. ''No.''

''I mean, I know kids move. I felt Cassie's baby when—''

''Cassie. Your brother's wife, right?''

''Uh-huh. She's due any day now, but when I was visiting them a while ago, the baby was kicking and Cassie let me feel...'' Cullen frowned. ''Sweetheart,'' he said softly, ''I'm sorry. It just really hit me that you don't know anything about my family except the little I've told you.''

''And I told you, I understand.'' Her smile wobbled around the edges. ''The thing is, that there's probably never a good time to tell them that you had to get married.''

He looked at her as if she'd lost her mind. ''I don't intend to tell them that,'' he said gruffly.

Marissa nodded. What else had she expected him to say? She didn't know how he could raise a child without his family learning about it but then, she didn't know his family. He'd made it sound as if his brothers and sisters were close, but maybe they weren't. Maybe you could have a family and never tell them anything about your life. Anything was possible.

The only certainty was that she'd been a fool to think last night had changed anything.

''Of course,'' she said, sitting up and swinging her legs to the floor. The shirt she'd worn last night lay on the floor near the doorway. Was there a way to get there without letting go of the blanket? She'd never felt more naked in her life.

''Marissa?''

''Yes,'' she said briskly.

''Where are you going?''

''To get dressed. Well, to take a shower. Then I'll get dressed. And make some coffee. Some breakfast. Some—''

Cullen reached for her and pulled her back against him.

''I don't want breakfast.'' He nuzzled her hair aside, bit

lightly at the nape of her neck. "The only thing I want is you."

"Cullen." She drew a steadying breath. "Last night was—it was very nice. But—"

"Very nice?" He gave a soft, sexy laugh as he turned her to him and framed her face with his hands. "Come on, sweetheart. You can do better than that."

"What do you expect me to say? It was…fun."

His mouth thinned. "Fun," he echoed. There was a dangerous edge to his voice.

"Yes. And you're right, having—having sex once in a while will probably make our relationship easier to—"

Cullen crushed her mouth beneath his. Marissa cried out, held back, tried not to let herself feel the kiss, but she couldn't. She wanted this. Her husband's arms. Her husband's kisses.

Her husband's love.

Tears rose in her eyes.

He would never love her. But she could love him, just as she had all these empty, lonely months. Love him, make love to him, take what she could and hold it hidden in her heart.

"Cullen," she whispered, winding her arms around his neck, and kissed him back.

Long moments later, he drew her head to his chest and gently stroked his hand down her spine.

"It was more than sex," he said quietly. "I—I care for you, Marissa."

Of course he did. She was carrying his baby. She'd seen the look on his face, after he'd felt his son move this morning. Oh, what she'd give to see such love in his eyes for her, too.

"And you—you care for me, too." His hand cupped the back of her head and he urged her face up until their eyes met. "You do, don't you?"

Marissa nodded. "Yes. You're—" *You're everything a*

woman dreams of. ''You're a good man, Cullen O'Connell. What woman wouldn't care for you?''

A muscle danced in his jaw. If she'd made such an admission yesterday, it would have shocked him. Today, it left him feeling empty. He didn't want his wife to think of him as a good man. He wanted—he wanted—

Cullen cleared his throat.

''If we try, we can make this marriage work.''

She nodded again. ''Yes.''

He kissed her, gently this time, brushing his lips lightly over hers, and then he smiled.

''Did I hear you say something about breakfast?''

''You did,'' she said, smiling back at him.

''I don't suppose…''

''What?''

''Ah, it's nothing.''

''What's nothing?'' She drew back and raised her eyebrows. ''What were you going to say?''

''Well, I don't want to boast, but—''

''But?'' she said, laughing.

''But, I make a damned fine omelet.''

''Good.'' She grinned. ''Because I have to warn you, O'Connell, I'm lousy in the kitchen.''

His grin was sexy and unabashedly male. ''Yeah, but you're terrific in bed.''

''Compliments won't change a thing,'' she said primly, even as she smiled. ''I'm still the world's worst cook.''

''Ah.'' Cullen put a finger under her chin and lifted it. ''But you're a great law student.''

''Yes.'' Her smile dimmed. ''Well, I used to be…''

''And you will be again. When we get back home, I'm going to introduce you to some people I know at Harvard Law.''

Oh, what he'd give to see that light blaze in her eyes just for him!

''Really?''

He nodded. ''Absolutely. Until then, we're going to need

some sustenance. Here's the deal. I'll do the eggs if you'll play student.''

Marissa wrinkled her nose. ''What the heck are you talking about?''

Cullen grinned. ''The best law students are logical and imaginative.''

''Yes, but—''

''They're good at reading stuff and figuring out what it means.''

Marissa rolled her eyes. ''Honestly, Cullen—''

''But some things are just beyond a man's comprehension. Even if he's a lawyer. You understand?''

''No,'' she said, pushing gently against his chest and scowling at him, ''I do not understand! What are you talking about?''

''Biscuits.''

''Biscuits?''

''Uh-huh. See, I came up here one weekend last winter when it was cold as the Arctic. Snow, ice… Anyway, Peggy—''

''The female half of the couple that watches this place for you…''

''Right. Peggy laid in some supplies, the way she usually does. And one of the things she included was a box of biscuit mix.''

''Be still, my heart,'' Marissa said, slapping both hands against her breast. ''You make great omelets, and you also know how to bake?''

''I've never baked a thing in my life. And once I read those biscuit instructions…I knew I never would.'' Smiling, he laid his forehead against hers. ''I figure maybe you'd like to give it a try.''

Marissa ran the tip of her tongue over her bottom lip. ''Because you never could convince another woman to come here with you and read those directions?''

Cullen clasped her face and lifted it to his. ''Because I never wanted to share this place with anyone until you,'' he said huskily. He kissed her, a slow, soul-stealing meeting of mouths that made her giddy with pleasure. ''I guess you could say we gave this bed its test run last night.''

That wonderful look he'd seen in her eyes a little while ago was there again. This time, he thought, this time, it was for him.

''That's lovely to know.''

He gave her another of those grins that all but melted her bones.

''What do you say? I'll do the eggs, you'll do the biscuits. Deal?''

''Just as long as you understand the biscuits might turn out to be hockey pucks.''

Cullen grinned and put a hand over her belly. ''Hey, what have we got to lose? Get the kid used to the game early, like his old man.''

Marissa laughed. ''Now you're going to tell me you were a star on the ice.''

''Well,'' he said, flashing another smile, ''maybe not a star but I was damned good. Actually, my game was football. Sean was the one who was the hockey star.''

''Your brother.''

''Uh-huh. My kid brother. Keir's the oldest. And there are the girls, of course.''

Keep smiling, Marissa told herself, even if you never lay eyes on these people.

''Of course,'' she said politely.

''Fallon. She's a model. Well, she was a model but she got married last year and… It's a long story.''

''Yes,'' Marissa said, even more politely, ''I'm sure it is.''

''And there's Megan. And Briana. Meg's an accountant, but she's not like any accountant you've ever met. I mean, how many CPAs do you know who're into sky-diving?''

''Not many,'' Marissa said, working to hang on to her smile.

''And Bree.'' Cullen snorted. ''I swear, there's not a

practical bone in her body. She's our Dr. Doolittle. You know, talks to the animals… Hell, they're a tough bunch to describe. You'll just have to figure them out for yourself when you meet them.''

''Yes,'' she said again, ''I guess… When I meet them?''

''Keir, first. He and Cassie only live a hundred miles away. Less, really.'' He cocked his head. ''I've got a great idea. How about paying them a visit when we leave here?''

''Well. Well, I—I—'' Marissa hesitated. ''You said—I thought you said you weren't going to tell them that—that you and I had to get married.''

''And I won't.'' Cullen smoothed a tumble of jet-black curls back from his wife's cheeks. ''We'll tell my family the truth, sweetheart,'' he said softly. ''That we met months ago, that we wanted to be together but that—well, that life got in the way somehow and we didn't find each other again until a couple of weeks ago.'' He smiled as he stroked his thumb over her parted lips. ''Is that all right with you?''

Marissa swallowed hard. ''It's very all right with me.''

''Great. In that case, we've got a lot to do. Breakfast. A drive to the harbor, so I can introduce you to the 38-foot lady in my life. We'll take her out for a cruise next time we're here.''

''I don't know. I mean, I don't—''

''You'll love her,'' he said, waving away her objections, ''once you get to know her.''

''But not today.''

''Nope. Like I said, we have stuff to do. Food. The harbor. Got to hit a few shops, so we can buy you some sexy clothes.''

''Sexy?'' Marissa laughed. ''Clothes do not look sexy on pregnant ladies.''

''They will, on my lady.'' Another kiss, this one long and sweet. ''And then,'' Cullen said softly, ''we'll pay a visit to Keir. How's that sound?''

Marissa stared at him. It sounded like a fairy tale come to life, but she knew better than to believe in fairy tales.

"Hell," Cullen said, "I'm an idiot. That's too much for you, isn't it? Here you are, probably exhausted, and I'm running off at the—"

Marissa lifted her face and pressed her mouth to his.

"I'm not the least bit tired," she whispered. "It all sounds wonderful."

"You sure? Because if you want to take it easy—"

"Cullen."

He could tell by her tone the discussion was over, but he knew how to get the last word.

"Change of plans," he said. "We'll spend a couple of days here."

"Honestly, I'm not—"

"I know. We'll still drive to the harbor, do some shopping." Gently, he eased her down against the pillows. "But Keir and Cassie can wait a couple of days. There are better things to do first."

Marissa laughed softly, looped her arms around his neck and kissed him.

"How about breakfast?" she said softly.

He cupped her breast, feathered his thumb over her nipple and she caught her breath.

"How about it?" he whispered thickly.

"It can…" Her voice broke. "It can wait, too."

He dipped his head and licked her flesh. "Your nipples are the color of roses."

"They're more sensitive than ever," she whispered back. "The baby—"

"Am I hurting you?"

"Oh, no. No! I love it when—yes. When you do that. When you—oh. Oh, Cullen…"

Marissa's breathless sighs were all the answers he needed, and when she reached for him, closed her hand around his rigid flesh, Cullen rolled onto his side, turned her to him and drew her leg over his hip.

"Look at me," he said hoarsely. "I want to see your face as you take me deep inside you…"

His words, his touch, the feel of him entering her, excited her almost beyond endurance. She cried out, kissed her husband's mouth, gave him complete possession of her body, her soul…

And showed him, the only way she dared, that what she was really giving him was her heart.

CHAPTER TWELVE

THEY awoke to a morning of bright blue skies and golden sun.

Indian Summer had come to Nantucket Island. Warm days. Cool nights filled with passion.

Marissa lost all her inhibitions in her husband's arms. Cullen was an incredible lover: romantic, giving, demanding. His lovemaking could be as dangerously wild as the sea, as sweetly tender as the wildflowers that bloomed on the moors. For the first time in her life, Marissa felt free...

Free, except for being unable to say the three simple words that were in her heart. If only she could say "I love you" to Cullen.

Still, she was blissfully happy.

They strolled the beaches, all but deserted this time of year. He teased her about the shells and bits of sea glass she picked up, but he was the one who tucked them into his pockets and carried them home for her.

They drove to the harbor and the slip where his boat was docked. Marissa took one look at the sleek vessel, another at the look in her husband's face, and changed her mind about not liking the ocean and sailboats.

"Can we take her out?" she asked.

Cullen hugged her, said he loved knowing that was what she wanted but now that he thought about it, he'd rather wait until after the baby was born.

"It'll be easier for you then, sweetheart," he said, and she smiled and said yes, it probably would, and reminded herself that it would be silly to weep with joy just because he'd mentioned the future. He'd done it before, but only in terms of their child. This was different. She knew it was a little thing, but it made her happy.

Everything made her happy.

The little restaurant he took her to, where the captain greeted him by name.

"This is my wife," Cullen said.

The man kissed her hand, beamed at the sight of her belly and offered her a single, perfect red rose after seating them at a table.

Another first, she thought, almost dizzy with pleasure. Cullen hadn't introduced her to anyone before. *This is my wife,* Marissa kept thinking, *this is my wife…*

Were there any more beautiful words in the English language?

They strolled the cobblestones on Main Street, peering into shop windows. Cullen bought her clothes, soft-as-silk cotton drawstring trousers and loose, gauzy tops, more of them than she could ever wear. He bought her handmade sandals because she admired them and gold earrings for the same reason. She learned not to say a thing was pretty in hopes it would keep him from buying it for her, but that didn't work because he bought things for her, anyway.

"I don't need all this," she said, a little breathlessly as the bags and boxes piled up in his car, and Cullen grinned and kissed her and said needing the stuff had nothing to do with wanting her to have it.

They bought an elegant picnic lunch and ate it at Brant Point, watching the boats round the point in a gentle wind. At Jetties Beach, they munched on hot dogs and potato chips while they watched the windsurfers skitter across the water. Because she couldn't drink wine while she was pregnant, they toasted the spectacular sunset at Madaket with ginger ale in champagne flutes.

And when they returned to Cullen's house each evening, he undressed her slowly, lovingly, and made love to her until she wept quiet tears of joy.

Oh, yes, she was happy. So happy it terrified her.

Could it last? The question plagued her in the middle of the night and when Cullen awoke and found her standing at the window, staring blindly out over the sea, she told him she was up because her back ached instead of telling the truth, that it was her heart that was aching.

"Let me help you, sweetheart," he said, and he carried her to bed, turned her on her side, gently rubbed the ache away until his hands turned a little harder, until his mouth replaced his hands, until she could think of nothing but how much she loved him.

One morning, at breakfast, she asked him about the brother he'd mentioned visiting. She phrased the question with care—she didn't want to pry if he didn't want her to—but Cullen sat back, smiled and started talking about all his family.

He told her stories about his brothers and sisters that made her laugh, but she sensed the loneliness of his early years when his father dragged them all from town to town in pursuit of a dream.

"I must be boring you with all this," he finally said.

Impulsively, she took his hand, brought it to her lips and kissed his knuckles.

"How could I be bored," she said softly, "learning these things about the man I married?"

He gave her a look she couldn't decipher and she wished she could take back the words, because she feared what he might have heard in them. So she turned it into something simpler and said she was always interested in the details of people's lives and he gave her another look and said that wasn't very lawyer-like. They both laughed and the moment passed.

In the end, lying in his arms late one night, soothed by the sigh of the wind and the heartbeat of the sea, she told him about herself. The father she'd never known. The mother she'd never understood. The emptiness of growing up on the fringes of polite society and the first small victory when she'd passed the entrance exam for the honors high school her mother had said would never accept her.

Cullen was so quiet that she thought he'd fallen asleep. Or, rather, that she'd put him to sleep with her babbling. While she lay there wondering what on earth had made her tell him all that stuff, he suddenly rolled above her and kissed her until her mouth felt sweetly swollen.

"You're wonderful," he said softly. "Wonderful. And I—and I—"

She waited, heart pounding.

"And you?" she whispered finally, framing his face with her hands.

She saw his Adam's apple move up and down as he swallowed. "And I," he finally said, "hate to leave here tomorrow...but we have to, sweetheart. I wish we could stay longer, but I have a court appearance coming up."

Why did she feel like weeping? "Of course," she said brightly. "I understand."

Cullen kissed her again. "We'll stay longer next time."

"Next time," she repeated, but somehow, even as he began to make love to her, she found herself wondering if there would be a next time, or if these few days were all they'd ever know of happiness.

They flew to back to Hyannis the next morning, picked up Cullen's car and set off for Keir's home in Connecticut. And as the miles flew past, Marissa kept hearing her mother's voice whispering slyly in her ear.

Nothing lasts. Get that through your head, Mari. Nothing ever lasts, especially if you're stupid enough to hope it will.

BY THE time they crossed the Massachusetts border, Cullen was a wreck.

Marissa had come up with a dozen reasons for changing plans and heading to Boston, so he knew she was nervous about this visit, too.

Yeah, but no way could she be as nervous as he was.

Hartford, 60 miles.

The sign flashed by before he could really process it. If Hartford was sixty miles away, how far was Keir's vineyard? Ten miles? Twenty? Why in hell hadn't he paid more attention to the details the times he'd been to Deer Run? Why hadn't he noted where it was by comparison to a city like Hartford?

Why would he have bothered? Who gave a damn about things like that?

He sure as hell didn't.

The only reason it mattered now was so he could figure out how long he had before he parked in the driveway at his brother's place, stepped out of the car and said, *Hello, Keir, and man, have I got a surprise for you!*

He glanced at Marissa, seated beside him, back straight, eyes pinned to the road ahead, hands folded tightly in her lap… Except, she didn't really have a lap anymore. She had a belly. A baby belly. A belly bursting with baby.

I'm punch-drunk, he thought, and snorted. Marissa looked at him.

"Did you say something?"

Cullen shook his head. "No. I'm just…" He drew a breath, huffed it out. "We'll be at Deer Run soon."

She looked at him, then at the road.

"You'll like Keir. Well, maybe not right away. He can be… But you'll love Cassie. She's terrific."

Marissa nodded. After a couple of minutes, she cleared her throat. "Cullen? Are you sure you don't want to phone your brother again?"

"I phoned him already."

"Yes, but you told him you were coming to see him and that—and that you had a surprise. I mean, it's your family and you know best, but—"

"I know what I'm doing."

She looked at Cullen. Her husband sounded positive, but he looked like a man on his way to a dentist who didn't believe in anesthesia.

"Suppose I stay in the car? So they don't see that I'm pregnant. Not right away."

"Now, there's a great idea. We drive up, Keir and Cassie come outside, I introduce you and then I tell them you're going to stay in the car while I go inside. 'No,' I'll say, 'that's okay. Marissa likes cars better than houses. We'll have supper, sit around, whatever, and after you guys are tucked in bed, I'll sneak her in.'"

She looked at him and made a sound that was almost a laugh. "All right, that wouldn't work."

"No," he said calmly. "It wouldn't."

"Then—then how about this? We go inside, we talk for a while, sort of work our way around to the fact that we're—that we're married."

"Uh-huh. And do we get to that bit of information before or after they notice you're pregnant?"

Marissa glanced down at her stomach. "I guess they'll see that right away."

Cullen figured it was his turn to laugh, but he couldn't. How come going to visit Keir had seemed like such a fine idea right up until the second they got in the car and he pointed it west?

"Yes," he said, "they will. And unless my brother's taken a bottle of stupid pills lately, he's going to figure out, real fast, that there's got to be a reason I'm paying him a visit with a pregnant woman in tow."

"I'm not exactly 'in tow,'" Marissa said coolly.

"It's just a figure of speech."

"It's *your* figure of speech, just like the idea of this unannounced visit is *your* idea." She folded her arms. Maybe her hands wouldn't shake so much if she did. Maybe she wouldn't be so terrified if she got just a little bit angry. "Frankly, I think you should have handled this differently."

"Like how?"

"I don't know. Write him a letter."

"Excellent plan," Cullen said sarcastically. "*'Dear*

Keir, How're the grapes doing this year? How's Cass? Oh, by the way, I've got a wife and she'll be giving birth to my son in four months.'''

His son. Were they back to that?

"How about re-writing that letter?" Marissa said, her voice trembling. *"'Dear Keir, Guess what? I made this huge mistake and now I'm paying for—'''*

Cullen put out his arm as if to make sure her seat belt held, then made a hard right, pulled onto the narrow shoulder of the road and turned to Marissa.

"Did I say I made a mistake?"

"You didn't have to say it."

"If I want to tell you I made a mistake, I'll tell it to you. You got that, counselor?"

Marissa looked away from him. She wanted to make a mocking response but if she said anything at all, she was afraid she'd start to cry.

"Marissa? You understand?"

"Yes," she said, and then, to her chagrin, she burst into tears.

Cullen cursed, hauled her into his arms and held her tight.

"Don't cry," he said roughly, pressing kisses into her hair. "God, I'm sorry, sweetheart. I'm so sorry." Gently, he swept the hair back from her temples. "I told myself this would be easy and the truth is, it won't be. But we'll get through it. Okay?"

She nodded. Her nose was running, her eyes were tearing, she looked like a whale and she was going to meet the man her husband described as his tough-minded, sometimes-difficult-to-deal-with big brother.

"We'll get through it."

Marissa's voice wobbled, but the proud lift of her chin almost killed him. Cullen pulled a handkerchief from his pocket.

"We will," he said firmly, drying her eyes. "Everything's going to be just fine." He brought the hankie to her nose. "Blow." She did, noisily, and he smiled at her. "Keir's a good guy. He'll be surprised but he'll get past it. You all right now?"

"Yes," she lied, "I'm fine."

"Good." Cullen dropped a quick kiss on her mouth and drove back onto the road. "Because I just recognized where we are. We'll be there in ten minutes."

Marissa was quiet as he made the turn onto the long drive that led to Deer Run. It was a good thing, too, because he couldn't have responded to anything she might have said, not with his stomach in his throat.

Whatever had possessed him to do this? She was right. He should have phoned or written or sent a message by smoke signal. Anything but just turning up cold to break his news.

It was only that yesterday, all the yesterdays since they'd reached Nantucket, showing up on Keir's doorstep had seemed the best way to tell his brother that he was married, that his wife was pregnant, that it was okay because he was happy.

That he'd married Marissa because it was the right thing to do and now—now, he was crazily, insanely, head-over-heels, forever-after in love with his own wife.

Holy hell!

He was in love with his wife.

How could that have happened? When? Why? Forget that. "Why" was a dumb question. Why did a man fall in love with one particular woman? Because he did, that was all. Because she was special. Beautiful. Brilliant. Tough. Gentle. Independent. And God, he loved her, he'd probably loved her since the night he'd first made love to her.

"Cullen?"

He had to tell her. But when? Not now, with the stone mansion at Deer Run looming ahead. When *did* a man tell his wife he'd fallen in love with her?

"Cullen?"

Marriage was one thing. Love was something else. And

he wasn't going to open himself up to her, pour out his heart unless he was a thousand percent sure she felt the same way.

"Cullen!"

He swung toward her. To hell with waiting. With being cautious. "Marissa," he said urgently, "I have to tell you something…"

"Look," she whispered, pointing straight ahead.

Keir was maybe half a dozen feet away, standing at the foot of the stone steps that led to his front door.

"Cullen," he called, his face creased in a big grin.

By the time Cullen stepped from the car, went around to the passenger side and held out his hand to Marissa, Keir's grin had changed to a puzzled smile. And when they walked toward him and Cullen said, quietly and carefully, "Keir, this is Marissa. My wife," Keir wasn't smiling at all.

"MORE salad?" Cassie said briskly, holding the earthenware bowl in her hands like a temple offering as she looked around the dining room table.

Keir and Cullen shook their heads. Marissa didn't even look up from the plate of untouched food in front of her.

"Well," Cassie said, even more briskly, "in that case, it's time for dessert. French apple pie. Sounds good, don't you think? I made it myself, too. I found the recipe in a magazine a few days ago and then I saw all these yummy new Granny Smiths at the farm stand up the road, so—so I'll just clear the table."

Marissa lurched to her feet. "I'll help."

"Oh. Oh, no, that's okay. I mean, you're probably tired. I mean, you're—"

The women's eyes met. "Pregnant," Marissa said flatly.

"Pregnant," Cassie repeated. "Just like me."

Keir looked up. *Not* just like you, his cold expression said.

"Fine," Cassie said quickly. "You can help me clear.

Matter of fact, you can help me put up the coffee. High-test for the guys, decaf for us because—''

''Because we're pregnant,'' Marissa said, her tone defiant.

Keir looked at Marissa again and she returned the look in kind. Did he really think he was going to intimidate her? There wasn't a thing anyone in this house could say would hurt her…

Except what Cullen had started to say just as they got here, what he'd tried to say again when they had a minute alone.

What he would say, once the evening was over.

Marissa snatched up her plate, went around the table and collected the others. Nobody had eaten. Nobody had attempted conversation. Keir hadn't said three words to her. He didn't have to. Those telling looks said it all.

And Cullen… Cullen looked like a living, breathing example of the old saying about being between a rock and a hard place.

Just for a moment, her heart softened.

He was trying his best, she had to admit. He'd held her hand all through the first awful minutes of their meeting with his big brother, slipped his arm around her as they climbed the steps to the front door of the stone mansion, rubbed his hand up and down her spine when Cassie came out of the kitchen, looking happy, hugely pregnant…

And shocked at the sight of her brother-in-law with a pregnant woman he introduced as his wife.

Alone in the room Cassie had shown them to, Cullen had taken her hands. Oh, if only he'd drawn her into his arms!

''I'm so sorry,'' he'd said. ''So sorry, Marissa.''

She'd nodded, not trusting herself to speak.

''I did this all wrong,'' he'd said, sounding fierce and angry. ''Damn it, I got it wrong from the beginning.''

Yes, he had. From the beginning. She'd known it. If only she'd been able to make him see it.

''But I'll make it right. I swear it. It's just not going to be the way we thought.'' He'd gotten this terribly serious expression on his face and said that he had something to tell her later.

And she'd nodded again because she knew what it was.

Their marriage was a disaster, never mind the last few wonderful days on the island. Sex was sex and responsibility was responsibility, but that didn't mean he'd had to marry her.

No question but Cullen knew that now. He'd made love to her, laughed with her, and maybe those things were okay, but he should never have married her. She was wearing the expensive clothes he'd bought her, the sandals, the gold earrings, but none of that changed the bottom line.

She didn't belong here, and her husband knew it.

She didn't fit in. Standing at the foot of the steps, looking up at his brother's cold face, the stone walls of his home rising behind him, she'd finally faced the truth.

These people were rich. They had Position and Power with capital Ps.

She was a Perez. A Mex. A *Chicano.* She had nothing. No position, no power, just a father she'd never known and a mother whose hobby had been bars and men.

She had no business in a setting like this or in a family like this. And Cullen had finally realized it.

''Marissa?''

She blinked. Cassie was standing in the doorway, a little smile on her lips.

''Did you want to bring those dishes into the kitchen?'' she said softly.

Marissa nodded. She felt Cullen's hand brush hers but she didn't look at him, she just kept putting one foot in front of the other until she was safely in the next room. Cassie gave her a pitying look. Damn it, the last thing she needed was pity, especially from an ivory-tower princess.

''Oh, Marissa,'' Cassie said, ''I'm so sorry...''

''Don't be ridiculous. There's nothing to be sorry for.''

"There is. My husband's behavior... He's just, well, surprised, that's all. Once he's had time to think—"

"Frankly, I don't give a damn what he thinks, now or later. I don't give a damn what you think, either." Marissa dumped the dishes in the sink and turned on the water. "As far as I'm concerned—as far as I'm concerned—"

She burst into tears.

"Oh, honey!" Cassie turned off the water and led her to a chair at the kitchen table. "Here." She yanked a wad of tissues from her apron pocket. Something metallic clinked against the tile floor and she bent and retrieved it. "There it is," she said. "I wondered what I'd done with the key to the SUV." Marissa hiccuped and Cassie tossed the key on the table and handed over the tissues. "You cry all you want while I go tell that dumb husband of mine—"

"No!" Marissa grabbed Cassie's hand. "Please don't. Cullen'll come in, he'll see me crying..."

"Why do you think I carry around those tissues?" Cassie said with a little smile. "Pregnant women cry all the time."

"Not like this." Marissa wiped her eyes. "I don't want him to know I'm upset."

"He knows already. He's upset, too. Heaven only knows what he's saying to Keir right now."

"I know what he's saying," Marissa said. "That he finally figured out our marriage was a huge mistake and that he's going to end it as soon as we get back to Boston."

"Oh, honey, no!" Cassie sat in the chair across from Marissa and reached for her hand. "He's crazy about you. Anyone can see that."

Marissa gave a watery laugh. "You mean, he's crazy to have married me. *That's* what anyone can see—especially your husband."

"Listen to me, Marissa. I love Keir dearly, but this is one of those times when he's being a pigheaded idiot."

"Cullen and I are wrong for each other, Cassie. It's sweet of you to try and make me think otherwise, but—"

"Keir's just surprised, that's all. He's very protective of

his brothers. He'll come around once he realizes how much Cullen loves you.''

''Cullen doesn't love me,'' Marissa said fiercely. ''He only married me because I'm pregnant.''

''Marissa. Honey, a man doesn't have to marry a woman because she's carrying his baby.''

''Cullen was determined to do the right thing.''

''Well, of course. He's an O'Connell.'' Cassie smiled and squeezed Marissa's hand. ''What I meant was, he could have acknowledged your baby as his, provided for his support, for your support. He didn't have to take you as his wife. The fact that he did means—''

''It means he got carried away with doing the right thing.''

''It means you matter to him.''

''I don't.''

''Marissa—''

''We only spent one night together!''

Cassie blinked. ''Well, okay. I mean, it's unusual, sure, but some women get pregnant really fast and—''

''You don't understand. We only knew each other that one night.'' Marissa's face colored but she kept her eyes on Cassie's. ''I met him,'' she said steadily, ''slept with him, and never saw him again until I was almost four months pregnant. When he found out, he said we had to get married. And now—now, we both know it was a mistake. I know that's hard for you to understand. It must have been so different for you and Keir…''

Cassie laughed.

''It was different, all right. I despised him. He disliked me. The only thing we had in common was this overwhelming urge to climb into the sack together.''

Marissa's eyes widened. ''Are you serious?''

Cassie sighed, patted Marissa's hand and sat back in her chair.

''I'll tell you the entire story someday. For now, trust

me when I tell you that I wouldn't have bet ten cents we'd have fallen in love with each other.''

''Really?''

''Really. Hey, Mr. Keir O'Connell, entrepreneur, and Ms. Cassandra Bercovic, ex-stripper? Don't look like that, honey. It's the truth. I used to strip for a living.''

''That didn't bother Keir and his family?''

''Oh, it bothered Keir, but he got past it. As for his family…he loves them like crazy and so do I. They accepted me with open arms, but if they hadn't, that wouldn't have stopped him.'' Cassie leaned forward. ''You hear what's happening in the next room? The raised voices? Assuming my husband's crazy enough to tell *your* husband he thinks this marriage was a mistake, I guarantee you that *your* husband is telling *my* husband what he can do with that opinion.''

Marissa felt her heart lift. ''You think so?''

''I know so. That's how our men are. Independent. Tough. And fiercely loyal to the women they love and marry.''

''I told you, Cullen doesn't—''

''I think he does,'' Cassie said gently. ''As for you…you're head over heels in love with him, aren't you?''

''Yes,'' Marissa whispered. ''Yes, I am.''

Cassie patted her hand again, cocked her head and smiled. ''The yelling's stopped.''

''Is that good?''

''Well, I haven't heard anybody bounce off the walls so yeah, it probably is. They've gotten past the shouting and now they're talking. Or waiting for us, so that Keir can apologize.'' She pushed back her chair. ''What do you say? Shall we join our men?''

Our men. Marissa's face lit as she rose to her feet. ''I'd like that.''

Together, the women walked into the pantry and toward the closed door to the dining room. Marissa touched

Cassie's shoulder just as Cassie cracked the door open. She needed one last minute to compose herself…

"…believe you did such a dumb thing," she heard Keir say.

Cullen's sigh carried the length of the room. "I know. It was worse than dumb."

Cassie swung toward Marissa, lips parted, but Marissa held up her hand. Cassie sighed, shook her head and stepped back so that it was Marissa who stood with her ear to the door.

"You're an attorney. You're supposed to know better than to get yourself into a mess like this."

"Look, spare me the lecture, okay?" Cullen's chair scraped as he pushed it back from the table. "I just admitted, getting married like that wasn't smart."

"I hope you left yourself some kind of out."

"Of course I did. I drew up a contract, added a clause that said the marriage was reviewable every two years."

"And?"

"And, tonight I'm going to tell her that the clause, the whole damned contract, is meaningless. I don't need two more years to know what I have to do."

"Now you're talking sense," Keir said.

Cullen added something, but Marissa had stopped listening. Eyes brimming with tears, she pushed past Cassie and ran into the kitchen.

"Marissa," Cassie said, "wait…"

But this was Cassie's ninth month. She was big as a house. Worse, she was clumsy. That was how she felt, anyway, as she waddled to the kitchen and wove through the chairs they'd left standing away from the table.

By the time she reached the back door, Marissa and the car key that had been lying on the table were gone.

CHAPTER THIRTEEN

CULLEN stared at Cassie as if she were speaking another language.

"Marissa did what?"

"She took off. How many times must I say it? Your wife's gone."

"Gone where? How?"

"I don't know where. And I already told you how. She took my key to our SUV."

Cullen shot to his feet. All at once, the message was getting through. It hadn't, at first, because it was so preposterous. Your wife took a stack of dishes into the kitchen, your sister-in-law ran in fifteen minutes later and said…

"My wife ran away?"

"Thank you, God," Cassie said dramatically, lifting her eyes to the ceiling. "Yes, you big jerk. She ran away."

The color drained from Cullen's face. "What happened?" he demanded. "Why'd she run?"

"She ran," Cassie said, her tone caustic as she thought back to a similar night in this very same house, "because the O'Connell brothers have the habit of saying things that sound bad within earshot of their women. You idiots sit here talking about what a mistake it was for Cullen to marry Marissa, how he's going to tell her tonight that the marriage is over—"

"What?"

"Oh, don't look so innocent, Cullen O'Connell! I heard you. More to the point, Marissa heard you. All that bull about how you built yourself a little exit clause into a marriage agreement, how you know now that marrying her was a mistake, how you have to tell her you want out…''

''That's what Marissa thinks I said?'' Cullen said numbly.

''That's what she heard. So did I.'' Cassie's eyes shot sparks. ''To think I was in there, defending you. Telling her not to cry, when all the time… She's crazy about you, Cullen. Are you blind? Couldn't you tell?''

Cullen got a strange look on his face. ''She said that? That she's crazy about me?''

''What is it with you men? Stupid, as well as blind!'' Cassie glared from her husband to her brother-in-law. ''She's a wonderful woman. Are you incapable of seeing that?''

He'd been incapable of seeing a lot of things, Cullen thought. And now, his wife—his pregnant wife—was out there, in the dark, on a road she didn't know.

Cullen ran for the door. Keir went after him.

''Cull? Cull, wait. I'll go with you.''

The door slammed. Cassie put her hand on her husband's shoulder and he turned toward her.

''He'll need help…''

Cassie shook her head. ''He won't.''

''Yeah, but—''

''He'll catch up to her and when he does, if he's anything like you, he'll do just fine.'' She smiled as she slid her hands up her husband's chest. ''It may take him a while, but he'll convince her that he loves her. You convinced me, remember?''

Keir smiled back at his wife. He put his arms around her and linked his hands at the base of her spine.

''You're a devious witch.''

''Uh-huh. And it's only one of the things you love about me.''

He kissed her. Sighing, she leaned back in his embrace. ''You were awful to Marissa.''

''Yeah. Well, I thought she'd scammed him.''

''He should have punched you out.'' Cassie grinned. ''Of course, if he'd done that, I'd have had to slug him with a skillet, but he should have done it, anyway.''

''He came close, after you and Marissa left the room. He chewed me out, said the only reason he hadn't done it sooner was because the two of you are pregnant, and he didn't want to upset you by taking me apart, limb by limb.''

''Did you mean it when you told him he'd been dumb to marry Marissa?''

Keir shook his head. ''You heard the tail end of the conversation. I started to give him hell. I said it was ridiculous to marry a woman he hardly knew, that he should have come to me for advice.'' He tilted Cassie's chin up. ''He told me to mind my own business.''

Cassie smiled. ''Smart brother-in-law I've got,'' she said softly.

''And then he told me he loved her, and I said, well, that was different. And he said he hadn't told her yet, that he'd written this unenforceable clause into an unenforceable contract and that he was going to tell her that the bit about reviewing their marriage every two years wasn't just impossible, it wasn't going to happen because—''

''Keir?''

''—because he was never going to give her up, and I said—''

''Keir!''

''Yes, darling. I know. But it'll be okay. She can't get very far before he overtakes her.''

''No. It isn't that.''

''What is it, then?'' Keir brushed his mouth over his wife's. ''You want me to apologize to Marissa? I will, of course, the minute they get back.''

''It isn't that, either.'' Cassie said. ''It's the baby.''

''What about the baby?''

''He's coming.''

''Well, sure, but we still have almost two weeks—''

Something hot and liquid gushed over his feet. Keir went rigid. ''Cass?''

''The baby's coming now,'' she said, with a look in her eyes he'd never seen before.

''Now?''

''Right now,'' Cassie whispered.

Keir swung his wife into his arms, dug the keys to his sports car from his pocket and headed for the front door.

''Wait! I need my suitcase.''

''The hell you do,'' Keir growled, heading out into the night.

CULLEN drove fast, faster than was smart considering the narrow road and dark night, but that was okay because Marissa was on this road, too.

If anything happened to her…

No. He wouldn't think that way. Nothing bad could happen. Not now. She loved him, Cassie said. God, he hoped she did, enough to forgive him for the monumental ass he'd been.

He should have hauled Keir out of his chair five minutes into the evening, told him to start treating Marissa right or he'd beat the crap out of him.

But how could he, with Cassie sitting there, looking as if she were going to give birth any minute?

He should have leaned across the table, taken Marissa's hand and said, so they'd all hear him, ''Marissa, I love you.''

But how could he, when she might have answered, ''So what?''

Cullen stepped down harder on the gas.

Except, she wouldn't have said that. If he hadn't been so thick-skulled, he'd have figured things out for himself. What she felt for him glittered in her eyes whenever she smiled at him. It infused each whisper each time they made love. Walking the beach holding hands, lying in his arms in front of the fire... If he hadn't been so afraid to figure out his own feelings, he'd have been able to read hers.

She loved him.

When he found her, he'd tell her he loved her every hour on the hour for the next fifty years. The next hundred years. If only she'd listen. If she'd believe him. If...

Red taillights winked in the darkness ahead.

"Marissa," Cullen said.

He stepped down harder on the gas, blinked his lights. Marissa speeded up. Was she crazy? The road got even narrower here. With trees standing sentinel on either side, there was no room for error.

He blinked his lights again. "Slow down," he muttered, "damn it, Marissa, slow down!"

She went faster. Hell! What now? If he kept pushing, she'd just increase her speed. He dropped back, even though it was the last thing he wanted to do.

The lights ahead vanished. Cullen's mouth went dry as he tried to come up with a reason. Was there a bad curve up there? Some kind of drop-off?

No. He remembered now. There was a curve—that was why he'd lost Marissa's taillights—but it was an easy one. And just past it was the shoulder where they'd stopped on the way to Deer Run.

The lights came into view again. Cullen checked for traffic, sent up a prayer to whatever gods might be in the vicinity, stepped on the gas, sped ahead and passed the SUV. When he saw the shoulder, he stood on the brakes, turned onto it, jumped from his car and stepped out into the road.

He'd left her plenty of time to see him and to stop. Not that he gave a damn about what might happen to him; he just didn't want her to have to brake hard, or do anything to endanger herself or their unborn baby.

He knew when she spotted him. The SUV slowed—but she wasn't going to stop. She was going to swerve around him.

''Marissa,'' Cullen shouted, ''Marissa, sweetheart, I love you!''

She couldn't have heard him, not over the sound of the car…

''I love you,'' he said, and after what seemed forever, Marissa swung the wheel, pulled onto the shoulder of the road and turned off the engine.

Cullen couldn't hear anything but the thud of his heart. The night was as silent as it can only be on a narrow country road. He took a deep breath and started toward the SUV. When he reached it, he grasped the door handle.

It was locked.

''Marissa. Sweetheart, let me in.''

She wasn't looking at him. She was staring straight ahead and he knew she'd have folded her arms if she could, but there wasn't that much space between her belly and the steering wheel.

''Marissa. I love you.''

She didn't answer. Didn't so much as look at him. He could hear the faint tick-tick of the cooling engine over the beat of his heart. He thought about the way she'd been driving, too fast, too hard, and what might have happened to her.

This time, when he tried the handle and called her name, anger roughened his voice.

Anger, at least, was an emotion he could deal with.

''Damn it, Marissa, open this door!''

She swung toward him. ''No!''

''Open it, or—''

A car came roaring down the road. Cullen looked up as Keir's Ferrari raced past, slowing just long enough for him to see Cassie give him a thumbs-up through the open window as Keir tapped the horn.

''Go for it,'' she yelled.

Cullen turned to Marissa. ''You hear that?'' he shouted. ''Cassie knows I love you. Keir knows it, too. The only person who doesn't know the damned truth is—''

The door opened. "Stop shouting," his wife said crossly, but not crossly enough to hide the catch in her voice. "You'll wake everybody up."

"There's nobody here but the damned cows."

"You're making enough noise to scare them silly." She hesitated. "What's all this nonsense about you loving me?"

"What's all this nonsense about you *leaving* me?" Cullen said gruffly.

"It's not nonsense, it's the first intelligent thing I've done since you came shouldering your way into my life."

"You're not leaving me, Marissa."

"I already have."

Cullen clasped her shoulders. "I'm not letting you leave me!"

"Did I spoil your plans? I know you were going to be the one to say, 'Goodbye, it's been interesting, but I'm ready to admit I made a huge mistake, and—'"

"I love you."

"Well, that's too bad, O'Connell, because it's too late for that. Listen and listen good, because I'm only saying this once. I'm the one who made a huge mistake. A gigantic mistake. A humongous mis—"

Cullen pulled her into his arms and kissed her. She struggled, but not terribly hard, and she started to cry even as her mouth softened under his, and that was when he knew, without question, that Cassie was right.

His wife loved him.

He took her by the shoulders again and held her just a couple of inches away.

"You love me," he said.

"Don't be stupid!" Tears were streaming down her cheeks but when he tried to wipe them away, she jerked back. "Why would I love a man who just told his brother how he's going to get rid of me?"

"What I told him was that I was going to get rid of that ridiculous piece of pseudolegal paper I showed you when we got married."

''You made a mess of things, you said.''

''I did. I shouldn't have forced this marriage on you.''

''Damned right, you shouldn't. Every good lawyer knows the importance of consultation.''

''What I mean is, I shouldn't have come at you as an attorney.'' His voice softened. ''What I should have done is woo you with flowers, told you what was already in my heart—''

''You don't have a heart,'' Marissa said, but not very convincingly.

''Well, I admit, it took me a while to find it. But I have one, sweetheart, and it's filled with love for you.''

''Ha!'' Marissa said, but he could see the glitter in her eyes that he'd been stupid enough to ignore until now.

''I love you. And you love me. And I'm not letting you move from this spot until you admit it.''

''In that case, O'Connell, you're in for a long wait,'' Marissa replied, and ruined her answer by throwing her arms around his neck and kissing him. ''I love you with all my heart,'' she whispered against his lips. ''And I always will.''

Cullen felt a sweet sense of relief. Knowing his wife loved him was one thing. Hearing her say the words was another.

''I should have told you.''

She smiled. ''Yes,'' she said gently, ''you should have.''

''Yeah.'' His voice roughened. ''So I'll just have to tell you I love you morning, noon and night for the next hundred years, to make up for it.''

Marissa leaned back in Cullen's arms and smiled. ''Only three times a day for a hundred years? Doesn't sound like an appropriate damage award to me, counselor.''

Cullen grinned. ''You're a tough negotiator.''

''I try,'' Marissa said sweetly.

He stroked his hand over her belly. ''You hear that, pal? Your mom's going to be one heck of a fine attorney. Maybe she'll even agree to come on board at my firm.''

Marissa laughed softly. ''Is that a bribe?''

''Maybe,'' Cullen said, his smile fading and turning slow and hot and filled with promise. ''On the other hand, I can think of some very creative forms of bribery to try, once I get you back to our room at Deer Run and into bed.''

Her answering kiss took his breath away.

''If it's really, really creative,'' she whispered, ''I might just be tempted.''

Cullen helped Marissa into the SUV, got behind the wheel and started the engine.

''What about your Porsche?''

''It'll wait till morning.'' He reached for her hand, lifted it to his mouth and kissed her palm. ''Making love to my wife won't.''

Marissa thought about telling him that he was doing it all over again, making decisions that involved her without consulting her first…

But a smart lawyer knew that if the opposition came up with a plan you liked, the thing to do was smile and accept it.

THEY took their vows again, The Right Way.

Marissa Perez became Marissa Perez O'Connell on a clear-as-crystal late winter day in the glass-enclosed sunroom of their home on Nantucket Island. She wore a long, lovely white wedding gown; Cullen wore a tux, but their newborn son was the star attraction.

He was perfect. Ten fingers, ten toes, a shock of dark hair, and it seemed as if his eyes were going to be the same gray shade as his mother's.

In other words, he was beautiful.

So was Cullen, Marissa thought, and told him so, after the ceremony, right in front of his brothers, who were his best men, and they groaned and hooted so much that Cullen turned a bright pink.

''I'll get you for this,'' he whispered as he drew her close, and Marissa gave him a little smile that was so perfect and sexy that he just had to kiss her, right then and there.

His sisters and Cassie were Marissa's maids of honor. She'd come to love all the O'Connells, from her husband straight through to his warm and wonderful mother, Mary, and Mary's husband, Dan.

She told them that when Cullen was showing off his son and Briana, Fallon and Megan went into the bedroom with her to help get a snag out of her hem.

"I love you guys," Marissa said, and sniffed.

"For heaven's sake," Bree admonished, "don't cry or you'll ruin your makeup."

They all laughed, because they were all crying, and then Fallon got down to business, whipping a tiny tube of fast-drying glue from her beaded purse.

"I'll just put a drop on the hem," she said, kneeling in front of Marissa.

Bree grinned. "Ah, the things a woman learns during the years she's a supermodel."

Everybody laughed again. Seconds later, the little group trooped from the room. All but Megan, who hung back.

"You guys go on," she said. "I want to run a comb through my hair."

The door swung shut. Megan sighed and looked into the mirror.

Her new sister-in-law looked so happy. So did Cassie and Fallon, Cassie cuddling her baby, Fallon with her own pregnancy just starting to show, all of them gazing at their husbands with stars shining in their eyes.

Was something wrong with her? Was she the only woman on the planet who didn't want to get married? The only woman who didn't think she needed a man and babies to make her complete?

There was a light knock on the door.

"Yes?" Meg said, quickly brushing her hands over her eyes, which were, for some unaccountable reason, suddenly feeling prickly.

The door swung open. ''Hey,'' Sean said, ''you okay, sis?''

''I'm fine,'' she said, looking at him and smiling.

He held out his hand. ''Got to stick together, kid, considering that there are only three of us O'Connells still sane enough to be single.''

Megan laughed, took his hand and hurried along beside him to go and join the fun.